Your Child Left Behind

Mel Conner

Dedication

This book is a work of fiction.... well, mostly. In certain cases, names have been changed to protect the ignorant.

I would like to thank the following people for reading early manuscripts of <u>Your Child Left Behind</u> and offering invaluable advice: Chuck Woolfolk, Gene Openshaw, Mike O'Neal, Richard Conner, Leigh Conner, David Conner, Jana Slovic, Frost Freeman, Cheyenne Cordell, Lydia Moland, Theresa Harrington and Bruce Ramsey.

Thanks to Gene Openshaw for allowing me to use lyrics from "Without a Limit".

Thanks to Ward Brannman for the cover photo.

I would like to thank the staff and students of Kamiakin Junior High for inspiring me to write this book. And while we're at it, thank you a thousand times over for providing me with a thoroughly satisfying career.

I would most of all like to thank my lovely wife Donna, who took the back cover photo, and who convinced me to write this book as a work of fiction, rather than as the exceedingly lame "History of Kamiakin" that I had originally intended.

Part I: 1978

Chapter 1 – September

I look back on 9th grade with a mixture of horror, disbelief and amusement. Two weeks into the school year, Mr. Krabke, my 1st period US History teacher, told us that every other industrialized country in the world had, unwisely in his opinion, switched to the metric system.

Johnny Boe took issue with that. "Well, that only applies to foreign countries."

"Nuh-uh," said Josh, "what about Canada?"

Just to keep the ball rolling, Jake disagreed. "Canada's not a foreign country."

"Uh-huh," said Jeff, "they're part of Russia."

And Johnny Boe brought it home. "Yeah, and they're a buncha fags."

I laughed, but not specifically at that last line, as they assumed; it was the entire sequence that cracked me up. And so began my association with the J boys, who could thereafter count on me to be an appreciative audience for their antics. For my part, it was an alliance I would neither have sought nor foreseen, but being the new kid at school, I could not afford to be picky.

The Krabman turned pale, and then crimson. Bracketed by distractingly tiny ears, his jumbo, middle-aged forehead was glowing. "Do you really believe...? How can you...?" Had that tic in his cheek been there before? Or had Johnny Boe and his crew caused it? In either case, from that moment on, the twitch kicked in whenever The Krabman encountered a stressful situation, like 1st period. One day I overheard him talking to our VP in the cafeteria, referring to our class as "prison prep history".

Why would anybody choose to become a teacher? And, more to the point, why would anybody choose to teach at Fernwater Junior High?

Waiting at the bus stop that first Tuesday in September, my next-door neighbor Jake had told me we'd be attending what was called an open concept school. "Ain't gonna be like your old school," he warned me. "Hey, if you wanna hang around with me and my.... Leo, anybody ever tell ya you sound like Kermit the Frog?"

Entering Fernwater Junior High, the first thing you noticed were the walls – there weren't any. You could see from one end of the school to the other. Picture a Kmart, minus the Blue Light Special. Of course the band room and the wood shop were walled in, as was the centrally located office; apparently the principal and secretaries needed some peace and quiet to do whatever it was they did.

The school was held up by a hundred or so brick pillars, arranged in a rectangular grid. All that separated one classroom from the next was a six-foot-high, ten-foot-long movable chalkboard, or maybe two of them. Every so often, an Egg McMuffin or a vegetable would come sailing over the wall, and paper airplanes passed by overhead with regularity.

The heavy duty carpet appeared to have been dyed a splotchy mix of salsa, sand and one of those Campbell's cream-of-something soups, like mushrooms, asparagus or celery. It was an ingenious color scheme, able to camouflage any and all spillage. So when the last bite of a goopy hot dog flew into our room one morning and came skidding down the aisle, the mustard-and-ketchup-coated wienie left no detectable stain.

I sat in the back with the J boys. Oddly, there were no chalkboards set up behind us as a boundary, so we were basically sitting in a hallway. Kids would stop to visit until The Krabman chased them away with his standard "Let's move along now."

To fully grasp the lunacy that was Fernwater Junior High, you first have to get a sense of the noise level. With 700 kids in one building – most of them within earshot – the simple sounds of closing books and opening binders and sharpening pencils and blowing noses created a constantly shifting background clatter. Add in the racket of three dozen teachers lecturing or leading discussions. Shoot, you could hear Miss De Waart's cheery screech three rooms away. If a nearby class had a substitute, the noise level would double or triple, as surrounding teachers raised their voices to climb above the racket. And when teachers took their classes to the library, things would grind to a halt in every classroom along the way, as friends waved to one another or swapped greetings and insults. Had Fernwater been populated with monks or mutes, the design of the school might have worked just fine, but our student body was made up of yappy, fidgety adolescents, spiced with a smattering of J boys.

There was one switch that operated the lights for our "house" – that's what we called each cluster of six classrooms. So on Movie Day, we'd be watching, say, a documentary about the Mayflower, and it would be all washed out by the fluorescent lights blazing overhead, so my buddies and I would get a game of cards going or start a pen fight, writing on and gouging each other's arms. The Krabman would be working at his desk with his head down, so he never saw us. My guess is that he didn't want to.

The first time the science class next door showed a movie, we heard all about how the surface temperature of the sun is 10,000 degrees. Now, who figured that out and how the heck did they do it? As dramatic music played in the background, I pictured solar flares erupting and hydrogen atoms fusing. All the while I took notes while The Krabman rattled on about Pilgrims and their turkeys. I became adept at multitasking, though at the time I was unfamiliar with that term; back then it was used as a descriptor of computer design and operation.

One day the teachers on both sides of us showed movies. Against The Krabman's objections, the lights in our house were turned off, and the competing soundtracks cranked up, leaving our teacher to shout at us in the near-darkness about Manifest Destiny.

Halfway through class, I whispered, "Here she comes." Miss De Waart, our 3rd period science teacher, was making one of her frequent trips to the office.

"Target acquired," said Johnny Boe, removing a baggie of

BB's and a straw from his jacket. "Christ, you could show the CinemaScope version of <u>Butch Cassidy and the Sundance Kid</u> on her ass."

Johnny was the leader of his band of troublemakers. His head swiveled as if welded to a gun turret, constantly scanning the room, wild-eyed, for an opportunity to create a ruckus. He wasn't out to cause trouble himself, necessarily. Rather, he was a catalyst, looking to set off his pals. The son of a cop, he had to be careful about bad news finding its way home. He referred to his dad as a "bad guy with a badge".

Johnny's shot missed its mark, but he was motivated, having failed the first science test of the year. His second shot scored a bulls-eye, and Miss De Waart, aka "Misty Wart", spun around and cast her evil eye into the murky gloom of our room, hoping to nail the little thug who had assaulted her backside. Johnny Boe passed the blowgun and ammo to Jake, who nailed Misty Wart on her return trip.

By week's end, the J boys had come up with a scoring system: three points for students passing by and ten for teachers. They each got the blowgun for five minutes per round.

Unlike my new pals, I was used to doing well in school; the previous year in Olympia, I had gotten a 4.0 and received a Perfect Attendance Certificate. I was not ready to take on a teacher, so I passed up my turn with the blowgun, but kept stats for my new friends: total points, percent accuracy and consecutive hits.

As if I needed more distractions, there was a pair of smokin' hot blondes sitting in the classroom behind us and off to the right. The one with the Farrah Fawcett hair – I never did learn her name – sometimes wore a pleated black mini, and on those days I left 1st period with a kink in my shoulder from craning my neck, trying to catch a glimpse of her or her legs.

I don't think the blondes ever caught me staring, but their math teacher did. Mrs. Skibbitz, an ancient woman with piercing blue eyes, would often position herself in the middle of the hall to stand guard. And though my back was to her, I could sense her presence; all of us could. Radiation from those all-seeing eyes scorched the back of my neck and shivered down my spine. We would stop whatever trouble we'd been causing and shrink down in our chairs, which of course was an admission of guilt. So we'd sit up straight again, and now it looked like we were being antsy.

Even The Krabman avoided her scrutiny; he'd look up, down, left, right, behind him – anywhere, in hopes of warding off Mrs. Skibbitz' sorcery.

Mr. Marvin Steiffel, our vice principal, wanted to be my friend. He told me so. After spotting me hanging around Johnny Boe one day, he fell in beside me on my way to math class. He wasn't short, but he walked in hurried little half-steps, making it look like he was doing his damnedest to keep up. He asked about my last school and if I had hobbies. When I told him I loved baseball, we talked about the Mariners, who, in their second season, were at that point 31 games back.

Then he said, "Have a good year, Leo Haldini. If I need to discipline you, I want us to have a friendship first."

I liked Steiffel, sort of, at least at first. He'd shoot the bull with us between classes, and he led cheers at pep assemblies alongside the cheerleaders. He liked kids. But here is the thing that weirded me out: He'd see me in the hall and call out something like, "Yo, Leo, how was your weekend?" Then he'd crack up. But when someone, even another adult, said something hilarious, he stood there stony-faced. He made me nervous.

The mascots for the other schools in our district were bears or wolverines or eagles. We were the Fernwater Terns. I had no idea what a tern was, but I assumed it must be something ferocious. Our school motto was painted in ornate white letters on the brick wall above the front doors of our school:

ONE GOOD TERN DESERVES ANOTHER

Being unfamiliar with that saying, I had no idea what it meant, so I did not recognize it as a fairly good pun. Hanging in the foyer was an old banner that read: Tern out for football.

One night I asked my dad what a tern is. Without saying a word, he shifted his recliner to its upright position, carefully refolded the Seattle Times and pulled a volume of the World Book Encyclopedia from the bookshelf. Mom looked up from her crossword puzzle and smiled – she loved it when Dad and I shared these moments. He thumbed through the encyclopedia, found the desired page and then read the first paragraph aloud. We discovered that a tern is a bird, closely related to a seagull. That was plenty of information for me, but Dad handed me the book and nodded.

"Oh, it's my tern now?" I said, forgetting that my dad considered puns to be a frivolity. Mom covered her smile, not wanting to aggravate him.

I read the next paragraph and handed it back to Dad. It was an effort not to say: Here, let me tern the book around for you. At his behest, we read about Caspian terns and sooty terns, all sorts of terns; I learned more about terns than a person would ever have reason to know.

At one point I slipped and said, "Time to tern the page."

Dad scowled, Mom hid another smile, and I found myself wishing that my Uncle Marco was there; he would have laughed himself silly.

My family moved to town in late August so that Dad could live closer to his older brother Marco, hoping to preserve a connection to the village on Lake Como in Northern Italy where they'd grown up. The Haldini brothers had immigrated to the US at or near the end of World War II; the details were murky. When my wild, good-natured uncle settled down for good – "No, really I mean it this time" – in Oxley, a suburban dairy town southeast of Seattle, my dad moved too, as he had done several times before.

Mom, my sister Ella and I followed in their wake.

Marco took me see the Mariners in late September, and we were engrossed in the game until the M's gave up six runs early on, at which point I asked Marco how he liked his job at the dairy.

"If it ain't one thing, it's an udder," he said with a chortle. Seeing that I didn't understand that word, he mimed milking a cow with both hands and said, "It's an udder nightmare."

I responded with: "One Good Tern deserves an udder." I had no idea what that meant, but it was gratifying to get another chortle from him.

He asked how I liked school. I told him we didn't have walls and about how my pal got beaned by a flying kumquat. My uncle was skeptical, so I upped the ante, telling him about Movie

Day Madness, the BB blow gun and Misty Wart's <u>Butch Cassidy</u>-sized ass. I saved the Russian Fags story for last. My uncle laughed more raucously with each misadventure, but every time he'd respond with something like: "Oh, how you exaggerate," or: "You spin a good yarn, Leo; I'll give you that," or: "In junior high? No!"

But that's the thing; I was not exaggerating. There was no need to. Unless you saw Fernwater with your own eyes, you simply could not believe it. Oddly, the people who did see it every day thought nothing of it; most of my classmates had attended open concept elementary schools, so they naturally believed that they were attending a real live school. And my teachers acted like their jobs fell within the bounds of normal.

Johnny Boe, Jake and I skipped lunch one day and headed out to The Crash, a small clearing in the woods beyond the football field. Typical of the Pacific Northwest in early fall, it was warm at noon, and sunlight filtered through the maple trees that were just beginning to turn. Couples were playing what Johnny referred to as "tonsil hockey". Others bought and smoked dope. "Terning on", it was called at Fernwater. A few, like me, were hanging out, soaking up the cool of the dangerous kids.

Jake told me that every few months, Vice Principal Steiffel discovered the location of The Crash. He would then round up a group of "troublemakers, truants and transgressors", and assign them Saturday School, meaning they had to work from eight until noon, clearing away brush around The Crash, thereby rendering it useless as a hideout. But within a week, a new Crash would pop up.

Jake assured me that it was easy to keep ahead of Steifel. And that was true, at least for Jake. He was a nondescript kid – average height, average weight, drab clothes, drab brown hair. By design, everything about him was average and drab. He could bash in a clock with a baseball bat in a busy hallway and then disappear into the crowd in four seconds; when questioned later by our VP, no one could say who did it. Whereas the other J boys were always finding trouble, Jake made sure that trouble never found him. A couple months later, I would nickname him "Jake the Invisible Boy".

But Steiffel got lucky that day; he leapt from behind a cedar and cried, "Gotcha!" just as Johnny Boe lit up a doobie. Jake and I hid inside a tangle of blackberries and watched the VP haul our buddy away. We followed at a distance and waited outside the front doors.

Looking at our motto again – One Good Tern Deserves Another – I wondered if it had to do with birds mating. Nah; if that were the case, they'd have written: Two Good Terns Deserve Another.

Given Marvin Steiffel's hard-line stance on drugs, I was surprised to see Johnny Boe come swaggering out of the office a few minutes later with his chest all puffed up, crowing, "Me and Marv cut a deal."

We pumped him for details, but that was all he'd say. This was not the first time I'd seen Johnny wheeling and dealing with our VP. How did he do that? I was impressed and envious, and I hoped to pick up some tricks from him.

Were they – or *we* – felons in the making? Or just idiots? Mostly we were doing what unsupervised kids do when left, well, unsupervised. My own mischief-making was low key. I would chuck things over the wall, like an eraser or an orange – never anything hard or pointy – or I'd graffiti my desk with major league baseball stats or Flying V guitars. And though my pals caused more of an uproar than did I, it all seemed harmless. It was just good clean fun.

We were not criminals…. well, not yet, anyway.

Chapter 2 – October

I was a wallflower in 2nd period English. Mr. Hester was ex-military, and he spoke in a manner befitting a drill sergeant. He didn't get riled up easily, but when he did, his eyes enlarged the slightest bit and took on an intensity that gave me the willies. Everybody from jocks and cheerleaders on down were terrified of him. Rumors about him were always circulating.

Johnny Boe claimed that Hester had done time in Alcatraz for breaking a student's finger in four places. "Why else would he keep a pair of rusty pliers in his desk?"

And everybody knew about Korea: Hester had sustained a head wound from shrapnel, and a metal plate was implanted behind his left ear. The story was accepted as fact, by all except Josh McLowan.

For months, I thought his last name was "McClown"; that was how everyone pronounced it. He was a stocky kid with a tuft of muddy brown hair sticking straight up, like a fuse. I thought of him as a human firecracker. He was into medieval weaponry; he'd sit there with his shoulders all hunched up, fashioning a miniature crossbow out of rubber bands, paper clips and Popsicle sticks, while referencing an article he'd ripped out of a *Scientific American* from the library. Another day he'd pull out, say, a torn-apart calculator and try to fix it. He never could.

McClown was the only one of us brave enough, or dumb enough, or crazy enough to take a crack at disproving the existence of that metal plate in Hester's head. So Johnny Boe swiped a magnet from science class one afternoon and gave it to McClown the next morning, along with instructions and a wager: "I'll bet you five bucks it sticks."

McClown approached Hester's desk with the magnet concealed in the palm of his hand. He asked about a poster on the chalkboard, and when Hester turned his head, McClown waved the magnet back and forth next to his ear. We were disappointed when the magnet did not stick.

"See?" McClown said upon his return. "That metal plate business is a pile of happy horseshit."

But Johnny Boe held his ground, maintaining that Hester the Molester's hair was thick enough to "deflect the beam".

"Oh, that's bogus!" McClown protested for the rest of the period, but he never did get his five bucks.

Other teachers were content to have McClown occupied and sitting silently, pleased that he was not stabbing a classmate in the neck with a pushpin or setting a comic book on fire and then chucking it into the trash can. But Hester assigned detentions if we didn't "Stay focused, people". So McClown kept his little projects hidden under his desk until Hester turned his back to write on the board.

Whenever McClown borrowed a pen – he rarely brought one himself – it would stop working after two minutes, three max. If he took it apart to fix it, he'd usually ended up covered in ink. One time he pulled the cap off an ink cartridge with his teeth and wound up with a mouthful of black ooze. He walked up to Hester, opened his mouth and said, "Ahhhhhhhh."

Our teacher said resignedly, "OK, go get yourself cleaned up," and gave him a hall pass. McClown gave Johnny Boe a high five with the back of his hand on his way out.

I kept my head down, pretending to read Animal Farm. My goal in 2nd period was to go unnoticed. I caused no trouble. None of us did, except for McClown.

Six weeks into the school year, Hester switched from writing on a chalkboard to using an overhead projector. I suspect he made the change so that he wouldn't have to turn his back on McClown. Mr. Hester set the overhead projector on a cart, and because our room didn't have an outlet, he ran an extension cord into The Krabman's room.

The first day Hester used the overhead, he taught us how to diagram sentences, which I kind of enjoyed, though I never would have admitted it to the J boys. Halfway through class, Hester stopped in mid-sentence when his overhead went scooting across the room. He grabbed the cart and stopped it, but as soon as he let go, it took off again. He followed the cord next door, where The

Krabman was teaching 7th graders – sevies, we called them.

I got up and peeked between two chalkboards. A kid was hiding under a table, extension chord in hand, reeling in the overhead like he was playing tug-of-war. He was having a blast.

Hester walked over to him and screamed, "Stop it!" The classes around us fell silent instantly. The sevie curled into a fetal position and sobbed. My teacher laid into him: "Do not disturb my class! Do that again, you and I are going to have a problem!"

The Krabman sat at his desk and twitched his cheek.

I got back to my seat one second before Hester returned. It was spooky, hearing silence at Fernwater. No one moved. No one spoke…. well, no one except for McClown, who viewed our teacher's outburst as his cue to go berserk. He tilted his head to one side and then rolled it around and around, while making a gurgling sound in his throat that sounded like a crow with indigestion. He'd been fiddling with a bunch of pipe cleaners and accidently knocked them to the floor. Reaching down to pick them up, he tipped over his desk, kicking Johnny Boe in the head on his way down.

"You retard!" yelled Johnny. "The hell're you doin'?"

Hester picked up McClown's desk, with him still sitting in it, and slammed it to the floor. He whispered, "Sssstop it. Nowwww!" It was easy to read his thoughts: If you and I were in prison right now, and if I had a pair of rusty pliers….

Seeing the look in his eye, no one, not even McClown, doubted the existence of that metal plate in Hester's head.

During the ten-minute break after 2nd period, Johnny Boe tried to get Jeff Mori to pull the fire alarm in the cafeteria. Jeff was a scrawny kid with splotchy skin and a perpetual half-smile plastered across his face. He would have pulled the alarm, had Jake not been standing off to the side, shaking his head.

"Coupla wimps," said Johnny. He took out a pack of Camels and lit one, then took a drag and passed it around. I was last in line, and I ordered my fingers not to take it, but they did not listen. This being my introduction to smoking, I was still coughing my lungs up when the VP busted us. Johnny and Jake had seen him coming and split, leaving McClown, Jeff Mori and me to take the fall.

Steiffel hauled us into his office and told us we were suspended for two days. As he flipped through his rolodex of student phone numbers, I started shaking. Mom would not be pleased, but my dad.... Oh God, what would he say? What would he do? I had absolutely no idea – I had never been in trouble before. Oh God, Oh God.

And yet, a jolt of excitement went through me as well. Here I was, *in trouble*, hanging out with the hoodlums, the J boys. And others had watched us being hauled into the VP's office. Hell, those smokin' hot blondes had seen me.

Steiffel called my house first. Nobody was home, and this was before anyone I knew had an answering machine, so I relaxed; Judgment Day was postponed. The VP moved on to Jeff and then to McClown. Jeff's mom answered right away and showed up four minutes later, looking like a used-up, worn-down female version of her son. A bony woman with chapped lips and a scaly patch on her forehead, she wore the trademark Mori half-smile, though in her case it had mutated into a half-grimace. I had this vision of her sitting by the phone all day, cigarette in hand, waiting for the VP to call.

McClown's stepdad strode in behind her. "Der Fuhrer" was a burly guy whose one eyebrow traversed his forehead with not the slightest drop-off in the middle. McClown was visibly disappointed; he'd been expecting his mom to show.

"Der Fuhrer is a total loser," he'd once told me. "He's been in between jobs for two years."

When Steiffel announced our suspensions, Jeff's mom jumped all over him. "This is my son's first smoking offense – same for Leo Haldini there – and since Joshua McClown got a second chance, I expect the same treatment for my son Jeffrey."

How could you argue with that? Our VP assigned Jeff a Saturday School and then said, "Josh McClown, this is your second offense – I am suspending you until Friday."

McClown's stepdad leaned in and then made of a show of resettling himself. "Now just hold it; hold it right *there*. Lemme see if I got this straight: Jeff gets a Saturday school, and my son gets the boot? For the same offense? Chrissakes, they was smoking the same damn cigarette!"

Steiffel clenched his fists, and I imagined him telling his

wife that evening: They've turned on me, Krabigail. I swear, I do some little asshole a favor, and all of a sudden I got my nuts in a sling. Fix me a whiskey sour, wouldja? And make it a double.

The meeting concluded with the expectation that all three of us would report Saturday morning at eight o'clock sharp.

As we left the office, McClown said, "Thanks, Dad." That was the first and only time I ever saw Der Fuhrer smile.

That night, with prodding from my mom, I fessed up to Dad. My greatest fear was then realized, as he shifted his recliner to the upright position, then refolded the Times and started in:

"Son, let's talk about making choices...."

Oh dear God. No, please. Whenever he addressed me as "son", I was in for his endless growing-up-during-the-war speech:

"Decisions you make when you're 14 stay with you always. It's not enough to go along and get along...."

My eyes lost focus and my ears went numb.

McClown, Jeff Mori and I showed up in The Crash at a quarter past eight. In rehearsal for trick-or-treating, Jeff wore a Chewbacca mask from Star Wars, so this might have been the Saturday before Halloween. It was a cold, gusty morning, and the VP pointed out which bushes were to be trimmed and which were to be cleared away.

Shivering in a white, short sleeve shirt, he said, "I will be in my office, but I'll be back to check on your progress. Mori, take that off."

Jeff removed his mask, but not before attempting a Chewbacca howl, sounding like a walrus that took a header into a cement mixer.

Jeff enjoyed physical labor, and McClown hated it less than housework or homework, so we jumped in enthusiastically, ripping out blackberry bushes and pruning vine maples. Jeff was the most productive of the three of us – surprising, given that he usually had the attention span of a goldfish. After watching for two minutes, Steiffel nodded with approval and left.

McClown was good for maybe fifteen minutes, at which point he grabbed a rake and brandished it as a spasticated knight might wield a defective sword. "En garde, ye scoundrel!"

Jeff snatched up a shovel, and the two of them went at it.

vays said: It's all fun and games 'til
at she should have said was: It's all
gets skewered with a rake.

ked up, so Steiffel couldn't hear
McClown pounding on the doors, screaming, "Mori's got holes in
his head!"

Jeff stumbled through the woods and into the street, waving
his Chewbacca mask, blood dripping from his temple. I followed,
trying to pull him out of the road with one hand, while trying to
flag down cars with the other. The first few vehicles swerved
around us, accelerating as they did so.

Lucky for us, a pickup pulled over and the driver rolled
down his window. "What's goin' on?"

Jeff was confused, more so than usual. "Uh, my friend
gave me a smoke, and me and McClown and Leo Haldini – that's
him over there – are s'posta cut down the forest...."

"Both of you, hop in the back. Try not to bleed on my
chainsaw."

After a ten-minute drive to the hospital, I thanked the guy
and led Jeff into the ER. He wasn't all that bright, but he was
impressively loyal to his friends. He told a nurse, "We were, uh,
playing in the woods. I got poked by a branch."

The soft-spoken black woman examined his five evenly-
spaced puncture wounds and said, "Either you're stupid, or you
think I am. Look at me." Jeff stared at his feet. "*Look* at me." He
finally raised his head, and she said in a firm but kindly voice,
"What.... happened?"

Jeff was a rotten liar and he knew it; he came clean.

"Geez Louise!" she said. "How do boys ever survive
childhood? I'll need to call your folks."

"What time is it? Nine? Uh, Mom might not be up yet."

Ms. Mori came fizzing into the ER twenty minutes later, a
frightful bundle of nerves and twiddling fingers. After making a
brief, boisterous fuss over Jeff's stitches, she bustled us out the
door and into her maroon Buick LeSabre.

Inspecting herself in the rearview mirror, she moaned, "I
didn't have time to put my face on. And with my hair like this...."

She steered with her knees, holding the rearview mirror
with one hand and applying lipstick with the other. After hitting

the first pothole, she had a bright red streak across her cheek.

"Ohhh, fiddle dee fuck and fiddle dee doo!"

We roared into the school's bus lane, past the "exit only" sign, tires squealin'. With Jeff hanging out the window to point the way, his mom jumped the curb and floored it. We sped across the football field, her maroon Buick bearing down on Steiffel. He dropped his pruning shears and crouched down in the middle of The Crash, arms akimbo, ready to dive into a blackberry patch if she didn't slow down or turn away.

At the last instant, she slammed on the brakes and spun the wheel. We skidded sideways over a clump of ferns, stopping five feet shy of a massive red cedar, behind which McClown had taken refuge.

"All *ri-ight!*" Jeff cackled. "Bitchin', Mom!"

She was chewing out our VP before we even got out of the car. "How in holy hell did my son end up in the ER while under your supervision? Can you explain that to me?"

With bold strokes of red lipstick emblazoned on her cheeks, nose and right ear, Ms. Mori lives in my memory as a mescal-crazed Apache warrior whose war paint had been applied by an aged squaw with palsy and poor eyesight. And with her black hair up in pink curlers and bunny slippers on her feet, she was a force to be reckoned with. Steiffel's confusion served to enrage her all the more.

"Oh, so you didn't *know* he was in the ER." She advanced, jabbing a bony, accusatory finger at his chest. "What have you been doing all morning? You don't give a hot patootie about these kids!" She was nose to nose with him now. "Well?"

Steiffel's voice cracked when he asked, "Will someone tell me what is going on?"

Jeff began his story, and McClown tried to interrupt, knowing his buddy would either tell the truth or, worse, get caught in a web of lies and then have to come clean. But Jeff was wound up; he told Steiffel all about their battle, jousting and sidestepping as he went.

He finished up with: ".... and then the doctor sewed my head back together."

Ms. Mori lit into Steiffel again. "Of course they're gonna horse around if you don't supervise 'em! Of course they're gonna wage war if you provide 'em with weaponry! Of course my son's gonna end up in the ER!"

The VP stood with head bowed, nodding. McClown and I kept sneakin' looks at each other; it was all we could do to keep from cracking up.

A few drops of rain hit us, and Ms. Mori ordered us to "Get in, boys!" Jeff hopped in the front, and McClown and I piled in the back. She revved the engine, popped the clutch and spun a donut in the soft ground, churning up a rooster tail of rocks and dirt.

Steiffel was a half second late jumping out of our wake, and he ended up with a faceful of mud and twigs. He spit out a bit of muck and wiped a hand across his forehead. Jeff's window was still down, and we heard our VP yell, "God damn it!"

The clouds chose that moment to unload, drenching him instantly. Steiffel looked down at his grubby shirt and hurled the injurious rake against a tree, snapping the handle in two.

"Goddammmitttttt!"

Ms. Mori spun another donut and then floored it. The Buick's V8 growled as we took off down the length of the football field. Jeff donned his Chewbacca mask and howled gleefully. McClown and I rolled down our windows and stuck our faces into the downpour, whooping in celebration of our rescue from Saturday school.

Jeff shouted, "You rock, Mom!"

Ms. Mori responded by yanking the steering wheel back and forth, causing us to fishtail, and tearing up the soggy field. As we approached the end zone, she called out, "Ready, boys? Are you *ready*?" Passing between the uprights, she brought both hands up as we all bellowed, "Touchdown!"

What was it that nurse said? Oh, right – Geez Louise!

For the next week, Jeff got away with murder. Steiffel was terrified of his mom and her maroon Buick LeSabre, and Jeff strutted around like he had a stack of Get Out Of Jail Free cards in his pocket. At lunch, he threw a soggy enchilada at me, missed, and pasted Penny Prismark in the forehead. A perky blonde, Penny had a big golden star stuck on her notebook. I imagined that she had kept and catalogued every one of her gold stars from elementary school.

She huffed and puffed and cried out, "Mr. Steiffel!"

"Hey, now!" said our VP. "None of that, Jeff!"

We boys echoed him. "None of that, Jeff!"

Jeff was late to school four days in a row, and each time Steiffel escorted him to class, threatening him with: "Your last warning, mister; I mean it!"

The Friday after catching a rake in the head, Jeff got busted for fighting at lunch. He was all skin and bones and gristle, but he could fight like a cornered badger. He got knocked on his can, but not before bloodying the nose of a kid that outweighed him by thirty pounds. The VP called Ms. Mori to tell her that he was suspending Jeff.

She roared into the cafeteria five minutes later and made a beeline for Steiffel. "My husband and I are teaching Jeff to stand up for himself, to stand tall and proud."

According to Jake, Mr. Mori had left the previous spring to work the fishing boats in Alaska. Jeff and his mom held out hopes of his return.

Steiffel relented. But when Jeff got in another fight after school that day with the same kid, the VP kicked him out for three days. His mom pleaded for leniency, but Steiffel finally held his ground.

Jake and I were waiting for Jeff as he came out of the office. With tears streaming down his face, Jeff turned to Steiffel and whimpered, "Some friend you turned out to be."

Chapter 3 – November

On Lab Day in 3rd period Science, McClown and I performed actual experiments, that is, we'd get partway through Miss De Waart's cookbook directions and then set them aside, adopting more of a let's-see-what-*this'll*-do approach.

One day he brought a little bottle of Clorox from home and said, "Let's add a smidge of this."

He poured the bleach into the beaker we had simmering over the Bunsen burner, and a noxious brown cloud billowed up, setting off the sprinklers, a crime for which we were never forgiven by the Big Hair Girls.

The day we worked with levers and pulleys, McClown added rubber bands and fashioned a crude trebuchet; he said they were used to lay siege on medieval castles. He had smuggled in a pocketful of worms, and we launched them at our buddies across the room. This is what passed for entertainment. One of the worms hit the window and stuck, and Johnny Boe offered a nickel to anyone who'd eat it. Without hesitation, Jeff picked the worm off the glass, tossed it in the air and caught it in his mouth.

"Mmmmm!" he said. "Sushi!"

Jeff Mori would do pretty much anything for Johnny. Example: Jeff was the one who finally got nabbed for using the blowgun. When the VP walked into class one day, Johnny nailed him in the forehead and then tossed the baggie of BB's onto Jeff's desk. Jeff didn't rat out his friend though; he told the VP he'd gotten the BB's from his brother who had enlisted in the army the week before.

Jeff's problem – well, one of his problems – was that he looked guilty. He usually wore a cock-eyed smirk, like he had just, oh, say, hawked a loogie in some kid's math book and then slammed it shut. Of course, he frequently did pull stunts like that, but just as often the guilty party would be Johnny Boe or McClown. Jeff usually got busted though, because he'd laugh at their hi-jinks, and his cackle stood out like chewed-up fingernails on a movable chalkboard.

Steiffel called Ms. Mori and found out Jeff didn't have a brother in the army. Matter of fact, he doesn't have any brothers at all. So Steiffel busted him for lying as well. He was ready to suspend him, but Jeff's mom showed up and bawled her eyes out in the VP's office. Jeff told us all about it later: his mom whimpered about how her son's spaniel got hit by a car.

"Actually," she had told Steiffel, "Blitz got hit by several cars, and by the time I got there, the crows had picked him over pretty good."

I said to Jeff, "Oh man, your dog got run over?"

"Well, yeah. Only it happened three years ago."

Misty Wart was a chubby, cheerful 28-year-old who inexplicably wore short skirts and sang snippets of hippie songs like "born to be wiii-i-ild" as we entered class. The chalkboards in her room featured psychedelic posters from the 60s, and with a straight face she proclaimed Fernwater to be the grooviest school in the district. While lecturing, she'd sit on a table with her legs dangling over the edge. We boys found the opportunity confusing: sneak a peek, or not? She was kind of gross, but still....

In retrospect, it strikes me how cartoonishly perverted we were in the way of virginal 14-year-old boys. Of course, Johnny Boe would have denied his status as a virgin, and McClown fed us some far-fetched tale about "gettin' some" with a second cousin at a McLowan Fourth of July get-together, which prompted Jake to comment: "Now that's what I'd call a close-knit family."

McClown told us with a leer that he couldn't wait for Thanksgiving; Jeff advised him to bring along some mistletoe.

It was rumored that Misty Wart acted as a consultant for NASA. One day while leaving 3rd period, I listened in on an exchange between a few of my classmates:

"I didn't understand that bit about solar systems."

"Yeah, I can't believe how smart she is."

"I wish I was that smart."

Dad would have been appalled at their assessment of Misty Wart. One evening I had asked him to look at my science test; he responded by holding up his newspaper and shaking it. "Jimmy

Carter wants to get rid of our nukes! Think the Soviets will give up theirs? Jimmy – what kind of name is *that* for leader of the free world?" He brought his recliner up and reached for the test. "Let's have a look." I pointed out a question that I'd missed and he read it aloud. "How many hours are there in a light year?"

Dad, being a structural engineer, was offended. He squinted and read it again.

"This doesn't even make sense," he said. "A light year is a measure of distance; hours measure time."

"That's what I thought too."

"Well?"

"Well, what?"

"Well, you went over this in class, right?" He shook the test. "What happened when you pointed out her mistake?"

"I didn't do that. Nobody did. Dad, nobody corrects her."

"Oh? And why is that?"

I couldn't tell if his growing fury was directed at my teacher's incompetence or at my own spinelessness. Either way, I regretted showing him the test.

"Dad, she has a Ph.D. in…. something. I don't want to be, um, disruptive."

He stared intently into the cold dark fireplace. I feared he would douse my test with lighter fluid and set it ablaze. His eyes glazed over, but he soon resumed his surly inspection of the test, and seconds later he leapt to his feet. "Now what the hell is this?"

With soap bubbles dripping off her elbows, Mom rushed in to see what had set Dad off.

He read another test question aloud: "Patrick McSweeney weighs 140 pounds. Explain why his mass would change if he were standing on the moon. Calculate the change."

"I know, Dad…."

He began to read it again. "Patrick McSweeney weighs…. Holy shit on a shamrock!"

"Now Gianni," said Mom, drying her hands on her apron. "I wish you wouldn't use that kind of language."

When Dad cussed, he usually did so in Italian, so as not to offend my mother. The first time Johnny Boe had come over, Dad was swearing at a soccer ref on TV. "Ma che cazzo fai, coglione?" What the fuck ya doing, you wiener? Unbeknownst to my parents,

Uncle Marco had translated Dad's more colorful phrases for me.

Later on that day Johnny told me, "Haldini, your dad is so cool. He looks like one of those old Mafioso guys."

That was quite the compliment, coming from Johnny. He never said anybody was cool. He had more respect for me after that.

My father pushed on. "Weight, not mass, varies because of changes in gravity."

"Dad, her specialty is chemistry or biology or something, not physics so much."

I found myself defending Misty Wart, though I wasn't sure why. It's not like I was filled with school spirit; none of us were, except for the cheerleaders, a few teachers, and some girls on the softball team. Maybe I was afraid Dad would show up at school and grill Misty Wart on her knowledge of – oh, I don't know – the moons of Jupiter. I wouldn't put it past him. Or maybe he'd challenge her to a debate. Or a leg-wrestling match. There were a dozen ways he could make a spectacle of himself, any one of which would lead to my embarrassment, if not ostracism.

Dad took a pen and paper out of the coffee table, saying, "I am going to write a letter to your.... your teacher, such as she is."

And that is my father. He has two modes of expression: sad but civil; and royally pissed, ready to take on the devil herself, who was currently teaching science at Fernwater Junior High.

While Dad wrote and cussed under his breath, I explained the issue to Mom, who considered herself more of a "fine arts kind of gal". She couldn't see what the big deal was. Having been born at the beginning of the Great Depression, her life was now bountiful by contrast, a gift for which she was ever thankful. Minor mistakes were to be overlooked.

"Now Gianni," she said, "anyone could make a mistake like that."

"Science teachers shouldn't. Jesus, anybody who's ever taken physics...." Dad focused his displeasure on me. "Son, this De Waart woman...." Oh God, here we go. "Authorities must earn your respect. People who get their way because they are in positions of power rather than because they live by reason and justice.... You must stand up to them, regardless of age, yours or theirs. Chi tace acconsente." Silence gives consent.

He was getting himself worked up now. "God knows I had to take a stand during The War. The *Resistenza* was not going to give up easily. You're concerned about being *disruptive*, for God's sake? Son, sometimes disruption is necessary...."

The frustrating thing was that I wanted to hear about how Dad fought Mussolini and the Fascists, and how he was disruptive, but his stories wandered all over the place, and before he ever got around to any heroics or actual fighting, he would always bring it back to: Leo, you need to Take A Stand.

Misty Wart asked McClown why he wasn't doing his assignment. He'd been fiddling around with a box of paper clips, trying to make a rhinoceros or a stagecoach or something.

"We drove back from Spokane last night, and didn't get home 'til one. I'm too sleepy to concentrate." Our teacher wasn't buying it, so he upped the ante. "These chairs are hard as a rock; and I've got a hemorrhoid the size of a lemon."

Jeff asked, "What's a him roy?"

"You're a hemorrhoid," said Johnny Boe.

"Am not!"

I blurted out, more loudly than I intended, "Well, he's sure a pain in Misty Wart's ass."

My pals giggled and snorted into their fists.

"Leo," said Misty Wart, "thank you for not using that kind of language." Though it was a mildest of reprimands, it was the first I had ever received at school, and my face turned hot. But the satisfaction I got from watching my pals laugh and repeat my line outweighed my shame.

An office TA walked in at that moment with a blue slip, a ticket to see the VP. Misty Wart read out three names with undisguised glee: "Johnny Boe, Josh McClown, Jeff Mori."

The summons to the office was expected; they'd been caught gambling at lunch, and would now be facing detentions, if not suspension. Before heading out the door, Johnny grabbed Jeff by the shoulders. "Let me do the talking, Mori. Don't say a word. You gotta *maintain*."

Jake called out, "Good luck, men," and I marveled at how masterful he was at avoiding trouble. He had been gambling too, but the instant before the other boys got nailed, he rotated in his seat and proclaimed, "And *that* is why the Mariners stunk it up."

The kid next to him registered surprise that somebody was suddenly talking to him, but it looked like he was taken aback by Jake's anti-Mariners sentiment. I had seen Jake pull this kind of stunt before; when he saw the VP coming, he'd peel away from his pals, leaving them to fend for themselves. Johnny did this too at times, but he was not as wary or watchful as Jake.

Here were the differences between the J boys: Jake never got caught; Johnny Boe got caught, but he'd weasel his way out of trouble; and the other two got caught and disciplined regularly.

I know we were only three months into the year, but here was the thing about Jake: He never got busted. Never. He didn't cause much trouble in class, at least openly, but between classes or after school, he'd break a window or set a roll of TP on fire and roll it down the hall, just for kicks. Every so often, a teacher would actually *see* him do it, but nobody – no custodian, no secretary, no administrator – ever apprehended him.

"How come you never get busted?" I asked Jake one day after he lobbed a chili dog across the cafeteria.

"I got my Six Rules," he said, and listed them for me:

#1 LOOK ORDINARY. Jake had an amazing ability to melt into a crowd. He didn't strut like a jock or talk like a stoner or dress like a preppie. By design, he looked like "just some kid".

#2 DON'T JOIN DRAMA CLUB. Or yearbook staff, or stage band. Don't turn out for sports. Few teachers knew Jake, and he never asked or answered questions in class.

#3 GET BY. Jake did just well enough academically to avoid the attention of teachers, counselors and the principal. He was getting a C- in every class.

#4 GO SOLO. He stole ten test tubes from science one day, then crushed and scattered them beneath the wheels of teachers' cars. I felt honored to be the only one who knew the cause of the sudden rash of flat tires. And when Fernwater's jazz band, No Stone Unterned, hung up their banner in the main hallway, Jake asked me to stand guard, while he altered it with a red felt pen to make it read: No Unstoned Tern.

I assumed he was tightlipped because Jeff could never keep his trap shut; I didn't discover the actual reason until years later.

#5 KIDS ARE NOT THE ENEMY. He aimed his pranks

at teachers or the VP, whereas Johnny had a mean streak – he'd grab a mousy sevie and get McClown to padlock him to a trashcan by his belt loops. Jake seldom broke Rule #5, but when he did, he had his reasons. Prime example: Jeff threw a party the day after Thanksgiving, and when his mom made a run to 7-11 for more snacks and sodas, Johnny Boe pulled a few of us guys into the can and pissing into her bottle of shampoo. Jake retaliated for Jeff by pissing in a bottle of beer and switching it with Johnny's. Again, I was honored to be the only one in on Jake's prank.

#6 STAY HOME ON PICTURE DAY. This was his true stroke of genius. According to Jake, when teachers see an unfamiliar kid screwing up in the hall, they find his picture in the previous year's annual – the librarian kept old yearbooks on her checkout counter – and report him to the VP. In Jake's case, there was no visual evidence that he ever attended Fernwater.

My mom came home from a PTA meeting one night and told my dad and me that Vice Principal Steiffel had addressed discipline issues at Fernwater. One student in particular was causing problems, but they could never catch this "invisible boy".

Huh? Huhhhh?

Dad bowed his head and rubbed his temple with three fingers, muttering something about "invisible boys". He was subject to spells like this; during a conversation or the evening news, he would latch onto a seemingly random phrase, which would thereby induce an hour-long paralysis of mind. If he went six months without one of his "zone-outs", I'd get suckered into thinking he was done with them, making it all the more disheartening when they returned.

Mom regarded him with affection and helplessness, both of which she seemed to hold in bottomless reserve.

I returned to my homework, but this business about the "invisible boy" kept intruding, and it finally dawned on me that Steiffel was conducting a manhunt – or maybe "boyhunt" is more apt – for Jake, my next door neighbor. I had not realized it until that moment, but I was proud of him. I was proud to be his friend. Jake the Invisible Boy had it all figured out. And if he could figure it out, then maybe there was hope for me.

Chapter 4 – December

In 4th period Geometry, I excelled, partly because the J boys were not in my class – they were taking lower level math – and partly because I looked at math as puzzle-solving, but mostly because I liked Mr. Farley; he was easy to follow, yet his class was challenging. Also, his "classroom" was located in a relatively quiet corner of the building, meaning that he could lecture without having to yell.

After Thanksgiving break, Mr. Farley taught us the Pythagorean Theorem: $a^2 + b^2 = c^2$, where a, b, and c are the side lengths of a right triangle. Being a baseball fanatic like myself, he then posed a series of questions:

It's 90 feet between bases. How far is the throw from home to second?

A shortstop fields a ball halfway between second and third. How far is the throw to first?

A batter runs 22 feet per second. It takes the 1st baseman 4 seconds to field a ball and tag first. Will the batter make it to first base?

"Depends," said Penny Prismark, who sat in front of me. "How cute is he?" She swiveled her head like an owl and winked, to make sure I got her joke.

Worse, I sat next to Delores Pearle, who suffered from a seemingly perpetual cold and profound gastrointestinal distress. One day she belched and sneezed simultaneously, causing her tangle of red hair to shake ferociously. She then giggled, though I couldn't tell whether she was embarrassed or amused. Penny snorted in revulsion and scooted her desk away.

Ten minutes later, Delores hiccupped and coughed, and followed up with a hiccup-belch combo and another giggle. Should I be frightened, disgusted or impressed? Being fascinated with Bodily Function Noises, I set out to list all possible pairings of her BFNs:

b = belch   c = cough   s = sneeze   h = hiccup

bc   bs   bh   cs   ch   sh

There. I counted six possibilities, and sure enough, those of us sitting around her were treated to each combination over the course of the next few days. I know this because I checked them off each time her head detonated.

And yes, I am well aware of what a bizarre human being I was at age 14.

Then one day, Delores sneezed, belched and hiccupped simultaneously. I went back to the original list, and added all of the possible three- and four-element combos:

bcs   bch   bsh   csh   bcsh

That brought the total to 11. I was pleased with my mathematical prowess. Yes, I was quite pleased, until the first time Delores farted. And this was no dainty girl fart. No sir; she let one rip! She then burped and farted, compelling Penny to move her desk away farther.

My list needed to be revised, expanded, updated. Adding an "f" to the list of BFNs, I systematically listed all possible combinations. There turned out to be 26 of them:

bc	bs	bh	bf	cs
ch	cf	sh	sf	hf
bcs	bch	bcf	bsh	bcf
bhf	csh	csf	chf	snf
bcsh	bcsf	bchf	bshf	cshf	bcshf

OK, now we're gettin' somewhere. Again, I checked them off, one by one, as various orifices would erupt. This was getting tricky, however, because with certain combos, it was not obvious which parts of her disturbingly prolific body we were hearing from. Still, I kept at it, as I began to appreciate the power and beauty of applied mathematics.

My satisfaction, however, was short-lived: What if Delores

should introduce a new BFN to the mix? If she starts cracking her knuckles, would that count? Probably not; it's a fully voluntary action. But what about yawning – should I count that? Yes, I'd have to think it would. How about giggling? Maybe.

This was getting complicated.

"Mmmm, reminds me of how my mother's kitchen smelled." Dad closed his eyes and practically drooled in anticipation.

Sitting at the kitchen counter on a rainy afternoon, he and I breathed in the aroma of tomatoes, mozzarella, basil, garlic and whatever secret ingredients Mom had slipped into the lasagna. When my parents got married, Granny Haldini had sent my mom several recipes from The Old Country. Lasagna had become our family favorite. Mom, like my grandmother, served it with spare ribs simmered in a spicy tomato sauce until it fell off the bone.

Dad and I started up a game of chess, and we shared a rare and idyllic half hour. When I made a crafty move, he'd inhale sharply, then grunt and say something like: "Good one," or "Didn't see that coming." It didn't take much to please me.

While waiting for him to make a move, I spotted Jonathan Livingston Seagull lying on the counter and asked what it was about.

Mom thought before answering. "Seeking a higher purpose in life, even if it means being banished from the flock".

Dad nodded. "Sometimes you have to tell the flock to go take a flying leap."

I thought that was pretty clever, but his annoyance made it clear he was not joking around. The flock? Who is, or was, his flock? And why would he tell them to take a flying leap? Mom rubbed his shoulders for a few seconds, and he nodded once, a begrudging acknowledgement of his misdirected surliness.

Who is my flock? I wondered. My family? The J boys? My school? And as for seeking a higher purpose.... Huh? I had no idea what that could possibly mean. I thought about our school motto – One Good Tern Deserves Another – and now I wondered if it had something to do with seagulls – or people – being nice and having friends. Was I a Good Tern?

Being a 14-year-old goofus, I did not dwell long on these questions.

Watching Dad salivate, I said, "Mom, you better serve me and Ella first, otherwise we're not going to get any."

"Five more minutes," said Mom, smiling contentedly as she tossed the salad. "By the way, Leo, 1st quarter grades came today." She wiped her hands on her apron and handed Dad a letter.

"It's about time." He set down his glass of red wine, and tore the envelope along the perforation. "Let's have a look." He leaned toward me so we both could see:

Geography	1.0	B
English	1.0	A .
Science	0.8	C
Geometry	1.0	A
Art	1.0	A

Fernwater Junior High had a unique two-grades-per-class system. The quantity grade showed *how much* work was done. In four classes, I had completed all of the required work, thereby earning one credit in each. The quality grade was a measure of *how well* that work was done. In Science, I averaged a C for the four units out of five I had completed.

Dad scowled and growled and grumbled his way across the kitchen, churning up the tranquil air and grinding away at Mom's contentedness. He dug a pen out of the junk drawer and circled "Science" on my report card. Our grading system had been explained to him before, but this was the first time he'd actually seen a report card. He asked about the .8.

"Chemicals got spilled on my lab report," was how I put it. "It needs to be redone."

"How much time do you have to redo it?" he asked. "A light year?"

"I'll have it done by the end of the week."

"And your friends – how were their grades?"

"I didn't see all their report cards."

That was true; I had only seen Johnny Boe's and Jeff's. We stopped by Johnny's house that afternoon, just as the mailman came. Knowing how dismal his grades must be, I was surprised at how upbeat he'd been.

"Yeah," Johnny boasted as he ripped open the envelope. "My dad's gonna give me five bucks and say, 'Kick ass report card, Jonathan.' He thinks I'm doing great."

"Why's he think that?" I asked.

"Check it out, lads."

Geography	0.2	B
English	0.2	C-
Science	0.2	C
Gen. Math	1.0	B
Art	0.7	A

"What do you mean, doing great? You only got 2.3 credits out of 5."

"Yeah, well, my dad, the Bad Guy with a Badge, asked me about those decimals two years ago. I told him they were computer codes, and not to bother with them."

Jeff dug his wadded-up report card out of his back pocket; it showed four "0.0's" for his quantity grades. He was passing Art.

"Jesus, you moron!" said Johnny. "Haven't you figured it out? All you gotta do is pass one unit per freakin' class, and that's your letter grade."

Jeff shook his head. "Won't work. Mom spends a lot of time in Steiffel's office. He told her how the grades work. Fiddle de fuck and fiddle de doo!"

Johnny's scam seemed too easy. "But what about the letter they sent home in September?" I asked him. "You know, the one that explains the grading system; parents had to sign and return it."

"Oh, you mean the letter I opened before Dad got home? The letter I forged his signature on? You mean that one?"

I looked at his report card again. "What is Gen. Math?"

"General Math, me and Jeff are takin' it. No offense, Mori, but it's math for boneheads."

"How'd you get into it?" I asked. "You're pretty good at math."

Johnny gave us a crooked smile. "I failed the placement test last spring, on purpose. General Math is easier than Algebra, and way the hell easier than whatever you're taking, Haldini."

Jeff looked like he'd found out there was a party coming, and he was the only one without an invitation.

Johnny took pity on him. "There's a way out, Mori."

Jeff was leery. "Yeah? How?"

"All you gotta do is check out a book from the library and then lose it."

"But…. but then I'd have to pay a fine."

Johnny put his hands on Jeff's shoulders. "Right! But then you forget to pay the fine.

Jeff was trying to understand; he really was. "But then I'd have to…. what happens then?"

"They penalize you by not sending home your report card."

Jeff's eyes flew open. "Woo hoo! Woo hoo hoo hoooo!"
`He had just been told, in effect, that he never had to do homework again. He broke into an idiotic hula dance and a tuneless version of that "Alo ha eeee" song.

Dad set aside my report card, and we sat for dinner. Dad raised a glass of red wine to toast Mom's lasagna: "A Mio Miele." To My Honey.

He had a tendency to slip into his native tongue whenever he became sentimental or angry, or got a little sloshed. In this case, reminiscing about his mother's kitchen had gotten him all dewy-eyed, and he was agitated by what he perceived to be the frivolous nature of American schools. He was also well into his third glass of wine.

It struck me as odd that Dad, who spoke dreamily about his homeland, had completely shed his accent, as if trying his best to fit in here, whereas Uncle Marco had not lost any of his native inflection. In part, that could be attributed to the difference in their ages; being three years Dad's senior, it would have required more effort for Marco to lose his accent. But it seemed like he didn't care about losing it; he was happy to bring a bit of Italy along as part of his being.

I considered Dad to be a conundrum – that was a "word of the day" in English class. He always talked about how hard it was, growing up during The War, yet he harkened back to those days as some sort of golden era. And though his accent was gone, we kept an ornately framed photograph hanging in the dining room from

The Old Country.

In the photo, the perimeter walls of a grand Italian villa are enmeshed in a lush web of bougainvillea. In the distance lies Lake Como, nestled in the precipitous foothills of the Alps. One wing of the villa had been badly burned, and I was often tempted to ask about growing up there, but I always shied away, deterred by the prospect of sitting through, again, the speech that begins: Son, when I was growing up during The War....

Mom dished up a hefty serving of lasagna for each of us, starting with my 6th grade sister. Ella guided her long, straight black hair behind her ears with her index fingers and dug in.

Primed by the arrival of 1st quarter grades, Dad was curious about Fernwater. "Leo, do I understand correctly that your school does not have walls?"

"The band room and woodshop have walls; and the office. Otherwise, classrooms are separated by chalkboards." My mouth watered as Mom passed me my dinner.

"Isn't it noisy? How do you hear your teacher? What do they hope to accomplish by that?" He turned to Mom. "*Why* did they build the school that way?"

A devoted PTA member, my mother had read flyers that explained the Philosophy of Fernwater. Being open-minded, she was willing to try most anything; or at least she was willing to have her son try it. Dad tended to be more of a conventional sort.

While dishing up his lasagna, Mom explained, "Kids learn at different rates; some move through the material more quickly than others. The school is open, so kids can be grouped depending on their need. Some days, they will be arranged in small groups; other days, lectures can be given to as many as sixty students. The walls are movable so as to allow a variety of configurations."

It sounded reasonable, I guess. Or at least it would have, had I not seen Fernwater with my own eyes.

"Here you go, Gianni," said Mom. "Dig in."

Dad thanked her and picked up his fork. "Leo, how often do the walls get moved?"

"They don't," I replied through a mouthful of pasta and cheese.

Ella asked, "Am *I* going to Fernwater next year?"

Mom forced a smile. "Yes, sweetie."

Dad set down his fork, and asked, "So, when the bell rings, class begins just like at a normal school?"

It was difficult for him to simultaneously talk, eat and stew about the state of the world. He could handle any two of them well enough, but could never manage to juggle all three.

"Well, no, Dad, we don't have bells."

"I think I'd like that better," said Ella. When things got tense, she spoke in her cute little girl voice, in an effort to lighten things up. It never worked.

Dad folded his hands and placed them under his chin. "Why are there no bells?"

The lasagna was hot and tasty. I squeezed an "I dunno" out the side of my mouth.

Massaging his forehead, he looked to Mom for an answer.

She was not as sure of herself now. "Well, the thinking is that some classes require more time than others, and bells would limit flexibility." She looked at Dad's untouched plate. "Gianni, eat." She added in a sing-songy voice, "I put in *lotsa mozza* rella."

Dad forked off a bite of lasagna and asked me, "Are some classes longer than others?"

"Nope," I said.

He lifted the forkful of lasagna. Melty cheese dripped back onto his plate. "So 1st period starts at 8:00 and ends when?"

"About 8:50. Mom, would you dish me up some more?"

Dad put down his fork. "What do you mean by '*about*'?"

It was a relief, listening to my dad ask questions that laid bare the goofiness of Fernwater. Misty Wart, Steiffel and on a good day, even The Krabman were gung-ho on our school, which somebody had nicknamed "Oxford of Oxley", a reference that none of us kids understood. By acknowledging the lunacy of my day-to-day existence, Dad was unwittingly providing me with an excuse for my increasingly hellish behavior.

Sometimes disruption is necessary – those were my dad's exact words, and being 14, I was perfectly willing to misinterpret them. I thought, Hell, I'm no more bonkers than the people who run the madhouse. And though I was still fairly well-mannered at school – a Good Enough Tern, by comparison to the J boys – I reveled in the lack of adult guidance and supervision.

I said, "The clocks at school aren't set together."

"They're not synchronized?" Dad picked up his original forkful of lasagna and pointed it at me. The cheese firmed up before my eyes.

"Right. But they're within a few minutes of each other."

"How do you know when class is supposed to start? Or end?" He turned to Mom again.

"When the principal is asked questions like this, his response is that Fernwater is moving away from cells-and-bells. He says, 'Kids won't bounce off the walls if there aren't any.' They are expected to take responsibility for their own learning. The principal is....'

"Frigato in capo!" Fucked in the head.

Mom tried to bring the conversation around to something we could deal with right away. "Leo, this science lab you need to make up – can you take care of it tomorrow before school?"

"No. Doors don't open for students until five, maybe six minutes before 1st period."

"I should know better," said Dad, "but I am going to ask: Why is that?"

With a lilt in her voice, Ella said, "We get to go into our room whenever we want."

Mom spoke softly. "The principal is afraid.... concerned, rather, that if students are let in earlier, the school will be vandalized."

"Mi sta sulle palle!" He's standing on my balls! At least, that's the literal translation. In everyday life, Uncle Marco says it means: He's pissin' me off!

Ella asked what that meant.

Dad ignored her. "It was 28 degrees Monday morning!" His voice was rising, in pitch and volume. "Hell, it was snowing! Did they let you in early then?"

"No, Dad, they never do."

"Minchioneria!" Foolishness.

Ella said, "I don't think I'd like that." I glared at her and shook my head.

Dad narrowed his eyes. "What else should I be asking?"

Boy, where to start? How about Mr. Hester's overhead zooming across the room? I began the story as if I were telling it to my uncle, but watching Dad's mood darken, I ended up sticking to just the facts. He was not entertained in the least, especially when Ella started giggling and choked on her lasagna.

Dad's voice was now ominously calm. "What else?" At this point, all I hoped for was that he did not zone out.

I told him about the paper airplanes and gummy bears that came flying over the walls. I didn't mention my participation in such monkey business, but Dad was no dummy; I did my best to look innocent, but he stared me down, and my blush and sudden squirminess gave me away.

Ella clasped her hands together. "That sounds like fun!"

Dad put down his unused fork again. He placed his elbows on the table, fingers kneading his temples. "Go on," he whispered.

I left out most of the good stuff, that is, stories that would incriminate me or my pals. So my parents never heard about the blowgun or the Russian fags or my mathematical wizardry as it pertained to Delores Pearle's sinuses and digestive tract.

"Well," I said, "there's a kid in science that's failed every test so far, and he got a C- for 1st quarter."

It was true; if you failed a test in Misty Wart's class, or, for that matter, most classes at Fernwater, you could re-study and re-take the test. It might not be exactly the same one, but it would be pretty close. The highest grade you could get on a re-test was a C-, but Jake didn't mind.

I went on. "Sometimes I can hear three movie soundtracks at once, which is cool because, if one of them is boring…."

"Enough!" Dad exhaled, folded his arms, and looked dejectedly at his room-temperature plate of lasagna. The cheese had congealed on his forkful of pasta. He asked in a weary, though determined voice, "When and where is the next PTA meeting?"

The noodles in my stomach knotted themselves up into one big disagreeable lump.

Chapter 5 – January

Child psychologists will say that one's basic personality takes shape by age five, framed by genes and filled in by environment. But looking back on 9th grade, my psyche was still in a riotous state of flux. As I moved from class to class, my personality adjusted itself according to subject matter, comportment of my teachers, and whoever happened to be sitting next to me. I was an unmolded lump of clay with a flexible ethos, willing to be and become most anyone. So in 1st period History, I was a goofus; in 2nd period English, a non-entity; in 3rd period Science, incompetent; and in 4th period Geometry, a star. To describe my various personalities, I considered amending our World Book Encyclopedia, to include several new species of tern: Good Tern, Good Enough Tern, Idiotic Tern, Wrong Tern, and so on.

My pals and I couldn't wait to get to 5th period Art. Miss Blohmeyer, whose name, of course, we shortened to "Bloh Me", was a fox. Bursting into her room one day, we found her standing on a stool to get materials from the upper shelves of a cabinet; I liked to think she was posing for us. She jumped lightly to the floor, and I marveled at how somebody that old – she was thirty at the time – could be that agile. Having performed as a figure skater with Ice Capades, she moved with the easy grace of an athlete. She favored long, loose-fitting dresses and wore her long blonde hair up in a bun, all of which somehow served to accentuate her California Girl good looks. In my mind's eye, I swapped out her dresses for those sequined barely-there skirts favored by skaters.

Miss Bloh Me greeted us as she did each day with a pleasant "Hello, boys," and we slobbered like St. Bernard puppies. We were attentive in her class and even respectful, except for Jeff Mori, who tried to get her attention by acting like a jerkwad. Whenever she turned her back, he stuck out his tongue and wiggled it up and down, in and out, side to side.

"Tickle your ass with a feather?" he'd mumble, hoping

she'd whirl around and ask indignantly: What did you say? And he'd be ready with his practiced reply: Particularly nasty weather.

But even with her back turned, Miss Bloh Me always knew what he was up to. Did she have mirrors set up? One time he had his arm cocked, ready to nail McClown in the head with a goopy paintbrush, and she turned around at exactly the right instant to stop him. Jeff yawned and pretended to be stretching. She didn't say anything, but she knew. She *knew*. She had this way of looking past him that shut him up for a few minutes, but then he'd do something dumb, like carve the word "fuk" or "dik" into a table, and he always got caught, because his spelling was noticeably worse than everyone else's.

Johnny Boe brought in three squares of fruit-filled green Jell-O from the lunchroom and handed them off to McClown, figuring he'd put them to good use. Seeing that my pal needed a distraction, I pointed at the ceiling in the far corner and called out, "How did *that* get in here?"

When everyone turned to look, Jake held open Penny Prismark's purse while McClown dumped in the Jell-O. She was bubbly, indiscriminately so, and therefore considered to be worthy of our scorn. She brought to mind Brutus, my sister Ella's cocker spaniel; he'd hump the foot of anyone who walked through our front door, and he'd do so with a great deal of enthusiasm, regardless of how the foot was shod or to whom it belonged. Dad's loafers were no more and no less appealing than Jake's mom's stilettos. As Ella explained to hapless guests, "Brutus has an itchy tummy."

Several kids looked back at me and said, "What?"

I squinched up my eyes and said, "Oh, it's nothin'."

Penny reached into her purse ten minutes later and pulled out a handful of green ooze that had sullied her make-up, money, and a fake love letter that Johnny slipped in there earlier. He had signed Jeff's name to it, encircling it with little hearts.

"Eeeuuuwwww! Miss Blohmeyer!" She held up her slimy green hand for all to see and handed the letter to Miss Bloh Me, while Jeff cackled away.

Penny glared at him and said, "No gold star for you!"

Miss Bloh Me scowled as she read the letter silently, and

then she wrote him up an after-school detention. As usual, we let him take the heat for the Jell-O and love letter.

And that was a typical Fernwater day: Johnny brought the Jell-O, I provided a diversion, McClown did the dirty work with an assist from Jake, and Jeff got busted. What a team!

The Krabman came in to borrow butcher paper near the end of 4th period, something he did on a regular basis. Johnny Boe shook his head in disgust. "I can't believe Miss Bloh Me is ridin' the bologna pony with that doof."

Always one step behind, Jeff Mori asked, "What's a blony bony?"

"Isn't it obvious?" said Johnny. "I mean, just look at 'em." Miss Bloh Me had The Krabman in a friendly headlock. "Yep, definitely doin' the wild thing." Seeing Jeff's confusion, Johnny said, "Jesus, Mori, you airhead! Mori – what kind of name is that anyway? Is it short for Moron?" Johnny then punched him in the shoulder; that's what passed for affection between the J boys.

Jeff responded with a half-smile and a return punch. "Uhh, it's Canadian or something."

Watching our teachers horse around, I became nauseous at the thought of Miss Bloh Me riding The Krabman's bologna pony. Although, seeing as how she'd been an ice skater and he a track star at the UW – at least that's what he was always telling us – I guess it made sense that two jocks would hit it off. Still....

Johnny got distracted by a group of girls on the other side of class; they were giggling about the phrase "No Unstoned Tern", which had become our unofficial school motto.

Miss Bloh Me was still yukkin' it up with The Krabman, so Johnny snuck over to talk to Lucy Sparkett, the most conspicuous of the girls. Juicy Lucy wasn't pretty, but boy, was she hot. She looked like she was 23 and flaunted a teased-up mound of coal-black hair that would have prompted Uncle Marco to declare in mock reverence, "The bigger the hair, the closer to God."

"Psssst." The kid next to me handed me a folded-up note with Johnny Boe's name on it.

Johnny was still flirting with Lucy, so Jake said, "Lemme have a look." He opened the note and showed me. It was from Penny Prismark, printed in big boxy capital letters, nothing like the flowery script I had expected.

Johnny, I know you wrote that note – Jeff doesn't spell that good.
It was sweet, what you said about my teeth lined up like Chiclets.
But no, you scamp, my lips aren't lonely! I'm stoked for the
dance. Are you going?
                                    Later gator, Penny   xxx ooo

Jake scribbled a response: Save me a slow dance – Boe.
He refolded the note and sent in back across the room.

See how ghoulishly we treated one another? Even our
friends. Especially our friends. And yet, even at the time it struck
me how brilliant was Jake's maneuver in its moral symmetry – just
as Jeff had unfairly borne the consequences of Johnny Boe's fake
love letter, so now Johnny would bear the fallout from Jake's
bogus response, though the nature of that fallout had yet to be
determined. This incident solidified my understanding of Jake's
role amongst the J boys; while Johnny was their self-appointed
ringleader, it was Jake that meted out a crude sort of tribal justice.

Now, whether Penny was treated fairly is another matter.
According to Jake, she had dumped him the year before, after
"going out" for three days, and that was how he justified his deceit.

Johnny was still chatting up Lucy; I couldn't hear what
they said, but she wrote on his arm with a black felt pen and gave
him a smile that announced: Saddle up, Boe; I am ready to breed.
He returned to his seat and flexed his not-yet-developed bicep, on
which the words "No Unstoned Tern" were written, surrounded by
little black hearts.

For many at Fernwater, it was nice to have a school motto
they could finally get behind.

Walking to my next class, I ran into Johnny Boe and Juicy
Lucy groping one another. She grabbed his hands, guided them
around her body, and planted them squarely on her ass.

I was tempted to shout: Hey! *I* am ready to breed!

Lucy Sparkett was all hips, hair, chest and mascara; she
jiggled and bounced her way across the cafeteria, secure in the
knowledge that her every gyration was tracked by boys and girls
alike. Eying Johnny Boe, she slowwwly skimmed her tongue

across her glossy upper lip, and headed for the door leading out to The New Crash.

"Gotta go, lads," said Johnny with a sleazy grin. "Got me a date with my little cock socket." He stood up and said, "I need a diversion, Mori; go pull the fire alarm, would ya?"

Johnny made this request frequently. As had become his habit, Jeff looked to Jake the Invisible Boy for counsel.

Without waiting for a response, Johnny muttered, "Coupla pussies," and crammed the rest of his cheeseburger in his mouth.

McClown heaved an open carton of milk over his shoulder as a distraction for his buddy. Within seconds the cafeteria became a blizzard of airborne mashed potatoes and fruit medley. Johnny weaved his way across the lunchroom, staying out of Steiffel's line of sight, and then he slipped out the door.

As usual, Jeff was confused. "What's a cock socket?" We eyeballed him until he said, "Oh!" It was at this point that he also made sense of "riding the bologna pony" – "Ohhh!" – and "doin' the wild thing" – "Ohhhhhhhh!" A goofy smile spread across his face, and he tapped his head three times with a forefinger. "Got me a little plan."

On the bus the next morning, Jeff bounced up and down all the way to school. "Wait'll you see what I did!" he kept saying. "Just wait and see!"

As we entered the loading zone, all faces were pressed against the bus windows to check out his handiwork. The previous night, Jeff had returned to school with a flashlight, a brush and a bucket of white paint. Just below our motto, "ONE GOOD TERN DESERVES ANOTHER", he had written "crabmn fux blomire" across the front of the school. The letters were all crooked, but they measured four feet tall and stood out nicely on the brick wall.

As he got off the bus, Jeff began shadow-boxing and singing the theme from Rocky: "Buh dut.... duhhh! Buh dut.... duhhh!" He stopped when he spotted Johnny Boe, who was clearly unhappy with the graffiti. "What?" asked Jeff.

A crowd was gathering to admire new artwork; this was supposed to be Jeff's moment of glory. "Whaaat!" he wailed.

Johnny snarled, "Look, numb nuts. Steiffel's gonna think I put you up to this."

"Hey, men," said Jake. "Check it out."

The Krabman's car was pulling up behind our bus, with his wife driving. The assembled students turned to watch him get out of the passenger's seat. His confusion was evident, so the crowd parted, giving him and his wife a clear look at the graffiti.

Mrs. Krabke's hands flew up, and her mouth flew open: "Oh, my goodness!" Her foot slipped off the brake, and she rammed the back of the school bus.

The Krabman stuck his head in the still-open car door and said, "I'm sorry. Honey, I am so sorry!" He then straightened and scanned the crowd. There was only one kid at who spelled that poorly, and pretty much everyone knew who it was.

The Krabman thundered, "Jeff Moriiii! Where are youuuu?"

Again the crowd parted, leaving Jeff standing alone, hunched over, trying to will himself into a state of invisibility.

"Moriiii, you worthless little turd!"

Jeff shrieked and took off around the corner of the building, with The Krabman in hot pursuit. Until that moment, we had all assumed our teacher had been lying about his track scholarship. Boy, was he fast! The crowd followed, some hoping Jeff would get away, and others hoping for The Krabman to make a diving tackle, but most of us would be perfectly happy either way. As The Krabman closed on him, Jeff ducked into the cafeteria, and he did escape, temporarily, by hiding in the girls' can. But twenty seconds later, the door crashed open and four girls emerged through a curtain of cigarette smoke, dragging my buddy by his ankles across the cafeteria. Jeff thrashed his arms and begged for mercy.

"This way, ladies," said The Krabman, directing them toward the VP's office. He motioned for Johnny Boe and me to follow, thinking we may have witnessed the crime.

Entering the VP's office, I was even shakier than Jeff, and I wasn't sure why; it wasn't me that defaced the front of the school. But just the thought of telling Dad about this incident made me queasy. Jeff was twitchy until Steiffel informed him that his mom was on her way. That information would have unnerved most kids, but Jeff was confident that she'd be able to come up with a perfectly reasonable explanation for his behavior, i.e., a lie, that would get him off.

"Pretty speedy, Mr. Krabke," said Johnny.

The Krabman was in a sour mood, but how could he pass up an opportunity like this?

"You know I ran track at U Dub," he said. "School record for the hundred would've been mine, if they hadn't switched to meters. I had a step on that fellow from Idaho until the final two yards."

"Really?" Johnny reeled him in like a rainbow trout; he made it look like child's play. And now that he had regained control of the situation, I relaxed.

"Record would have been mine." Twitch, twitch, twitch. "What next, metric football? Imagine Howard Cosell on Monday Night: 'First down and ten *meters* to go.' Football is an American institution, and just because they use meters in Europe...."

Jeff's mom skulked into the VP's office, eyes darting furtively. She was followed by Miss Bloh Me, whose attitude was, in Ms. Mori's eyes, "unreasonable and unforgiving". Jeff's mom tried to cover for him, saying they had both been home all night. Her alibi might have held up, had Jeff not reminded her that she had gone out to a bar with a "colleague". She screeched at him to shut his stinking pie hole, at which point he pled guilty, and because he had painted on brick, the wall would have to be sand-blasted.

Ms. Mori took out her checkbook and asked, with pen poised, "How much this time?"

We were supposed to be making model cars out of clay. Jake molded his lump into a dog that was, as McClown put it, "all teeth and teats".

Jake held up his sculpture. "Guess who this is, Haldini, The Krabman's wife or his mom?" When I didn't answer right away, he said with a shrug, "Same bitch."

Giggling, I asked the kid next to me if he had The Krabman for history. A high-strung sort to begin with, he looked around nervously for Miss Bloh Me, who was helping a girl on the other side of the room. He sized me up through sheepdog bangs, and in a low voice, he said, "This is my only class." My confusion was evident, so he added, "I only come for lunch and 4th period."

"How do you get away with that?"

"I leave my house in the morning, like I'm coming to school, but then I don't get here until lunch. And I leave after Art; Mom doesn't get home until five."

I was learning all sorts of stuff at Fernwater. "How did you work this?"

He looked around again before answering. "First day of 2nd quarter, everybody was picking up their schedules, but they didn't have one for me. So I went to the counseling office, and there were forms on the counter that said 'add/drop classes'. The lady had her back turned, and I figured: What the heck? It's worth a shot. So I snagged one and filled out the part saying I should be in Art 4th period. Then I forged the counselor's signature."

"You know you'll get found out though." I regretted the words even as they were leaving my mouth; here was a kid who had figured out how to ditch school for two months and I'd just cut him down.

"Yeah, I know," he mumbled through a guilty grin. "But this is fun city, man; I leave at 7:26, like I'm catching the bus. Then I sneak back through the woods and crawl in through my bedroom window. I wait for Mom to split for work and then I go fishing or ride my bike around. When it rains, I watch TV."

"Why only 4th period?"

"Because I like Miss Blohmeyer." He stopped smiling and swallowed thickly. "A lot."

"My name is Mrs. ...." Our sub's name got swallowed up in the chatter and laughter and clatter of chairs. Louder this time, but just as timidly, the spindly woman said, "I am filling in for Miss Blohmeyer."

Jake said she looked like Olive Oyl. Like a pack of coyotes circling a lamb that had strayed from the herd, Johnny Boe and the boys smelled fear. I can't remember exactly how it happened – I had not yet begun keeping a journal – but within five minutes, the sub was hunkered down beneath her desk, and every time she poked her head up, my pals pelted her with clay. Jeff started singing, and the other boys joined in:

I'm Popeye the sailor dude

Throw clay at the substitude

I cheered them on and laughed as loudly as anybody, and up to this point, that had been good enough for my buddies. But Johnny Boe had been dropping hints as of late that I needed to have a stake in the game.

"You play baseball, don't ya, Haldini?" He handed me a wad of clay and said, "Here; I wanna see you nail Olive Oyl."

How could I resist? My first shot caught her on her upper lip, and I was mobbed by my friends. McClown initiated me into the club by punching my shoulder, and I gave it right back to him. Prior to that moment, I had not quite fit in; I was the newcomer that did well in school, whereas the J boys were all first class fuckups. Johnny and Jake managed to squeak by, but McClown and Jeff were each failing four classes.

Whenever they had cranked up their "mayhem machine", as McClown called it, I egged them on from the sidelines. Not that I was a model student, not at all; I was perfectly willing to peel an overly ripe banana and huck it over the wall into the next classroom, but when it came to dumping Drano into The Krabman's gas tank or stealing dope out of lockers, I sat out. And that had been OK with them.

But now I was one of the gang, and ready to cause a little mayhem of my own. In the words of my father: Sometimes disruption is necessary.

Chapter 6 – February

"Leo Haldini, you're up!"

I stepped to the podium and launched into an account of the Boston Tea Party, while The Krabman, sitting off to my left, assessed my report. I held a squirt gun in my right hand, keeping it low so the podium hid it from his view.

Penny Prismark sat in the middle of the front row, a'grinnin' and a'winkin' at me while I gave my speech. She was perky, annoyingly so, and she had a crush on me, which didn't mean much, seeing as how she had the hots for most of us guys at one time or another. And though I was hornier than a two-peckered tom cat, as Johnny Boe put it, the thought of smooching Penny turned my stomach.

I squirted her in the face.

She yelped, earning her a reprimand from The Krabman: "Now let's be quiet during Leo's presentation."

"Yes, Penelope," I said in a snooty tone, "please treat your classmates more respectfully." I resumed my speech, took aim and let her have it. More yelps. The Krabman glared at her, and I stopped my barrage long enough for her to wipe her face, but I kept on talking: "That night the colonists threw 45 tons of tea into the harbor. This was not your caffeine-free herbal variety; the fishies didn't get much sleep that night...."

And so it went: squirt, yelp, glare, wipe.... squirt, yelp, glare, wipe.... And the entire time, I ploughed right on through my speech.

Sitting in the back row, Jake, Jeff and McClown were in silent hysterics, doing their best not to ruin the moment for me. The Krabman never did figure out what I was up to. How could he not know? I suspect the reason we caused him trouble was that he was oblivious to so much that went on around him. To our twisted 14-year-old brains, that made him unworthy of our respect. In my father's words: Authorities must earn your respect.

I finished my speech and took a bow, to wild applause from my pals, all except Johnny Boe. He gave me a snarly look, the same one he'd given Jeff after that little crabmn-fux-blomire stunt. The look said: Hey, numb nuts, The Krabman's gonna think I put you up to this. Or.... was Johnny pissed that he *hadn't* been the one who put me up to it? This was my show, and he didn't like somebody else call the shots.

The Krabman gave my boisterous buddies a withering stare and introduced the next kid, who was set to talk about the history of American currency. The Krabman prefaced the speech by pointing out that we honor presidents by placing their pictures on coins and bills.

Just to kick things off, Johnny Boe asked, "Is that Dick Nixon on the quarter?"

Before The Krabman could answer, McClown said, "Nope. Nixon's dead."

Jake the Invisible Boy knew better, but he kept the ball rolling: "No, he's not. Tricky Dick's on the dollar bill."

Jeff didn't hesitate. "I thought the guys on dollars died."

And Johnny Boe brought it home. "That's right, and all the people on coins are still alive."

The Krabman's cheek twitched like a flipper on a pinball machine. Though I laughed along with some of my classmates, my conscience jolted me. Watching the J boys torment him, and knowing that I had just made him look like a fool, I was reminded of the time I caught a fly, then methodically pulled off the wings on one side and watched it spin in erratic circles. Of course, I had only been six years old at that time. I could no longer use age as an excuse. Or could I? In a decade, maybe I'd look back and think: Ah well, I was only fourteen; what can you expect?

Johnny Boe, back in the driver's seat, looked around in satisfaction. Jeff, though, gave me a quizzical look; he had no idea what I was laughing at. He had not been tormenting The Krabman, at least intentionally. He had no idea who Nixon was.

Like my pals, I was a social retard. Even so, I was aware that The Krabman was perilously close to his breaking point. Most of the students in 1st period class had been failing most of the tests, and to his credit, it bothered him.

One day The Krabman began lecturing on the lead-up to World War II: "At the beginning of the war, there were three Axis nations: Germany, Italy.... and the interesting thing about Italy is this...." And away he went. He did this often; he would intend to name three or four items, but then he'd get stuck on item two and never circle back to where he was. A decade or two later, we would suspect Attention Deficit Disorder as the likely cause of such behavior, but at the time, we just thought he was a dingbat.

On this particular day, however, his dinginess was OK with me; having heard only tidbits of my dad's childhood, I looked forward to learning about Italy's role in the war. But the noise level in the school was louder than usual, so I called out, "Can't hear you, Mr. Krabke."

He looked around the class to see who was causing the ruckus, but nobody was; a few of us were tuned in to his lecture, one kid was reading a novel, two were writing notes, some stared off into space, and so on. The Krabman's voice had been drowned out by laughter from another class, and Hester's lecture next door, and a movie soundtrack from somewhere, and Mrs. Skibbitz' sub was trying to settle a dispute between those smokin' hot blondes.

The Krabman took a deep breath and shocked us by asking, "How many of you want to learn?"

For most of my classmates, he was asking, for the first time, a relevant question. Half a dozen hands, including mine, hesitantly rose.

"Anybody else?" He had obviously expected to get more takers. "Nobody? Going once, going twice.... OK, those with raised hands, come sit up front."

We did so, displacing all but one kid in the first row.

"Later, dude," said Jake.

It was an awkward moment. Though I had become part of the J boys' circle, there remained differences between us, and we all understood that. Still, this was the first time I consciously put space between us.

The Krabman directed those of us sitting up front to form a semi-circle around him. He was officially giving up on the other 25 students. That was the point at which the class completely fell apart, and it happened like this:

The following Sunday, Jake the Invisible Boy and I were invited to spend the night at Jeff Mori's. My folks were leery about letting me sleep over on a school night, but we were painting our living room and the fumes gave me a headache, so they relented. I did not mention that Jeff had been suspended for breaking a window, on a dare from Johnny Boe.

Ms. Mori worked as a bingo caller at the community center two nights a week, so we were on our own. Had Mom known that, she never would have OK'ed the sleepover. We boys put the time to good use, prank calling teachers until <u>Goldfinger</u> came on at 9:00. Jeff made "a ton of popcorn" and poured a melted stick of butter over it. He and I debated who made the best Bond; I favored Sean Connery, whereas he argued that the old movies look corny next to the ones starring Roger Moore. Jake settled the debate once and for all by saying: "Who cares who plays Bond? <u>Goldfinger</u> stars Pussy Galore."

Ms. Mori stumbled into the kitchen at 11:00. She elbowed aside two piles of unopened mail and plopped a bag of groceries on the counter. She took out a bag of Fritos, a package of Oreos and a quart of ice cream; I got the sense this was standard fare in the Mori household.

"Help yourselves, boys." She sat down at the kitchen table, ran a hand through her wispy hair and rested her face in her hands. "I could sleep for a week."

While Jake and I broke open the snacks, Jeff laid a hand on her shoulder and said, "Hey."

She lifted her head and smiled faintly. "Hey to you too." She patted her bony thighs, and Jeff sat on her lap, like a 2nd grader might. Guiding his head onto her shoulder, she wrapped her arms around her adolescent son and rocked him back and forth, quietly humming "The Battle Hymn of the Republic". He wasn't self-conscious at all about Jake and me being there, and I half-expected him to suck his thumb. I had no idea what to make of the whole lullaby scene on Planet Mori – cool or completely bizarro?

After Jake and I ate half the ice cream and all the Fritos, we carried our sleeping bags down the hall to Jeff's room and got set up for the night. Jeff slept with a night-light on, and we stayed up, telling dumb jokes and eating Oreos until well past midnight.

"B.... 13!" My eyes snapped open. Had I dreamt that?

"G.... 12!" It came from outside Jeff's room.

Jake sat up. "The hell is that?"

"O.... 30!"

"That's my mom," said Jeff apologetically. "She has bingo nightmares."

"B.... 14!"

Jake whispered in response, "B.... quiet." Jeff and I covered our mouths so our laughter wouldn't wake his mom.

"I.... 23!"

"I.... can't believe this," said Jake. "N.... credible."

Jeff and I were literally rolling on the floor. The bingo-fest from next door stopped but Jake kept going:

G.... whiz, your mom's a crack-up! O.... my God! "

"Johnny won't believe this," I said. Jeff was still laughing, but it was suddenly an effort.

In the murky glow of the night light, Jake pretended to yawn. "Naw, don't tell him." I was surprised to hear him say that; Johnny would have gotten a kick out of this.

That night I dreamt of Jeff, Jake, me and Steiffel as a little kid. The four of us cut class to go fishing. The dream wandered around, seeming to last for hours. I've forgotten most of it, but I remember that a flying fish – except it was a barracuda – jumped out of the water and bit our mini-VP on the ass, then grabbed Jeff and hauled him into the lake. Steiffel Junior threw him what he thought was an inner tube, but it turned out to be a tire that sunk straight to the bottom, taking Jeff with it. Jake dove in after him, but came up empty-handed.

Ms. Mori rousted us out of bed. "Let's go, I'm late again." She had begun waitressing the week before. She kissed Jeff on the lips and said, "I'll see if I can bring home some of that ravioli you like."

Jake and I got dressed while Jeff dished up the rest of the ice cream. The moment his mom walked out the front door, McClown slipped in the back. She had banned him from the Mori household – understandable, given the five scars that adorned the side of her son's face.

McClown spied a half-full bottle of Jack Daniel's on top of

the refrigerator. He grabbed it and staggered around the kitchen, blustering like a drunken pirate. "Aye, mitey! Gissome grog or I'll 'ave ya keel-hauled fer sure!" He opened the bottle, took a whiff and grimaced. "Smells like ye bin swimmin' in the bilge!"

Jake began chanting, "Drink! Drink! Drink!" Jeff and I joined in.

McClown, never one to disappoint an audience, took a swig. His eyes glazed over, but he managed to choke it down.

"Aye, and a fine lot ya rrrrrrrr!" he said, squirting the words out the corner of his mouth. In addition to chanting, we were now clapping as well. McClown took another swallow and belched, then he stashed the bottle in his denim jacket and careened around the kitchen again. He closed one eye and scrunched up that side of his face.

"Mori, ye scurvy scallywag! Suspended, arrrrr ya?"

"What's a scully whack?"

I gathered up my books and coat, and tried my best to be a Good Tern by lying to Jeff, saying I was jealous of him getting to stay home. We left him standing in his doorway, looking like an abandoned pup.

By the time the bus dropped us off at school, McClown was polluted, and staggering no longer required effort. He raised an imaginary glass and toasted, "Here's ta swimmin', wit' bow-legged women!" He was singing and dancing around and being totally obnoxious, but it was a hilarious performance.

He did his best to hold it together during 1st period, but every few minutes, he'd belch and get a case of the giggles. The Krabman moved him closer to the front of the room and then did his best to ignore him.

Halfway through class, there was a commotion that could not be ignored: McClown vomited, in his lap, on the floor, and right down the back of Penny Prismark's floral print blouse, cut low in the back. She leapt up, shrieked and spun around, spraying chunks on everyone sitting nearby. They in turn fell out of their chairs and scattered. Sickly though he was, McClown began to laugh, causing him to heave again, this time on Penny's shiny black shoes. Prior to this moment, she had been unable to envision what was oozing down her back, as the contents from McClown's stomach blended in agreeably with the carpet's color scheme.

"He barfed!" she squealed. "He barfed on my shoes! He barfed on my blouse!" The Krabman tried to calm her down, but she took off, shrieking, "He barfed on me!"

After watching her disappear down the hall, Johnny Boe swatted McClown on the back of the head and called him a jerk off. His irritation confused me, because there was absolutely no chance of him being blamed for his pal's drunkenness. No, this was something else; Johnny had been acting erratically as of late. He had been upset the day I squirted Penny and now he was bothered that McClown vomited on her. It occurred to me that.... could it be? Yes, Johnny Boe liked Penny Prismark. He would never admit it to us – or, who knows, maybe even to himself – but he did; he *liked* her.

McClown heaved once more, and the whiskey bottle tumbled out of his jacket. Before Jake could kick it under a desk, old Mrs. Skibbitz from across the hall hustled in and snatched it up. Without saying a word, she looked around at the traffic jam of vomit-covered desks, and then regarded each of us students with a withering eye. Silence.

"Well?" she shrilled. "Hop to it!"

We had the desks back in order in fifteen seconds, and she then turned her evil eye on my teacher, who ordered McClown down to the office. To avoid her incendiary gaze, The Krabman studiously reviewed his notes. Mrs. Skibbitz returned to her room, but not before spraying the room with one last scattershot glare.

McClown returned three minutes later, claiming that the secretary wouldn't take him without a referral. The Krabman said that he had run out of forms, and sent McClown down to the office again. On his way down the hall, The Krabman yelled at him to "Tell 'em to smell your breath!"

Mrs. Skibbitz regarded our teacher as she would an impenitent child.

I was called down to Steiffel's office to act as witness. It was a task I hated, because, like Jeff, I didn't want to rat out my friends. So, as I had done several times before, I lied. I stuttered and stumbled through a half-baked tale about McClown getting, um, uh, food poisoning at um, a.... a.... an.... Andorean restaurant. Steiffel scowled at that, but apparently his understanding of geography was no better than mine, and he let it pass.

"What about the bottle?" he snarled.

"Had no part in that," I mumbled. "Smell my breath."

He opened his mouth to scold me, but McClown's stepdad showed up at that moment, protesting as he barged through the door: "You can't give a kid the boot because he has a touch of stomach flu."

Steiffel plunked the whiskey bottle down as evidence and gave him an I-dare-you-to-challenge-this look. Even without incriminating testimony from me, McClown was suspended for a week. He had screwed up one time too many.

"Marvin Steiffel, that weasel," McClown told us guys later on. "Ol' Marv stabbed me in the back." That day he reverted to calling his stepdad "Der Fuhrer".

On the first day of 2nd semester, The Krabman walked into class looking like he'd been sucking on a lemon. We hadn't even done anything yet and his cheek was twitching like crazy. I noticed something peculiar – he'd suffer one large spasm, and then follow it up with two smaller ones. He was twitching in 3/4 time.

"Somethin's up," said Jake.

I thought maybe The Krabman was dreading McClown's return from suspension. Or maybe he was uptight because of the three inches of snow that had fallen that morning; we were amped up by the prospect of being sent home early.

Our class settled down, sort of, and The Krabman announced, "I.... I made.... Well, a mistake was made."

His 3/4 twitch brought to mind my Uncle Marco singing "That's Amore" with his thick Italian accent: When.... the.... moon meets your eye like a big pizza pie.... Geez Louise, what a dorky song, but somehow Marco managed to make it cool.

The Krabman explained, "In September, I was given the syllabus for the year, and I thought.... Actually, I was *told* that it was the syllabus for 1st semester." His eyes flicked back and forth nervously, scouring the room for trouble spots.

"So?" asked McClown, unhappy to be back after his week off. "What's that got to do with anything?"

Johnny Boe, always one step ahead, said, "It means that The Kra.... that we've already covered everything we're supposed to cover this year." Faces registered bewilderment from the back of the room and frowns from the front.

The Krabman went on, "I was not informed that US History is a two-year course, and I mistakenly…. Well, Physical Education, as you well know, is my area of expertise, having received a track scholarship from the U."

I turned and whispered my favorite Uncle Marco saying to the J boys: "He is sweating like a leeetle peeeg een a beeeeeeeg blanket". The Krabman ignored their laughter.

Johnny called out with a wicked grin, "So, Mr. Teacher, what now? We gonna watch movies? We gonna watch a lot of movies?"

"No. Class, we are going to…."

"Incoming!" yelled McClown.

A snowball thrown from who-knows-where splatted against the chalkboard and dripped down across the day's reading assignment. As if that were a normal, everyday occurrence, The Krabman went on: "We are going to start over from the beginning; we will cover the material again."

Penny Prismark, sitting in the front row, began to ask the obvious question: "But what about those of us…?" Realizing that The Krabman was on the verge of tears, she stopped.

So we pretended it was September, and we started in with the Nina, Pinta and Santa Maria. Again. Up to that point, we had thought of our history teacher as being cranky, clueless, and mind-numbingly boring. But I had given him the benefit of the doubt; after all, he was a PE teacher teaching history. I now realized that he was simply incompetent. What would my dad have said, had he been sitting here? I had visions of him as a kid, rallying the partisan forces hiding in the forest and inciting them to revolution.

The upside of The Krabman's mistake was that the goof-offs got a do-over. As he pitched it to them: "This is your chance to tern over a new leaf. Heh, heh, heh."

Johnny and McClown actually passed all of the tests the second time around, and because credits were issued according to the number of units passed, as opposed to semesters completed, they each ended up with a full year's credit in US History.

And I, as a reward for having passed all of the tests and completed all of The Krabman's assignments the first time around, was required to sit through the same lectures, watch the same movies, re-hand in the same assignments, and take the same damn tests. I even gave my same speech on the Boston Tea Party, but Penny was no longer sitting in the middle of the front row, so I left my squirt gun at home that day. Even that small pleasure was denied me.

It was in Mr. Krabke's class that I perfected my ability to tune out the world. I began to write down the tall tales I was inventing in the VP's office, except that I toned them down to make them more believable. Only in retrospect is it clear that I was practicing for the next time I got called down to act as witness for the J boys' shenanigans.

Soon I began writing short stories. My first effort featured five boys who go hiking in the Cascades; they get lost and live off berries and bark. They build a crude shelter out of pine boughs and fern fronds. They hunt bunnies, paint their faces and finally turn on one another.

Now, everybody knows that if you get lost in the mountains, you find a river and follow it downstream until you come to a road or a town. So in order to make the plot work, the boys wanted to stay lost. It wasn't much of a story. And to make things worse, I realized halfway through that it was a knock-off of Lord of the Flies, which we were reading in Hester's class.

I thought about re-writing that book, featuring people I knew. I would cast Johnny Boe as Jake, the leader of the outlaws, and Piggy, the victimized kid, would be played by…. who? Penny Prismark? Or maybe Jeff Mori, except that Piggy was smart and chubby. How about Ralph? He was the boy who fought against the tribe's descent into lawlessness.

That was a problem; none of my classmates resembled Ralph. Hmmm, maybe my dad, as a young man could play Ralph. He was big on "fighting the good fight" and "taking a stand" when it came to important issues.

At that time, however, I had little understanding of exactly which issues he considered important.

Chapter 7 – March

If it seems odd that I remember those days in such detail, it must be understood that 9th grade was a formative year for me. Repercussions from decisions I made echoed through my life for decades. Newly formed friendships and enmities effected long-term change. Memories from those days, some yet to be processed, will arise of their own accord and percolate through my mind for hours. A series of short interactions with my English teacher stand out in my memory as pivotal:

Still spooked by Mr. Hester, I tentatively approached him after class. "How did Golding come up with the plot for Lord of the Flies?" Before he could answer, I changed the question: "How do authors write a book like that, something original?"

"I've never written a book," he said. "But I imagine it's like, say, playing baseball."

How could he possibly know about my interest in baseball? Uh-oh. What else does he know?

He let me sweat a minute and then said, "You have a Mariners' logo on your notebook."

Oh.

He said, "The way to get good at hitting a baseball is to practice hitting balls, over and over and over. Same way with authors – they write and write and write, and most of it gets tossed, but eventually, hopefully, they come up with a keeper." He gave me a penetrating stare. "Why? Have you written something?"

I looked around before answering. "Well, yeah, but I haven't really finished it."

Tell ya what, Leo," he said, and in that one moment, his spookiness dissolved. "Why don't you bring me in a story? I'll read it, and then we'll talk about it."

The following Monday, I brought in a four-chapter, ten-page story about two boys who hitchhike to California; they pick apples and cucumbers to pay their way. Leaving Disneyland, they get picked up by an escapee from a mental institution. He's driving a stolen car and he talks non-stop about how important it is to break out and break away and break free and break the cycle before life breaks you. He almost drives off the road several times because he keeps craning his head toward the boys and asking, "See what I mean? Do you see?" But he buys them lunch at a truck stop and turns out to be a nice guy. The story fizzles at the end; one kid returns home, and the other just keeps going.

Two days later at the end of class, Mr. Hester called me up to his desk, saying he wanted a word with me. Oh God. Naturally I wondered what kind of trouble I was in.

He dismissed class and then, seeing my anxiety, he said, "I finished your story. Thank you for letting me read it."

I breathed a sigh of relief. "What did you think?"

He gave me a great response. "I found myself wishing that I knew the main character. Oh, and that escapee – man, he had me spooked." Hester gave me an appraising look. "What was your inspiration for the story?"

Was he asking if I wanted to run away? Because I didn't. Jake the Invisible Boy, on the other hand, was kicking the idea around: Haldini, what say you and me hit the road, just the two of us, hitchhike down to LA, live on the beach. Running away? No no, think of it as an unauthorized vacation.

I told Hester, "Oh, I daydream a lot in The Kr.... Mr. Krabke's class, because...." I stopped short of telling him we were repeating 1st semester. He gave me a curious look, and I asked what I could do to make the story better.

"I have three suggestions. First, learn how to describe your surroundings; bring your reader *inside* the story. Second, keep a journal."

"What do I write in it?"

"Thoughts, observations about friends, family, the world.... I don't know, funny stuff that happens. Write down enough so that you'll be able to make sense of it ten years from now, because, trust me, you'll forget most of it if you don't write it down." He gave me a moment to mull that over. "Thirdly, you should read."

When I asked for recommendations, he took a copy of Huckleberry Finn out of his desk and tossed it to me. "Try this, but it won't hurt my feelings if you return it unread."

A week later, I returned <u>Huck Finn</u> after school and told Mr. Hester I liked it a lot.

He said, "I thought you might. It's a good traveling story." We talked about our favorite parts of the book and why it's still widely read a century later.

There was a pause, and before I could stop myself, the words came pouring out of my mouth: "Do you have a metal plate in your head?"

I had never heard an adult laugh that hard. The veins stood out on his forehead. "Where did you hear that?"

"Everybody knows that story." My face was on fire. "About how, you know, how you fought in Korea."

He laughed again, and then narrowed his eyes; he was deciding whether to tell me the story. Finally he said, "I fought in *Vietnam* when I was *twenty*. My God, how old do you people think I am?" He grunted and shook his head. "I was out on patrol during monsoon season. You have to feel rain like that to believe it; imagine a guy up in a tree with a fire hose. Anyway, we were hiking through the mud, and all of a sudden the trail gave way. I slid down a hillside and bonked my noggin. Got stitches right here." He pointed to a spot behind his ear. "Got a medal for that; injured in the line of duty." He leaned back and put his hands behind his head. "Yeah, I know all about the metal plate story. Next thing you know, they'll be saying I spent time in prison."

My eyes popped open and I gulped. He laughed again, every bit as hard as the first time.

"Yeah," he said. "I've heard that one too."

"So you didn't break a kid's finger with rusty pliers?"

"Oh, is that how the story goes now?"

"Why don't you set the record straight?"

"I've heard the stories, and I know some kids are afraid of me." My face reddened again, but I was the one who laughed this time. "Truth is, I don't mind kids being scared; it makes my job easier." He paused. "Are you going to tell your pals I don't have iron in my skull?" Before I could answer, he said, "Ah, what the hell; maybe it's time to lay those stories to rest. Madness comes, madness goes." He paused again. "By the way, I know about that stunt McClown pulled with the magnet, waving it back and forth by my head. That was pretty funny – it was all I could do to keep from crackin' up."

I realized right then why I never messed around in his class; he was onto us. "You said you haven't written a book," I said, "but did you ever want to?"

"Yeah, I considered it, but never got around to it. I wrote some stories about my time in the service though."

"Could I read one?"

"Yeah, if you want. One good turn deserves another."

"Ummm, I've been wondering: What does that mean?"

He nodded and sighed, like he got asked this every day. "'Turn', spelled with a 'u', means something like 'favor'. So, if you do me a favor, I should do one back."

Ohhhhhh. This is what it must feel like to be Jeff Mori.

The next day he brought in a twenty-page story, typed, but before handing it over, he said, "Look, this is not finished, so don't be too critical. At some point, I want to weed some things out, and the story wanders, but at its core, there might be something good."

A week later I stopped by after school and told him, "I read your story twice, and I think about it every day."

"Leo, that is just about the highest compliment you could pay me."

At that moment, I was cast forward several years, providing me with a glimpse of how a post-adolescent friendship might look.

Baseball season had started up, and Mr. Farley was playing sports trivia with the jocks before Geometry class. He asked, "What team has won the most World Series?"

"Yankees?"

"Nope; the damn Yankees. Who has the single-season home run record?"

"Roger Maris."

A kid protested. "Yeah, but that record should belong to The Babe; they only played 154 games back then."

They nailed every question until Farley asked, "OK, the last major leaguer to hit .400?"

When no one replied, I offered up: "Ted Williams, 1941."

They turned to see who had intruded, and Farley said, "Haldini, good man."

"You play ball, Haldini?" This kid had blonde hair and

thighs as big around as my chest.

"Yeah, I played shortstop last year. I don't got a lotta power, but I switch hit pretty good." I had grown six inches in the past six months, but only put on twenty pounds.

He looked me up and down. "I play short, but we need somebody at second. Wanna try out?"

Weird question – schools have a no-cut policy. "For the school team?"

"Yeah, right," another boy scoffed. "Like we'd really play for Fernwater."

The blonde kid pulled me aside. "Don't mind him. We play in the city league – better players, longer season. Tomorrow afternoon, 4:00 at Oxley Field – can you make it?"

And so began my association with a new crowd. I was trading up.

Every day I left Mr. Farley's class, increasingly confident that I could learn anything I'd ever want to. That's the main thing I remember from Geometry. Well…. that, and Delores Pearle's gastronomic and respiratory afflictions, though she had given us a respite the past few weeks from the pyroclastic sneezes, farts and belches with which she had subjugated her corner of the room. Speaking of which, I had taken to heart Hester's advice about keeping a journal; here is one of my more bizarre early entries:

Did Delores have a change of diet or change of heart? She's an inactive volcano, dormant or extinct? Or would that be "ex-stink"?

We've all heard those accounts of disasters from crusty old-timers that begin like this: I recall a morning in '79, must've been mid-April. The day dawned clear, with a little nip in the air. I was sitting in Geometry class when Mt. Delores, with absolutely no warning, rumbled to life.

Mr. Farley told us to take out our assignments, and Delores responded with a simple belch-sneeze pairing. He flinched and glared in her direction, but said nothing. It was not clear if her outburst was a rogue wave or the beginning of a tsunami. But when she followed it up with a more demanding cough-fart-belch combo, Farley, a soft-spoken man, asked, "Do you need a cork?"

That was the only time I remember him clowning around.

His question elicited snickers from around the room. Delores blushed, but the pump was primed – so to speak – and she was back in business. She let loose an unimpressive sneeze, followed up with a hiccup-sneeze-belch combination that would've rattled the walls, had there been any.

Mr. Farley strode back to her desk and said calmly but firmly, "That is *it* – the next sound I hear from you will be your ticket out of class. Understand?"

Penny Prismark heaved a dramatic sigh. *"Thank you*, Mr. Farley."

I appreciated his efforts to rein Delores in. On some days, it was hard to hear myself think. But seriously, how can you expect someone to all of a sudden stop sneezing? And really, can you just decide not to cough? Or belch? Maybe. How about farting? Usually, at least audibly. But Geez Louise, did he expect her to intentionally put the kibosh on a bout of the hiccups? C'mon. His ultimatum was appreciated, but simply not reasonable.

The Krabman assigned us the task of learning the US presidents up through the Civil War. Having already memorized them back in November, I resumed working on the Delores Pearle Problem. For the past couple of months, I had been searching for a formula relating the number of BFNs to the number of combinations.

# of BFNs	1	2	3	4	5
# of combos	0	1	4	11	26

I pored over the tables I'd made and fiddled around with a variety of equations, hunting for patterns. Finally, through a mix of perseverance and luck, I hit upon the elusive formula:

if n = # of BFNs
then # of combos = $2^n - (n + 1)$

I basked in the glory of my discovery. Or, as Farley might have asked, was it an invention? I was so enamored of my solution that I didn't notice The Krabman sneaking up on my flank. He snatched up my papers, filled with calculations and equations involving belching, farting, coughing, hiccupping and sneezing.

"For the love of God, Haldini! What is this?" He flipped through the pages and made indignant clucking sounds with his tongue.

I was mortified. It's one thing to be a twisted little pervert; it's another for the whole world to find out about it.

"Who's your math teacher? Farley? Let's you and me take a walk!" Walking down the hall, The Krabman held up the papers and spat: "This is disgusting!" His ranting disrupted other classes, but that didn't stop him. He marched me up to Farley's desk – this was his plan period – and proclaimed, "Mr. Haldini here is using class time to do…. this!"

He held up my papers as a DA would present a bloody steak knife with the perp's fingerprints on it. The Krabman paced back and forth, hands clasped behind his back, as if presenting an open-and-shut case to a sympathetic judge.

Meanwhile, Mr. Farley perused a sheet of paper with "The Delores Pearle Problem" written at the top and my formula at the bottom. He grimaced, nodded and mumbled to himself, "Hmmm. Hmm? Oh, hmm."

The Krabman ranted about the Youth of Today, while his face twitched furiously in 3/4, bringing to mind a favorite tune of my parents, The Blue Danube Waltz. "Kids today are uncouth and undisciplined, not to mention unhygienic! And another thing…."

He flailed his arms like a rookie symphonic conductor with his toe stuck in a socket, in a manner that I'm sure would have left Johann Strauss unimpressed.

It soon became clear that Farley was not offended by my work. On the contrary, he was testing my formula by performing calculations of his own. He massaged the back of his neck and muttered, "Hmmmm, uh-huh, yes…. what? Oh, uh-huh. This is a nice piece of work, Haldini."

Realizing that he was not going to recruit Farley for his cause, The Krabman grabbed me by the elbow and steered me back toward his classroom, all the while snarling and grumbling. I snuck a look over my shoulder at Farley – he was too professional to flash me a peace sign or give me a thumbs-up, but I swear he smiled in that one second before The Krabman spun me back around. Passing Mrs. Skibbitz' class, she gave him a dirty look, but he was beyond caring.

As we entered our room, McClown called out, "If you're not gonna be here to teach us, Mr. Krabke, you got no right to test us on this stuff."

"Hey!" said Johnny Boe, pointing a stern finger in his pal's direction. "Young man, if Mr. Krabke wants any crap out of you, he'll squeeze your head!"

The lights at Oxley Field were only partially visible through the cold mist. Though spring had officially begun, playing baseball at night in the Pacific Northwest in March can be a miserable experience. We were down seven runs by the third inning, and both teams just wanted to get it over with. The only thing that made the game tolerable for the dozen or so hometown fans was listening to my dad shower the ump with Italian expletives; he'd had a rough day and wanted to share his misery.

"Ma che cazzo fai, coglione?" What the fuck ya doing, ya wiener? The other parents shivering in the stands had no idea what he was saying, but they egged him on anyway.

In the top of the fourth, I charged a bunt, bare-handed the ball and flipped it sidearm to first. I thought I had him by a step, but the infield ump called him safe. Following my dad's cue, the fans on the home-side bleachers booed and gave the ump a group thumbs-down.

Dad yelled, "Figlio di puttana!" Son of a bitch! "Figlio di puttana!" Other parents picked up the chant, though they had no understanding of its meaning.

I led off the bottom of the fourth, and the ump immediately called two strikes on me – the first pitch flirted with the outside corner, but the second was belt-high down the middle.

"Figlio di puttana! Figlio di puttana!" The ump glared up at my father, obviously the leader of the insurrection.

The next batter watched the spectacle from the on-deck circle. "Who *is* that guy?"

"That's my dad!"

"Cool!"

The next pitch was high and outside, but I reached for it and drove it down the first base line. I rounded first as the right fielder chased down the ball at the fence. I passed second just as the ball reached the cut-off man, who gunned me down at third with five feet to spare.

When the ump called me out, my dad ran down the stands and shook the wire mesh on the backstop. From my vantage point at third base, he looked like a caged baboon.

"Arbitro bastardo!" Ump, you're a bastard! Dad thought he was safe, swearing in his native tongue. But disguising an insult with the word "bastardo" is about as effective as Clark Kent hiding his Superman identity by donning a pair of glasses; it only works in comic books. The ump reared back and pitched his right arm forward. Until that moment, I didn't know that spectators could get tossed from a game.

"Stand up to the damn ump!" Dad shouted at our coach. "The man is a tyrant!" The coach ignored him, which only served to further enrage my dad. "Credo che diventero pazzo!" I think I'm going crazy!

Mom cajoled Dad into leaving. On their way to the parking lot, he was still urging other parents to "Take A Stand! Figlio di puttana!" But his charming swear-at-the-ump-in-Italian had long since lost its appeal.

On my way back to the dugout, I asked our first base coach, "Who *is* that guy?"

Chapter 8 – April

When good, normal stuff happens, it doesn't make for effective story-telling. When you're swappin' tales at a party, it's more interesting to hear about the kid who filed off his fingerprints to fool the FBI than it is to listen to some bonehead talk about how great his 9th grade math teacher was.

Bad luck for you. But I promise not to drag this out, and I'll get to that business about the fingerprints as quick as I can.

Mr. Farley took complex ideas and broke them down until they were understandable, with one notable exception: One day he took a poll, asking us which number was larger, .9 repeating or 1. Most of us said 1 was larger.

"OK, then," he said, "how much larger?"

We offered up a variety of answers, some reasonable, some clever and some just plain nutty:

".1 repeating."

"The more 9's you add, the closer you get to 1, but you'll always come up a teensy-weensy bit short."

"No, you'll be an eensy-beensy bit short."

"The difference is infinitely small, but not zero."

"An infinite number of zeroes, with a one at the end."

"That's an interesting approach," said Farley, writing .00000000....1 on the board. "What do you think?" He waited.

Finally a kid said, "If you have an infinite number of zeroes, there won't be a last place to put the 1."

"Well said." Farley then showed us a proof that $.\overline{9} = 1$, the guts of which went like this:

$$\frac{1}{3} = .\overline{3} \qquad \frac{2}{3} = .\overline{6} \qquad \frac{3}{3} = .\overline{9}$$

And since $\frac{3}{3}$ equals one, then $.\overline{9}$ has to equal one.

A kid offered up weakly, "But that's not right."

"Then find a problem with my proof."

The next day several of us tried to debunk his logic. He showed us another proof that trumped our objections. We debated this issue off and on for the rest of the year. Most of the objections we offered up were some variant of: But they *can't* be equal. There's always going to be a gap.

Finally, an elegant brunette who rarely spoke raised her hand. "You're playing with us; you know they're not equal, and on the day you retire, you're going to send a letter to every student you ever had that says, 'Ha! I was only kidding about .9 repeating being equal to 1.'" When the class broke into raucous applause, the girl stood and clasped her hands over her head, like a prize fighter that had KO'ed her opponent.

Farley attempted not to smile.

As for Delores Pearle, the coughing stopped, as did the hiccups. We heard no more colossal sneeze-fart combos belching forth from her corner of the room. Meaning what? That she'd been sneezing on purpose? That she had chosen to hiccup and belch simultaneously? I developed a whole new respect for her.

Or, was she now holding it all in? Would we have some sort of warning, a harmonic tremor, before she blows? I made up a story to tell my sister: "Yeah, this girl exploded today! Body parts everywhere; index finger here, jawbone over there, gizzards hangin' off the flag, I actually caught one of her eyeballs." Ella was gullible, and I liked to think my story-telling was getting better. Now, if only I could keep a straight face.

Delores' gastronomic and respiratory ailments had subsided, and nobody was happier about it than Penny Prismark. A different sort of trouble, however, awaited her as we left Farley's class one day.

Lucy Sparkett bellowed, "Prismark, I am gonna rip your tits off!" She'd heard that Penny was flirting with Johnny Boe, and by God, she was gonna put an end to it. Juicy Lucy added, "Well, if you had any, I'd rip 'em off!"

Nothing draws a crowd like calamity. The previous weekend, there had been a car wreck in front of Jake's house at midnight. Neighbors I'd never met, or even seen, poured out of their homes, wearing pajamas and bathrobes, to watch policemen and firemen pry an old man out of a station wagon that had wrapped itself around a cedar tree. What a weird scene – a group of moms, after an hour of idle, somber speculation as to the cause of the wreck and the extent of the man's injuries, ended up swapping recipes for peach cobbler.

A ring formed around the two girls instantly, and though Johnny Boe was not in my class, he showed up to watch immediately. He had a knack for finding a brawl. Cupping his hands around his mouth, he half-whispered, half-yelled down the hallway: "Girl fight!" He pushed his way to the inside ring of bystanders, none of whom made a move to stop the coming battle.

Fights between boys were cool in their own way, but they rarely lasted more than a punch or two. But watching girls go at it, that was something to see! They did throw punches, of course, but only as a means of introducing themselves. Lucy then grabbed Penny by a fistful of hair and kicked her in the shin.

Penny broke loose by biting Lucy's wrist, and then hissed, "You're sssuch a ssskank! What would he want with *you*?"

It was unclear whether she was simply defending herself or fighting for the rights to Johnny. By the smug look on his face, I'd say he assumed the latter. To my eye, though, he was trying hard to act triumphant. His dopey grin reminded me of the time the dentist gave my dad too much Novocain and one cheek got stuck in the "up" position.

Lucy charged and kneed her in the stomach. With hands clasped, she then pummeled Penny repeatedly on the back of the neck and shoved her to the floor. Juicy Lucy screamed at her, punctuating each word with a strategically-placed kick to the back, butt or thigh. "Stay! Away! From! Johnny! *Boe!*"

Mr. Farley shot out of his room and broke it up. "Down to the office, both of you! Lucy, walk ahead of me, Penny, behind!"

"She hit me back first!" cried Lucy. She planted a wet, sloppy kiss on Johnny's lips, and then ran to the office, to make sure Steiffel heard her version of the story first.

On the bus ride home that day, I asked Jake about Lucy.

"Yeah," he said, "she got a decent set of gazoongas, don't

she?"

"One Good Tern deserves an udder," I said.

Jake laughed and said, "My aunt and uncle own a dairy farm; Auntie will love that one. As for Juicy Lucy, she was a straight-A student in 8th grade, captain of the softball team and student body Vice Prez. Model student," he sneered. "She spent last summer in Texas with her aunt and uncle. They own a tavern and had Lucy to tend bar for them. She drank a lot, dropped acid and fried her brain. Nobody recognized her when she returned."

"C'mon," I said, "she can't look that different. And 14-year-olds can't tend bar."

"I got something to show you; you can make up your own mind."   .

We got off the bus and headed over to Jake's house. He thumbed through his annual from the previous year and pointed out a picture of a pretty – no, gorgeous – face, full of confidence and contentment, framed by cascades of thick blonde hair. I pictured the Lucy I knew – the black hair, the scar on her cheek, the I-can-kick-your-ass-and-you-know-it attitude.

"But, that's not even her," I protested.

"See what I mean?"

I checked the name again and gaped at her picture until I saw something in the eyes that linked her up with the girl I knew.

"Bummer," I said.

"Oh, I don't know," Jake replied. "Kinda like her better how she is now."

Here is what I remember from my first Fernwater dance: sevies playing tag in our dimly lit gym; 8th grade girls fleeing into the restroom in tears because of a slight from some boy or a tiff with a friend; we freshmen were dancing or making out in dark corners, acting like we owned the place; anyone left over was an 8th grade boy, standing around with hands in his pockets, utterly lost.

On a poster hyping the dance, someone had scrawled: TERN IT UP!

Jake and I looked up in awe and envy at the band, with their monstrous amps, shiny drum kit and long floppy hair, playing a mix of Rush, Aerosmith and Styx on a two-foot-high stage. We couldn't hear the vocals all that well, but the band was awesome anyway, until they lit into a Bee Gees' tune, at which point they were drowned out by chants of "Disco sucks!" and "Cisco ducks!" from all except for the cheerleaders in Honor Society.

Since receiving that save-me-a-slow-dance note, Penny Prismark had been pursuing Johnny Boe, willfully oblivious to his involvement with Lucy Sparkett. When Penny spied him on the dance floor with his hands up Juicy Lucy's blouse, she set up camp directly beneath the sole overhead light in the gym and began blubbering away, while a gaggle of her friends did their best to console her.

Given the degree and volume of her emotional upheaval, it came as a surprise when she asked me to dance ten minutes later. Without waiting for an answer, she grabbed my wrist and hauled me out to the middle of the gym. I was embarrassed – this was Penny Prismark, after all – but also flattered – this was a girl, after all. In need of perspective, I looked over my shoulder at Jake. He shrugged – whatever, dude.

The band began playing the Stones' "Miss You", a medium tempo tune, and I figured I could get through this by shuffling my feet and flailing my arms. I was horrified and thrilled when Penny put her arms around my neck. I placed my hands on her slim waist and we lurched through a wobbly series of turns, the timing of which was completely unrelated to the beat.

OK, I can do this, I thought. But just as I began to believe that, Penny leaned back, looked me in the eye and then pressed her lips against mine. The previous year I had kissed a girl, and I recalled her clenched-up little tongue darting in and out, probing and pleasing. Kissing Penny reminded me of that time Dad tried barbecuing oysters, and I sucked one down on a dare from Uncle Marco. He laughed himself silly when I started gagging, and he said they'd grow on me.

To make matters worse, Penny was looking out the corner of her eyes. I broke off the oyster kiss to see what had caught her attention, and there was Johnny Boe, thirty feet away, looking in our general direction but over our heads, up at the band. It was not clear to me if he saw us, but he nudged McClown and the two of them cracked up.

Penny went to kiss me again, and I pitched in, figuring it

would be good for me to get used to an oyster doing calisthenics in my mouth; maybe it would grow on me. But this time she kissed me with eyes closed and crotch crushed against mine. Her tongue firmed up and caressed my lips in a pleasurable way. We began to move in sync, driven by the insistent guitar riff playing off the pulsing disco beat, while the singer moaned Mick Jagger's bluesy lament: "What's a matter witch you, boy?"

There was a slap on my shoulder, and I turned around to tell Johnny to beat it. But there was old Mrs. Skibbitz, wagging her finger and hollering, "No neckin', and no pettin'!" She led Penny away by the elbow, scolding her as they went: "A man will never buy a cow if he can get his milk for free. Now, in my day, we used to do the jitterbug...."

I retreated to my spot next to Jake, who informed me that Johnny Boe had sicced Mrs. Skibbitz on us. "He was watching you and Penny like a hawk," he said with a self-satisfied grin. "He didn't enjoy that one bit."

I replied with a partial truth. "Makes two of us."

Johnny joined us a few minutes later, and he slugged me on the shoulder, harder than he normally would. I slugged him back, harder than I normally would. Case closed.

The following Monday morning, I passed Penny in the hall, and we avoided one another. Whew! It was a relief to know she wasn't going to be pushing for more suckin' face. However, contrary to what I told Jake, I had enjoyed kissing her, once we got past that weird oyster stage.

Fourteen is a perplexing age. How could I be feeling relieved, sad and horny all at once? This was the first time I had experienced such a stew of emotion and physiological commotion. Or maybe it was simply the first time I knew it was happening.

"My fingers are sore." That was Jeff Mori's whiny excuse for not taking notes.

Mr. Hester put down his overhead pen and folded his beefy arms. "Why are your fingers sore?"

With no trace of embarrassment, Jeff said, "I filed off my fingerprints last night." He didn't mention that Johnny Boe had given him the idea.

Hester paused, knowing he would regret getting drawn into

one of these dialogues with Jeff. But, hey, this kid filed off his own fingerprints. Really? How could you resist that?

Hester said, "OK, why did you file off your fingerprints?"

"Because the FBI has my prints." Johnny had told him so.

"Why do you believe that?"

"The FBI has everybody's prints." Again, Johnny Boe.

Mr. Hester was in too deep to back out now. "No, I think they just have fingerprints of government employees and known criminals on file." He paused for Jeff to consider that, and then asked, "Are you a government employee?"

"No."

"All right," said Hester; we were getting somewhere. "Are you a known criminal?"

Jeff mumbled a tentative, "No."

"But...."

"But the police think I am."

Hester looked away and took a deep breath. Again, how could you possibly resist?

"Why do they think you're a criminal?" asked Hester.

"They think I torched a school in Tacoma."

"Did you?"

"No!"

"But...."

"But they think I did."

"And why do they think that?"

Jeff knew he'd said too much, but it was too late now. "Because I was with the guy that did it."

"And that was....?"

Jeff looked around frantically. "Uh, I don't remember his name. Um, or hers!" Before Hester could follow up, Jeff blurted out, "But the FBI does have my fingerprints on file! 'Cause I, uh, I wasn't born in this country."

"Where were you born?"

"Japan.... I mean, Brazil!" The class was spellbound.

Hester continued, "OK, so your mom is a Brazilian?"

"A brazillion? No. Heck, she's only about 36, maybe 40."

Hester shut his eyes and roughly massaged his temples, then continued with his lecture.

McClown, sitting on the other side of the room from Jeff

and me, wanted a piece of the attention his buddy was getting, so he began throwing pennies at Jeff. Every few minutes, we'd hear a "tink" or a "thunk" or a "thud" as a coin bounced off, respectively, a desk or a chalkboard or Jeff's forehead. When McClown ran out of pennies, Johnny handed him more. Try as he might, Hester could not catch McClown in the act.

I was conflicted; I didn't want to rat out my pal, but his antics were growing tiresome, and Hester had turned out to be a decent guy. Besides, I was afraid an errant throw might poke my eye out. Nah, leave it to someone else to snitch on McClown.

While deciding if and how to let Hester know who was bombarding us with pennies, he did two remarkable things. First, he looked me straight in the eye for two seconds and gave the smallest possible shake of his head. Did I really see that? Yes, I did! I was off the hook! He then walked over to Jeff and squatted down so the two of them were eye to eye.

He said in a concerned tone, "McClown isn't throwing at *you*, is he?"

Thinking he was being loyal to his friend, Jeff whispered, "Oh no, he's throwing at…. at the flag."

I thought sure Hester would let McClown have it right then, so I was surprised when he walked back to the front of the room. But before resuming his lecture, he gave McClown a look that asked, Am I gonna hafta get out my rusty pliers?

The frequency of tinks, thunks and thuds decreased, but they didn't stop.

With ten seconds to go in class, Hester walked over to McClown and lit into him. "You are not going to throw things in here! You are not going to act like a jerk! You are not in 3rd grade! If I wanted to babysit, I'd be teaching kindergarten!"

McClown sat with head bowed, weeping. Kids from surrounding classes gathered to watch Hester take him apart. Having timed his assault for maximum effect, he saved his Killer Question for last: "Do you act like an idiot in all your classes?"

McClown hesitated. "Yes" would be an admission of full-time idiocy. "I don't know" would invite a repetition of the question, with a louder and slower delivery. He mumbled, "No."

"Oh, so you only act like an idiot in *my* class?! You think you can get away with that in *here*? Let me spell it out for you…."

Walking into 2nd period the next morning, the class was subdued. McClown entered with eyes downcast. My classmates were undoubtedly contemplating the existence of that nonexistent metal plate in our teacher's head. In contrast to the dour mood in our room, there was a commotion coming from the sevies next door, where The Krabman had a sub. Hester was becoming more annoyed by the minute.

Halfway through class, the sub strutted into our room, planted puffy hands on her hips and huffed, "Someone from *this* class just threw a piece of paper into *mine*."

All eyes turned to Hester, and then to McClown, who held up his hands in mute protest.

At that instant, a cascade of wadded-up papers flew over the chalkboard into our room from hers, followed by waves of hilarity. It was not a question of *if* Hester would dismember someone; it was simply a matter of whom.

"What in the world?" The sub scurried back to her room and lit into her class. "You should be ashamed of yourselves! If I was your teacher...." She stopped in mid-sentence, recognizing a lost cause. She slammed a book down on her desk, picked up her purse and stomped away down the hall, grousing as she went: "Miserable little slime balls!"

Hester turned his back on us. His shoulders began shaking, and a smattering of tentative chuckles arose as we realized he was stricken with a bout of silent laughter. Turning to face us thirty seconds later, he rubbed the protruding veins on his forehead and wiped his reddened eyes. He looked at each of us, and stillness descended as we looked to him for a cue. He attempted to quash a smile, then snorted twice and burst into a howl of laughter. Everyone joined in immediately. Well, everyone except for McClown.

And that substitute was never heard from again.

Entering the cafeteria at lunch, Jake the Invisible Boy showed me a "boneless" sticker he had taken off a pot roast at Safeway. When Steiffel exited the staffroom, Jake walked up beside him, said hello and gave him a friendly slap on the back. The rest of us greeted him in a similar way so that later on, our VP wouldn't be able to say who had planted the sticker. For lunchtime entertainment, we watched Mr. Boneless police the cafeteria. When he confronted a sevie about leaving trash on a table, I called out, "C'mon, Mr. Steiffel, don't be so *hard on* him."

Our VP waved me off with a smile.

Jake said to me, "Don't get *cocky*, young man."

The moment Steiffel was out of earshot, we cracked up. Johnny Boe spit a mouthful of clam chowder all over Jeff.

Old Mrs. Skibbitz exited the staff room, cigarette smoke billowing out behind her. She paused to watch Mr. Boneless roam the cafeteria. She made a move to approach him, just as a trio of passing girls giggled and called out in sing-songy voices, "Hello-oooo, Mr. Steiffel."

Lucy Sparkett sashayed up to him and cooed, "I feel so safe around you."

Lucy's friend adjusted his tie and patted him on the chest. "Lookin' fine today, sir!"

Mrs. Skibbitz threw her hands up in resignation and left.

Our VP looked proud to be part of the "Fernwater Family". And suddenly I had a vision of Steiffel as a sevie, walking into class with zits, a bad haircut and a "KICK ME" sign taped to his back. I was overcome with a sense of.... what? Guilt? No, because I hadn't really *done* anything.

Only in retrospect am I able to navigate the adolescent swamp of disquieting sensations and burgeoning empathy that coursed through my being at that moment. Back then, had anyone pressed, all I would have been able to say was that I felt rotten.

And so began my transition to adulthood, and the long crawl up and out of my 14-year-old reptilian brain.

Chapter 9 – May

Being tardy to Miss Bloh Me's class had never been an issue; we boys fell all over each other trying to be the first one into her room. But one day McClown hit upon another way to get her attention; he strolled into class one minute late.

Pointing to the clock on one of the brick pillars in her room, she said, "Tardy, Mr. McClown; you'll be cleaning up tables in the lunchroom tomorrow."

"Bummer deal," said Jeff.

But McClown scanned the wide open school and pointed out another clock 25 yards away that was three minutes slower than the one in her room. "Nuh-uh, I'm early! And hey, I gotta whiz like a water buffalo! Be right back."

He took off for the boys' room and made it back with five seconds to spare, at least according to the slower of the two clocks.

The girls realized right away that tardies were a thing of the past. The next day, when several girls trickled in late, Miss Bloh Me scowled but said nothing. As the school year wound down, they arrived later and later, until one day Lucy Sparkett moseyed in six minutes late. Miss Bloh Me gave her a detention slip.

Juicy Lucy pointed at one her friends and said, "What about her? She just came in 15 seconds ago."

Miss Bloh Me gave an exasperated sigh and said, "You're right." She retrieved the detention and ripped it up.

The next day both girls came in eight minutes late. Miss Bloh pretended to ignore them, but I could tell it bugged the hell out of her. Time had been officially deemed to be relative.

Jeff was still using his "Tickle your ass with a feather" line on Miss Bloh Me, hoping for a chance to use his "Particularly nasty weather" comeback. But one day he got careless. At one of those random moments when an entire roomful of people stop talking at the same moment for no apparent reason, Jeff said, a bit too loudly, a bit too clearly, and standing a bit too close to Miss Bloh Me's desk, "Tickle your ass...?"

He got that far and realized his mistake. She stood up and calmly slapped his face. SMACK! Had there been walls, it would have echoed. Whoa! What happens to a teacher who hits a kid? In class!

That night I told my parents about the incident. Dad didn't even bother to look up from his newspaper. "I have no idea why she did it, but I'm sure that little weasel had it coming."

Mom furrowed her brow and cocked her head, but she ended up nodding in agreement.

Walking into class the following day, Jake called out, "Schmmack!" Jeff Mori's face reddened as if it had just been backhanded. Miss Bloh Me turned away, but not in time to hide a smile.

Word got back to Ms. Mori about The Slap, but she let it go. As a matter of fact, everyone let it go, which surprised me. It took me a while to figure out that Miss Bloh Me got away with it because she was respected, by students – well, most of us – and other teachers and parents. At least my folks had given their seal of approval. Mom liked her because she encouraged creativity. Dad okayed her because she was a disciplinarian; at least that's what he said, but I caught him ogling Miss Bloh Me at parent conferences.

The day we began using water colors, Miss Bloh Me spoke of the importance of choosing complimentary colors. She then frowned at Lucy Sparkett, whose bright red lipstick clashed with her green eye shadow, which in turn clashed with her skimpy pink skirt. Her lemon yellow belt clashed with itself. Top it all off with a mountain of frizzy hair dyed jet-black and she became the visual equivalent of chewing tin foil on Halloween.

But don't get me wrong; she was still hot.

When she got up to borrow eye liner from a friend, Miss Bloh Me ordered her to "Park it, Sparkett!"

Neither of them made the slightest effort to hide their mutual dislike. Lucy was used to getting attention from boys, and now she had competition. From a teacher, for God's sake! Lucy and Johnny Boe were still an item, though intermittently, and she didn't appreciate him getting all moony-eyed over Miss Bloh Me.

Juicy Lucy began blowing bubbles – she'd been chompin' on four sticks of Bubble Yum – and she attached one of her more impressive bubbles to a pair of Mickey Mouse ears, which in turn got attached to Jeff's head. He yanked off the ears and tried unsuccessfully to pick the gum out of his hair. With Lucy's friends pointing and giggling, Miss Bloh Me cut off a lock of Jeff's hair, leaving him with a noticeable bald spot above his left ear.

When Johnny and McClown joined in the laughter, Jeff folded his arms on his desk, plopped his head down and bawled. Jake reached out a hand toward his buddy, but yanked it back before the other boys saw him – compassion was not exactly our strong suit, and anyone showing outright kindness might just as well tattoo "KICK ME" on his own forehead.

And then it hit me: I was not the only one who perceived himself as living out there on the periphery of our social circle. Jeff did too, and probably Jake as well. It was weird; *most of us* considered ourselves to be on the outside, looking in.

Miss Bloh Me hauled Lucy behind a brick pillar and laid into her. We couldn't hear much of what was said, but Lucy did not return. When she didn't show up for Art the next two days, I asked Jake where she'd gone.

"Miss Bloh Me cut her a deal; she told her not to come back."

"Huh? Where does she go?"

"Sunny days, she catches some rays out in The Crash. As long as she doesn't cause trouble or get noticed by Steiffel or the fuzz, Miss Bloh Me's gonna give her a passing grade."

"Can she do that?"

"Don't know if she can, but she's gonna."

Lucy managed to stay off Steiffel's radar, at least during 5th period. But one day after school in the gym, before a staff-student basketball game, she snuck up behind The Krabman and yanked his shorts down around his ankles. Jock strap and all. Full moon over Fernwater. Embarrassed, angry and indignant, he pulled up his shorts and ordered Lucy to follow him to the office. He collared Jeff and me to act as witnesses, in case Steiffel didn't take his word for what happened.

We sat silently in the VP's office until Lucy's mom showed up ten minutes later. Steiffel began, "Mr. Krabke, will you tell us what happened after school today?"

Jeff blurted out, "She pantsed him!"

"Tell me what you saw," said Steiffel.

Jeff held up his hands, curved into hemispheres. "Two lily white cheeks, nastiest buns you ever saw, and...."

Our VP interrupted him. "Lucy, please tell us your side of the story." The Krabman shot him a dirty look.

This was Juicy Lucy's opening, and she charged on through it: "I was walking behind Mr. Krabke, and I guess I tripped. I reached out to grab something, and I must have grabbed his shorts. Accidentally." She batted her mascara-caked eyelashes at him. "I really am sorry."

"Lucy," said her mom. "Are you telling the truth?"

"Mo-om! Yes! I tripped and...." She covered her mouth to hide a guilty smile, but her story was blown. "OK," she said with a giggle. "I did it, I pantsed him."

There was a two second pause, and then her mom, Jeff and I lost it. A few seconds later, even Steiffel was laughing. And it was a genuine laugh. The Krabman stomped out in a huff and missed out on seeing Lucy get suspended.

For the last month of school, whenever I ran into Steiffel waiting by the bus zone to greet students, I said, "G' mornin'," and meant it.

My pals and I walked out of school one misty afternoon, and Johnny was intercepted by a lanky, loose-limbed kid a couple years older than us. "You Boe?" he asked.

Like a tough guy in a gangster movie, my buddy straightened his shoulders and stepped forward. "Who's asking?"

"I am." The guy had long arms, and he belted Johnny in the gut, doubling him over. "I'm Penny's brother," he said, and delivered a swift uppercut to the jaw. "Good to meet you."

In response, Johnny spit out a string of bloody slobber that hung off his chin and then dribbled down his chest.

"Don't mess with my sister." The guy slapped Johnny upside the head and turned to leave.

Penny Prismark had seen the entire interaction, all ten

seconds of it. She pounded her brother on the shoulder and yelled, "You brat!" She then bent over Johnny and asked, "Are you OK? Oh my gosh, you're bleeding!"

"No shit, Sherlock."

With two notable exceptions – her theatrical meltdown at the dance, and the time she got barfed on – Penny was irrepressibly buoyant, even when confronted with blood, snot and drool.

"We have to get that cleaned up!" She pulled a hanky out of her purse and began to fuss over him.

"Just back the hell off," Johnny grumbled.

"I'm so sorry," said Penny, not backing the hell off. "Oh, this is all my fault; he found those letters you wrote me."

"What notes?"

Uh-oh. Jake's save-a-slow-dance note had been such a hit that he'd been sending her fake love letters every few weeks, signed with Johnny's name. My favorite was a poem that rhymed "cushy pillow" with "pussy willow".

"You know," said Penny. "Like the one about me having a, um...." She blushed and lowered her voice. "About me having a bubble butt."

Eying her with contempt and confusion, Johnny hawked a bloody loogie on the sidewalk. "Must've been a different Johnny, girl. But now that you mention it.... Turn around, would ya?"

She straightened her arms and clenched her fists. "Ooooooh, you are such a nerd!" She stalked off.

Watching her go, Johnny Boe wiped his chin, smearing blood across his jaw. "Bubble butt, bubblehead."

"And a butthead brother," added Jake.

Jeff chanted, "Bubble butt, bubble head, butthead." He cackled and repeated it.

Johnny started laughing, and all of us joined in. He'd pause every so often to swallow or choke or spit out some blood, and then he'd start right back up again. When he saw Steiffel headed our way, he recognized his chance to regain control of the situation; he turned away and ran two bloody fingers diagonally across his face.

Our VP said, "Time to get on the bus, boys."

McClown cried out, "My God, it was awful, Mr. Steiffel! The birds came out of nowhere! Went straight for his eyeballs!"

"Whose eyeballs?" Steiffel spun around, searching the sky. "What birds?"

Johnny turned to face him. "Peckers, sir, a flock of 'em." He grabbed the VP by his shoulders. "You've never seen so many peckers in one place. OK, maybe *you* have, but I haven't."

The VP shook loose and sourly regarded the red stains on his white shirt. "They attacked you? Why would they do that?" He took a step back and shook his head in an attempt to clear it. "Johnny, you're.... you're bleeding!"

"Just a flesh wound, sir. Better board up your house. You don't want a pecker getting anywhere near Mrs. Steiffel. You might want to pick up some of that.... uh, what's it called?"

With no hesitation, McClown said, "Pecker-b-gon."

"Yeah, that's it. Better get yourself some, Mr. Steiffel."

The next day in The Krabman's class, Johnny Boe caught Penny staring at him with pity, which was absolutely the last thing he wanted from her, or from anyone, for that matter. He glared at her and mouthed the words: Fuck off.

Two minutes later, I watched her wipe a tear from her cheek. Johnny saw it too; he bashed himself in the side of his own head with the butt of his hand three times.

When talking with us guys, Johnny Boe had taken to conveying our art teacher's name as a request: Miss, Bloh Me? He put forth the theory that she'd given Lucy the boot so she could have him all to herself. With his girlfriend out of the way, Johnny was free to try a more straight forward approach with Miss Bloh Me, who he had kept "simmering on the back burner".

He sauntered into class one afternoon and asked her, real casual-like, "What're you up to this week-end?"

"My cousin's getting married on Sunday. Other'n that, not much. How 'bout you?"

"Not much." Pause. "Wanna catch a movie Saturday afternoon?"

He was so smooth. How did he do that? He was asking a *woman* out on a date, a *hot* woman. His brother lived in a frat – did he give Johnny lessons? Could *I* get lessons? I looked around to see if Penny Prismark was watching, but then remembered she was absent, which might be why he'd picked this particular day to hit on our teacher. Was he keeping Penny simmering on a back burner too? Or did he not want to hurt her feelings? Or was he afraid she'd have another meltdown? No, he'd have enjoyed that.

As smooth as he was, however, Johnny Boe was no match for Miss Bloh Me.

"No, thank you," she said with a distracted air, but then brightened immediately. "Hey, I ran into your mom in Kmart last week. She was buying you underwear – 34 Hanes, right?"

Johnny slunk away like our cocker spaniel Brutus, the time Mom spanked him for chewing up her undergarments. My pal was nowhere near as invincible as I had once thought. He slouched in his chair silently until class was dismissed.

"Haldini, today never happened, right?"

I nodded and took one last look at Miss Bloh Me on my way out. It was nuts to imagine that he'd ever had a shot with her.

Before Art class the next day, Johnny Boe waved me into the office. He waited for our dowdy secretary to hang up her phone and then asked, "Ma'am, is that a new sweater?"

"This old thing?" Dressed uniformly in rumpled beige, she made a sound that was equal parts snort, laugh, and cough. "What can I do for you boys?"

"Miss Blohmeyer asked us to get pencils for her."

She swiveled in her chair and opened a cabinet. "How many would you like?"

"I believe she said eight boxes."

"Take 'em. And there's an electric sharpener behind you."

"I'm sure Miss Bloh Me…. Blohmeyer would appreciate that. Thank you, ma'am."

When we got to class, Johnny passed out the pencils to me and the boys, and we began launching them straight up at the foamy acoustic ceiling tiles. About one out of every ten stuck, eliciting an unfathomably gleeful response from whoever threw it. When Jeff got his first one to stick halfway through class, you'd have thought he had hit a walk-off home run.

The ceiling soon sprouted a forest of rubber-tipped stalactites. Surprisingly, we had not been caught; on most days, Miss Bloh Me had eyes in the back of her head.

But she was onto us after all; with one minute left in class, she strutted over to Johnny and smiled warmly. "296-4155," she cooed. "One good turn deserves another."

He perked up. "Yeah?"

Had she changed her mind? Hope took flight. But then she jerked her thumb toward the ceiling, causing him to stammer, "Wha.... what's that number?"

"King County Sheriff's Office."

He swallowed. "That's where my dad works." Hope took the form of a woodpecker with a bad wing.

"Oh, *is* it now?"

Johnny was close to panic. His woodpecker had taken a nosedive.

Miss Bloh Me said, "You have fifteen minutes to remove the pencils from the ceiling, *all* of them."

"How am I gonna do that? I have to catch the bus."

She shook her head.

He looked at us guys, one by one. "Well, do they have to help?" We kept our heads down, pretending not to listen. "Do you have a ladder?" he asked.

She shook her head again. He looked up at the pencils and then down at his feet. His Woodpecker of Hope was road kill.

Miss Bloh Me leaned forward and broadened her smile. "296-4155."

Chapter 10 – June

Jake walked out of science class, pale and shaking. My buddies and I crowded around, and he whispered, "I *saw* it!"

We knew right away what he was talking about. Misty Wart had worn a polka dot skirt that day, a *short* polka dot skirt. Sitting on a table at the front of the room, she'd been scissoring her legs back and forth, and occasionally crossing them.

Jake shuddered. "It's gonna be the priesthood for me." His eyes lost focus. "She doesn't wear panties. It was all grody!"

It was unnerving to see Jake the Invisible Boy in distress.

Johnny Boe stretched an arm roughly across his shoulders and shook him. "Jakie boy. Women – gotta get 'em before they fossilize. C'mon, let's eat outside. Fresh air will do you good."

He was talking about eating lunch in the courtyard in front of the school. But my dad was supposed to pick me up for a dentist appointment in a couple minutes, and since his ejection from my baseball game two weeks earlier, I was embarrassed to be seen with him.

So I blurted out, "I think the cheerleaders are doing their new routine in the cafeteria."

That did the trick. They lit out, and as soon as they were out of sight, I took off out the front exit. My dad, sitting in his Fiat Spider, the priciest Italian-made car he could afford, rolled down his window and motioned me over. Walking across the bus lane toward the parking lot, I looked over each shoulder to see if I'd been seen; the only other person in sight was Penny Prismark, fifty yards behind me. I hustled to get in the car and then bent over to fiddle with my shoelaces.

Penny's mom called out from the car next to ours, "Hi-iii, Penelope!" She was an older, louder and, though I would not have thought it possible, more cheerful version of her daughter. "How was school, honey?"

Dad shifted into reverse and began to let out the clutch. I

kept my head down.

"Great, Mom! Especially science; Miss De Waart is so smart, we don't even know what she's talking about half the time!"

Dad pushed the clutch in.

"Oh honey, I'm so happy you have good teachers! Gold star for Fernwater!"

The Prismarks drove off, and Dad shifted into neutral. He asked if I shared that girl's assessment of my science teacher.

Still reeling from the repellent image of Misty Wart and her chubby, polka dotted thighs, I lifted my head and responded with a feeble: "Ummm, I don't know."

Dad clenched his jaws and inhaled loudly through his nose. "Leo, this De Waart woman, just because she cannot speak clearly does not mean she's smart. Inability to communicate is not a mark of intelligence." He gripped the steering wheel until his knuckles turned white. "Son...." Oh no. Please. ".... if you don't stand up to ignorance, you give it permission to exist, to fester, to breed. When I was growing up, people in the *Resistenza* knew how to fight." I drifted in and out of his narrative. ".... decisions you make when you're 14.... Authorities must *earn* your respect.... We didn't have it as easy as you...."

He finally noticed my glassy eyes and asked, "How many days of school left?"

I answered right away. "Ten and a half."

He let out the clutch and grumbled, "Praise the Lord."

At the beginning of Science class, Jeff Mori ripped open four pink packets of Sweet 'n' Low. Holding two in each hand, he poured them down his gullet. He told me with a grin what I already knew: "Mom loads up her purse at the restaurant. I need a little pick-me-up around noon."

Misty Wart halted her lecture on continental drift and asked Jeff to read Sweet 'n' Low's warning label. He eyed the packet, scrunched up his face and scratched his head. He then handed it to me, and I read aloud: "This product contains saccharin, which has been determined to cause cancer in laboratory animals."

"Not a problem," he declared triumphantly. "I'm not a lavatory animal."

Misty Wart was noticeably less cheerful than she had been

in September. She harrumphed and turned to write on the board. Jeff opened ten packets, dumped them all in his mouth, puffed up his cheeks and tilted his head back. Using the butts of his hands, he pressed in on his cheeks, sending up a cloud of artificial sweetener. He reminded me of a puffball fungus, a spherical mushroom that grows in the forest. When stepped on, they send out a fine mist of spores.

Misty Wart turned back to face the class and noticed that Jeff had opened up yet another pink packet. She surprised him with a question about plate tectonics: "Jeff, what is the longest fault line on the West Coast?"

In similar situations in the past, one of us would feed him the right answer, so he had no reason to doubt Johnny Boe's whispered cue, "Uranus".

"Yer anus," Jeff responded, bewildered but pleased with the J boys' laughter.

"You're a *crack* up, Mori," said Jake with downcast eyes. Ever since The Polka Dot Skirt Incident, he spent most of Science class staring at the floor.

"Gettin' to the *bottom* of things now," said Johnny.

I thought, but didn't say: Don't be such an ass, Boe.

Jake countered: "I *rectum* yer right."

"Wrecked 'em?" asked Jeff.

The lasting image I have of Jeff Mori is this: a human puffball fungus, head tilted back, mouth filled with artificial sweetener, palms poised by his cheeks.

The last week of school, there was an incident that shook the town of Oxley. Someone pulled a fire alarm at Fernwater Junior High at the end of lunch, and on the way to answer the call, a fire truck ran a red light and plowed into and over a VW bug. The 73-year-old driver, our mayor's father, was killed instantly. He had neither heard the siren nor seen the truck.

Our VP, the fire marshal and the police launched a lengthy investigation, interviewing dozens of students. The mayor offered $2000 for information leading to arrest. Naturally, I suspected my buddies: Johnny Boe or McClown, whose willingness to raise hell knew no bounds; or Jeff, on a dare from Johnny; or Jake, who was most likely to get away with such a stunt. Jake, however, didn't do it – he and I were buying yearbooks at the time the alarm was pulled on the other side of the school.

Between classes that afternoon, there was a lot of whispering back and forth between my friends and me: Did you do it? No, did you? No way. Well, who did then? Got me.

Johnny Boe convened a meeting in the Crash after school that day. When three girls approached, Johnny shook his head with authority, and they beat it.

"All right," he said. "Who did it?"

He was bothered, for reasons not hard to guess. It was widely known that he'd been prodding Jeff all year to pull the alarm, and if any of us were to get fingered, Johnny would receive his share of the blame, especially considering that his dad was a cop.

But I wondered if there was another reason behind his anxiety; Johnny Boe wanted – or needed – to be the one calling the shots. Yes, Jake the Invisible Boy had been acting unilaterally all year, but the other J boys were not privy to a lot of his pranks.

"Who pulled it?" asked Johnny, looking at each of us in turn and getting angrier by the moment. "Who.... pulled it?"

I went with the obvious answer: "Maybe it was somebody else. Jake and I were at the office when the alarm went off." I then asked Jeff and McClown where they were.

"With me," snarled Johnny, meaning that Jake and I were the ones under scrutiny here.

"There ya go," said Jake. "Must've been somebody else."

"Yeah," said Johnny. "Must've been."

But he was clearly not convinced. And knowing how much he liked running the show, I shuddered to think what his next move might be. I didn't have to wait long.

The location of The Crash had eluded Steiffel for two months. Situated in a little sinkhole out behind the woodshop, Johnny Boe frequently reminded visitors to pack out their empty bottles, cigarette butts and used rubbers. From a post inside a rotted-out stump, lookouts could spot the VP coming from a hundred yards away, giving us time to clear out.

One warm, cloudy morning before school, Jake the Invisible Boy took his turn standing guard inside the stump while a dozen kids grabbed a quick smoke or copied homework.

"I thought acid came in tablets," said Jeff Mori, his eyes fixed on the vial of hydrochloric acid that McClown waved hypnotically before his eyes. Johnny Boe had lifted it from Misty Wart's room the day before.

McClown took an eye dropped out of his shirt pocket. "Sometimes," he said, "but acid trips are better using liquid. C'mon, Mori, hold out your tongue."

"Let's wait until after school."

"Nah. Look at the bottle; it's only 30%. See? It'll be a short trip."

Jeff squinted, trying to make sense of the label. "30%? Is that a lot?"

"Nah. That means 70% is not acid."

Jeff hesitated one last time, then opened wide and said, "Ahhhhhhhhhhhh."

I waved my arms, trying to get Jake's attention, thinking we could step in and to put a halt to this madness. But he missed my signal, so I stepped forward to stop McClown. Too late. He removed the eye dropper from the bottle and emptied it onto the tip of Jeff's tongue.

Jeff smacked his lips. "Not bad; tastes like….. Ow! Hey! Yowwwww! Water!" He lit out for the creek running along the boundary of the school grounds, screaming and stumbling over tree roots. "Water!"

Jake took out after him.

"Enjoyin' your trip, Mori?" McClown laughed and howled and danced in circles.

A snippet of Dad's speech played in my head: Son, if you don't stand up to bullies….

I knocked the acid out of McClown's hand and yelled, "Youuuu fuckwit!"

I had never been in a fight, and he knew it. Though I had five inches on him, he was built like a bulldog. He tensed, ready to pop me, but at that moment, I didn't care. One good turn deserves another. Adrenaline, exhilarating and powerful, surged through my body, and I punched him, hard, in his left eye. The agreeable *whump* of knuckles on skull felt good. McClown fell on his butt.

Ohhh, so *this* is what Dad's been talking about all these

years. He'd been right all along about how satisfying it is to fight the good fight, to stand up to a bully and take him down. In an instant, it became clear how my father had developed his taste for fighting.

Triumphantly and defiantly, I strutted back and forth in front of McClown, daring him to rise. He made a move to sit up, but fell back on his elbows when he sensed the rage in my eyes. And I saw what may have been fear in his. Or maybe, for once, he realized he was a fuckwit. His ultimate humiliation came when he looked up at Johnny Boe, smug and smirking, back in the driver's seat, his gleeful eyes asking: Could I have scripted this any better?

I hated that son of a bitch. Had I punched the wrong guy? Though McClown had committed the atrocity, it was Johnny that put him up to it. Still, Johnny hadn't *done* anything.

Riding a wave of fury and adrenaline, with no one else to slug, I ran, aimlessly. I sprinted across the football field and into the woods, finally collapsing into a massive clump of sword ferns. Any satisfaction I'd gotten out of punching McClown trickled out of me.

I wondered how Jeff was doing, that dumb ass.

My friends and I had always been peripherally aware of the differences between us, but that day we faced them head on. McClown, sporting the beginnings of what would become a magnificent black and purple shiner, took his seat next to Johnny Boe in The Krabman's class. They seemed surprised when Jake and Jeff chose to sit on the other side of the room. Jeff sucked on an ice cube he'd gotten from a secretary, after telling her that he burned his tongue on hot cocoa. Nursing an A-, I sat in my usual spot at the front of the room, kneading my sore knuckles.

Johnny tried to cajole his pals into sitting with him: "What's the deal, guys?"

To him, sending Jeff on an "acid trip" was good clean fun, not so different in flavor or severity from the abuse he and McClown had been heaping on Jeff all year. And maybe Johnny figured that my altercation with McClown, though it had lasted all of one second, would forever be the moment around which we all would bond: Hey man, remember the time Leo knocked McClown on his ugly ass? Remember that?

That morning's sequence of events brought about a lasting reconfiguration in my circle of friends, and it wasn't just me that sensed the shift. Though Jake the Invisible Boy was a trouble-maker, he lacked the mean streak that Johnny and McClown so valued in one another. In Jake's eyes, they had clearly crossed some undrawn line of decency.

As for Jeff, he was a happy-go-lucky buffoon, a puffball fungus, blundering from one train wreck to the next. Above all else, he wanted to belong. Somewhere. Anywhere, to keep from being left behind.

I imagine that Johnny Boe considered me too constrained, too uptight, unwilling to break a pointless rule or two. Whereas I had a different perspective on his savagery: Having Taken a Stand, I was ready to move on. The J boys and their mayhem were behind me.

Or so I thought.

Chapter 11 – July

On July 2nd, it was already 70 degrees by nine in the morning, and Jake the Invisible Boy asked Jeff and me to ride bikes out to his aunt and uncle's dairy farm. I was about to turn him down when he mentioned that Johnny Boe and McClown were not invited.

We stopped at a fireworks stand and bought up a small arsenal of firecrackers, Roman candles, smoke bombs and the like. We then headed east out of Oxley on the winding, two-lane road with two-foot-wide shoulders. We rode single file when the logging trucks blew past at 60 mph, but as soon as the traffic thinned out, the three of us, for sport, tried to run each other off the road, laughing and cussing and spitting at one another.

After an hour-long ride, we pulled up in front of a weather-worn farmhouse with a spacious wrap-around porch. Auntie welcomed us with brownies and lemonade. Jake and I thanked her and raved about how good they were. We were surprised that Jeff only ate half of one brownie – he was usually a hog for sugar.

When Auntie left the room, he showed us where the acid had corroded the tip of his tongue, which was now knobby and forked at the end.

"I can't taste sweet," he said, without the slightest regret, and he was not looking for pity. He was simply stating a fact, as if losing a piece of your tongue is a normal part of anybody's day. He added, "Doesn't hurt anymore."

We emptied our bags of explosives on the table and planned our assault on the world.

"Outside with that!" Auntie barked.

We packed it all up and dumped it out again on the porch. We lit fire-crackers, waited for the fuses to burn down and then threw them at one another. The only mishap came when Jeff waited too long to launch.

"Fiddle de fuck!" He grabbed his hand and winced.

"You OK?" laughed Jake. "Let's see."

Jeff showed us his reddened fingers. "They won't fall off, will they?"

The numbness wore off after a couple minutes, at which point we lit sparklers and had a three-way sword fight. Next we fired off bottle rockets, aiming for passing cars; we would light the fuse when a car was still a quarter mile away and then hide behind the sprawling maple in Auntie's front yard. We tried that for an hour, but never got the timing right. We crawled under a barbed wire fence, stuck firecrackers in cowpies, lit the fuses, and ran for it. Jeff blew up an anthill with a dozen firecrackers stuck together with a single fuse.

Once our ammo was used up, we hit up Auntie for more brownies and lemonade. Sitting around the kitchen table, Jake said he wished he could live out here on the farm.

"Well, we need the house painted," she said. "And the fence needs fixing. Interested?"

"Oh, man! I sure am! But how much would you charge me to stay here?"

"Silly boy – we'd be paying you!"

Jeff was not happy with this talk of his best friend being gone for the summer. "How long does it take to paint a house?"

Jake ignored him and pumped a fist in the air. "Oh, that is copacetic! Thank you!" But then he slumped in his chair. "I don't know if Mom will go for it."

At that, Jeff looked hopeful.

"I've already talked to her," said Auntie. "She'll be happy to get rid of you. Just kidding! I'll warn you though; it's going to be hard work."

Jake nodded enthusiastically, whereas Jeff looked like his dog had been run over.

We stopped by Kmart on the way home so Jeff could pick up an AC/DC album. "Hey Leo, do you know about their discount?"

He looked at Jake and cackled, having recovered from hearing that his pal would be going away for two months. Jeff was nothing if not resilient. What did they know that I didn't? If we could get a discount, then, yeah, count me in; record companies were making a killing.

"I'll show you how to save a coupla bucks," Jeff assured me as we locked up our bikes.

On our way back to the music department, Jake couldn't stop talking about his good luck, getting to live and work on the farm. "You think I'm a slouch, Leo, but this ain't gonna be like school; this is gonna be *real* work."

I picked out the first Van Halen album, which had come out the previous year; since hearing "Eruption", Eddie's smokin' guitar solo, I'd been hitting up my folks for lessons. Jeff grabbed ACDC's Dirty Deeds Done Dirt Cheap and then lifted Stan Wolowic and the Polka Chips from the Special Deal bin.

I was horrified. "What's *that* for?"

"Check it out," he said with a cackle. "Today's Blue Light Special." He then swapped the price tags on the two albums and then put Stan Wolowic back where he found him.

"Jeff, you spaz," I said. "The tag's all wrinkly. Give me that." With no thought to what I was doing or why, I pressed on the price tag and rubbed.

"Excuse me." I looked up into the unsmiling face and closely cropped blonde hair of a huge man; in my memory he is a block of granite, as wide as he is tall. The lapel of his dark suit displayed a security badge.

"Both of you, come with me." His voice left no room for refusal.

A cold fear coursed through my veins. I looked around for Jake, but of course he was long gone. Jeff and I followed the guy to a stockroom at the back of the store.

"Sit," he told Jeff, and motioned to a box of canned peas. "I know you."

"I was just...."

"Don't." The guy leaned forward, daring Jeff to speak. "Same question I've asked you before: What were you thinkin'?"

"I knew it was illegal, but I didn't know it was wrong."

Huh? Huhhhhh? Welcome to the curious, audacious world of Jeff Mori, a place where logic and everyday sensibilities don't apply in any recognizable way, where legality and morality are discrete entities.

But the *way* he delivered that statement made it almost sound reasonable: Yeah, I messed up, he seemed to be saying, but

I'm not guilty or bad or mean, just dumb.

The guard waved at a forklift twenty feet away. "Sit over there. Wait for the police."

Police? Oh, God! This cannot be happening. The police?! C'mon, it was Jeff; he was the one.... What will my mom say? And Dad.... Oh God, oh God! Does this go on my record? What about college? Is this a felony? Do universities accept felons?

The man focused his attention solely on me and motioned to the box of canned peas. I sat down with a thump and looked up into that humorless face.

He said, "Name."

"Leo." Pause. "Haldini. Uh, Leo Haldini."

"I know you too." His eyes narrowed; mine grew huge. He didn't say anything for a good ten seconds, and I was sure he was trying to get me to piss my pants.

"You play on my son's baseball team," he said. "He's your shortstop."

"Who is...? Oh, yeah.... uh, I play second."

"You could stand to pick some better friends." He jerked his head toward Jeff.

"Sir, I've never stolen...." But those heartless gray eyes looked straight into me. "Well, I took plums from the neighbor's tree at my old house, when I lived in Olympia, and...."

He held up a palm the size of a catcher's mitt. "I will make you a deal." Another excruciating pause. "You tell your father what happened today. And if I meet him at the ball field, I will ask if you spoke with him." He let that sink in. "If you cannot agree to that, I will turn you over to the cops when they come to pick up Idiot Number One." He hooked a banana-sized thumb at Jeff.

"I promise to tell my dad.... I mean, my father." My voice cracked when I said it.

"Now go on home."

"Thank you, sir," I said, gushing sincerity.

I struggled to my feet and stole a glance at Jeff, his face clouded in utter confusion. He didn't speak or wave, but his expression was reproachful, as if he could not believe that I would leave him. The last few weeks, he had worn this expression often. He seemed to be asking: Wait; where you goin'? How'd this happen? Hold on. Do I still get the Kmart discount?

I felt sorry for him, and my conscience poked at me halfheartedly, prodding me to stay and see if I could help him out of this fix. But that inclination was trumped by an instinctual desire to get the hell out of there. Now. But don't run. I had almost made it to the door when the security man bellowed, "Heyyy!" Oh God, oh God. I turned to face my tormentor.

"You and my son," he called out. "That was some double play you turned the other night."

Halfway home, the terror wore off and I toyed with the idea of keeping the incident to myself. But that night at dinner, the whole fiasco tumbled out. While I confessed, Dad's eyes were riveted on the photograph of the fire-damaged Italian villa, his expression shifting from surprise to anger to disgust and finally arriving at agony. Ordinarily, when he cycled through the dreary silence of his internal landscape, Ella would try to lighten things up with a joke, delivered in her little girl's voice, but this time even she knew to keep her trap shut. I had no idea what Dad was going to do or say, but whatever it was, I wished he'd get it over with.

Finally he said in a soft tone, "Growing up, I took some things from good people worse off than I. It's not a pleasant memory, son. Decisions you make when you're 14...." His voice fizzled, and I hoped he did not zone out. Seeing regret in Dad's eyes was unfamiliar ground for me. For the first time in my life, I found myself wishing for his growing-up-during-the-war speech, the unabridged version.

Beseechingly, I said, "I am sorry."

The heartache in my father's eyes ran deeper than did my own, and though it would be another quarter century before the source of that heartache was brought to light, it was his willingness to bear his sorrow that accorded him the fortitude to assuage my own grief.

Laying his hand squarely on mine, he said, "Leo, you are a fine young man."

Listening to my father's unusually gentle tone, I realized the forgiveness I sought had been granted.

We made up a rained-out game on the Fourth of July. The shortstop and I turned a nifty double play to end a rally in the top of the fifth, and Mom yelled, "Nice goin', Haldini!"

Trotting off the field, I spotted the Kmart security guy seated two rows above and off to the side of my parents. Ever since my father's outburst two months before, they had taken to sitting off by themselves. The big man pointed at my folks and then looked me in the eye. I stopped and nodded my head once, signifying that I had come clean with them. He offered up a tiny salute; my business with him was finished.

Entering the dugout with my teammates clapping me on the shoulder, it occurred to me that my business with Johnny Boe and the gang was finished as well. Jake the Invisible Boy had always been my connection to them, and he would be working on his aunt and uncle's farm all summer. It was liberating, knowing that I had willed myself to break away from the J boys. Then it hit me:

Hey! Today is Independence Day; I will claim it as *my* Independence Day as well. The flock can go take a flying leap.

Chapter 12 – August

A week before Ella was to enroll as a 7th grader at Fernwater Junior High, my dad, with Mom and a dozen parents in tow, descended on the school board. The way Mom told it to neighbors and family at our end-of-summer barbecue the following Sunday afternoon, I pictured the angry mob from an old Frankenstein movie, torches in hand, lightning lacing the midnight sky, storming the mansion in a downpour. Sometimes disruption is necessary.

But the skies were clear on the day of our party, and Mom rhymed her weather report: "Eighty degrees, with a westerly breeze."

Dad brandished a spatula and tended steaks, wearing an apron he'd gotten from Ella on his birthday that read: I don't need a recipe – I'm Italian.

My mom, a non-confrontational sort, bragged about their assault. "I was burstin' with pride when Gianni took 'em to task for – I have the whole thing memorized – using our children as guinea pigs in a lame-brained experiment that never had a snowball's chance in hell of teaching them to read, write and think. Anyone with half a brain could have seen that.'"

Dad looked up from the glowing briquettes and forced a crooked smile.

Mom gazed at him with nothing short of adoration and continued on. "The superintendent started to interrupt him, but Gianni marched up to the front of the room...." She pumped her arms forward and back. "…. and slapped a petition down on the big oak table. He declared, 'Here are names of fifty parents who demand to see bells installed, walls put up, and this imbecilic grading system done away with at Fernwater.'"

Jake's dad added, "Then he hauled out his staple gun and stapled the petition to the table! Klouh! Klouh! Klouh!"

Many of our guests had attended the board meeting, and they all agreed that was exactly how it went down; they clapped and cheered and pounded Dad on the back. Mom smiled, though she'd have preferred to leave out that business with the staple gun, which I was not alone in thinking was the best part of the story. And Mom made no mention of the restraining order against my father; he was not to set foot in the district office, nor was he to speak to members of the board.

I sat at a picnic table across from Uncle Marco. He patted his wife's bottom affectionately and said to me, "Lei ha un culo belle sodo." She has a firm butt.

When I laughed, she smacked him on his chest. "What's this old goat sayin' about me?"

"Mia seconda moglie," said Marco, "una tavola da surf." Something like: My second wife had an ass like a surfboard.

"I don't know," I said, with as much innocence as I could muster. "I don't speak Italian."

"Maybe not," she said, "but you understand it."

She grabbed a dill pickle and cocked her arm. Still giggling, I shielded my face.

Marco snatched the pickle from her. "Hey, don't waste that!" He lowered his voice and leered at her. "You and me, we could have some fun with this." He gave me a wink.

"You old goat!" But now she was laughing too. "You will ruin these kids!"

Jake's mom took a camera out of her purse and asked my parents to pose in front of our wisteria-covered arbor. Mom draped herself all over Dad, smiling like she'd won the Publishers Clearing House Sweepstakes. He made a valiant effort to grin.

Marco said, "In the Cinque Terre, there is a hiking trail overlooking the Mediterranean; very beautiful, very romantic. The trail is called Via dell' Amore, Path of Love." He gestured at my parents. "Leo, your mother is my brother's Via dell' Amore."

Watching Dad socialize, I considered him to be a passably good host, though he spent an inordinate amount of time tending the barbecue, staring into the red hot coals of his own private little hell. Since laying siege on the school board, he had reverted to his default setting, a pervasive melancholy. I had seen him complete this cycle before: from sad, to raging crusader, and then back to sad, or sadder.

The Friday before Labor Day, I hiked the two miles to Fernwater High, looking forward to getting oriented at my new school. Having signed up for college prep courses, I would not be seeing much of the J boys, except for maybe my neighbor Jake. He had called the week before to say he wouldn't be back until the morning that school starts.

"I love it here, Haldini. There's bullshit, yeah, but it's *real* bullshit, not like what Johnny and McClown been pedalin'. They got their hooks into Jeff again – can you believe it? Three fuckin' stooges. How you doing?"

I said I'd been palling around with guys from my summer league team. We had managed a seven-game winning streak, and we floated the Cedar River in inner tubes when the thermometer broke 90. Our shortstop, the security guard's son, asked me to join his Boy Scout troop.

Passing by the junior high, I was happy to say good-bye to it. My year-long party with the J boys had been an educational and social experiment, from which I had walked away unscathed and hopefully wiser for the experience. My 9th grade year was good for some laughs, but at some point it had become the same joke being told day after day.

"Hey! Haldini!" Mr. Hester was approaching, about to turn into the school parking lot.

"Hey!"

"Have a terrific year!"

"You too!"

"Got three words for you: inside the story! Bring your reader *inside*!" He waved and was gone.

I missed him already. I was keeping a journal, and I had re-read Lord of the Flies. I thought back to the story I'd written about my pals and me getting lost in the Cascades. How do I bring the reader inside? I took a last look at the school. Hmm, bring your reader inside. Hey! Hester had not intended it this way, but what if I moved the story *inside* Fernwater Junior High? Just like in the book, upon landing on the island/school, I had reveled in the lack of adult supervision; the halls were lawless, the students savages. On the island, the descent into barbarism had to happen gradually; otherwise the change would not have been acceptable, even to children. What I could not understand – and, as I write my memoir, what I still cannot understand – is this: Right out of the shoot, Fernwater must have been a zoo, or, as Dad put it: "Chaos incarnate, a seething cauldron of ineptitude."

In whose eyes had that passed for normal?

I realized that Fernwater had not suffered from a lack of rules, not at all. Rules *always* get written; it's simply a matter of who writes them. For the most part, the Fernwater staff had failed in their bid to maintain order, so Johnny Boe and his crew gladly stepped in and filled the vacuum by imposing an order of their own, savage though it may have been.

For Ralph in <u>Lord of the Flies</u>, deliverance would come only by leaving the island. Could I now see a bit of Ralph in myself? Would the J boys ever escape their island? Hard to say.

Approaching Fernwater High, I passed through a stand of cherry trees and took the brick steps two at a time. The excitement of the first day of school outweighed the sad realization that summer vacation was over. Though apprehensive, I was ready for a challenge.

Upon entering, however, I looked around in horror and disbelief, but no amusement. I had not asked, and no one had bothered to tell me that I would be attending an open-concept high school! Aarrrrrgghhhhh!

Part II: 1994

Chapter 13 - September

The excitement of the first day of school outweighed the sad realization that summer vacation was over. At least that's how it was for me, and, I suspected, for many of my 9th graders. I stood outside my classroom to greet my 1st period Geometry students, many of whom I'd had in class the previous year.

"Mr. Haldini, did you get my postcard?"

"Not yet. Hey, Calvin, you been playing guitar?"

"Hours a day; how 'bout you?"

"Hours a day."

"Hey Gramps, you got some gray in your beard."

"You're confused; that's blonde."

"Haldini, I'm stuck with *you* again?"

"Hiya, Jaime, nice shoes…. psych!"

"Hey Teach, nice hair – you cut it yourself?"

"Hey! You're jealous cuz *you* don't have a cool mullet."

I intended to start off the year in a businesslike manner and then loosen up over the course of the next month or so. But as I finished calling roll, a girl from the previous year poked her head in the door and called out, "Hi, Fuzzface."

So much for my businesslike facade. "Calvin," I said, "any words of wisdom?" He reminded me of the kid in the "Calvin and Hobbes" cartoon, in appearance if not temperament.

Stroking an imaginary goatee with his thumb and index finger, he said, "If it's green and wriggly, it's biology. If it stinks, it's chemistry. And if it doesn't work, it's physics." A lot of us had been waiting for just such an excuse to laugh.

"Good stuff," I said. "And welcome back. By the way, if I ever have to discipline any of you, understand that you will be listening to polka, at high volume for an extended period of time."

I hit the play button on my cassette player, where I had Stan Wolowic and the Polka Chips cued up. Following a short accordion intro, Stan and his female back-up singers tore into the verse with gusto: Roll.... out.... the barrel! We'll have.... a barrel.... of fun! First-timers in class were horrified. The others considered it funny, though sick and twisted.

I turned off Stan and said sternly, "Think what that could do to your brain."

One of the first-timers was leery. "Do you listen to that?

"Friends don't let friends do polka. OK, let's clear away the cobwebs from summer. Try this problem." I drew an 8x8 grid and a domino on the chalkboard.

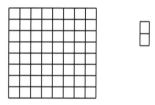

"How many dominoes it will it take to cover the grid?" Everyone saw immediately that it would take 32. I then erased two squares at opposite corners.

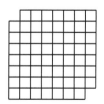

Again, I asked how many dominoes it would take to cover the grid. Somebody tossed out an answer of 31. I asked why.

"62 squares divided by 2 equals 31."

"Makes sense," I said. "Everyone draw this grid, and show me how the 31 dominoes could be arranged."

Nathan was removing a chessboard from his backpack; he would be able solve the problem in two seconds. I shook my fist at him and he agreeably put it away.

The previous year, Calvin brought Nathan in before school to meet me, and I had gawked at his wild, curly black hair. He was building an instrument, he told me, a flute-like contraption that could play two notes at once. He thought that I, being a musician and a math guy, might have some insights. He and Calvin came in to chat every so often, and the three of us developed a budding camaraderie.

After working for a few minutes on the domino problem, a kid said, "I don't think it can be done."

"Me neither," chimed in others.

"Here's the deal," I said. "Either come up with a solution, or else come up with a convincing argument why it can't be done."

After a couple minutes, a kid said, "No matter how you arrange them, there's always one domino that won't fit."

"How do you know?" I asked. "Have you tried all possible configurations?"

"Well, no, but it seems like.... hmmm...."

"Anybody come up with a solution?" Silence. I turned to Nathan. "May I borrow your chessboard? OK, everyone look at this board and think about the problem. Silently." A minute later, I called on a dark-skinned girl with huge brown eyes.

Radiating confidence, she said, "Each domino covers one white square and one black. When you remove squares from opposite corners, both will be white or both black. Either way, you have an uneven number of white and black squares. So it can't be done."

"Well explained. What was your name again?"

"Anjuli."

"You're Kali's sister?"

"Yeah, and she told me not to believe any of your taxi driver stories."

"Oh, she of little faith."

"But she said you were her favorite teacher.... well, her favorite junior high teacher.... well, her favorite junior high math teacher.... well, her...."

"OK, OK, I get it. Tell her she's one of my favorite Costa

Rican slash Pakistani students. Where did your parents get your name?"

"Mom found it in a trashy romance novel."

"Nice to meet you." To the class, I said, "Most of you tried a guess-and-check approach, and that's often effective, if a problem can be done. If it can't, how many configurations would you have to test out?"

Somebody said, "Too many to count?"

A boy said, "You could do it, but it wouldn't be any fun."

A likeable Jamaican wise guy named Jamie said, "Unless you were Mr. Haldini, and didn't have a life."

"By contrast," I said, "Anjuli's method was powerful and abstract. That mode of thinking, using proof, was developed by the Greeks some 2300 years ago. There were highly developed civilizations before the Greeks – the Egyptians, for example, were accomplished engineers, and they built those amazing pyramids – but their understanding of mathematics was not as abstract or powerful."

If someone had told me when I was 14 that I would one day be teaching at Fernwater Junior High, I'd have jumped out the window of a speeding school bus. By now, I should be playing guitar in a reggae band in Jamaica, or writing my third novel, or.... or.... Yet there I was, beginning my eighth year at Fernwater, and for the most part, loving it.

For most educators, they make a decision to teach, whereas in my case, it was a calling. Arriving at Western Washington University in Bellingham in the fall of 1982, I planned on getting a degree in journalism. But my direction in life changed abruptly when Mom enticed me home one weekend with an offer of lasagna and laundry service. At that point, my jeans practically stood up by themselves, and my socks.... Let me explain it this way:

On Halloween, my roommate over-imbibed and passed out face down in the third floor hallway of Higginson Hall; he was literally on his lips. My neighbors offered to help drag him back down to our room.

Not being in great shape myself, I slurred, "Lemme try sumpin' firz. Turn 'im over, jinnelmen." Standing on one leg, I took off a shoe and a sock, and promptly took a tumble. I sat up giggling and reverentially draped the sock across my roommate's face. "Blesh you, child."

He sat up twenty seconds later, gaggin' and cussin'. He held out my sock like it was a week-old possum carcass. "Jeeees Chriz, 'Aldini! Somepin' die in yer shoe?" He retched and threw the offending sock at me. "Somepin' die 'n' not go ta heav'n?"

I went home for the weekend with a black plastic garbage bag of laundry and a monstrous appetite. On Sunday afternoon, I was playing guitar in my room when Ella, then a sophomore at Fernwater High, barged in, looking distraught. She plopped herself and her open Geometry book down on my bed.

"Can you help me with proofs – I don't get 'em."

I thought back to Farley's class. "Think of it like building a bridge: You don't start at one end and build all the way across; you start from both ends and work toward the middle."

She showed me the one that was giving her fits, and we talked about working forward from what she knew, and then working backward from where she had to end up. That left one missing step in the middle, and by that point the solution was obvious.

"Oh, that wasn't hard," she said. "It was almost fun, like a puzzle. I wish *you* were my teacher. Mom says dinner's in twenty minutes and you better be hungry."

Watching Ella leave my room with a relieved smile, I bid my journalistic aspirations good-bye. In exchange for helping my sister with one geometric proof, she unwittingly shed light on the phrase "Higher Purpose". I had never experienced such a moment of absolute clarity; I would become a teacher.

Though happy for me, Mom was concerned that my decision was made too quickly.

Dad feared that I was making a mistake from which I might not easily recover. He held journalists in the highest regard, considering them indispensable in calling out the crooks, his standard reference to politicians.

After graduating with a teaching degree from Western, I was restless, and spent a year wandering around India, living on the cheap. The next July, I returned home to visit Ella. She had married her high school sweetheart and moved into my parents' house in Oxley, after Dad convinced Mom to move back to Italy, at least temporarily. He said he wanted to be closer to his ailing father. I had visited my folks at Lake Como on the way home from India.

Ella picked up her six-month-old daughter and asked me, "How's Gramps?"

"Oh, he's fine. I think Dad used him as an excuse to move back to The Old Country. You know how he got all weepy-eyed, talking about the food and vineyards."

"And the war and poverty," Ella added with a shake of her head. "It's weird if you ask me." She nodded toward the photo of the Italian villa. "Did you see the place where Dad grew up?"

"I asked to go see it every day, but he kept saying, 'Let's wait 'til the weather clears,' even though it was warm and dry. Then it poured my last two days there."

"How's Mom?"

"Oh, you know. Plop her down on a beach in Bangladesh, and she's happy as a clam. Give her five minutes and she's settled in. Dad, on the other hand, is becoming a full-time grump." I shook my head. "I think they brought the wrong baby home from the hospital. I don't see myself in either one of them."

"That's because you don't have kids yet. But when you do – OK, *if* you do – don't be surprised when you open your mouth and Dad's voice comes out. Because I do see him in you, Leo. You get contentious like he does."

It was all I could do to stop myself from saying: I do not! Which of course would have proved her point brilliantly. Ella gave me a see-what-I-mean look.

She went on. "The moment I had Lucia, I swear I became our mother." Ella made kissy noises that brought a smile to her baby's face, and I saw what she meant. "It's spooky," she said, "but kinda cool too. Here, hold her. I need to start dinner."

Lucia promptly sneezed all over me, but won me over with an impish smile.

I'd been applying to districts all over Washington State, but as yet I had received no offers. When my sister mentioned that Fernwater had an opening for a math teacher, my stomach gurgled in response; memories of ninth grade were replete with cheap laughs and hooliganism.

"At least go look at it," she said. "You'll be pleasantly surprised. I promise."

I scoffed at that, but agreed to go look.

While in high school, I had visited my old junior high teachers on occasion. Due in large part to my father's "lobbying efforts", bells and synchronized clocks had been installed, and a few more clapboard walls were erected every few months, forming an ever expanding labyrinth of tiny, windowless rooms, some of which had no ventilation, and some of which lacked heat.

"I guess it's better, having walls," Ella had told us one winter evening. "But you can see your breath in Hester's room."

In 1983 the Seattle area suffered a 3.7 earthquake, a piddling jolt, but powerful enough to open up a 30-meter-wide, 10-meter-deep sinkhole beneath Fernwater Junior High. The quake rolled through just before dawn, and Ella, upon seeing the wreckage of her old school on the morning news, cut class and went to check it out. A high school junior at the time, she called to fill me in:

"The cafeteria got swallowed up, the music wing caved in, and brick pillars toppled like dominoes. Kids had picnics on the lawn with donuts and Slurpees. Word got around that the school would have to be rebuilt from scratch, and after a half-assed attempt at looking bummed, teachers were literally dancing in the street. You should've heard Dad. He was *giggling*, Leo. No, really. He kept saying, 'Fernwater, an educational sinkhole!'"

Having promised Ella that I'd go look, I visited Fernwater Junior High the next morning and was pleasantly surprised; the blend of brick, glass and massive wooden beams gave the building a solid but airy feel. Reuben Rapp, the roly-poly exuberant VP, showed me which room would house the new hire and then gave me a tour of the modern, but traditional school. I found the prospect tempting. Still, this *was* Fernwater, and I feared that accepting the job might be a tern for the worse.

Entering the counseling office, we ran into Miss Bloh Me. In her mid-40's now, I would no longer have described her as a fox.

"Haldini!" she spat. "I remember you!"

Reuben Rapp eyed me suspiciously.

I cursed my impossibly bad timing. "Miss Bloh.... meyer? Uh, hey, it's nice to see you."

She planted her hands on now sizable hips and craned her head toward me. "You hung around with Johnny Boe and his pack of rats! You were the one...." Then she cracked up, and I saw the sparkle that had so captivated me fifteen years earlier. "Had you going, didn't I? What are you up to?"

"Applying for the math position," said my prospective VP.

"Math, huh? I always pegged you as a writer." She turned to Reuben. "Ask Felix about him – he'll give Leo a glowing recommendation." Responding to my confused look, she said, "Felix Hester, although kids call him Uncle Fester now. He used to talk about you; said you'd go far. He's still here, you know."

"He *is*? And you – you're still teaching?"

"Welcome to my humble abode." She spread her arms and twirled gracefully. "I've been counselor here for.... oh, gosh, four years." A sign hung above her office door in flowery lettering:

Mrs. Blohmeyer
Sage of the Age

"Mrs.? You got married?"

She laughed easily. "I got hitched 25 years ago."

"Then why did we call you *Miss* Bloh.... meyer?" I almost blew it that time.

She stared me down, making it clear that she had long known about her nickname. "That is a very good question," she said. "Winnie De Waart is still here too, and Betty Skibbitz." She laughed at my widened eyes. "Betty's got a lot of mileage left in the tank."

The VP jerked his head, indicating for me to follow. "Let's head over to the main office. I want you to meet my boss."

Thirty seconds later I was shaking hands with the principal, Mr. Krabke. Yikes! First Miss Bloh Me and now The Krabman; Beauty and the Beast!

"Long time, no see." To clarify, I added, "I was in your class, 78-79."

"Oh, yes; right!"

But he clearly did not remember me, which was probably just as well, giving my history at Fernwater. He wore running shorts, and sweat trickled down his larger-than-I-remembered forehead.

"Excuse my appearance," he said. "I just went for a five-mile jog."

"Good to see you're still running. You ran track at the U Dub, didn't you?"

"Indeed I did. Record for the hundred would be mine if they hadn't gone metric on me."

On the wall above his desk hung a banner reading:

> FERNWATER TERNS
> out the best students!

We talked for maybe a half hour, and he proclaimed to his secretary, "We will not do better than hiring an alumnus of Fernwater, still the district's flagship school."

I would be living close to Ella and teaching next door to Mr. Hester. The school had walls and a good vibe. How could I say no? I went back to Ella's, updated my resume', and accepted the position that day, with one reservation: Felix Hester used to talk about you, Mrs. Blohmeyer had told me. Said you'd go far.

Go far? I'd be working at the same place I attended junior high. Geez Louise.

"Next problem," I said to the class. "Suppose you have 27 cubes glued together to form a larger 3 by 3 by 3 cube, like so."

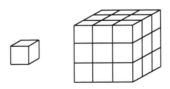

"Now, if you drop the large cube into a bucket of paint, and then pull it out, how many of the 27 little cubes will have no painted faces? One painted face? Two painted faces? Three? Go ahead and figure that out."

I looked around the room and noticed that Nathan just

happened to be holding a Rubik's Cube. He grinned triumphantly. I borrowed his cube a minute later, and we all discussed the solution. That night's assignment was to find the corresponding answers for cubes measuring 4 x 4 x 4, 5 x 5 x 5, and N x N x N.

"OK, next," I said, "I have a probability puzzle for you."

Nathan took dice and a deck of cards out of his backpack.

"Geez Louise! What else you got in there?" I rummaged through his pack and hauled out what appeared to be the remnants of a radio. "What's this gizmo?" I held it up for all to see.

"That's a receiver, in case Calvin steals my backpack." He removed what looked like a remote control from his shirt pocket. "I click this button, the receiver beeps, and I can find where he stashed it."

Everything he had said would generally indicate a high degree of nerdiness, but somehow he managed to project an aura of cool eccentricity.

"Show him your coat!" said Anjuli.

Nathan stood and opened his long black overcoat, revealing a set of socket wrenches, a miniature Frisbee, a wooden flute and bulging pockets.

"Are you running away from home? By the way, we're calling you 'Gizmo' from now on. "

"Show him the key!" said Anjuli.

"All right, Miss Trashy Romance Novel," I said, "don't go encouraging him."

Gizmo dug into a pocket and produced an ordinary-looking key.

"I will probably regret asking," I said, "but what does that open?"

"That's a master key. I can open any door in the school."

This was no longer fun or funny. "Where did you get it?"

"The librarian gave it to him," said Calvin. "He had to; Nathan is…. *Gizmo* is the only one in the school who knows how to fix computers."

"Wait a minute. I've been teaching here six…. no, seven years, and I don't have a master key!" I mumbled to Gizmo, "Give ya five bucks for it."

Chapter 14 - October

I held up a nut and bolt for my 2nd period 8th graders. "I need to tighten this nut on this bolt," I said, and then held up a wrench. "Suppose a 1/2 inch wrench is too small and a 3/4 inch wrench is too large. How do we go about finding a wrench that's in between? Find as many as you can."

Cruising the room, I was struck by the wide range of abilities, from 4.0 students to three kids unable to multiply 2 x 8; one boy had no idea what multiplication even meant. Most of them, though, if they applied themselves, had the knowledge base to be successful. Two minutes later, I asked for solutions.

Only one kid raised his hand. "Just try all the wrenches."

"That would work," I said, "but it might take a while. Anybody have a faster way?"

Gemini, a stuck-up brunette who smelled like a chimney and looked like she was 18, answered with a perfectly straight face. "I'd just use my scissors."

Now, there are many ways to respond to answers that are inaccurate or incomplete. If a kid gave an answer of 3/8, I might ask if that's reasonable, and somebody would point out that 3/8 is less than 1/2. I'd ask, "How do we know one fraction is smaller than another?" And away we'd go.

A girl once gave an answer of 2/3. A boy responded that wrenches come in halves, fourths, eighths, sixteenths and so on. I asked how she'd gotten her answer. She said, "I averaged the tops and bottoms of the fractions and got 2/3. Does that always make a fraction in between the other two?" We were off and runnin'.

A kid will sometimes respond with a question of her own: "What do you call it when the bottoms of fractions are the same?" We would then talk about common denominators, and how that relates to the wrench question.

One time the resident wise guy suggested we use a crescent wrench. I asked him to explain how they work. He said they're adjustable, and I asked how many fractions there are between1/2 and 3/4. The wise guy's question turned out to be a great lead-in to a discussion of infinity.

Yep, there are many effective ways to respond to student responses. Looking stunned and drooling out of the corner of my mouth is probably not one of them, but in the case of the "I'd just use my scissors" answer, it was the best I could manage.

Halfway through class, I got a new student named Robby Gibb, a confused-looking little guy with half-inch-thick glasses. He started working a problem, made a mistake, erased it and ripped a hole in the paper, crumpled it up, meandered up to the front of the room, threw the paper at the trash can from three feet away and missed, bent to pick it up, tripped on a shoe lace, got up, left the wad of paper on the floor, wandered back to his desk, smacked a kid on the shoulder for laughing at him, knocked his own notebook on the floor, picked it up, stood up again, broke his pencil in two and chewed off the eraser.

I watched, enthralled and then growled at him, "Siddown. Your job today is simple: Don't make me crazy."

At lunch, I visited the counseling office to get some background on Robby. He'd been enrolled by his mother, the registrar told me, but we had not yet received his academic records. I called the contact number, but got a "number has been disconnected" message.

The next day, I asked Robby which school he'd been attending, and which math teacher he'd had. That afternoon I called the teacher to ask about him.

She replied, "I didn't have that student in class."

Sometimes students use both parents' last names. "How about Robby anybody? Or Rob? Robert?"

"Nope. Sorry."

The following day, I told Robby that the teacher had said he was not in her class.

"Well, I *was*."

I looked him in the eye. Was he playing me? It didn't seem so. "Can I get your phone number?"

He crinkled up his nose and mussed up his already mussed-up hair. "We just changed it. I don't know it by heart."

It took me a week to sort it all out. "Robby Gibb" was really "Joe Clarke". His mother had been concerned that his reputation as a goofus would precede his arrival at Fernwater. And, as a fan of the Bee Gees in disco's heyday, she had developed a crush on Robin, youngest of the Brothers Gibb, when he reached up for that big falsetto note on "Stayin' Alive". By enrolling her son under the name "Robin Gibb", she was paying tribute to the musical genius of her first love, as well as launching a preemptive strike against teachers' preconceptions of her son's abilities.

Robby had no idea what a Bee Gee was, but he liked the idea of being someone else.

Whenever possible, I tried to connect our curriculum with real life. I drew a crude map of the neighborhood around the school on the board, indicating where the Safeway, fire station and 7-11 were located.

"Who wants to volunteer their home address?" I asked.

Only one student had her hand up. "1834 22nd Ave. NW."

I wrote it on the board and traced a route on the map with my finger. "You hang a left out of Fernwater's parking lot, take a right here at the Safeway, and then…. I'm not sure; the roads back here twist and turn. I think you take a right, and your house will be a couple of houses down on your left.

"Close," she said, "we live in a cul-de-sac. You take a right, and we live at the end."

"OK, next."

Jeremiah, younger brother of wise guy Jaime from 1st period, giggled his way through his address. He was hyper, but likeable. His parents had moved here from Jamaica when he was an infant.

"That's an easy one," I said. "Left out of the parking lot, right on 36th, left in two blocks, and your house is here on the corner."

Jeremiah said, "That's kinda creepy." The girl sitting next to him asked if I was right. He cast a suspicious eye my way. "Yeahhhh…. How do you do that?"

"I worked part-time driving taxis in college. Before you pick up passengers, you have to learn how addresses work. So

look at Jeremiah's address: 3702 NW 14ᵗʰ. Since the NW comes
before the street number, that means he lives on an east-west,
horizontal street. I drew x- and y-axes on the board, and labeled
the origin in the center.

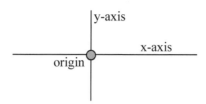

"For where we live, the origin is where?   Where's the
center of our world, address-wise?"
      Students tossed out "the high school", "New York" and
"my girlfriend's".
      "The courthouse is our origin," I said. "Next to the new
stadium – how many of you have gone to a game there?"
      Only two hands went up, which surprised me; I had seen
several of these kids at Fernwater High football games. But this
class was hard to read; they did their homework, and all but three
had passed their first two tests, yet the atmosphere in the room was
oppressive, and I had no idea why. By contrast, my 6ᵗʰ period 8ᵗʰ
grade class was relaxed and energetic; it crackled with a glandular
hum. But when someone cracked a joke in 2ⁿᵈ period, kids looked
around to see if it was OK to laugh, as if seeking permission.
During class, they were hesitant to interact with me, which was
odd, because most of them joked around with me or at least said hi
as they entered my room. And it was the same way when they left,
but once the bell rang to start class, they clammed up.
      "Jeremiah lives 14 blocks north of the x-axis," I said. "Now
look at his house number: 3702. The 02 is even, so he lives on the
north side of the street, and it's a small number so he lives on the
corner. How about the 37? Guesses? No? That's how far west he
lives from the y-axis."
      Jeremiah asked, "Did you ever pick up a psychopath?"
      "Not exactly. But I drove at night, and you pick up some
interesting characters." I told them about picking up a man who
had just robbed a 7-11, and about how the police pulled us over
and nabbed the guy. Expecting questions, I was surprised by a

room full of blank looks.

But after class, kids crowded around my desk and peppered me with questions:

"Did they handcuff the guy?"

"Did he have a gun? Did you try to outrun the cops?"

"Did he look like that guy in Silence of the Lambs?"

Class chemistry is an elusive thing.

In most professions, people go to work and do one thing at a time, i.e., they pound a nail, defend their client, or write software. Teachers, however, rarely get to do just one thing.

The bell was about to ring in fifteen seconds. I felt a surge of adrenaline, a sense of: It is SHOW TIME. Unless I was firing on all cylinders, it would be a longgggg day.

"Take a seat," I called out while scanning the room: A girl is crying, Robby Gibb is asking me why his calculator won't work, Gemini is blowing spit bubbles off the tip of her tongue, and Jeremiah is gigglin', wigglin' and foaming at the mouth – he has apparently forgotten to take his Ritalin again.

A thickset girl stood next to her desk. "Anybody see Jurassic Park?"

Gemini answered immediately. "Yeah, it was stupid."

"Yeah? Well, *you're* stupid!"

Gem stood up. "Did you just call me a hoochie?"

"What if I did?"

Gem was now inches from her face. "Fuck you!"

"Fuck *me*? Fuck *you*!

It had escalated so quickly, there hadn't been time to stop it. I came unglued. "Heyyyy!" Several kids jumped. "Outside of school, you can talk anyway you want, but don't bring that in here!"

Gem asked, "Are you in a bad mood?"

"I wasn't one minute ago! Outside!"

When she turned to spar with the other girl, I placed my hand on her shoulder and guided her toward the door. Once in the hall, I said, "Talk like that again, and I'll send you to the office."

She folded her arms and adopted a look of monumental boredom. "Fine."

"Do you understand?"

She looked off down the hall. "Whatever."

"No, not whatever!"

This was the moment at which I should have backed away. But my father's Prime Directive was deeply embedded in my psyche: Stand up to bullies. Of course, looking back on that day, I am struck by the irony of the situation: It was me doing the bullying.

"I want a yes or no!" I demanded. "Do you understand?"

"Did you hear what she said to me?"

"Gem! I don't want to hear the word "hoochie"."

"Why don't you talk to *her*?" And then, under her breath, she said, "That ho-bag."

"You're not going to talk like that. You can sit out here today and I'm calling your mom tonight."

"Fine, but she'll back me up – this is harassment."

"Do you act like this in all your classes?" While she was working up a smart-ass comeback, I returned to my room.

"Do you act this way in all your classes?" asked Uncle Fester, grinning broadly as he came through my door at the start of lunch. He wore braces now, and his hair had grayed, but he was still built like a tank.

"That's *my* line," he said. "I'm thinking about copyrighting it. I heard you talking in the hallway during 2nd period."

"Oh, yeah, uh, this kid was being a pain in the ass. Sorry if I disturbed your class."

"It's OK; that's my plan period."

"I didn't know I was so loud."

His smile faded. "Oh, I'm pretty sure they could hear you downtown. Or at least down in the office." That got my attention. He said, "I'm one to talk, I know; I remember unloading on a few kids in the old days."

"Yeah, I remember you going after Josh McClown; boy, he had it coming."

"That was a doozy; it made my top ten. You know, I got a certain satisfaction from reaming a kid when he got out of line, but let me say two things: One, the administration started a file on me; and two, I am a happier man than I used to be."

"But, are you happier because you don't yell, or the other

way around?"

"I'm happier and I yell less because Fernwater is a better place to be – flip sides of the same coin."

It was odd, teaching across the hall from my own junior high teacher, but he had been a great resource, especially during my rookie year. A teacher's first year is, in a word, *hard*. I spent too much time on trivia and didn't leave enough time for the big ideas. Kids pushed me, to see how far I'd bend, or if I'd break. And a single quarter of student teaching had been woefully inadequate in preparing me to handle 150 kids a day.

In October of my first year, Fester could see that I was wearing down, and he took me out for a beer after school. He asked how I was doing, and then he let me bitch and moan. Ten minutes in, I told him I was thinking about calling it quits in June, and he said exactly the right thing:

"I know how difficult it is; believe me. I remember. But I wish I could show you two videos: my first year of teaching, and your second." He let me absorb that and then went on. "My first month on the job, I had a fire and a stabbing in my class, and an 8th grader dropped out to have a child. I do not mean to trivialize your anguish, Leo, but one year from now, I promise, you will look back on today and laugh."

During 5th period, I got an email from Reuben Rapp, our VP: Please meet with me and Gemini's mother today at 3:00.

Hmmmm.... that sounds ominous. What had happened in the ensuing two periods since I'd kicked her out? Had Gem called home? Had her mother come roaring into the office, ala Ms. Mori, and raised a stink? Had Gem told Reuben I picked on her? She had used the word "harassment"; is there a more frightening word in the English language?

I know what my father would say: Stand up, son. Don't let them take advantage of you.

Dad's imaginary advice notwithstanding, my mind kicked into overdrive during 6th period, conjuring up one nightmare scenario after another: Did she say I *touched* her? Because I had – I put my hand on her shoulder for five seconds. Did she say I *pushed* her? I hadn't, but would she say I did? And I had repeated the word "hoochie" – did she say I was calling her names? Did she go to a special ed teacher and report that I had not made allowances for her disability, ADD? Or maybe I'd be raked over the coals for being a sexist pig. *Was* I a sexist pig? Would Reuben start a file on me?

Gem and her mother breezed into the VP's office at 3:23. Reuben Rapp, a heavyset, congenial fellow, looked at the clock to signal his annoyance, which failed to register with either of them.

Gem's mom looked like she might be a model; she was cadaverously thin and eye-catching in a vacuous, exotic way, but not the least bit attractive. She could have used a double bacon cheeseburger. Her mascara had been applied with a bricklayer's trowel.

Reuben made introductions and then asked me to state my concerns.

I began, "She said 'fuck you' in class today. Yesterday she told a girl she suffered from a case of pussy breath. She stole a kid's wallet last week. And she's failing, due to a lack of homework."

There. That should do the trick.

"Excusing me," said Gem's mother in an accent of undetermined ethnicity. She could have been from just about anywhere, from Persia to Puerto Rico. Regarding me imperiously, she said, "I am understanding Gemini is not to have learning in the school. Is not important, for she not to be graduating."

Whoa. In meetings like this, parents usually vowed to ride herd on their kid. Or they made excuses or blamed teachers. Every now and then, a parent would say: You know, I didn't do much homework either when I was growing up. Most dismaying of all were the two moms who put forth the shudder-inducing opinion that girls are not as good at math as boys.

But this mother had a unique approach: "When Gemini seventeen, she can marry prince for my country."

I studied her again. She could have been Italian or Greek. Do they have princes in Greece?

Reuben leaned forward. "We expect Gemini to complete homework and follow school rules."

To which her mom replied, "17, we go back, she will becoming princess."

Gem had certainly developed the proper attitude to be a princess. There was no trace of that smug look that says: Told you so. No, she took her mother's proclamation as a statement of fact; in three years, she'd be living in a palace, as was her due. Homework was beneath her.

After the meeting, I returned to my classroom, where Anjuli Torres had sketched a rough world map on the board. She was drawing in little flowers at various spots – Rome, New York, Costa Rica, San Francisco and several places in Africa.

"Hey kid, what're you up to?"

"These are the places I want to go, as soon as I graduate."

"Good for you – it's a big, bad, beautiful world out there."

"Have you travelled much?"

"I've been to India and Europe, and around the US some."

"I'm so jealous. I can't wait." Her entire body slumped. "Mr. Haldini, life sucks."

"Yeah, I can see how you'd think that."

"What?" Anjuli's face registered surprise and more than a touch of indignation.

"Well, you're not too bright, you're too pale, you're not pretty, and – let's face it – your sense of humor needs some work."

She tried her hardest not to smile, and ended up frowning and laughing simultaneously.

"Mr. Haldini, do you think I'm hard to get along with?"

"Let me put it this way: *No.* Why would you even ask?"

"Kali called me a bitch this morning."

"Whaaat? I thought you and your sis were pretty close."

"We are. Well, we were, but all of a sudden she's picking fights with me."

"Any idea why?"

She looked away. "I don't know."

"But you have a guess. Come on – spill."

"Let's see, you want to hear about her skanky new friends? Or her sudden taste for vodka? And she's failing 2nd year alg."

"*Kali?* Here, sit down. What's goin' on?"

"I don't know. She's been asking me to party with her, and so far I haven't, but they're pressuring me. What do I do?"

"Let's try a little experiment. How do you think I would

answer that?"

"You'd tell me I have to live my own life." I nodded and she asked, "How come you don't give me advice? Everybody else does."

"If you were incompetent or dumb, I'd be glad to give you advice." She mulled that over. "Anjuli, you are intelligent and good-hearted; you don't need me telling you what to do."

"Live my own life, huh?" She slumped again. "It sounds so simple."

"It *is* simple; it's just not easy."

She stood and looked out the window at the hazy sky. "I'm worried about her."

"Then it's a good thing she has you. If I were 14, I'd want you as a friend."

She looked absolutely lost. "Aren't you and I friends?"

"Yeah," I said tentatively, and then thought back on the fledgling friendship I had begun all those years ago with Felix Hester. "Yes, I guess we are."

Chapter 15 - November

Ninth grade Pre-algebra can be hell on wobbly wheels. These classes tend to be stocked with kids who have failed math and school and life for years, and they're understandably pissed about it. Their anger can manifest itself as vandalism, fighting, skipping school, or "just saying no" to homework. When I first heard Pre-alg referred to as "Granola Math", I didn't get it.

A veteran teacher explained with a guilty smile, "You know, fruits, nuts, and flakes. And that's just the parents."

Every year, Fernwater held an open house one evening at the end of 1st quarter; parents followed their kids' schedules, spending ten minutes in each class. For my Geometry class, 28 parents showed up to find out who was bending the minds of their children.

For Pre-alg, however, only two mothers showed. When the bell rang at the end of the ten minutes, one of them sidled up to me and twitched her nose like Samantha on *Bewitched*.

"My daughter wasn't kiddin' when she said her math teacher was cuuu-ute. Would you like to come over for a drink later on? I make a dangerous Martini."

She was pleasant enough and pretty, in a giddy, I'll-try-anything-once sort of way. Her laugh had acquired that gravelly quality you get from frequenting smoky bars. Uncle Marco, an occasional horse rider, would likely have assessed her like this: She looks like she's been ridden hard and put away wet.

But it would not be clear whether he was advising me to leave her be or go for it.

I thanked the mom for her offer, but said I had plans, which was true – teachers were going out for drinks afterwards. Two minutes later, I spied her sneakin' out to the parking lot, looking over her shoulder for our VP.

Many parents of pre-algebra kids blow off Open House, because they're tired of hearing about how rotten their kids are doing in school, or how rotten their kids are, period. Some parents forget about Open House, and some never hear about it in the first place. Some have their own unpleasant memories of school and they have no desire to relive them. Given their parents' lack of involvement, it's no surprise that pre-algebra students are often disagreeable and disengaged, and most of them function academically between a 4th and 7th grade level.

How do they get behind? Some suffer from poor health and resultingly poor attendance. Some pretend to suffer poor health. Maybe the dad lives in Ohio, Mom tends bar at night, and the kid stares at a TV eight hours a day. Maybe Dad is nomadic, and his kid changes schools every few months. One student had just gotten off the plane from Brazil, speaking only Portuguese. Another lived with her aunt in a Ford Pinto, and you can see how studying by the overhead light could be a handicap.

One kid, according to his mom, fell off the roof when he was five. "You know," she told me, "he was never quite the same after that."

I am convinced that some students – maybe three or four percent – would be better off working as an apprentice, learning cooking, carpentry or plumbing. These kids, most of whom end up in Pre-alg, simply hate, hate, *hate* sitting in a desk – they squirm, they slouch, they stab a classmate in the head with a pencil so they can get suspended, hoping to get a break from sitting in that damn desk.

This year's group, however, was a pleasant aberration. Though several were frustrated and felt disenfranchised, there was a core of kids that were healthy in body and mind, and their attitudes rubbed off on everyone else. They had not done well in math for the usual array of reasons, but they had not given up, and it was my job not to give up on them.

For pre-alg students, basic arithmetic – dividing fractions, or calculating sales tax – is about as pleasurable as chewing sand. So when we began a unit on surface area and volume, we used the metric system, to make the calculations easier.

I began, "Everybody put your fingers as close together as you can without touching them. That's about a millimeter. Now, the fingernail on your pinky is about a centimeter wide, or ten

millimeters. Hold up your pinky. By the way, that's how you
metricly flip somebody off. Hey! No need to be rude! OK, for a
meter – that's a hundred centimeters – hold one arm up and out to
the side." I struck my finest John Travolta pose from Saturday
Night Fever, which, oddly, they were familiar with. "It's your
basic disco move. Show me." It looked like 1978 all over again.
"A meter is roughly the distance from your outstretched finger to
your opposite shoulder. That's not exact, because we're not all the
same height, but it's close."

I then asked them to figure the quantity of paint needed to
paint the room, given that one liter covers ten square meters.

This exercise may sound straight forward, but the thought
of measuring and estimating terrified them: How accurate do I
have to be? What do you mean by "close enough"? How do you
know when to round off? Do we use millimeters or meters? How
do we know if we're right? Do we paint the floor? How about the
windows – do we paint them?

The source of their anxiety? Here is my theory: If their
folks had asked them to measure and paint their room, most of
them could have done it, and they'd know not to paint the floor or
windows. But for these kids, a math class bears no connection to
the real world.

As one boy asked: "I get how to add fractions, but who
made all this up?"

At first I thought he was asking about the history of math.
But then I recognized it as something else – for him, there was no
logical necessity to mathematical processes. They're like the rules
to Monopoly; some guy just made 'em up, and they could have
been completely different.

I allayed their anxiety as best I could and then instructed
them to measure the room. "I want you to work in pairs, but pick
somebody you work well with. If you're a goonball, don't pick
another goonball to work with."

Wrong Way waved her hand. "What if we don't know if
we're goonballs?" I had nicknamed her the previous year when
Fernwater was playing our final basketball game of the season, and
she scored a basket for the opposition.

"If you don't know, then you probably are."

Nikolai, a blue-eyed kid with a Ukrainian accent, asked,

"Am I a goonball?"

"Nikolai, if you look up 'goonball' in the dictionary, it would have your picture right there." He smiled proudly. "But you're a likeable goonball." I passed out meter sticks, along with the admonishment, "No sword fights."

At the end of class, Wrong Way bounded up to my desk. "Mr. Haldini, we're studying adjectives in LA. If you had to pick one adjective to describe me, what would it be?"

Without hesitation, I said, "Effervescent."

"What does that mean?

I pivoted my chair and pulled a dictionary off a shelf. "Here, look it up."

She thumbed through the pages. "How do you spell it?"

"Effervescent – two f's."

Twenty seconds later, she cried in her ever cheery voice, "Here it is! It says, 'Giving off gas or bubbles'." Her smile burst like an overfilled balloon.

"Fitting," I said.

"Hey! You can't call me that!" She raised the dictionary over her head, and I raised my arms in defense.

"Read the next definition," I told her.

"It says, 'Showing liveliness or exhilaration'. What does 'exhilaration' mean?"

"Effervescence."

She threatened me with the dictionary again.

The bell rang at that moment, and I said, "Time to go, Miss Effervescence. You don't want to be late."

She flipped me the metric finger as she skipped out the door.

I stood in the hallway for a few minutes after school, to make sure sevies weren't getting stuffed into lockers.

"See ya, Pinball." He was a slight kid with a low IQ and a sweet disposition. I'd given him the nickname after watching him navigate the narrow halls, like he was getting knocked around by the bumpers of a pinball machine. Oddly, he seemed to enjoy it.

"I caught my pants on fire today," yelled Pinball, as he caromed off a locker and disappeared around a corner.

"I hate when that happens," I said to myself, then called

out, "Ladies, good luck today." Our volleyball team was off to a great start; we were playing the only other 3-and-0 team in our conference.

"Thanks, Haldini."

"Yo, Jaime, hands off." He was playfully throttling his brother Jeremiah. Bright and mischievous, they were a handsome mix of Black, White and Carib Indian.

Jaime threw his hands up and laid an arm across his brother's shoulders. "Aw, Mr. Haldini, he's my kid bro; I don't want him to feel neglected."

"Please," said Jeremiah, "neglect me."

A pair of girls from 3rd period walked by and metricly flipped me off. Geez Louise!

A group of boys and girls passed by, critiquing the movie The Crying Game. "Dude!" said one of the boys. "That chick had a wiener!"

Down the hall, an unfamiliar redheaded boy shoved a kid in the chest. It wasn't a friendly, messing-around push. They were squared off, ready to go at it.

"STOP!" I have a really loud voice, and it shocked them, long enough for me to step between them.

Red recovered quickly. "Why should I?"

"Because I just told you to; you got a crappy memory?" My dad would have loved that line. "And I'm hauling you down to the office if you don't walk away nowwww."

Fortunately, they left in opposite directions.

A soft-spoken boy from my afternoon class had been waiting for the halls to clear. "Mr. Haldini, you said you're giving me a B for the quarter."

We entered my room and I consulted my grade book. "That's right, you've earned a B."

He stood there, rocking back and forth. "My parents won't let me get B's."

"I can show you your test and homework scores."

Back and forth, back and forth. "You don't understand." That last word was pronounced slowly, like I was a dimwit. "My parents won't allow it."

"But they don't determine your grade; you do."

"Can my dad call you?"

"Sure."

But his dad never called, and this kid, who, up to that point had been quietly engaging, rarely spoke to me after that, and he never again looked me in the eye. I would occasionally greet him on his way into class, and he'd mumble something that sounded like "Good morn".

Or it could have been "Kid porn"; hard to say.

Increasingly, kids expected to be given A's. When a student earned less than that, it was interpreted more and more frequently as an insult, a personal attack, an arbitrary defilement of one's character that should therefore be retroactively negotiable. Over the course of the past eight years, I'd seen an increase in the pressure that is exerted on students, and collaterally on teachers, to get and give out high grades.

An interaction with a student that autumn left me shaking my head. A girl with a mop of orange-streaked hair asked me what her 1st quarter grade was going to be.

I referred to my grade book. "You have a D+."

She replied confidently, "Uh, that won't work for me."

What an odd response. It's something you might say when you're arranging a dentist appointment and the receptionist asks, How about Friday at two? Uh, that won't work for me.

"Tough luck," I told her. "That's the grade you've earned."

She twirled a sprig of orange hair around her little pinkie. "What can I do for extra credit?"

"I don't give extra credit; you already know that. And the quarter ended yesterday; it's a little late to start worrying about your grade."

"But I'm gonna get grounded for the next two weeks."

"OK, here's what you do." She leaned forward hopefully, and I told her, "Build a time machine and go back two months; do your homework."

Judging by the tears welling up, she thought of me as an unsympathetic ghoul. I had no problem with that assessment.

My interest in grade inflation and statistics led me to the counseling office, where I asked the registrar if she could tell me the number of A's, B's, C's, D's and F's given out school-wide that 1st quarter. It was none of my business, I guess, but somebody needed to analyze the grades we were handing out.

The registrar delivered a print-out to me the next day that included the distribution of grades, by department and also by individual teachers within each department. I was appalled to find that 51% of grades given out school-wide were A's. How could that be? Here is what I found out:

    * Students in honors classes got out mostly A's, which made sense; these kids tended to be bright and conscientious;

    * Most Special Ed students got mostly A's, the thinking being that these kids were not college-bound, and a heap of A's would provide a much-needed boost for their self-esteem. But SpEd kids are no dummies – they know which A's are knock-offs;

    * Electives teachers handed out mostly A's, the rationale being that since these weren't required academic courses, their grading systems should be "relaxed"; and

    * PE teachers gave out mostly A's, because, hey, it's PE.

The day before Thanksgiving, I stopped by Safeway on my way home and spotted Robby Gibb coming up the nuts and chips aisle.

"Howdy," I said. "Help ya find anything?"

His thick glasses magnified his bulging eyes. "You.... you look like my math teacher."

"Hello-o? Hi, Robby."

Though I would not have thought it possible, his eyeballs bugged out further. "How do you know my name?"

Apparently he thought.... what? That we teachers live in our classrooms, subsisting on deliveries from Pizza Hut?

"Robby, it's me, Mr. Haldini."

He tilted his head to the side, as if the proper perspective would allow him to make sense of this madness.

"How do you know my teacher's name?"

He tilted his head the other way, and just when I thought he had come to grips with the surreality of my presence in a grocery store, he made the mistake of looking in my shopping cart, only to discover six-packs of beer and toilet paper. Whaaaaat? This was simply too much! His eyes, unable to enlarge any further, focused on the faraway, and I left him standing immobile next to a display of Fritos. He reminded me of Data, the android on Star Trek, the time he had his emotion chip deactivated.

"See you tomorrow, Robby." I considered picking up some rubbers or Preparation H and then cruising down that aisle again, but thought better of it; I imagine Child Protective Services takes this sort of incident seriously.

Two minutes later, I was on my knees, checking out the selection of turkeys, when a serious voice behind me said, "Can I help you find anything?"

"I'm fine, thanks." I turned and looked up at a smirking brunette. "Anjuli, you goofus." I stood and turned my attention to the toddler in her arms, a chubby boy with dark gleaming eyes and wavy black hair. "Hey, is this one of the mutants?" That was her and her sister Kali's term for their four younger brothers.

"I'm a mootut," he said proudly.

"Yes, you are." Anjuli affectionately swept the hair from his eyes and kissed his forehead. "This is Mini Mutant."

"And how old are you?" I asked.

He thought a moment. "I'm two no mo'."

Anjuli laughed. "He had his third birthday last week."

"Very clever." I reached out my palm and he slapped it. "What a cutie! Hmmm, he doesn't look much like you." In my mind, those two statements were unrelated, but they sure as hell didn't come out that way.

"Oh well, thank you very much." She gave me a playful shove. Mini Mutant took a swat at me too.

"I didn't mean that you're not...." I sighed. "Let's pretend I didn't say that."

"You mean I should pretend that you didn't mean to say that I'm not uncute?"

"You are enjoying this way too much."

"I'm a mootut!" her brother bellowed joyfully.

Anjuli smiled smugly and pointed behind me.

"Hi, Mr. Haldini." It took me a moment to recognize the pleasant, concerned face. I'd had her son in class the year before, and her daughter was currently a pre-alg student. The girl was reserved, but respected by her classmates. Currently, she was getting a C in class.

"Catch ya later, Mr. Foot-in-your-mouth," said Anjuli as she walked away. Mini Mutant gave me an enthusiastic wave.

I scowled and waved, and then asked the woman about her son. She talked about how well he was doing in high school and thanked me for asking. She then furrowed her brow and said, "I almost don't want to bring this up.... But my daughter thinks you don't like her."

"What? She's such a sweet kid."

"I know. But she says everybody in class has a nickname and.... well, she doesn't." She said it in a non-accusatory manner. "She thinks you don't like her, and I know that's not true, but...." The woman choked up.

"Ohhhhhh," I said in a barely audible voice. It's easy to forget how fragile these 14-year-old creatures are.

I told her, "She's not the only one without a nickname."

While that was true, it was also wholly irrelevant. Before she could respond, I offered to come up with a nickname for her daughter.

"You know, that would be great," she sniffled, but then looked alarmed. "But don't tell her I talked to you. Gracious, she would never forgive me!"

"I promise." I held up the three fingers of my right hand, Boy Scout-style.

"Thank you. For all you do." She squeezed both my hands and left.

Two days later at the beginning of 3rd period, the mother entered my room to drop off her daughter's lunchbox, much to the girl's chagrin.

I told the kid, "That's it; we're calling you 'Lunchbox' from now on."

Mom and daughter looked horrified, but only for a second. They then bestowed upon me matching smiles. Lunchbox scored a 94% on her next test and 100% on the one after that. As a matter of fact, she aced every test for the rest of the year.

Why could it not always be that simple?

Chapter 16 – December

Leaving Barnes and Noble one cold, clear afternoon, I ran into Jake the Invisible Boy. He had with him a copy of <u>A History of Philosophy</u>, which came as a surprise – as a kid, I had never seen him open a book, let alone buy one. After helping him move into an apartment the day after high school graduation, we parted ways, and I had not seen him since.

We stood outside the bookstore and chatted about the old days. Though he looked pretty much the same, he seemed relaxed; only now did it register how shifty-eyed he'd been as a boy.

"Yeah," he said, "we were a bunch of punks. I should track down my teachers and apologize. Remember the time you squirted.... what was her name?"

"Penny Prismark."

"Right. The Krabman had no clue. Funniest damn thing I ever saw. I wonder where he is now. I hope he's not locked up in an asylum, chewing the carpet."

"I happen to know where he is. But hey, it's freezing out here. Wanna get a beer?"

"Sure. Where do you want to go?"

"Beats Workin'?"

"Good call."

I drove through a booming section of town, past what long-time residents of recently incorporated Oxley referred to as the Mega Mega Mall. Ten minutes later, I pulled in beside Jake, and we walked across the parking lot together.

Beats Workin' used to be a garage. On weekends, when they bring in a band, they put the drummer on the hoist and raise him up during drum solos. The place goes nuts.

Jake opened the door, unleashing a potpourri of smoke, sweat, beer and disinfectant. But the juke box was playing the title track from Dire Straits' <u>Brothers in Arms</u>, and the barmaid, an attractive brunette, waved and smiled, baring a mouthful of white teeth that stood out like day-glo in the dingy bar. Above a Ms. Pac-Man machine hung a one-eyed, six-point buck. The walls were adorned with Sonics team posters, year by year, going back to the '79 championship team. On the bar sat a jar of pickled eggs that, by all appearances, had not been opened in my lifetime.

We took seats at the bar and I bought a pitcher of Rainier from the toothsome barmaid.

Jake toasted, "To survivors of Fernwater."

We drank and then immediately returned to the subject of terrorizing our teachers.

"14-year-olds can be heartless," I said. "I know we were."

Jake considered that. "Yeah, we were, and the thing is, I can't remember why I was like that. My parents didn't beat me or lock me in the closet. But I wouldn't have blamed them if they had; I was pretty hard on them, always threatening to run away, or go live on Auntie's farm. But it wasn't my folks I wanted to get away from; I wanted out of that school, Haldini." He took a long drink. "You used to call me 'Jake the Invisible Boy'."

"Yeah. That school was screwed up; kids were allowed.... no, encouraged.... no, *trained* to be jerks and criminals."

"Maybe so, maybe so." He jerked his head up and down. "You know, in elementary school – you won't believe this – but I was a very good student. And then my first week at Fernwater, a 9th grader stole my lunch three days in a row, and I was afraid he'd pound me if I said anything, so I ate in the john for a month, until *that* kid got beaten up, and *he* stopped comin' to lunch. Freakin' madhouse. After that, I declared war; I hated that school, Haldini."

"It was entertaining for a while, but yeah, it got old."

"So, you said you had the scoop on The Krabman."

"Yeah, he's principal at our alma mater."

"No way! And you know this how?"

I smiled slyly, savoring the moment. "I am teaching.... at.... Fernwater Junior High."

Jake responded with a horror-stricken, whispered, "Noooo. Leo, oh, dude!" Obviously suffering a Fernwater Flashback, he slumped on his stool and let his head fall back. Staring at the ceiling, he let out a prolonged groan. "Why would you do that to yourself?" It was a fair question, given his experience.

"Believe it or not," I said, "I'm lovin' it.... except for the 3

P's – Politicians, Principals and Parents – they drive me bonkers."

I was fast losing faith in the ability of adults in my line of work to make rational decisions. The previous year, the district had decreed that all junior highs use one particular algebra text, which the teachers in my school judged to be lacking in rigor.

Betty Skibbitz, now 80 years old, considered the book to be full of gobbledygook. At a district meeting she hauled out a 35-year-old textbook and screeched, "Now *this* is how you teach algebra. Back when Kennedy was president...."

The response from Curriculum was: Thank you very much, but we need to standardize. Our decision is made.

A week later, when we went to order books, we discovered the text was out of print. The new district decree? Each school can use whatever text it chooses.

"Yeah," I told Jake, "it's maddening."

He didn't hear me. "Teaching at Fernwater," he moaned. "Oh, Haldini, that is karmic."

"How about you? What have you been doing?"

He partially recovered. "I paint houses. It's great in the fall, and hell on 90 degree days. I work inside during winter and spring." He poured us both another beer. "Business is real good. And get this: Jeff Mori works for me."

"Mori," I said, shaking my head. "How is he?"

"He's good. But it was touch and go for a few years. He dropped out at 17. Jesus, Leo, he couldn't read a job application. And did you know he's deaf in one ear? But he's OK now; he's got it figured it out. If he ever quit, I'd have to hire two people to replace him."

"Glad to hear it. And Johnny Boe?"

"Doin' time at Walla Walla, last I heard, but that was years ago. He went by the name 'Johnny Turboe' when he and Jeff were stealing cars. What an ass."

"How did you ever fall in with those guys?"

He shrugged. "They were troublemakers, so was I. And Johnny got beat up too as a sevie. But mostly.... Well, who else was gonna look out for Jeff?"

"What do you mean?"

"Remember how Johnny used to come struttin' out of Steiffel's office like a fuckin' peacock? 'Me and Marv cut a deal,' he'd say. Well, his part of the deal was rattin' out Jeff and McClown. And you too, a couple times." In response to my look of disbelief, he said, "Yeah, remember that time you guys got caught smoking? Johnny set that whole thing up."

"How do you know?"

"Son of a bitch bragged about it. He'd get busted for bangin'…. what was her name?"

"Lucy Sparkett."

"Right, he'd get caught bangin' Juicy Lucy behind the bleachers, and Steiffel would say he's gonna suspend him, and Johnny would say, 'Sir, I will be your eyes and ears.' Then he'd get Jeff or McClown to clog up and overflow a toilet, and he'd head right back to the office. Oh, and here's the best part – you know how Jeff was always getting in fights? Johnny would go up to some kid and say, 'You hear what Mori's been saying about you?'"

"I had no idea."

"Remember how I never wanted anybody around when I was gonna, oh, say, torch a trash can? Remember? Truth of the matter is that I didn't want Johnny Boe around – he'd have gone straight to Steiffel."

"Here's to better days," I said, hoisting my glass. "Say hi to Jeff for me, would you?"

"I will. Hey, he's got two kids, look just like him, cock-eyed grin and all. Yeah, Mori's doing good. Course, he's still got that gnarly spot on the tip of his tongue from that little stunt McClown pulled with the acid. He still can't taste anything sweet or salty."

"Crazy. He used to live on sugar and salt."

"I know. Weird, huh? He actually eats food now, and he's bulked up."

"How about McClown? How's he doing?"

Jake shrugged. "I hear he got his license back."

I sat in the kitchen that evening, reading a postcard from Mom:

Leo, I love Italy! Lake Como is lovely – the picture on the front doesn't do it justice. The food, the people are magnifico! Gianni saw two friends he hadn't seen them in 50 years! Of course, most of his neighbors from the old days have moved away, and some have passed on. We saw an opera in Milan – Norma, by Bellini. The sets, the voices are impressive. Your father was moved to tears, as Norma is filled with love, betrayal and a pagan plot to overthrow Rome. Grandpa's fine.

Love, Mom

I was startled by a knock on the window behind me. What the heck? I turned and saw two mischievous faces pressed against the glass. I flinched, eliciting gleeful shrieks from Anjuli and her older sister Kali. Pleased that they had scared the bejesus out of me, they high-fived one another and screeched again.

I opened the sliding glass door to let them in, pretending to be perturbed. "What are you doing?"

I had never seen the Torres sisters side by side; they shared the same huge dark eyes.

Kali hugged me and said, "I got my license last week. We thought you might like a visit."

"I am honored, but isn't it kind of late?"

Anjuli said, "We were coming home from youth group, and your house is almost on the way. We never go to sleep before 11:30 anyway."

Snooping around, Kali said, "Geez Louise, your house is kind of a mess."

"Hey! I think of it as being homey."

"You have a lot of books," said Anjuli. She picked out Caribbean, by James Michener. "Did you read this?"

"I did; I liked it. He writes historical fiction. Before he starts a book, he moves to the wherever the book is set and does research; then he writes a story that could have happened."

"I'm going to Haiti next winter."

"Feel free to borrow it. Or, what the heck, you can have it, as long as you promise to tell me adventures when you get back. Deal?" We shook on it. "Why Haiti?"

"I'm going with my grandma for two weeks. We're doing volunteer work with my church, building houses."

"Sounds like a worthy venture."

"Yeah, I can't wait. "

Kali pointed at my 12-string guitar. "Why does that one have so many strings?"

I picked it up and strummed a chord. "You play piano, right? The strings are paired up. Some are tuned in unison, some in octaves."

"Play us a song," said Kali. "Do you know anything by Nirvana? Kurt Cobain is my man."

I shook my head. "Boy, what a shame; he left too soon. Just think where he could have taken us musically."

Talented as Cobain had been, it seemed odd to idolize a man who took his own life. But taking into account Anjuli's concerns over her sister's partying and falling grades, it wasn't surprising that Kali looked up to the troubled singer.

Anjuli sat on the sofa and asked me to play my fave song.

"I don't know if this is my favorite," I said, "but here's one I like by my songwriter buddy." I launched into an upbeat number entitled "Without a Limit". The last verse goes:

Friends are gone as fast as you blink
As skipping stones in time must sink
Love them now, or forever think about it

As the song faded out, Kali looked distractedly out the window. Annoyed, Anjuli rose and elbowed her. They applauded.

"Uh, thank you very much," I said in a deep, cheesy Elvis voice, which they didn't get. "How did you guys find my house?"

Kali perked up. "Remember how you told us you drove a taxi in college, and how you had to learn how streets are laid out? We got your address out of the phone book and used what we learned in *your class*." She preened. "And you thought I wasn't listening."

"I am pleased," I said with exaggerated pride.

"Hey, were those taxi stories true? Like, did the cops really pull you over 'cause you had an ax murderer in the back seat?"

Anjuli joined in the grilling. "Yeah, that didn't really happen, did it?"

I feigned grievous insult. "I'm hurt that you would even ask. Actually, the guy had robbed a 7-11, and yes, he ended up in my cab five minutes later. Very few normal people take cabs at three in the morning."

Kali said, "I bet there are very few normal cab drivers at three in the morning."

"Touché." I broke out a round of Pepsis. "What kind of youth group were you guys at?"

Anjuli looked at her sister and asked, "Can I tell him?"

"Yeah, it's OK."

"See, Dad's Christian and Mom's a Muslim. They argue about how we kids should be raised. They talk about splitting up."

"Sorry to hear that. Do you think they'll reconcile?"

"I don't know. I want them to."

Anjuli seemed annoyed with her sister again. It would be another decade before I discovered the source of her annoyance, and if I knew then what I know now, I would have handled the girls' visit differently.

Kali said, "*We* want them to."

Anjuli looked back at my bookshelves. "So. How many of these have you read?"

"Oh, maybe half. How about you; do you read much?"

"Well, I like to read, but, with school and everything, I don't have time to. Isn't that weird? School takes up too much time to learn." Though she excelled academically, school was, for the most part, a burden to be borne. "Isn't that.... um, what's that word, Kali? Uncle Fester always makes a big deal about it."

"Irony," said Kali. "It's ironic that school gets in the way of learning."

"Right. Hey, Mr. Haldini, play us another tune by your songwriter buddy."

I met Carl Martin, my songwriter buddy, on a district picket line in 1992. He's bright, gregarious and bears resemblance to Booger from <u>Revenge of the Nerds</u>. After college, Carl joined the Peace Corps for two years; he taught English and planted gardens in West Africa. Upon his return, he visited a cousin in Seattle and instantly fell in love with our mountains, our lakes, our long, warm days and the color green. However, he first saw the Pacific Northwest in July, and didn't realize that we pay for our gorgeous summers with six months of sodden, soul-withering gloom. While Seattle winters may dampen my spirits, Carl spirals down into full-blown depression. SAD – Seasonal Affective Disorder, or, as he refers to it, Showers And Drizzle – descends each November and doesn't lift until the thermometer breaks fifty, which in some years does not happen until April. The maddening thing about our weather is that even though we might get only half an inch of rain on a given day, it often takes all 24 hours to fall. Even the name of my school, Fernwater, bespeaks green and wetness.

Every few weeks Carl and I would get together over beers to swap teacher stories and bitch about our bosses. A history teacher at Oxley Junior High, his standard refrain was: Administrators – can't they remember what it was like to teach?

Sometimes we got together to play guitar. He's written some terrific songs, and his slightly nasal voice fits them well. On one of those cold, damp afternoons when we Seattlites turn on our car lights at three in the afternoon, he showed up at my house with a left-over pizza from his staff meeting, along with his guitar and a new song he'd written.

"Leo, remember how it rained every day for three months straight last spring?" He strummed his way through a rollicking intro and then opened with these lyrics:

> It's rained for 90 days and 90 nights
> Noah never had it half as bad as Seattlites
> Eight months of November
> It's hard to remember
> The color of sunlight

After a middle section that dubiously rhymed "human mushroom" and "you gonna rust soon", he sang the last verse:

> I curse La Niña for bringing us this monsoon
> By March my fingers and soul had turned to prunes
> I have been wrestlin'
> With that age old question
> Why is the sky not blue?

Carl let the last chord ring and asked, "Got a beer?"

On the Saturday after Christmas, Gizmo, Calvin and Jaime

invited themselves over to my place to play Risk, the objective of which is to conquer the world. My fridge was stocked with soft drinks and I laid out fudge and cookies I'd received as Christmas presents from students. I brought in a load of firewood and got a rip-roaring blaze going. The four of us had played Risk before, but this would be our first all-night session. Gizmo's dad dropped the boys off in the early evening, along with sleeping bags, M&M's and Fritos. I talked to him for a few minutes, and then he turned to go, saying, "I'll pick them up at nine in the morning."

"Right-o, see you then."

He stopped and turned. "You sure you want to do this?"

"I plan on conquering the world tonight."

He laughed, waved and left. The boys and I got snacks organized; they completely covered my coffee table, so we set up the game board on the floor.

A Risk board is basically a simplified map of the world, and each player is allotted little wooden armies. Players roll dice to see who wins battles, and then armies are moved from one region to an adjacent one. A good game takes upwards of four hours to play. Along the way, we made pacts, deals and non-aggression treaties. We made a rule that you had to live up to the word, if not the spirit, of each pact.

At one point I vowed not to attack Gizmo in Brazil for the next two turns if he'd leave me alone in Europe on my next turn."

He agreed, and then, when I foolishly left to take a whiz, he made a pact with Calvin that I heard about later: If you dislodge Haldini in Italy, I'll leave you alone in North America for the next three turns.

Of all the mean, lowdown, rotten tricks....

We spent hours hunched over the Risk board, joking, propagandizing, threatening and negotiating. Jaime conquered the last country just before midnight.

We had been too engrossed in the game to notice that it was snowing. I turned on the patio light, and we felt the thrill that Western Washingtonians experience maybe five days a year. The boughs of Douglas firs, laden with snow, bowed down as if in worship. Transfixed by the beauty and purity of the white-washed world, we were humbled into silence.... for all of about fifteen seconds, at which point Calvin placed his hand inside his shirt

Napoleon-style and asked, "Ready to play again?"

"Dang right!" I replied. "I want my revenge. Let the war games begin."

"I wonder if they play Risk at the Pentagon," said Calvin.

"I bet they do," said Jaime, "or something like it."

Gizmo disagreed. "I bet they don't, because the one thing you learn not to do in Risk is spread yourself thin. The US is spread all over the globe, playing policeman."

"Good point," I said. "That's why I lost, trying to keep all you dictator wannabes in check."

I brought out another plate of fudge and opened a can of cashews, while we imagined how it would be, working in the Pentagon. We then launched another world war.

At four a.m., after fending off a sneak attack from Calvin and thwarting a diabolical double-cross from Gizmo, I prevailed.

It was a relief to see that the snow had stopped falling; as much as I liked these kids, the idea of getting snowed in with them held zero appeal. They spread out their sleeping bags in front of the fireplace, amid empty soft drink cans and potato chip bags.

"That was fun, guys," I yawned. "See you in the morning." I surveyed the wreckage one last time and trundled off to bed.

At a quarter to nine, I went in to wake the boys. They looked as wasted as I felt. After helping me pick up the trash, they packed up their sleeping bags and hauled them to the front door. We looked out onto the front lawn, where it had snowed several more inches.

All four of us yelled, "Snowball fight!"

Chapter 17 – January

On a dark, drizzly 35-degree morning, I entered school singing a song of Carl's:

> Feeble sunrise
> Faith, take flight
> Winter, stingy with her light

The song ends on a note of hopefulness and perhaps even redemption, but it sure doesn't begin that way. Arriving in the dark was bad enough, but because we had an afternoon staff meeting scheduled that day, I would also be leaving in the dark. So even if the sun did break through, I would not be seeing it. Adding to my despondence, our staff received a bulletin the day before, saying that because Christmas break had been extended by two weeks due to unusually heavy snowfall, our school year would be extended into July for the first time ever.

In college, I had often felt out of sorts in the winter, and I indulged in endless self-examination, trying to figure out: What.... is.... wrong? It was not until years later that I realized my malaise was due in large part to Seattle's leaden skies and short, soggy days.

Waiting in my mailbox was a letter from Maximillian R. Padgett. I growled, assuming he'd be lobbying me to raise his daughter's grade. Again. This letter was thicker than his first two. If I had any sense, I'd have passed it along to my principal. Instead, being a glutton for abuse, I opened it and began reading:

Dear Mr. Haldini,

As noted in my letter of December 13rd, my daughter indicated to me that she thus far has a C in Geometry for this semester. Through a proper analysis of her test and homework grades, I will demonstrate that she is deserving of, beyond any reasonable doubt, a B-, perhaps even a B. Your grading system is overly rigid and unforgiving of the reality that adolescents might have a bad day. I have enclosed a separate sheet with calculations that clearly show alternative grading systems that would more accurately reflect her effort, and moreover, her true understanding of the concepts and skills presented in an introductory Geometry course such as the one you teach.

After all, what is the purpose of education? If I may quote Socrates, for whom I have the highest regard....

That was his opening salvo, the top third of the first of four pages, single-spaced with tiny margins. Seething, I gave the other pages a quick glance and again considered putting the letter in my principal's box with a post-it note attached. Mediating staff-parent conflicts was part of his job. However, I had seen The Krabman cave under pressure from aggressive parents; the year before, I'd caught a boy cheating on a test and gave him an F. After a visit from the kid's whining mom, The Krabman insisted the boy be given another chance to take the test.

Besides, it was simply not in my nature to pass along a problem I could handle myself. My father's mantra played in my head: If you don't stand up to bullies....

I wanted to put Padgett in his place. I continued reading:

Mr. Haldini, here are alternate grading systems that provide a more accurate and honest assessment of my daughter's progress:
1) Toss out the lowest grade in each quarter. She would then have quarter grades of 83.5 and 82.723. Clearly then, she would be earning a solid B.
2) Toss out the lowest and the highest grades for the semester. Referring to my calculations on page four (4) of this communiqué, this scoring method results in approximately an 81%, placing her easily in the B- range.
3) Her lowest test grade was 51%, but that was two months ago. Learning mathematics is sequential process, and she scored significantly higher on two of her past three tests.

My God! How long did it take him to write this? If he had used that time to help his daughter with Geometry, she might be acing my class.

"Oh my, we're not off to a cheery start this morning," said Heidi Blohmeyer.

In my aggravated state, I was not even aware that she had entered the office. "Ever gotten a letter like this?" I asked.

She took a quick look and smiled. "Ah yes, Maximillian R. Padgett." She lowered her voice. "Or as the secretaries call him: 'Maxi Pad'. Yeah, I had the older brother in class." She took a closer look at the letter. "This looks familiar; I wonder if he has form letters at home; you know, copies with blanks for test scores, course and name of the offending teacher." She handed the letter back and placed a motherly hand on my shoulder. "Don't take it personally, Leo. His insanity has nothing to do with you. You are an excellent teacher."

Walking to my classroom, I continued reading the letter, but for entertainment now. Heidi had de-fanged Mr. Padgett.

I unlocked my classroom and felt that familiar, pleasant rush upon turning on the lights. Over the years, kids had drawn caricatures of me featuring an enlarged forehead, and I stapled them on the wall behind my desk. I scanned my Wall of Fame, a collage of student photos, some current and some past, and a wedding picture from a couple who had met in my class. Math/art projects covered the walls, and a paper-maché ogre hung from the ceiling.

I graded papers until 7:00 and then grumbled, "Time to call Maxi Pad." I calculated the girl's percentage again, then compared them with those of her classmates, and walked to the staffroom to use the phone.

"Padgett residence." He answered crisply, like he'd been up for hours.

"Good morning. This is Mr. Haldini from Fernwater. Do you have a minute?"

"Ah, Mr. Haldini, yes. Thank you for getting back to me. It is unacceptable for my daughter to receive a C in Geometry. She has always gotten A's in math. And she is a stellar student in her other classes."

"Mr. Padgett, your daughter is a good student. Geometry is a college prep class, and it's challenging. She needs to be asking questions in class. If she has more questions, she is welcome to come before or after school; I will be happy to help her."

"The bus doesn't get to school in time for her to come see you, and she turns out for basketball after school."

"I would be happy to write her coach a note."

"The *point*, Mr. Haldini, is that your grading system is disrespectful of students."

"My grading system was laid out clearly at Open House."

"Really, Mr. Haldini. Did you pass out copies of the policy at Open House?"

"No, but I…."

"Then how can you expect parents to remember the policy four months later?"

"I sent a copy home with your daughter; it was returned with your signature on it."

"I signed no such letter!"

Again, if I had any sense at all, I'd have referred him to The Krabman, but this was too tempting. "Well, you now have a second problem; your daughter forged your signature."

"You are dodging the issue!"

I wondered how well his tactics worked on others. "I have her grades in front of me, as well as those of her classmates."

"Yes?" I pictured smoke pouring out of his ears.

"Mr. Padgett, she has the lowest test average in her class."

"*Everyone* has a C or better?"

"Yes. That's not uncommon in with geometry students. They're advanced one year in math."

He cleared his throat and roared, "You flat-top faggot!"

This would have been yet another appropriate time to refer him to the administration. Instead, I snarled, "Nice alliteration."

"Mr. Haldini, I will be taking this matter up with your principal!"

"You are welcome to do so. By the way, your daughter is a great kid, and she…."

"Do not patronize meeee, Haldini! At what time does your principal arrive?"

"It varies, depending…." Click.

I ran to the office. The Krabman had not yet arrived, so I related my phone conversation to our head secretary, an older woman we called "Big Boss Lady". Her closet was apparently filled exclusively with Fernwater football jerseys.

"A flat top faggot?" she giggled. I had expected her to offer up a sympathetic ear, but watching her skinny body shake with laughter was much better medicine.

Big Boss Lady ran the school, and everyone knew it. When 1st period was set to start in five minutes and a substitute had not yet arrived, she'd dig one up. And the previous August, a bureaucratic snag delayed the arrival of new textbooks. "Let me see what I can do," she had said with a wink. "I have my backdoor contacts." The books were delivered the next morning.

She thanked me for letting her know about Maxi Pad, but told me not to worry. "Believe me," she said. "I have seen it all."

Just then, Maximillian R. Padgett, tall, tanned and in a tizzy, charged into the office like a wounded bull. He pounded a fist on Big Boss Lady's desk, demanding to see the Principal.

"No!" I shouted, advancing and ready for battle. "You will not speak to her like that!"

Big Boss Lady didn't say a word. She dropped her frail arm in front of me like a barrier at a toll booth. With her other hand she picked up her phone, dialed a number and punched the speaker button. A deep, officious voice answered: "King County Sheriff's Office."

Big Boss Lady handed the receiver to Mr. Padgett, who stammered into the wrong end for twenty seconds, then slammed it down and stormed out.

Big Boss Lady flexed her wiry little bicep and sang the jingle from an old Ajax detergent commercial: "Stronger than dirt!" Her body again shook with laughter.

I laughed along with her, grateful that she had saved me from my own idiocy.

And Maxi Pad? I never heard from him again.... well, not until his son arrived at Fernwater two years later.

With three minutes to go in 1st period on a Friday morning, Felix Hester poked his head in the door. "OK if I interrupt?"

"Sure," I said. "What's up?"

Several kids called out, "Hi, Uncle Fester."

He bowed and smiled, showing off a mouthful of orthodontia. "I have what would be a physics problem, I guess. If you have a guy with a rock, in a boat, in a lake, and the guy throws the rock into the water, would the level of the lake rise, fall, or stay the same?"

Silence fell, and I turned my eyes up to the ceiling, as I often did when working out a problem. A kid asked me if I knew the answer. Before responding, I saw that Gizmo was staring at me intently, and I realized he was offering to mouth the answer to me if I needed it. Of all my interactions with this kid, it was perhaps this moment that most wowed me.

"Yeah, I know the answer," I said, still baffled and blown away by Gizmo's ability to communicate nonverbally. How did a 14-year-old boy know how to do that?

"Preliminary poll," I said. "How many say the water level will rise?" Six hands went up, some with certainty, some with hesitation.

"OK, how many say the level will fall?" Three kids raised their hands, and they looked around for confirmation.

"And how many say the level stays the same?" A dozen hands went up this time.

"Great problem," I said to Fester and then called out, "Bell's gonna ring in 30 seconds. I want everyone to discuss this problem with a parent or brother or granny. We'll talk about it Monday." I turned back to Fester. "You'd have made a great science teacher."

He waved off the compliment and asked, "You going out for LEMONADE after school?"

That was staff code for "Let's Everyone Mosey Over 'N' 'Ave a Dos Equis". Heidi Blohmeyer had invented the acronym after making the rounds at Open House, whispering to teachers the words "beer", "nine-thirty", "Beats Workin'" and "more beer". After that evening, Heidi, as Fernwater's self-appointed social director, would announce over the intercom every few weeks: "LEMONADE at three-thirty, attendance mandatory."

"Yeah, I think we'll have a good turnout," I told Fester. The bell rang before kids could grill us about our after-school shenanigans. "Have a swell week-end," I called out.

Calvin regarded us warily. "Yeah, and have a swell time drinking 'lemonade'." He slashed a pair of quotes in the air.

On Monday, I asked if anybody had an answer to the guy-in-the-boat problem.

A boy in the back asked, "Doesn't it matter how big the rock is?"

I threw the question back to the class. The consensus was that "Size doesn't matter," which brought a few knowing grins. I ignored them.

Teri Zucati asked, "Hey, does this have anything to do with that Greek guy who jumped out of his bathtub and ran down the street naked yelling 'Eureka!'?" Cute, curious and irrepressible, I thought of Teri Zu an academic cheerleader.

I answered, "The story goes that Archimedes had.... insights while bathing."

Jaime asked, "Did he get arrested for.... you know, like, exposing himself?"

I could not resist. "No, he *bare*-ly got away." That drew the expected groans.

"Geez Louise!" cried Teri Zu.

An older-looking girl asked, "Did the Greeks believe that size doesn't matter?"

That drew some laughter, bringing us precariously close to crossing a line that I did not want to cross. Fortunately, this class understood where that line was drawn. Had this been a Pre-alg class, I probably would have squelched such a remark; otherwise they'd spend the rest of the period chortling about boners and chubbies and tools, oh my!

"The water level would stay the same," said Jaime. "The rock pushes down the boat, and that raises the level. But if you throw a rock in the lake, the water raises by the same amount."

Anjuli disagreed. "That sounds right, but it doesn't work that way in real life."

I asked, "How so?"

"I did the experiment last night."

"You went out in a boat? In the dark?"

"No, I filled up my kitchen sink partway with water, and floated a bowl with a rock in it. I marked the water level with lip gloss – raspberry flavored! Then I took the rock out of the bowl and put it in the sink. The water level went down."

Silence. None of the rest of us had thought to perform an

actual experiment.

"Clever girl!" My already considerable respect for Anjuli rose a notch. "By the way, which is a better way to prove things, by logic or by experiment?"

A kid pointed out that just because the water level went down for that rock, in that bowl, in that sink, it doesn't mean it's always true.

Gizmo countered immediately. "But we agreed that size doesn't matter, so she did prove it for all situations."

"OK, now that we're pretty sure that we know what does happen, I want everyone to go home tonight and figure out why."

Gizmo stuck around after class that day. "Haldini, when the rock is in the boat, the boat displaces the rock's *weight* in water. When the rock goes into the water, it displaces its *volume*. And since the rock is denser than water, more water gets displaced when the rock is in the boat. That's why the water level went down."

"Well done! Why didn't you say this in class?"

"I didn't want to give it away. I figured you'd want to torment them for a week or two." I realized again not only how sharp he was intellectually, but how socially adept he was.

"Mr. Haldini, I don't learn the same way as other kids. Once I understand an idea, I've got it; I don't need to do all the homework problems."

I had never heard a kid say anything like that. I thought back over the school year, and what Gizmo said was true: He understood concepts instantly, at a deep level. I asked what he was proposing.

"I'm not sure. I know teachers have to assign homework, but it's not all that interesting to me. But I like geometry."

"Let me think about this, and I will get back to you."

"Fair enough." He scurried out the door to his next class.

His words kept returning to me. He had aced every test, but his homework grade was dismal. Averaged together, he had a C+, which was disturbing – his grasp of geometric concepts and applications was exceptional.

That afternoon I ran into Gizmo in the hall and pulled him aside. "I have a proposal for you. I will require you to do half the homework problems; I will choose which ones. I will also assign you other problems, but let me warn you: they're going to be challenging. Interested?"

"Yes! Oh, this is awesome!"

I was pleased by his enthusiasm, and hopeful that we could manage this alternate way of doing business.

I said, "Understand that we will do this only as long as you continue to kick butt on tests. Got it? This is absolutely fair, what we're doing here, but I don't want to have ten kids coming up to me tomorrow, asking for the same deal. Feel free to tell Calvin, but don't advertise."

"Understood. Thanks, Haldini."

Chapter 18 – February

You can tell a lot about kids by how they answer to roll call on the first day. Half of my 2nd semester 8th graders were newcomers, and I made notations about them on my roster.

"Here."

"Here."

"Yo, call me J.J., would you? For Josh Junior." This kid was slouched down, ready to slide right out of his seat. Next to Joshua Jones's name, I put a "g", for "goonball".

"Here."

"Here." It was delivered quietly and seriously. I put a "b" next to his name – he'd make a nice little buffer between a pair of goonballs.

"Right.... over.... here!" Several kids laughed at Gemini's well-rehearsed tough grrrl posturing. I wrote "blc" next to her name, for "back left corner", which is where she would be sitting the next few weeks.

"Here."

"H-h-here." In September, I had made up the designation "ws", whispering snowflake, for this kid whose face was enshrouded in zits, anxiety and thick glasses. I had sat him at the front of the room. Since then, he'd grown several inches and his voice had dropped an octave.

"Here."

"Here."

"Here I am." Jeremiah said it with a giggle. I wrote "rfc", for "right front corner", the same place he'd sat all year. He was a nice kid, if rambunctious, and I wanted him right in front of my desk where I could keep an eye on him. But I also enjoyed chatting with him before class about soccer or reggae or whatever. If I gave him 20 seconds of my attention, he'd be fine. If not, he'd want 20 minutes.

"Here."

"Here." I met this kid in the lunch line the previous year. Even as a 12-year-old, she was articulate, confident and sassy. I wrote an "m" by her name. I wanted a bright student with a strong personality sitting in the middle of the room.

"Here." A girl with jet-black spiked hair, piles of purple eye shadow and big black boots was dispassionately eating her schedule. I put a "g" by her name, then erased it and capitalized it.

"Here." She might just as well have had "nice kid" tattooed on her forehead. I wrote "cf", for "center front".

And so it went. The word "here", depending on how it's delivered, is loaded with info. Sometimes, though rarely, I misread a kid completely – the girl with the boots turned out to be bright and personable, in an oddball sort of way, and conscientious about academics. I enjoyed being wrong about Bootsy.

I used the notations on my roster to devise a seating chart; more or less a divide-and-conquer approach. I knew half a dozen teachers who placed their Johnnys, Jasons, Jimmys, and Josiahs at the four corners of the room, and if there were Jeremys, Joeys, or Jeffs left over, we dispersed them as best we could and called it good. Remarkably, we had all come up with that method independently of one another.

Various theories were floated by staff members to explain the J Boy Phenomenon. Heidi Blohmeyer pointed out that there are a lot of boys' names that start with "J". Another teacher, a fan of numerology, claimed that there's an inherent mischievousness associated with the letter "J". Fester pointed out that whatever the source of J Boyishness, this was not a new phenomenon.

"For decades," he said, "Joe Blow has been joshing around, jackin' cars, jackin' off, jimmying locks while drinking Jim Beam or Jack Daniels, and writing books that purport to explain why Johnny can't read.

Three weeks into the semester, Jesse and J.J. Jones were acting squirrelly, more so than usual. Every few minutes, they'd make eye contact across the room and swap hand signals.

I approached Jesse and said, "I don't know what you're planning, but I've got one word for you: Don't."

He gave me an innocent look: What? Me? *Me?*

Halfway through class, Jesse was standing by J.J.'s desk.

When he saw me watching him, he high-fived his pal and returned to his seat.

One minutes later, Jesse approached my desk, his face the color of guacamole that had been left out on the counter all night. He was holding his stomach, and his throat and cheeks were convulsing. "I'm not.... I don't feel so good."

My God, he's ready to hurl! All over my desk! As I steered him toward the door, J.J. approached us, his face the same hideous shade of green.

Now what the hell is this?

"Get down to the restroom!" I ordered them. "Now!"

The instant they left my room, they erupted, spewing all over the lockers and floor. J.J. inadvertently threw up on Jesse, who attempted to jump back and then slipped on the now slimy tile floor. He executed a partial backflip and managed to vomit on the ceiling, a feat I would not have believed possible. He landed with a resounding thud on his back, knocking the wind out of him. He was now writhing on the floor, alternately gasping for air and blowing chunks.

I sent a kid to get our VP, who collected the boys and cordoned off the hallway.

I addressed my class. "I'm in a foul mood. It's got nothing to do with you, but do not mess with me today."

Laying out one's emotional state like this is the educational acid test – I would now discover the essence of our relationship: either they would help put me back together, or they would reveal themselves as a school of sharks, smelling blood in the water.

We were studying linear equations, and I again brought up my experience as a cab driver. "Here's how we got paid: When you get in a cab, the driver *drops* a small metal bar, which starts the meter running, but it doesn't start at zero. It starts at, say, three bucks, which is called the *drop*."

Bootsy raised her hand. "So you owe the driver money before you even go anywhere?"

"That's right."

Jeremiah was undeterred by the edgy tone in the room. "What a rip-off!"

I asked why the meter would not start at zero. It took a while to get an answer:

"Because cab drivers have to drive to somebody's house or the airport, and they get paid for it."

"Right. Now, cabbies also get paid by mileage. Let's say the driver gets $2.00 per mile."

Jeremiah was keeping the discussion going. "Are these numbers real?"

"No, these numbers are a bit high. For this first problem, I'm using nice numbers. So, three bucks for the drop, two bucks per mile. How much would a seven-mile trip cost?"

Most got an answer of $17.

"OK, how far could you go with $31 in your pocket?"

And so on. Eventually, the class collectively figured out an equation relating money (y) to mileage (x):

$$y = 2x + 3$$

In a kindly voice, Bootsy asked me to tell a cab driver story.

I was not in the mood, but the atmosphere was tense, and kids don't learn much from a surly teacher.

"OK," I said, "but it'll be a short one. I picked up a guy one night down by Oxley Park at 1:30. I asked where he wanted to go, and he said, 'Home.' He didn't know his address, but he knew how to get there: 'Take a left. See the Safeway there? Don't pay any attention to it. The road curves a bit. Now, take a right.... no, not yet. See that fire hydrant? Don't pay any attention to it. OK, stop right.... riiiiight.... right here!' He paid the fare, along with a hefty tip, and he got out. After driving him around for ten minutes, we were right across the street from where I picked him up."

"Was he drunk?" asked Bootsy.

"Didn't seem to be. Like I've said before, not a lot of normal people take a cab after midnight. OK, back to math."

"Hold it," said Jeremiah. "How do you get customers?"

"Good question. Sometimes we drove around busy areas, and sometimes we parked at the bus station, but mostly people called in and the dispatcher radioed us with an address."

"Gotcha." Jeremiah aimed two imaginary pistols at me and clicked his tongue. He was a kinetic bundle of hormones, and though the mood of the class was subdued, he was maintaining his normal, high-octane, good-natured approach to life. To his credit, he could read me pretty well, and had the good sense not to tangle with me. Still, he was looking for his opening….

While passing out the day's assignment, I looked over at Jeremiah, who was movin', groovin' and wielding an imaginary microphone. Out of sheer grumpiness, I opened my mouth to say something, but he beat me to it, launching into a disco tune by Alicia Bridges, a one-hit wonder from '78:

"O-oh, I love the night life, I love to boogie, in the disco, oh, AHHWHHWH, yeah…."

The high-pitched wail on the original sounded like an alley cat that had feasted on a good-sized carp and was now choking on a bone. I cannot imagine how or why, but Jeremiah reproduced that sound exactly. It was so unexpected, so random, so weird for a 14-year-old boy to even know that song that I laughed until the veins in my forehead protruded.

He was surprised and pleased that I appreciated his talent, such as it was. Squirrelly students like Jeremiah are accustomed to annoying adults with their hijinks. I got the impression it was a new experience for him, getting a teacher to crack up.

And a grouchy teacher at that.

Seated next to a secretary's desk at lunchtime, Jesse and J.J. studiously avoided my eyes; it may have been the first time they had done *anything* studiously. Gray and orange splotches adorned Jesse's shirt and pants. Opening the VP's door, I found Reuben Rapp in an animated debate with Heidi Blohmeyer.

"Sorry to interrupt," I said, "but what were those clowns up to?"

Sitting amongst a clutter of phone messages, kids' duffel bags and a machete he'd confiscated, Reuben managed a partial grin and waved me in. "I hope you haven't eaten yet, because this'll turn your stomach." He shut the door and motioned me to have a seat. "J.J. and Jesse have taken a disliking to a kid in your class, and…. Are you sure you're ready for this?'

"Bring it on."

How bad could it be? Shoot, I had lived in a college dorm.

"You know what ipecac is?" he said.

"Sure, you give it to little kids to make them throw up if

they eat something poisonous."

"Right. Well, Jesse brought a bottle of ipecac to school today. He and J.J. each took a swig, and they were waiting for the bell to ring. When the kid left your room, their plan was to vomit on him. Not being exactly Mensa material, they got the timing and dosage wrong. They chugged half the bottle."

I exhaled, closed my eyes and slumped in my chair. "What are you going to do with them?"

"That's what I was just explaining to Heidi. I want Jesse out of here."

"Then you're passing our problem along to someone else," she said. "We have a duty to help every student."

"We've made it abundantly clear that we want to help him," said Reuben. "He's made it clear that he's got no interest in learning. By moving him out, I'm betting that his followers will clean up their act. When a kid goes to a new school, it's a shock to his system; sometimes he wakes up and decides to become a student. We have two kids here now that were kicked out of other schools, and they've shaped up."

"And what about J.J. Jones?" she asked.

Reuben deferred to me. "How about it, Leo? What do you want me to do? I'd be happy to send him home for three days."

I considered that. "You know, it was Jesse that brought the ipecac. J.J.'s a pill, but he's manageable, and he's passing my class. How about you assign him an after-school detention?"

"You got it. Stick around, would you?" He opened the door and called the boys into his office. They sat, chins on their chests. "Boys, I'd like you to apologize to Mr. Haldini."

With heads dangling at half-mast, they mumbled in unison, "Sorry."

"Not good enough, not even close. Try it again; I want you to look him in the eye." He waited for their heads to come up. "Now, apologize."

J.J. said, "I am sorry for disturbing your class."

Jesse, still a sickly shade of greenish gray, said, "Sorry for ralphing."

Reuben opened the student handbook to the discipline section. "Jesse, this is your third major violation this year. You've been suspended twice. You've given us no indication you're here

to learn. You are expelled, as of today. Your mother is on her way
to pick you up. She will need to find you a different school. Do
you understand?"

"Yes, Mr. Rapp."

"Wait for her out front. Start making smarter decisions."

And that was how Reuben Rapp functioned. When a kid
got in a fight, or told a teacher to go fuck a porcupine, or hatched a
plot to barf on a classmate, our VP dispassionately referred to
Fernwater's discipline code. It was not *him* doing the disciplining.

"Joshua Jones," said Reuben. "This is your first major
offense, but it's a serious one. I was going to suspend you, but Mr.
Haldini talked me out of it. I am assigning you three after-school
detentions, an hour each time. And I will be meeting with your
father shortly."

J.J. breathed a sigh of relief. "Oh, thank you! Dad would
kill me if I got the boot."

"You can thank Mr. Haldini for that; he is One Good Tern.
Be in my office at 2:46 this afternoon, Josh. Otherwise I will
suspend you. Got it?"

"Yes, sir."

That was Reuben at his best. J.J. now viewed me as the
good guy; I had saved him from suspension. And if he got sent to
the office again, he'd have to deal with Mr. Rapp, the bad guy,
who sat in his office, just waiting for an opportunity to kick him
out – the VP was now someone to be avoided. It was a win-win-
win-win solution: J.J.'s behavior improved; students learned in a
more pleasant environment; I was a more effective teacher; and
Reuben would never again have to deal with J.J. Jones, that little
pill.

Stepping out of Reuben's office, I bumped into a hefty,
balding man who had been eavesdropping on our conversation. I
backed up, apologized and looked into the face of…. Josh
McClown? It took me a moment to recognize him; he'd put on
weight and there was a nasty-looking gash on his chin that
probably should have had stitches. It was just before noon, and he
smelled like a distillery. He didn't smile.

"McClown! What are you doing here?"

He hitched up his jeans. "I come to see about m'boy."

"Who's your boy?"

As if on cue, J.J. slouched out of the VP's office, but stood apart from us. He and McClown were clearly ashamed of one another's presence.

Ohmigod! J.J. – Josh Junior! He must have been using his mom's last name. The Joshes didn't look alike, but many of their mannerisms and personality traits were identical: the hunching of the shoulders, the fidgeting, the poor work ethic, the inclination to barf at school. Like father, like son! Was J.J. aware of the vomit-in-class chromosome buried not so deeply in the McClown DNA?

Hold on. Is McClown old enough to have a son in 8th grade? That would mean he.... Geez Louise! Back when we were schoolmates, I had assumed that his claim of "getting some with a second cousin" was all talk.

"If you're done here, J.J., get yourself back to class," said McClown. He took two steps toward Reuben's office and stopped.

"I'm sorry," he said, standing sideways to me with eyes downcast. "Not for m'boy – he gots to apologize for hisself. I mean I'm sorry for bein'.... wha' joo call me back then? A 'fuckwit'?" I started to say something, but he silenced me with a raised hand. "No, Haldini, you were right, and I *am* sorry."

For two seconds, I felt responsible for the sorry state of McClown's life.

The next day on his way into class, J.J. Jones apologized to me again. I asked why he had not mentioned that his dad went to school here.

He squirmed before answering. "Dad never told me much about when he was growing up, but my aunt tells stories at Thanksgiving. Dad was, uh, um.... a douche when he went to Fernwater, wasn't he?"

I didn't intend to laugh. "J.J., let me say this: Whatever your dad did or didn't do growing up has nothing to do with you. You get to choose for yourself what kind of life you'll lead."

Just when I thought he hadn't heard me, he said in a somber voice, "J.J. – Josh Junior. I never liked the 'Junior' part of my name. Or 'Josh', for that matter – it sounds like a joke."

Oh my, what a glorious opportunity! How often do you get the chance to remove a "J" or two from a J boy's name?

I asked, "What's your middle name?"

"Jackson."

Curses! Naming your son Joshua Jackson Jones Junior is child abuse. He didn't stand a chance.

"But I never really liked that name either," he said.

Furiously, I cycled through possible nicknames. Should I ask about his favorite actor? No, he'd probably say Jim Carrey or Johnny Depp. Favorite singer? No, he'd say Johnny Rotten.

"I've always liked 'Dakota'," he said. "That's what Mom wanted to name me."

Good enough for me.

Over the course of the next few weeks, with his partner in crime gone, Dakota's grades and outlook improved. I made a point of chatting with him about sports, music and friends.

But we never again spoke about his dad.

\-

The last tests to be turned in belonged to Gemini and the boy sitting beside her. With five minutes left in class, I began correcting. Gem scored a 75%, her best effort of the year. I was encouraged; though she still was not doing much homework, she had been more attentive in class the past couple weeks.

I next corrected the test of the boy sitting next to her, and one of his answers caught my attention; it was the same wrong answer as on Gem's test, and nowhere near the correct one.

I called the two students up to my desk and pointed out the "coincidence".

"I didn't cheat!" said Gem. "I didn't!"

I looked at the bewildered boy and then back at her. "Are you saying it was *chance* that you got the same completely wrong answer as the kid sitting next to you?"

"I don't know!" she said. "It could happen."

"Look," I said, "either you're stupid or you think I am."

"This is fucked up!" She turned and stormed out the door.

"Gem!"

With one minute left in class, I hurried down to the staffroom to call her mom. I deliberately spoke in a calm voice: "On several occasions she's tried to pick fights. She cheated today and used the words 'fucked up'."

Gone was the mom's imperious attitude from our conference earlier in the year. She spoke in a quiet, broken-down voice. "All right, I can be speaking at her."

I administered the same test that afternoon, allowing me time to correct tests from 2nd period. Oddly, the first test I graded contained the same wrong answer that Gem had given. I checked the work of one of my sharper students, and was unable to find her mistake. I worked through my own step-by-step solution and then almost swore aloud: Oh, damn it! My answer key is wrong! Damn, damn, damn!

When the bell rang at the end of the day, I hightailed it down to the VP's office. Heidi Blohmeyer entered behind me.

Reuben said, "Leo, I was just about to call you down. Gemini's mother just left."

I gulped and sat down. "Uh, what's goin' on?"

"Just a sec." Reuben shuffled through a stack of papers.

I had no idea what was coming, but whatever it was, my stomach dreaded it. I conjured up one nightmare scenario after another, most having to do with me getting fired or arrested. Regret and fear vied for top billing in my mind, and I began to zone out. Oh, so this is how it's been for Dad all these years.

Heidi handed me a withdrawal form. "Gem and her mom are moving back to Georgia, to live with Gem's grandparents." The blood drained from my face. "I know what you're thinking, Leo." Actually, she had not the slightest idea what I was thinking. "Cheating was just the final straw. She's smoking dope. She got in a fight last month. Dad just got out of jail. Want me to go on?"

I don't remember what else was said during that meeting. But I do remember what was not said; there were no confessions from me regarding my false accusation. If I hadn't been so quick, so eager, to accuse Gem, might I have eventually reached her? She had gotten a C on her test; maybe she was already on the upswing.

How would my dad have addressed the questions swirling around inside my skull? He might have referred to Gem as an "undesirable", an expression of revulsion and boundless scorn that made my skin crawl – it was a term I suspect he brought along from the Old Country. Then Dad might have added: The princess is gone. Your class will be better now. Look forward, Leo, always forward.

Never look back.

Chapter 19 – March

Overall, my pre-algebra students were doing poorly in most of their classes. If asked, many of them would say they felt little or no connection to school academically, athletically or even socially.

They had been left behind.

In an effort to provide a place of refuge – or at least to make math class less repellent – I sometimes started class by asking a kid: How did your soccer game (or drum lesson, or paintball war) go? Did you play well?

One day a student held up a clipping from a tabloid. "Mr. Haldini, there's a guy in France who sings Japanese backwards."

Another time I asked, "How many of you think Wrong Way should dump her boyfriend and go out with Nikolai?"

Every hand in the room shot up; it was a moment of unity. The shy, blue-eyed Ukrainian kid was embarrassed, but enjoyed our support. Wrong Way acted offended.

A week later, the bell rang to begin class, and she asked how old I was.

"Ancient. Take out your assignment."

"You're not married, right?"

"Be serious. Who'd have me?"

Another girl smirked and said, "I see what you mean."

"My mom wants to know...." Wrong Way blushed. "Mom thinks you should go out with my Aunt Cheri, that's her sister, she's cute and funny and has a Corgi, and she lives up on the hill above the new stadium."

The class took great pleasure in my discomfort; though, truth be told, I was more flattered than embarrassed. Wrong Way passed forward a scrap of paper with a phone number on it.

It was a luxury, having a class of 18; it allowed us to operate differently than in my other classes, which ranged in size from 25 to 35. In Geometry, I would often lecture or lead class discussions for 30 minutes or longer. With my Pre-alg class, I had to get in and get out – five minutes max.

Connecting a topic to money definitely raised my students' interest level. The Dow Jones had been rising steadily for some time, and I wanted my Pre-alg class to give the stock market a whirl. I called the Seattle Times circulation department to see if they would donate 20 copies of their paper once a week for a class project. I got an enthusiastic "yes" in response.

The following Monday I told my class, "Suppose you have $100,000 to invest. I want you to pick three stocks. Divide up the money anyway you like." I gave them a simplified explanation of how Wall Street works, and showed them how to read the stock market page.

I said, "Your assignment is to track your gains and losses until June. *Invest* yourselves in this project."

One kid got the pun. "Ha ha. Don't quit your day job."

Students chose stocks for a variety of reasons: one girl's dad worked at Boeing; one boy downed a half gallon of Pepsi every day; and three kids found stocks whose ticker tape symbols matched their initials.

The next Monday, everyone was excited to see who were the big winners and losers. As they calculated gains and losses, I walked around the room to field questions:

"How do people in real-life choose what stocks to buy?"

"How do people know when to buy and sell?"

"Mr. Haldini, do you own stocks?"

I prefaced my grossly simplified responses by saying that my own returns in the market had been dismal.

Wrong Way raised her hand and called out, "Boris, will you come help us?" I looked behind me. Who the heck is Boris?

"Boris," she and her friend said impatiently.

"What's the deal with calling me 'Boris'?"

Wrong Way gave me a devilish smile. "'Cause that's what you do: You bore us. Hey, my brother had shoes like that, back when they were in style."

Towards the end of Pre-alg one day, an unfamiliar guy showed up. He was not standing in the doorway so much as he was filling it. He only stood about five-ten, but he must have been pushing 350 pounds. He wore a faded t-shirt, on the front of which was emblazoned the picture of a band, The Pus Puppies. Sweating profusely and panting, he took a rest, using the moment to size up my class. He then lumbered over and handed me a New Student Form.

I introduced myself and said, "We have a test tomorrow. If you do well, we'll keep your grade. If not, we'll pretend you never took it. Deal?"

In a credible Marlon Brando imitation, he jutted out his jaw and said, "You make me an offer I can't refuse."

"Hey, that's pretty good; We're calling you Brando from now on. Deal?"

"You make me another offer I can't refuse."

He was unable to fit in a student desk, so I loaned him my chair and sat him at a table.

The kid sitting nearest to him mumbled, "Half man, half mayonnaise."

With no hesitation, Brando extended his hand to shake and said pleasantly, "Good morning."

The kid unsurely took the proffered hand and immediately groaned in agony.

Brando released his grip and said, still pleasantly, "It's nice to meet you."

Before there was a chance for me to intervene, their skirmish was over. I called the kid up to my desk and asked if his hand was OK.

He stretched his hand and wiggled his fingers. "Yeah, I guess so."

"You know you had that coming."

"I guess so."

At the end of the period, I stopped Brando on his way out. "That kid was out of line, but I don't want you hurting anybody in here. Understand?"

"I promise," he said and held out his hand. "Shake?" I hesitated, and that's when I heard him laugh for the first time, a deep, wheezing, joyful jowl-shaker that instantly won me over.

"C'mon," he said. We shook, and he gave me a chuck on the shoulder, saying, "Have a terrific day."

A month after being expelled for puking in my 8th grade class, Jesse the Ipecac Kid showed up in 9th grade Pre-alg, waving his new class schedule in my face. He explained his return to classmates before the bell rang: After moving in with his dad in Seattle, he was suspended for fighting on the first day at his new school. Three weeks later, he got booted from another school, at which point his dad announced, "Young man, I think your mother must be missing you." They loaded Jesse's clothes, TV, football and drums into his pick-up and then headed over to his mom's apartment. They got out and lowered the tailgate, but Jesse refused to remove his gear. His dad got back in and rolled down the window. He asked, "Sure you don't wanna lend me a hand?" Receiving no answer, his dad shifted into reverse, floored it and then slammed on the brakes, leaving all of his son's worldly possessions strewn across the pavement.

"My dad's a dickweed," said Jesse.

I felt for the kid; how could you not? But the moment the bell rang, Jesse snatched the assignment from the kid behind him and threatened to rip it in half.

"Jesse, give it back."

He gave it back, but one minute later, he shredded a piece of paper.

"Jesse, pick up the paper." My empathy for him was all but used up.

He picked up a handful of confetti and tossed it in the air. As it fluttered down, he treated us to a gruesome rendition of "White Christmas", all the while smiling like the demon child in The Omen.

"*Jesse,* stop singing. Pick up the paper and throw it away." He picked up two tiny pieces and threw them away. I ignored an urge to rip off his arm and shove it down his throat; Reuben had asked teachers to simply document infractions. Let him dig his own grave, he'd told us.

"*Jesse,* pick it alllll up."

He picked up three pieces this time, and then wrote "ACDC" on his forehead with a pen, backwards, so he could read it in the mirror he'd swiped from a girl sitting two rows away.

I was doing my best to ignore the tiny devil sitting on my shoulder, whispering, "If you don't stand up...."

One last try: *"Jesse*, give the mirror back!"

He smacked the kid next to him with the mirror, and told him to give it to "the wicked witch". He then removed a shoe lace and tied it around his wrist to cut off the circulation; his hand turned red and swollen.

"JESSE, UNTIE THE SHOELACE! I don't care if your hand falls off, but I don't want you bleeding on somebody!"

Teachers need to be understanding of the adverse conditions under which many kids are raised, and at times we make allowances for obnoxious behavior, but in Jesse's case.... well, I'll just say it: I didn't like him. I filled out an office referral with an abridged list of offenses and handed it to him.

Jesse snatched the referral and left, singing an ACDC song, complete with guitar lick: "You.... shook me allllll night.... long! Bair dair dair.... dair! Yeah, *youuuu*...."

When the lunch bell rang, I hoofed it down to Reuben's office and demanded, *"Why* is Jesse back?"

He shook his head resignedly. "You'll have to ask Mr. Krabke."

Our principal insisted that we not address him by his first name; early on he had let it be known that he considered such chumminess to be "inappropriately informal".

Reuben said, "But he's in a meeting right now with Jesse's mom and The HOSE."

My blood in a boil, I burst into The Krabman's office and asked why Jesse the Ipecac Kid was back. Reuben followed me in.

"Let's all just calm down," said The HOSE, our district's Head Of Special Education. He was an imperturbable man with a regal bearing.

His admonishment had exactly the opposite effect on me. "Why.... is Jesse.... *back?*" My question was aimed at no one in particular.

The HOSE answered, "Jesse's mother is appealing his expulsion, on the grounds that he is disabled."

"Disabled how?"

"He has been diagnosed with a fairly rare affliction: Pervasive Developmental Disorder Not Otherwise Specified."

"What is that?"

"I believe the title is self-explanatory."

Jesse's mom took over.   "Under the Americans with Disabilities Act, my Jesse is being discriminated against. Besides, he's always done so well at Fernwater."

"Lady! Your son barfed in my class!"

"I was told he became ill in the hallway."

"Ill, my ass! He hurled, he spewed! He blew major chunks! On purpose! He called a girl a 'droopy ass bitch'!"

"I'm glad you brought that up." She jabbed a finger at me. "Mr. Haldini here scolded my son, just for singing. Before class even started."

"There's a song about a droopy ass bitch?" asked Reuben.

"Jesse was practicing his rapping. You're out of touch."

Reuben grabbed my arm and coaxed me back to his office. "I didn't want to bring Jesse back," he said, "but his mom lobbed the phrase 'according to my lawyer' at the school board, and they consulted their legal team, who advised us to give her what she wants."

As Uncle Fester once put it, our district's central nervous system reacts epileptically to the prospect of a lawsuit.

"Why is he in 9th grade?"

Reuben shrugged, and I barged back into The Krabman's office. "Jesse failed my 8th grade class! Whyyyy is he all of a sudden moved *ahead* one grade?"

"He's old for his age," said The Krabman. "The lad is bored; he needs a challenge."

The HOSE handed me a sheaf of paper. "Here is a copy of his contract, outlining his rights and responsibilities at Fernwater."

Reuben dragged me back to his office. Scanning Jesse's list of infractions, he said, "What would you like me to do with him? Want me to suspend him?"

Skimming Jesse's contract, I said, "I'm not sure we can, unless he dismembers a classmate, and only then if it's another special ed kid."

Reuben looked beaten. "We been HOSED."

During lunch I wrote a letter to my parents, recounting the debacle with Jesse, Principal Krabke and The HOSE. Against my better judgment, I asked Dad if he had any advice for dealing with bureaucratic imbecility. I also asked Mom if she'd seen the villa where Dad grew up.

Wrong Way came to see me after school one day. "I hear you blew it with my Aunt Cheri."

I blushed, sighed and gave a dozen other indicators that confirmed her verdict. No use denying it.

"Word travels fast," I said.

Wrong Way had not lied about her aunt being cute and funny, not to mention smart, available and childless. The previous evening, I had invited her over for shrimp fettuccini, a Granny Haldini dish that Uncle Marco told me could be counted on as the ultimate aphrodisiac; resistance is futile. And Cheri had emailed me that morning, saying that Wrong Way informed her that the third date is considered "the kissing date".

To sum up, only a moron could mess this up.

After dinner we sat in front of my fireplace with a bottle of Chardonnay, listening to an Enya CD, which is, in a word, "soothing". This was the first time I'd seen Cheri wear make-up, and she wore a powder blue sweater that complimented her red hair and ivory complexion. I regaled her with teaching stories; the Russian Fags were of course a big hit, and my account of Jesse's return to Fernwater was horrifically entertaining, but I wisely steered clear of the Ipecac Kids. Cheri told me embarrassing stories of Wrong Way as a little kid, saying I should feel free to use them as ammo in class.

At midnight, Cheri leaned forward and asked if I wanted to have children. Though I assumed she was speaking in general, as opposed to suggesting that we get going on it straight away, I was thrilled and aroused by her question. But, like a moron, I couldn't resist telling one last teacher story:

The week before, Wrong Way had asked, "Mr. Haldini, do you have any kids?"

Nikolai pointed at my Wall of Fame, plastered with student pictures. "He's got hundreds of 'em."

Brando said, "If those kids are all yours, Haldini, you must be like Paul Revere."

All eyes turned toward him and most of us said, "Huh?"

Brando gave me a sly smile and said, "He was a Minuteman."

About half the class got that, and we cracked up. For me, it was one of those veins-popping-out-on-the-forehead moments. The kids who didn't get it were instantly abuzz, and one by one they came on board.

Everybody has their sore spot that you don't joke about, and I had just found Cheri's. She had previously been married to a man who sired a child with his mistress and then got a vasectomy, none of which she knew anything about until a medical bill arrived in the mail.

Cheri was out the door at 12:05, never to be seen again.

The depth of my sadness over her sudden departure surprised me, because I didn't really know her that well. And it would not have worked out between us anyway, because the truth of the matter was that I didn't want my own children. At the end of a school day, even a typically marvelous day, I had no desire to see another kid.

Now, teachers have told me: You will feel different when they're your own. Maybe, I thought; maybe not. Many of my colleagues handled the dual demands of teaching and parenting very well, though I've also met my share who functioned on constant overload. One teacher claimed that driving home in rush hour traffic was his daily hour of relaxation; the moment he opened his car door, he was "on", mobbed by his three young children, all of whom he adored.

Had I chosen another career, I would have wanted kids of my own. I even know who I'd have wanted to be their mother – Mira, my college girlfriend; she with the dark, quiet eyes and weird, wicked sense of humor. A year my junior, she was not pleased when I took off to see the world two weeks after graduation. When I returned to Bellingham a year later and discovered she was engaged to a truck driver, boy, was I was pissed, and I let her know it.

"If you wise up," I hissed at her, "I'll be at Dirty Dan's," and then I stomped out.

Her fiancé came home from a cross-country haul that evening, and he found me pouting and drinking brandy in the bar. A pudgy southpaw, he slugged me in the jaw. His engagement ring cut me right down to the bone.

Before I could even think about retaliating, he said matter-of-factly, "You dunce. Mira had no idea when you were coming home. Girl like that, you expect her to wait around forever? You lose. Here, wipe your chin."

Who could argue with that? I started growing a beard right away, to hide my stitches.

While all this was going through my head, Wrong Way looked around my classroom. "You may find it hard to believe, but I'm going to miss this."

"Yeah, three months and you'll be out of here."

She handed me a withdrawal form.

"Not you too! Whyyyy?"

I hung my head; this was the third withdrawal from 3rd period this month. The frustrating thing about Pre-alg was not my students' lack of skills or conceptual deficiencies, or even their poor work ethic. Rather, it was the revolving door aspect of the class; one kid would move away and two others would transfer in a week later. With a constantly changing roster, it's difficult to deliver a coherent curriculum or develop any kind of rapport. By contrast, my Geometry roster would likely be the same in June as it had been in September.

"Dad got a job in Boise," said Wrong Way.

"How come you tell me ahead of time? How come Cheri didn't tell me?"

"We didn't know we were moving until last night."

"I am going to miss you, Wrong Way, even if you were mean to me."

"I'll miss you too. And just so you know, Boris, you were my favorite teacher. Well, except for Uncle Fester…. and Mrs. Blohmeyer…. and the custodian and her wiener dog."

Chapter 20 – April

As usual, I stood guard duty outside my room after school. When Anjuli and Calvin passed by, I asked her, "How's that wild and crazy sister of yours?"

"Kali's doing better, at least in school; but she's still hanging around a bunch of losers."

"And how are you?"

Calvin gave me a cagey look and answered for her. "She's living her own life."

"Glad to hear it. Enjoy your afternoon."

Teri Zu came skipping down the hall a minute later. She grabbed my wrists and pulled me into my classroom. Closing the door behind her, she said, "Promise you won't tell my dad?"

By chance, I seemed to run into this girl and her father everywhere: Safeway, hiking in the Cascades, Mariners games.

"OK," I said unsurely.

"Ya ready?" She squealed with delight, then grabbed the bottom of her blouse and lifted.

No! No! Noooooo! This cannot be happening! No no no nononono…. My career flashed before my eyes.

She bared her navel. "See? I got my belly button pierced! Isn't that the best?" She lowered her blouse and said in a grave tone, "But I mean it – you can't tell Dad." She opened the door and scampered away. "Bye, Haldini!"

I collapsed into a chair and buried my face in my hands. 14-year-old females are bizarre, delightful, mystifying creatures, equal parts girl, brain, proto-woman and hormone factory.

Still wobbly, I stood up and spied two folded-up notes on the floor. I felt like a kid on Christmas morning. The first one, from one 9th grade girl to another, began: I'm happy for you and Jesse, but don't get infested with him.

Infested? Did she mean "infatuated"? Or maybe she meant "invested". Or maybe she means exactly what she wrote; Jesse the

Ipecac Kid was a skuzzy guy. I'd have to ask her about it tomorrow. It would embarrass her, but heck, that's part of my job. For once I looked forward to our staff meeting; everyone would get a kick out of this one.

The second note was from a girl in 1st period: Dear Jaime, it began, I was kidding about you having a tiny dick.

This was the kind of letter Johnny Boe used to get. Was it cause for concern? Or was it none of my business? And was it relevant that this girl was our Student Body President?

Gizmo poked his head in the door. "You seen my people?"

"Anjuli and Calvin? You just missed them; they headed that-a-way."

"Thanks."

A tall, well-groomed man entered the room and asked in a soft voice, "Mr. Haldini?" He introduced himself as the father of a boy in 6th period, a serious student with glasses in the second row.

"He's a nice kid," I told him. "What can I do for you?"

"My son doesn't like you," he said dispassionately.

Whoa! I waited, but he didn't elaborate.

"Did he say why?" I asked. "Did I offend him?"

"No, he just said he doesn't like you." His glasses slipped down his nose, and rather than pushing them back up, he tilted his head back, so that he was literally looking down his nose at me.

"He gets along fine with his other teachers," said the man, but he did not offer up further details.

"Would you like me to speak to him?" I asked. "Is there something I can do to make him more comfortable?"

"No. Not really." He didn't seem to be angry or upset. I'd had his older son in class the previous year, and he had excelled. The dad thanked me for my time, and then he left.

What was *that* all about? I'd just had a great day. I sat down again, feeling crummy. I blinked my eyes several times, as if that might erase the incident. I went over my interactions with the kid, none of which seemed unpleasant. I told myself not to let it get to me, but it did. I was left to stew in my own toxic juices until a commotion in the hall distracted me.

Two girls and a boy that I'd had in class three years prior burst through the door with arms splayed. "Ta-da!"

"Hey, hey!" I said. "Seniors, right? How's school?"

"It's fine, but we still miss you."

"Not as much as I miss you." Yes, I am well aware of how sappy this all sounds.

One of the girls, a six-foot brunette, ran her hand softly over my flat-top mullet. "Sorry; I had to do this."

"It's OK, I have strangers do that. Sit. Tell me stories."

They told me about their classes and sports and dating. Then the boy asked how I was doing.

"Fine, all things considered, but I just had a bizarre conversation with a parent." I relayed the exchange word for word, minus the student's name.

At the end of the story, the three of them looked at each other and cracked up. The girls said, more or less simultaneously, "Well, *we* love you."

"Thank you – I needed that."

The six-footer abruptly switched topics. "Mr. Haldini, I have a question about colleges."

"I love questions."

"I need to decide where to go next year. The UW has a better business school, but WSU has a better veterinary program. How do I decide where to go?"

We talked about both schools and then I suggested we try an experiment: "Which school do you think I'm going to say?"

She placed a finger on her chin. "Well, a business degree is probably more practical, but I love working with animals."

"And what would I say to that?"

"If I had to guess, you'd say I should go with what I love."

"Then maybe that's what you should do." I shrugged, then checked the clock. "Dang, I've got a staff meeting in three minutes. I wish I had a Get Out Of Jail Free card."

After a round of hugs, they bounded out of the room like a trio of gazelles. On my way out, I checked my Suggestion Box and found an anonymous scrap of paper: Haldini, I love how your hair poofs up in the beautiful sunshine.

Did anyone have a better job than me?

Betty Skibbitz had fallen asleep, as usual, during our weekly Wednesday afternoon staff meeting in the library. Her silvery head was still slumped forward, but she was beginning to stir. Most teachers awaited her revival with aggravation, while a few of us looked forward to it with relish.

Betty's back straightened, her head rose, and her mouth opened: "I had a student named Jimmy; Jimmy K, back when I taught kindiegarden at Fernwater Elementary. Hoover was president then, and Jimmy would go bananas when…. no, come to think of it, it was Roosevelt – Franklin, of course, not Teddy – oh, I don't know, but the point is, Jimmy K was a bastard, literally, and one day he brought a little can of turpentine to school…."

She had built up a head of steam, and her steely blue eyes swept the room, daring anyone to interrupt. Jimmy K was my favorite of her characters, imaginary though he may have been.

Annoyed, The Krabman looked for an opening, but her delivery was seamless. He had never worked up the nerve to say: Betty, stick a sock in it.

"…. and by golly, Jimmy K was a little jitterbug; you couldn't get him to do doodly-squat, so I'd ring up his father. He'd show up in this old crate and throw a hissy fit – he was pickled half the time. Couldn't do nothin' about that; this was after Prohibition…."

I admired Betty's stamina. She had been teaching math for…. well, seemingly for*ever*, and she was good at it, in an old school sort of way. A first year teacher once asked how she dealt with discipline problems, and she replied, "Don't have any."

For the most part, our staff was dedicated, educated and, unlike Betty, easily entertained. We got to school early, stayed late, corrected tests in the evening, coached, attended plays and high school football games on Friday night, read essays on Saturday and took classes during the summer.

"…. and I'd run into Jimmy K's dad at this joint down on Oak Street, and he'd fess up to molly-coddlin' Jimmy, then he'd slap five clams on the bar and holler, 'Drinks 'r on me!' But I'll tell you, sure as I'm sittin' here…."

Most teachers work their proverbial asses off, and take delight in doing so. Having said that, after seven hours of soaking up teenage goofiness, many of us had become the 14-year-old monsters whose behavior we bemoan in the staffroom at lunch. During meetings, we doodle, we make smart ass comments, or we nod off and then tell unending Jimmy K stories:

".... it was all a bunch o' hooey. See, you can't tell about some folks, because Jimmy K grew up to be a school teacher, as you old-timers are well aware...."

As Betty apprised us of The Wicked Ways of Jimmy the Literal Bastard, I spied a one-inch bit of string on the table, and laid down a challenge to Uncle Fester: "I'll give you a dime if you eat that."

The dare was so pathetic that of course he ate it. All of us at the table silently cracked up, and I paid up.

Fester whispered, "We are what we teach."

Stories about the metal plate in his head still circulated, but he was different now, more relaxed than when he'd been my teacher. And it was not just that I was interacting with him as an adult now. Kids no longer feared him. To the contrary, he was widely adored.

Betty Skibbitz paused to take a breath, and The Krabman immediately began reading stats from an overhead: "For each student, our school receives $3600 from the state. For each special ed student, we receive an additional $3400, for a total of $7000. The state provides special ed funding for up to 12.5% of our student population."

Setting aside his buffoonery, Uncle Fester asked, "So we have an economic incentive to label kids as special ed?"

"I would not put it so crassly," said The Krabman. "We have a responsibility to identify students with learning disabilities and label them as such."

Fester asked how many special ed kids we currently had.

"I've got those numbers right here." The Krabman placed another transparency on the overhead. "Our district population is 9458, of which 1182 have been identified as special ed."

Being a math geek, I hauled out my calculator. "That's 12.497%," I said. "So, if we were to identify one more student as special ed, we would not receive additional funds for that student. Is that correct?"

"That may be. Where are you going with this?"

The Krabman was twitching like a tasered tern. At this point, I'm sure he regretted bringing up the whole SpEd issue, but the district was making a Push For Full Transparency – widely known as PFFT – in hopes of getting more buy-in from teachers.

Fester stopped short of suggesting criminal behavior. "That's one heck of a coincidence. What percentage of our students have been identified as special ed in the past?"

The Krabman told the truth: "I do not have those figures in front of me. But two years down the line, we anticipate a, um, a....." He made a weird sucking sound with his puckered lips while searching for a word. ".... I guess you'd call it a 'situation'. Currently, more than 12.5% of upper classmen are in special ed; we have a surplus, if you will. But our lower grades are under the 12.5% mark. These anomalies average out right now, but in a year, and more noticeably in two, our district will be significantly below the mark." He let those facts sink in.

"And?" I said. "We'd expect variations from year to year."

Twitch, twitch, twitch. "We do a good job of identifying kids with ADD, ADHD, and ODD, and we...."

Someone interrupted. "ODD?"

"Oppositional Defiant Disorder. And there are several other disorders on the horizon that we are keeping an eye on."

"On the horizon?" I asked.

"Yes. For example, CDS is a promising candidate."

"CDS?"

"Administrators across the U.S. are seeing a rise in Chronic Disorganization Syndrome. And a handful of other afflictions in school-age children have not yet been officially recognized by the AMA. Though it's unlikely that all of these afflictions will pan out, our district, working in conjunction with neighboring districts, is creating a task force to monitor their status."

"So we are hunting for new disorders?" This was getting me worked up, and a saying of my dad's played over and over in my head: Authorities must earn your respect.

Fester gave me a warning glance: Insubordination will not look good on your résumé.

"We are not *hunting* for anything," said The Krabman. "We are simply keeping current with educational and medical trends around the world."

Winnie De Waart, my old science teacher, raised her hand. Shoulders slumped, eyes rolled and spirits fell. Fester referred to her as a "staff infection". She could derail a meeting faster than you can say "Betty Skibbitz". Gazing at the ceiling, Winnie fiddled with a mole on her chin. "Speaking of special ed," she said, "I met with parents on Monday 'til almost four; that's 45 minutes past our contracted time. I expect to be compensated, and I'd like us to adopt a policy that requires parents to leave the building by 3:15."

Another teacher protested, "But sometimes I need to meet with parents past 3:15."

"That sets a dangerous precedent, in which case the union will need to address the issue."

A staff will occasionally get stuck with a lemon, and it's impossible to fire him – or her, in this case – unless she's bashing a kid over the head with a three-hole punch, and only then if it's her third offense, and only then if there are witnesses. The well-funded National Education Association and its affiliates excel at providing job security for its members, even the occasional lemon.

In many professions, if you hate your job, you can put your nose to the idiomatic grindstone and tough it out. Not so with teaching, and particularly not with junior high. Rookies will routinely arrive home at the end of a grueling day with chunks of flesh missing. And if a beginner exhibits fear while addressing a room full of 14-year-olds, they sense it in a matter of seconds and go straight for the jugular.

It ain't pretty.

Most teachers that are ill-suited to the profession figure it out early on, and they bail. A few – and thankfully it's very few – try to tough it out for 30 years, and they end up twisted and lonely like our very own Winnie De Waart. Gone was her c'mon-people-now-smile-on-your-brother sentiment left over from the sixties.

The previous year, teachers had every so often opened the staffroom fridge and found bites taken out of their lunches. Tuna sandwiches were known to disappear altogether. A cookie might have a bite taken out of it, leaving a crescent moon; another would be nibbled into the shape of a bunny's head. By April, lunches were being plundered on a daily basis.

Our VP spent one morning camped out in the courtyard bordering the staffroom. Crouched down among the mushrooms, azaleas and sword ferns, he kept the fridge under surveillance. During 3rd period, Winnie De Waart entered the staffroom and began reading the Herald. When no one had come or gone for five minutes, she jumped up, yanked open the fridge, rifled through a lunchbox, opened a baggie, took two bites of a sandwich, dropped it back in the box, slammed the door and sat back down.

Reuben Rapp timed her raid – eleven seconds! He leapt from his hiding place and confronted her.

"What of it?" she bristled through a mouthful of meatloaf and sourdough. With a telltale cluster of sprouts poking out the corner of her mouth, she couldn't very well deny his accusation.

Reuben said, "I expect you to buy lunch for the owner of that sandwich, and I want you to apologize."

Winnie opened her purse, took out three bucks and tossed them on the table. "Here. *You* get 'em a new lunch." She wiped a smear of mayonnaise off her upper lip and then stood up to leave.

Reuben persisted. "I expect you to apologize."

"Now why would I do that? Why?" She looked him up and down through slitted eyes and told him, "I'm not apologizing to nobody. No way, José. You push this, I'll call my union rep; I will. My word against yours. If I was you, I'd drop it."

Most of us didn't hear the story until that June, at our end-of-the-year party. As a rule, Reuben was tight-lipped about staff conflicts, but once he had downed a few gin and tonics, we didn't have to push very hard for the gory details. Besides, Winnie was circulating a version of the story herself, wherein our VP had inexplicably confiscated *her* lunch.

After Reuben's Morning Amongst the Ferns, there had been no more stolen bites from sandwiches and cookies, but we were stuck with Winnie De Waart until Reuben, or his eventual successor, could contrive a way to move her to another school. She had taught in the district for 21 years, and she would most likely be with us for another decade as she coasted into retirement. With the union behind her, she was all but invincible.

Students talk about teachers all the time, and it's easy to tell if their gripe is legit. One morning before school, I asked Teri Zu which was her favorite class.

"Art, definitely Art…. well, next to yours."

We both rolled our eyes.

"And your least fave?"

She didn't hesitate. "That would have to be science with

Misty Wart."

"And why's that?"

"Because I like to learn; all the slackers have to do is mention child abuse, and away she goes. We get a free day."

Before The Krabman could address Winnie de Waart's grievance, Betty Skibbitz cried, "My gun! Somebody stole it!" She dug frantically through the pockets of her jacket.

The Krabman's twitch shifted into overdrive. "You have a gun?"

"I confiscated a gun today, but it's...." She checked her pockets again. "It's gone! Call the police!"

Guns at Fernwater – the thought brought back some ugly memories. The year prior to Reuben Rapp's arrival, there had been a growing gang presence in the neighborhood. Kids brought knives to school, dances got cancelled because of rumors of rumbles, graffiti sullied the walls, and gang-bangers took what they wanted. My school was turning into a war zone.

During an assembly on Reuben's first day, he made it clear there'd be no gang colors worn at Fernwater. "Bandanas are out. Saggin' your pants – out. Gang signs are grounds for suspension."

Having come of age during the 70s, the so-called "Me Decade", when you were expected to "do your own thing", I initially cast a wary eye toward these new rules, as did many of my colleagues.

His first week at Fernwater, Reuben identified five gang leaders at our school, and he leaned on them: "Commit to being a student, or find yourself another school." Many parents considered him to be despotic, and kids hated the pudgy SOB. They were used to cuttin' deals in the VP's office, and they did not appreciate this new way of doing business. But after four months, parents and students alike realized two things: If they did battle with Reuben, they would lose; and he was fair. No question about it, there was a new sheriff in town. He didn't particularly care if some kid hated his guts; at least that was the vibe he cultivated.

The day before Reuben's first spring break, a group of staff met for LEMONADE at Beats Workin', and he regaled us with a story about one of our gang bangers:

"Jalen jacked Mr. Krabke's car today at lunch and headed

for the hills. I heard about the heist just before it was supposed to happen, from a kid Jalen beat up, and I took off in pursuit. Ten minutes later, The Krabman's car.... oops, I mean, *Krabke's* car.... oops, *Mister* Krabke's car ran out of gas, and Jalen took off on foot across a muddy field. I backed up, floored it, jumped a ditch, and played cat-and-mouse with this knucklehead until he collapsed in a heap three minutes later. For being such a tough guy, he's got no stamina, absolutely none. I loaded him into the back of my pick-up, brought him back to school and called the cops to haul him off to Juvy."

The story elicited applause and raucous laughter. Reuben stood and took a bow. He never again had to buy his own beer on after-school outings.

When another gang leader was expelled for selling drugs on campus a week later, the kid's mom sent him back to live with his dad in LA. The bangers at Fernwater got the message and straightened up, more or less. Reuben not only removed the gang presence from our school; he vanquished it from the neighborhood. Single-handedly.

The morning after our staff meeting, Reuben addressed our student body in the gym about his expectations for 4th quarter.

"Now, I want you all to focus on three things." He paused, and it was obvious, at least to me, that he was just gonna make up a bunch of stuff.

"Here's the first thing." He paused again, to glare at a kid who was not paying attention. Silence descended over the 700 students sitting in the bleachers. The poor kid finally got a poke in the ribs from his neighbor, and he shrunk down, hiding behind a girl's peacock hair.

"The first thing…. is that you need to…." I wondered how he would finish that sentence, and, I suspect, so did he. "…. excel in academics". He talked about doing homework and the need to focus.

"The second thing…. I expect you to…. treat one another with respect and kindness." He elaborated on that theme, and then asked, "Wanna hear me sing?"

The gym erupted! Boos rained down from the stands.

Reuben crooned into the microphone: "Strangers in the

night, exchanging glances, lovers at first sight...." Kids on the top row of the bleachers stood and gave him a thumbs-down. Our VP rested a hand lightly on his flabby chest and swayed grotesquely. "What were the chances we'd be sharing love, before the night was through...." The top row of students stomped their feet.

A dozen parents were present, and their thoughts were easy to read:

What is he *doing?*

He'll never get their attention back.

What a dipshit.

They had apparently never seen our VP at work. Abruptly he said, "May I have your attention?"

Silence, instantly. One kid was two seconds late sitting. Reuben fixed him with an icy stare, and the kid pleaded silently for mercy.

"The third thing.... I want you to.... be appreciative of your folks and all they do for you. It's not easy being a parent, and you need to thank them every chance you get." He talked about his own kids and how much they meant to him. Considering that he had made up the entire speech on the spot, it was a masterful performance.

As kids were leaving, Reuben pulled a few of us teachers aside, wearing his loony I've-got-the-best-story grin. "You will not believe this. You know that gun Betty Skibbitz confiscated? She didn't realize that it was a fake, a toy. She put it in her jacket and then laid it on the back of her chair. Some kid swiped the gun, and she forgot about it until the staff meeting."

We all cracked up and breathed a collective sigh of relief.

"Reuben," I said, "you enjoy this job a little bit too much."

"I know what you mean. Here; watch this." He snapped his fingers twice at a random kid and said sternly, "I want you to consider the consequences of what you did yesterday."

The kid's face registered confusion, then surprise, then more confusion, and finally guilt, all in the span of five seconds.

"Yes, Mr. Rapp," he said and quickened his pace. The second he was out of sight, we all broke up again.

I said, "You, sir, are a very sick man."

Chapter 21 – May

Though 1st period didn't start until 8:15, students begin trickling in at 7:30. Some came to ask for help with their homework. Some came to hang out. Anjuli, Gizmo, Calvin, and Teri Zu often showed up around 8:00. Some days they had stories or questions for me; other times they talked and whispered and giggled amongst themselves.

One morning Anjuli held out a Tupperware container to me. "My mom said you dropped a not-so-subtle hint at parent conference that you like Indian food. Pakistani food is different, but it's even better. "

I unsnapped the container and inhaled. "Yes! I love curry! Thank you! And thank your mom too!" I took another sniff and set it aside. "You get an A in Geometry." She had a 97% average. "Heck, so does your mom."

Teri Zu had been practicing impersonations. "OK, who's this?" She drew a breath and forced herself to calm down, then threw her shoulders back, leaned forward, and strode across the floor, chanting in a deep voice, "Go-o-o, Huskies!"

All present cried out, "Uncle Fester!"

I asked her to do it again. Geez Louise, she was getting good. This time she exaggerated Fester's long strides. Other kids entered, and we all shouted, "Again!"

I asked if she could imitate other teachers.

She said no, but Anjuli pressed her: "There's one other teacher you can do."

Teri Zu scowled, trying to hush her up.

I said, "C'mon, let's see it."

Calvin goaded her: "No way you can get out of it now."

"Mr. Haldini," said Anjuli, "a bunch of us were over at Calvin's yesterday, and Teri Zu did a killer impression of you."

"Me? *Me*? But I don't have any behavioral weirdities."

"Show him," said Anjuli. "Give him the bad news."

Teri Zu asked me, "Promise you won't get mad?"

"I promise." I held up the three fingers of my right hand, Boy Scout-style.

Teri leapt up and stood behind the podium. She bent forward, vigorously massaged her forehead with her left hand, ran it straight back through her hair, and yanked up her jeans with her right. In a Kermit-the-Frog voice, she said, "Geez Louise, you guys!" The dozen kids present had a good laugh at my expense.

"I don't do that!"

Several kids shouted, "Ohhhhhhhh, yes, you do!"

"Really? *Really?*"

Gizmo had been debating music with a couple of buddies. He asked, "Mr. Haldini, do you think any of the music we listen to today will still be around in a hundred years?"

"Good question. Songs usually survive because they have interesting, catchy melodies. Tell me a current song with a great melody."

"How about Pearl Jam?" asked Jaime. "They're so rad." He sang the beginning of *Even Flow* that was true to the original; not an easy feat, given the unusual intervals involved.

"I love that song," said Anjuli, and then turned to me. "But jazz standards don't necessarily have catchy melodies, at least not the way they're played; they wander all over the place. Maybe the music from our time that gets remembered will have a great rhythm or beat."

A kid with the crotch of his jeans sitting at mid-thigh weighed in: "If that's the case, Run DMC will be around for a long time." Had his pants drooped one inch lower, he would have drawn the VP's attention.

Teri Zu was vehement. "No, rap will be gone in five years. My uncle says hip-hop is today's bubble gum music, whatever that is. He calls it 'bubble rap'."

Calvin asked me, "Would you say that polka songs have great melodies?"

"I'd say they're catchy, in a pestilential kind of way."

In a pouty voice, Anjuli said, "Mr. Haldini, I have to get braces tomorrow."

This is how these morning gabfests tended to go, careening from one subject to another.

"Do this." I gave her an exaggerated grin. She bared her teeth, looking off to the side self-consciously. "Geez Louise, they look straight to me. How long you have to wear 'em?"

"Geez Louise, my orthodontist says two years."

I pulled a rusty old pair of pliers from my desk. "Tell you what, if you get tired of them before the two years are up…."

"Eeuuuww!" She crossed her index fingers until I put them away. "I think it's neat that Fester has braces," she said. "What I don't get is my dad – he got braces, but he's already married."

"Whaaat?" Her comment served as a reminder that Anjuli was still a kid, albeit a mature kid.

"Let me get this straight," I said. "The reason people get braces is to nab a mate? You have got to be kidding."

An angry parent burst through the door. "Nikolai is here?" He approached my desk, walking ape-like, with arms and legs moving in tandem. "He is in here?"

"No. Are you his father?"

"Yesss, I am father," he said in a thick Ukrainian accent. "Nikolai is not to come home last night." He leaned over my desk and wagged a hairy, knobby finger in my face. "He in your class at afternoon."

"He is in my *3rd* period class. If you check in the office…."

"Not to be true! He in your class at afternoon! I know he stay herrrre for last night."

Had he been afraid or showed concern for his kid's well-being, I could've understood. But the goof was angry. At me! And he had called me a liar, in front of my students! Heat spread up through my face, as that familiar refrain echoed through my skull: If you don't stand up….

I stood, with fists clenched.

"Not to happen in Ukraine!" he griped and turned to go.

"Well, then, why don't you go back there?" I said.

But he was already on his way out, ranting, "Schools degenerate much for America".

Nobody said anything for a good ten seconds. I was dumbfounded.

Gizmo came to the rescue. "Teri Zu, can you impersonate that guy*?*" I hoped that Nikolai's dad didn't hear us laughing.

"Mr. Haldini?" A soft-spoken boy from 2nd period stood

off to the side, waiting with an open math book. "Could you help me?" He was almost apologetic.

"Sure. What can I do for you?"

"I got a lot of wrong answers on last night's assignment."

"Let's have a look." I skimmed over his assignment, then wrote a quadratic equation on graph paper and handed it to him. "Show me how you'd graph this."

He drew x- and y-axes and started plotting points. His first was correct, but the second one was off; he squared -3 and got -9. I pointed out the error, and how to correct it.

"Oh, that's all there is to it?" He looked over the other problems he'd gotten wrong. "It'll be easy to fix these." On his way out, he smiled and called out, "Thanks, Haldini."

Watching him leave, I thought about how unfairly teenagers were portrayed in the press. Newspapers and TV at the time presented your average 14-year-old as a gun-totin', dope-tokin', illiterate, promiscuous moron. Compared to my own generation, these kids were, as a whole, more appreciative, more curious and more ambitious.

I was snatched from my reverie by Teri Zu, who had worked up an imitation of Nikolai's dad. She stood with arms folded, talking to an empty desk in a gruff, sing-songy voice. "Nikolai, I know t'day that you play tricks at me! I know for shuuur you hide maybe und'rneat desk!" Most of my class had arrived by now, and they were howling. "Don't make me get pissed off on you!" She lifted the desk and peered underneath. "Nikolai! How you can be disappear?"

Later that day, word got around that Nikolai *had* spent the night in the school, on a dare. He'd camped out in the cafeteria with his Discman and a backpack full of sodas and Ho Hos. His dad had spent the night calling Nikolai's friends and cruising the neighborhood, finally showing up at Fernwater at eight o'clock. Because my classroom was the first one you saw coming in the back door, I had borne the brunt of his anxiety.

I called Nikolai's dad that evening and apologized for not being more cooperative.

"Is OK," he said. "He come home right away today."

At that moment, I remembered that Nikolai *had* been in my

classroom the previous afternoon to pick up an assignment for a sick friend. I apologized again.

"Is OK. Boys are to be boys."

I made the mistake of telling him he had a great kid. He replied that Nikolai was a work-in-progress and then proceeded to denigrate him, listing faults I had never seen in the boy. I tuned out his harangue and sorted through my mail; it was all junk except for a postcard from Mom:

Leo, The Leaning Tower of Pisa is spectacular! It only leans at five degrees, but looks like it's ready to tip over. You know the photo of the villa we had hanging in our houses over the years? I saw it! The bougainvilleas are molto belle! Your dad has written you letters (6 at last count!) addressing your educational concerns. But he gets upset halfway through and rips them up. He always begins: Authority must be earned. This must be frustrating for you AND Mr. Krabke. Remember when he was your teacher? Well, of course you do. Try to be understanding. I get concerned when Gianni's feistiness comes out in you.

Love, Mom

If your typical American watched my Geometry class come spazzing into the room, it would confirm every horror story ever printed in newspapers about the decline of public education. These kids were loud. They were rowdy. Three boys were trash-talking about their exploits on the basketball court.

Kids called out, "Hey, Haldini!" and "Yo, Teacher-dude!"

And then there was Teri Zu, shrieking and laughing uncontrollably. When I gave her the evil eye, she giggled her way through an explanation. "I was talking to Anjuli, but I accidently spit out my retainer and it stuck in her hair!" She recovered her retainer, brushed it off and stuck it back in her mouth.

I said, "God knows what kind of critters are crawling around in your mouth right now."

Anjuli leapt to her feet and slugged me in the shoulder.

The bell rang, and miraculously, all 33 of these monsters transformed themselves into a group of scholars. Massaging my shoulder and baring my teeth at Anjuli, I addressed the class: "Our federal debt is approaching the five trillion dollar mark. If you're not bothered by that number, it's because you don't understand how big it is." I wrote 5,000,000,000,000 on the board.

They had questions:

"Why doesn't the government print more money?"

We talked a bit about inflation.

"Who do we owe the money to?"

We talked a bit about bonds, and I presented a simplified explanation of how banks work.

"How do we get out of debt?"

I encouraged them, upon reaching voting age, to elect people who would spend no more money than we take in.

"All right, enough economics," I said, and turned on my overhead projector:

Would five trillion dollar bills fit inside this classroom?

If they would, what fraction of my room would they fill?

If they wouldn't, how many classrooms would they fill?

We took a preliminary poll – some thought five trillion bills would fit, some thought they wouldn't, and some weren't yet ready to hazard a guess.

I continued, "This is due Monday. You need to show your calculations. Explain how you got your answer. I have to read 33 of these babies, and your job is to not make me crazy, so write legibly. Questions?"

Anjuli was frowning. "Do we have to come up with the exact answer?"

"Nope. You have to come up with a reasonable answer." That brought some disgruntled looks. I asked, "What would be a reasonable estimate for the height of this room?"

"Nine feet."

"Three meters."

"Three and a half meters."

"OK," I said. "Now give me unreasonable estimates."

"Six feet."

"Six meters."

"Six bags of apples."

There was still hesitation on faces. One kid griped, "But we'll get different answers."

"Right. You have to convince me that your answer is in the right ballpark."

Teri Zu asked, "Do you know the answer?"

"Nope. I'm not even going to come up with *an* answer until all papers are handed in. So feel free to ask questions, but don't ask if you're right, because I don't know. Other questions?"

Gizmo asked, "Should we use the metric system or standard?"

"Whichever you like. But which one is simpler? Which is better?"

Teri Zu said, "I think inches and feet are easier."

Calvin disagreed. "Once you get used to it, the metric system is way easier."

"OK," I said, "here's a story from when I was in 9th grade. But I'm warning you, I'm going to use an inappropriate word."

"Ooooooooooh," came their response.

"I am not using this word to make fun of people; I'm making fun of anybody dumb enough to use it. OK, here goes: When I was in 9th grade, I had Mr. Krabke for US History. He told us that every other industrialized country had, unwisely in his opinion, already switched to the metric system."

Anjuli said, "The Krabman used to teach?"

"Yes, Mr. *Krabke* used to teach." I then proceeded to tell them the responses from the J boys. Each response got a louder laugh than the previous one.

"Well, that only applies to foreign countries."

"Nuh-uh, what about Canada?"

"Canada's not a foreign country."

"Uh-huh, they're part of Russia."

"Yeah, and they're a bunch of fags."

They were skeptical, so I explained about open-concept schools.

Anjuli asked, "But how did anybody learn anything?"

"That's the point; a lot of them didn't. OK, let's talk about why the metric system is superior. How many inches in a foot?"

"Twelve."

"How many feet in a mile?" After a couple kids ventured incorrect guesses, I said, "There are 5280 feet in a mile. How many feet in 17 miles?"

Jaime said, "A lot?"

"Right. OK, watch: There are 1000 meters in a kilometer. How many meters are there in 17 kilometers?"

Everybody said 17,000.

"How many in liters in 17 kiloliters?"

Everybody said 17,000.

"How many grams in 17.3 kilograms?"

Most said 17,300. Somebody asked why we don't use the metric system.

Gizmo knew the answer. "Because Americans are lazy."

"Bingo," I said. "As a whole, Americans are intelligent, creative and generous, but when it comes to change, we are lazy."

Teri Zu asked, "How do we measure the thickness of a dollar bill?"

"Good question. And good luck answering it," I said smugly and then said to the class, "Here are meter sticks and yard sticks. Get started."

Over the course of the next few days, we spent five minutes at the beginning of class discussing The Five Trillion Dollar Question. We talked about volume formulas and whether or not to take into account the little jag in the back wall, which of course brought up the issue: How accurate do we have to be?

On day three, Teri Zu reported that she had visited a bank and asked a teller to measure the thickness of a stack of a hundred dollar bills. "She looked at me kinda funny," she said, "especially when I shoved a ruler under the bullet-proof glass."

A week later, we were all stunned to discover that 5,000,000,000,000 dollar bills would fill up 20,000 classrooms, give or take.

Gizmo visited me after school, saying, "Mr. Haldini, I have something to show you."

As part of his alternative grading system, I had assigned him a problem involving the Pythagorean Theorem, his first task being to find as many Pythagorean Triples as he could. One such triple is 5–12–13, because $5^2 + 12^2 = 13^2$. I then wanted him to see what patterns emerge.

He started writing numbers on the board. "Here are a few triples. I've underlined them."

$$\begin{array}{ccc}
\underline{3 \quad 4 \quad 5} & \underline{5 \quad 12 \quad 13} & \underline{7 \quad 24 \quad 25} \\
3^2 + 4^2 = 5^2 & 5^2 + 12^2 = 13^2 & 7^2 + 24^2 = 25^2 \\
9 + 16 = 25 & 25 + 144 = 169 & 49 + 576 = 676
\end{array}$$

"Here's one pattern," he said. "If you take the first number in each triple and square it, you get the sum of the other two. So, in the first triple, 3 4 5, if you square 3, you get 9, which is what you get if you add 4 + 5. And the algebraic formula for these triples is:

$$x \quad \frac{x^2-1}{2} \quad \frac{x^2+1}{2}$$

"Whoa! Does that always work?"

"No, it only works when the second and third numbers are consecutive. But here are some other Pythagorean Triples:"

6 8 10   8 15 17   15 36 39

"These have a different pattern; in the first case, 6 squared is 36; that equals *double* the sum of 8 and 10."

"And that works when?"

"When there's a difference of two between the second and third numbers."

I watched with mouth agape as he laid out increasingly complex patterns. He then wrote the algebraic formula that hooks the whole thing together.

I applauded and said, "Well freakin' done! Wow!"

Gizmo allowed himself a moment of pride.

Calvin entered and gave the board a once-over. "Pretty cool, huh?"

Seeing my confusion, Gizmo explained, "I showed him all this stuff yesterday. But this isn't the best part."

"You have more?"

"No, but Calvin does. Take it away."

"Haldini, you know how you told us the Greeks were the first to prove the Pythagorean Theorem?"

"Right."

"Well, that's not true." He stood there a moment with a

sloppy grin. "My uncle sent me this article." He handed me a page ripped out of *Scientific American.* "The Chinese figured out how to prove it 1000 years before the Greeks."

The article presented archaeological evidence that the Chinese had beaten the Greeks to the geometric punch. While I read, Calvin drew two squares on the chalkboard, with four same-sized triangles inside each.

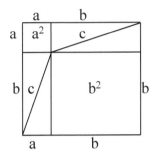 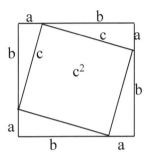

"Voila!" he said. "$a^2 + b^2 = c^2$."

Awestruck, I realized in a matter of seconds that it was a much simpler proof than the one the Greeks had devised. And it required no algebra to back it up – the diagram spoke for itself.

I asked, "Will you guys show this to our class tomorrow?"

Calvin smiled slyly. "What's it worth to ya?"

The school year was winding down, and I could almost smell summer. The clouds had finally parted, and each day the sun rose almost perceptibly higher in the sky. I had planned a month-long trip to East Africa, and couldn't wait to hit the road.

Still, there was a bittersweet quality to summer's approach. In a typical class, I figure that half the students enjoyed being there, and a few hated my guts, which left maybe a dozen that I was unable to read. But my 1st period class was special, and they knew it. *We* knew it. We were enjoying our time together, and that time was growing short. I felt privileged to work with this curious, diligent, sassy, kind, brilliant group of people.

Even at the time, I was acutely aware that *this* was the class teachers hope to have, at least once in their career.

Chapter 22 – June

"What is going onnnn?" Bootsy's mom wailed into the phone one morning. "I never thought I'd say this about my own daughter, but she's a.... a.... a bitch! What do I do?"

For the past two weeks, this cheerfully irreverent kid had been growling at the world

I said, "Eighth grade is a bear, isn't it? But whatever she's doing, unless she's drowning kittens or something, believe me, it's not uncommon."

"But, she's never been like this."

"Yeah, I've seen the change too. But she's smart and good-hearted; she'll pull out of it. I know it's hard, but whatever she's doing, you can't take it personally."

Easy for me to say; walking into 2nd period that day, Bootsy damn near bit my head off for saying hello. Before the bell rang to begin class, kids were kicking around career ideas for one another. I tossed in a few suggestions as well, some serious and some not.

Bootsy said, with attitude, "How about me, Haldini? Should I work in a PMS clinic?"

I froze; her question had trouble written all over it. I cycled through a progression of possible reactions, just like my dad would have done: Take offense? Scold her? Laugh it off? Yell?

But before I could respond, she cracked up and said, "Had ya goin'."

And just like *that*, she was back. It was as if she had consciously tried being someone else for a couple weeks, and decided she wanted no part of it.

"That was cruel, Bootsy!"

The bell rang and I opened class with this problem: "A farmer raises goats and chickens. He looks at his animals and counts 40 heads and 92 legs. How many chickens does he have?"

"Well, that's lame-o," said Jeremiah. "Why doesn't he just count the frickin' chickens?" Pleased with his rhyme, he repeated it with a giggle. "Frickin' chicken."

I shook my finger at him. "I'm warning you: You keep it up, I'm goin' home."

Two kids said, "See ya." Several others waved bye-bye.

Jeremiah challenged me with a dopey smile, saying, "Ooooooh, we wouldn't want thaaaat!"

I asked, "Do you know that 'Jeremiah was a Bullfrog' song?"

"I think so, yeah. That's an old geezer tune, right?"

"Right. We're callin' you 'Bullfrog' from now on, *if* that's OK with you. And if it's not OK, we're calling you that anyway. Deal?"

He spazzed out for three seconds, squirming wildly and waving his arms. "Deal!"

Many students tried a guess-and-check approach on the Frickin' Chicken problem. After a couple minutes I called on Bootsy to explain her solution.

She clomped up to the board in her big black boots, and wrote while she talked: "Since every animal has one head, we know the total number of animals is 40. So first I guessed 20 of each animal, but that would be 120 legs, which is too many, so we need more frickin' chickens. For my next try, I guessed 30 frickin' chickens and 10 goats...."

Two guesses later, she zeroed in on the correct answer.

"Well done. Anybody try it a different way?"

Dakota raised his hand. "It seems like you should be able to write equations, and I tried, but...." He held up a paper covered with seemingly random scribbles. ".... this is a mess."

"There is a way to solve this problem with equations. Here's a hint: Call the number of goats 'g' and the number of chickens 'c'."

A minute later, a kid said, "I have an equation: $c + g = 40$"

"I got that too," came a chorus of voices.

"Anybody get another equation?"

Robby Gibb raised his hand. "I'm not sure this is right, but.... $2c + 4g = 92$?" I looked at him with wonder. This was the spacey little kid who had not recognized me at Safeway.

"Well done." I high-fived him across the room, and he awkwardly but enthusiastically reciprocated. We talked about why his equation made sense; Robby offered up the observation that 2c represents the total number of chickens legs.

I wrote both equations on the board:

$$2c + 4g = 92$$
$$c + g = 40$$

Bullfrog suggested that we cut the top equation in half. "OK," I said, "Look at the two equations. What now?"

$$c + 2g = 46$$
$$c + g = 40$$

As usual, I called on the quietest kid with a raised hand.

"The equations are the same, except for the extra g in the first one. So g has to be 6."

"Good thinking. Here's a formal way of doing what you just did intuitively. I'm going to *subtract* the bottom equation from the top one. Like so."

$$(c + 2g = 46)$$
$$\underline{(c + g = 40)}$$
$$g = 6$$

We figured out there were 34 frickin' chickens and talked about why that method works. I gave them a similar problem, involving octopi and cows, with 13 mouths and 46 appendages.

A girl asked, "How many testicles on an octopus?"

Everyone laughed, except the girl.

I said, "For those of you who are zoologically confused, an octopus has eight *tentacles.*"

"What? Isn't that what I said?"

Giggling, the boy sitting behind her whispered in her ear.

"Ohmigod!" she squeaked, then buried her face in her hands and shook her head. She raised her head a minute later, but not before brushing her wavy brown hair over her face.

After they figured out the cow and octopus problem, I gave them one with birds and dragonflies, wings and eyes.

Near the end of class, I noticed Nikolai from 3rd period

standing unsurely in the doorway with one hand behind his back.

"You're early," I said.

He responded by handing me a withdrawal form.

"No!" I said. "Why?"

He and Lunchbox were my stars in Pre-alg.

"We're moving into Seattle."

"What if I refuse to sign this?"

He smiled, but didn't respond. Recalling his dad's early morning tirade a few weeks prior, it was hard to believe they were father and son. I asked if he was looking forward to this move.

"Not really." From behind his back, he brought out what looked like a cricket bat. He said, "Here, I made this for you in woodshop, in case a goonball ever gives you trouble." The words "STICK OF DOOM" were etched into the blade of the bat.

I hefted it and vowed to put it to good use.

"OK, gimme the damn form. Nikolai, you are a good man. I wish you well." My eyes were burning.

"You too."

He took the form, shook my hand and walked out the door. It happened so abruptly; there hadn't been time to say I'd miss him or to get his new address. And this was a year or so before email began to be widely used. Nikolai was gone.

I collected myself and said to the class, "Your homework tonight consists of one animal math problem. Who wants to be the hero or heroine?"

Several kids waved their hands. I said, "OK, here you go: Bootsy has a farm. And on this farm she had some bulls."

Several kids sang, "E-i-e-i-o."

"Right – Ol' McBootsy. She's raising bulls, unicorns, and flamingoes. And she counts 17 horns, 50 legs, and 20 mouths."

"Do flamingoes have mouths?"

"Yep. The question is this: How many of each animal does she have?"

When the bell rang, I was still dejected by the departure of Nikolai. I tried to cheer myself up by singing, "Ollll' McBootsy had a farm."

"E-i-e-i-o," came the response.

Bootsy sang back, "And on this farm she punched a geek, e-i-e-i-o." She and her buddies ran up and pummeled me. "With a punch punch here, and a punch punch there…."

Fending off their assault, I called out, "Hey! Somebody hand me my Stick of Doom!"

My 2nd period class had become an absolute jewel. After Jesse the Ipecac Kid got the boot, the atmosphere of the class had improved marginally. But when Gem moved away, the oppressive cloud hanging over our class lifted instantly.

I pictured her holding court in the cafeteria before school, her entourage looking to her for cues: What is funny? When do I laugh? Who can I talk to? That girl with the goofy red shoes? Yes, she's cool; they're phat. How about that skinny girl with the "boyfriend back east"? As if! She's so fugly; she needs a good stompin'.

Of course, Gem would generally leave the actual stompin' to someone else.

In 2nd period, her cues had been subtle, and her troublemaking under the radar, but Gem had definitely been the driver in my classroom. Many kids followed her lead, and not, I suspect, because she was a natural leader. Gem was just a bully. Still, she was a bully that I had falsely accused of cheating, and was now living on the other side of the continent.

On his way into class, I asked Dakota – aka Josh Jackson Jones Junior – if he played sports. He said he'd gone to a tennis clinic over spring break and planned to turn out in the fall. I mentioned that I used to coach tennis.

He squinted. "*You* coached? Uh, sorry, I didn't mean it that way. I mean, You *did*?"

"Nice recovery."

"Would you wanna play sometime?"

"Yeah, I'd give you a run for your money."

We played three times over the course of the next couple weeks. The first two times, I exploited his weak backhand and beat him handily. The third time, Dakota charged the net at every opportunity, daring me to drive it through him or lob it over his head. Tied six-all at the end of the set, we played a tie breaker, which he won four-two. I reached over the net and shook his hand.

"Nice game, dude."

"Thanks, but I got lucky.

"No, I played as well as I could, and you kicked my butt."

"Yeah, but you had the flu last week."

His efforts to explain away my mediocre play were endearing, though odd. Here I was, thinking Dakota could use a mentor, an uncle figure of sorts, and there he was, doing his best not to show me up. As he was busy cooking up excuses for me, I could not help wondering what it would be like to have Josh McClown for a dad.

The most gratifying aspect of teaching junior high is bearing witness to the profound transformations that kids undergo at that age. A student's maturation may be intellectual, social, emotional, artistic or physical in nature.

In September, the boy I dubbed "Whispering Snowflake" had been a skinny kid with oversized glasses, a humiliating case of acne and a spirit-crushing stutter. Now, nine months later, he had grown six inches, put on forty pounds of mostly beef, and was the star of Fernwater's track team. The glasses, zits, and stutter were gone, replaced with contacts, confidence and an easy laugh. He had also grown a full beard, to the amazement of his classmates. It was like having another adult in class. On the rare occasion when some kid was being a pain, he'd give him a knock-it-off look. As he left class one day, I was tempted to say: Hey, the staff is going out for lemonade after school. Wanna join us?

By contrast, the rest of my kids were just that – kids, and some were still little kids. At the end of class one day, I sat with my legs crossed at the front of the class, and Robby Gibb, who would have made a nice little 5th grader, asked, "Does Mr. Happy like it when you sit like that?"

I pulled him aside and told him that I would just as soon leave Mr. Happy out of class discussions. I then asked how his weekend was.

His bangs hung down almost to his nose. "Oh, perty good. I went over to my Uncle Jimbo's Saturday morning and we built a hovercraft. No, really. Me and Jimbo and my cousin Jasper made it out of plywood, Styrofoam, an old carpet, and parts of a vacuum cleaner." I could almost hear the Looney Tunes theme. He drew on the board as he talked: "We drilled holes in the plywood like so…. and attached Styrofoam to the bottom with fishing line.... The carpet was falling apart, so we…."

"Pack up your stuff!" I called out to the class.

"And thennnnnn…." Robby gave me a goonball smile as the bell rang. "We strapped my cousin Jasper onto a chair on the hovercraft, and tied it to my uncle's truck."

His tale brought to mind childhood fiascos in the Haldini family: One January I watched in horror as Ella and her sled vanished beneath a Greyhound bus. She slid out the other side unharmed, but for three seconds I thought sure we'd lost her. And I fell out of a Douglas fir from twenty feet high and walked away. But Geez Louise, we never tied our sleds to moving trucks or skydived out of trees!

Grimacing, I said, "And…."

"It worked!" he cried, but his triumphant smile faded instantly. "Well, it worked until Uncle Jimbo drove around a corner and the hovercraft hit a fence. Jasper went flyin'."

"Is he OK?"

"Oh, he's fine." His tone implied: Why wouldn't he be?

"Where was Jasper's mom when all of this was going on?"

Robby Gibb smiled sheepishly. "We wait 'til she's at work before we build stuff. Oh! She's flying down to California next month; we got plans to build a stun gun!"

Chapter 23 – July

My Pre-alg class was in shambles. This group that had started out so promisingly was limping toward the finish line. They were a highly transient bunch, even more so than usual. Several of my more successful students had moved away, their places taken by a collection of angry kids with spotty attendance. Once every few weeks, we'd have a full contingent of 17 kids in class; but the next day, ten might show. And the day after that, a different group of ten would come.

To make matters worse, because of our unusually snowy winter, make-up days took us well into summer. On July 1st, an 83 degree day, eight students came to class. Two sisters were visiting their grandparents in Mexico, one girl was crying in the counseling office, four kids were sick – at least that was their claim – and two boys were suspended for mooning a passing school bus. The driver was only able to provide "a partial description of the culprits, ho, ho, ho", but neighbors had watched the whole thing and were happy to provide Reuben with the boys' names.

Every ten minutes, Jesse the Ipecac Kid would snap a girl's bra or steal some kid's wallet or pop a zit in the direction of a classmate or…. or…. or…. But since acquiring a special ed label, and since he had not yet dismembered a classmate, my hands were tied.

Educators, politicians and scientists have debated for centuries about how best to handle the developmentally disabled, though in the 1800's, the more commonly applied labels were "idiots", "the feeble-minded", "mentally ill" and worse. At the time, these human beings were commonly housed in jails, reform schools and psychiatric institutions. They were often denied adequate food, basic hygiene and health care. It has only been in my lifetime that laws were written to insure that free education be provided for all children.

By the mid-1990s, the special ed debate boiled down to this: Some educators advocated placing SpEd students in self-contained classrooms and designing a curriculum commensurate with their cognitive abilities. Others advocated mainstreaming, i.e., placing most SpEd kids in a regular ed classroom, thereby providing them with stronger role models than they would otherwise encounter. Proponents of mainstreaming could quote research proving that slower students benefited from the presence of faster learners, but the sharper kids were not held back by their slower classmates. Uncle Fester maintained that the research is a load of hoo-haw, written by academics who had not set foot inside a primary or secondary school in decades. He feared that special ed might be the straw that breaks the back of public education.

Some argued that it was bad for a student's self-esteem to be placed in a SpEd classroom, and that debating point proved to be the factor that tipped the balance in favor of mainstreaming. According to Heidi Blohmeyer, kids were often mainstreamed in order to improve the self-esteem of parents, who no longer had to say: My son Jesse is in special ed.

Pinball, a good-natured, developmentally delayed kid, had a tough time adding single-digit numbers. I had little reason to believe he understood anything we studied, which could not have been good for his self-esteem. He was an outsider in a class full of outsiders. Nonetheless, I was expected to develop – or contrive, Fester would say – an individual grading scale for him.

For no reason – at least none that was discernible to me – Pinball would disrobe every so often and make a run for it. One morning during the last week of the school year, he began to unbutton, untie and unsnap his clothes.

"Pinball," I said calmly, "please stop,"

He whooped twice, leapt up, and hopped out the door, chanting, "I'm a kanga*woo*! I'm a kanga*woo*!"

Jesse shouted after him, "Hey Pinball, pull your head out!"

Pinball took off running and skipping down the hall. I gave chase, shouting, "Come back!" Off came his shirt.

"I'm gonna call your mom!" Off came a shoe.

"You're gonna get a detention!" Off came the other shoe, and he flung it at me, laughing.

"Your dad will be very unhappy with you!" He danced down the hall, while tugging on his zipper.

"I am going to call the President!"

Pinball stopped in mid-pirouette, and fixed me with a questioning look. Convinced that I was not bluffing, he collected his clothing, then sat down in the middle of the hall and got dressed. He returned to class and resumed his struggle with solving equations.

Upon our return, Brando called me over. "Mr. Haldini, did Ginny Klepto used to wear braces?"

"No, I don't think Ginny *Caletto* ever wore braces. Why do you ask?"

"Take a gander."

Ginny had a retainer stuck in her mouth at an odd angle, gamely trying to wrangle it into position with her tongue and a thumb. But no matter how she twisted her head or contorted her jaw, the retainer poked her in the cheek or gum or palate, causing her to flinch and grimace. If nothing else, I admired her tenacity. Afflicted with Fetal Alcohol Syndrome, Ginny Klepto would steal anything that wasn't nailed down: hats, money, chalk, retainer, you name it.

I approached her cautiously. "Hi Ginny."

She swallowed a mouthful of saliva. "Hi, Mither 'Aldidi."

"Whatcha got in your mouth?"

Another swallow, and a lopsided, drool-oozing smile. "Thad's by retaider."

"Oh? And when did you get your braces off?"

To buy herself time, she asked, "Huh?"

At that moment, Uncle Fester poked his head in the door and deadpanned, "Hey kids, free pony rides after school! Out by the Maypole!"

Ginny slobbered, "Mither 'Aldidi, where's our babe hole?"

Back in March, the stock market project had begun with great promise. My pre-alg kids were excited to see who was rakin' in the big money. But in early April, the Dow Jones, which had been climbing steadily, leveled off and took a nose dive, taking our project with it. Stocks lost value; students lost interest. I tried to convince them that this was part of the ebb and flow of the market.

Stocks would rebound, I told them, but it was a hard sell. By July, all but four students had misplaced their stock records.

Due to poor attendance, most students were playing catch-up; they were basically on a learn-at-your-own-rate program. I would present a five-minute lesson to the handful of regulars, and then move through the room, helping students on whichever assignment they were working, the problem being that I was outnumbered a dozen to one.

Help had come from an unexpected direction. 350-pound Brando had scored a 90% on his first test back in February, after being enrolled for one day. Because of health issues and poor attendance, he had been failing Algebra at his old school. Heidi Blohmeyer placed him in Pre-alg so that he could receive high school math credit for 2nd semester. Brando volunteered to tutor, and he made himself indispensable by explaining things in a kid-friendly way. He also learned a considerable amount in the process. Only ten of my original eighteen pre-alg students were left, and of the six that ended up passing, three of them credited Brando with their success.

Brando permanent impacted the way I taught. He figured out right away that if a kid knew his times tables up through 10 x 10, it was easy to teach him. Conversely, if a kid did not know those basic facts, he'd have trouble learning much of anything. And it was not simply a matter of handing the kid a calculator and saying: Here, multiply 7 x 9. It's crucial to know that 63 can be broken down into 7 x 9, something a calculator wouldn't tell you. Brando got five kids to construct times tables and then he talked me into allowing them to be used on tests.

The next year, on the first day of school, I identified which kids could not multiply 7 x 9 and then hooked them up with parent volunteers as tutors.

Unfortunately, Brando was still gaining weight, and he suffered a heart attack on July 3rd, the last day of school. When I visited him in the hospital the next day, he could tell I was upset at seeing him bedridden, so he entertained me with his Godfather impersonation. We had a good laugh and chatted for a while, but the second I left his room, I was blubbering like a baby.

Brando did not live to see his 15th birthday.

Jake the Invisible Boy and I were well into our second pitcher of beer at Beats Workin' when I happened to ask about his aunt and uncle's dairy farm.

"Still going strong." His speech was getting fuzzy, and something sinister rustled around behind his beery eyes. "Leo, I never told you why I was so hot to go live with them that summer. I had to get away from Johnny Boe and McClown. And Jeff too." Jake took a long swig. "People still wonder who pulled that fire alarm."

"Yeah?"

I wasn't sure I wanted to know what was coming next. When Jake had phoned me out of the blue and suggested we get a bite, I had no idea that he had a purpose for doing so.

He said, "That old man was driving along, minding his own business, and all of a sudden, BOOM! That fire truck mashed him flat." Jake struggled to bring my face into focus. "Johnny Boe told Jeff Mori to pull that alarm."

I imagined it all: Jeff following Johnny through the halls like a puppy, Johnny pointing at the alarm, saying, Go pull it, boy! Good dog! Yeah, that's it! Gooood puppy.

"But why?" I asked. "Why would Jeff do it?"

"At first he refused, but Johnny threatened to tell Steiffel that Jeff let the air out of The Krabman's tires – my handiwork, by the way. And Jeff, that dummy, he said he would."

Jake closed his eyes and the muscles around his mouth tensed, like they were trying to hold something in.

Finally he said, "I did it, Haldini. I pulled that alarm."

He's lying, I thought. But why would he do that? Ahhh, to protect Jeff. But looking into Jake's tortured eyes, it was obvious he was telling the truth.

"Why?" was all I could say.

"Because I knew Jeff would get caught if he did it. So I made him promise not to."

"Why was it so important to Johnny that somebody pull the alarm?"

"He had a test the next period, and he wasn't ready for it, meaning he hadn't gotten the answers from somebody in an earlier class. We evacuated the building, and he didn't have to take the test until the next day. Johnny aced it."

"Hold on; what are you talking about? You were with me that day. Remember? We were buying yearbooks."

"I could have been a career criminal, Leo. I'd have been very good at it." He closed his eyes again and gave a dozen small shakes of his head, like he was refusing to believe whatever reality he was reliving.

"Yeah," he said, "I bought a yearbook, at 11:59, one minute before 4th period started. I know the time, because I asked the secretary for a back-to-class pass in case I was late to Ol' Lady Skibbitz' class. That pass was my alibi, my Get Out Of Jail Free card. Skibbitz' room was close to the office, but I hustled my ass to the other side of school, pulled the alarm over there, and then hustled back and walked out with my class, making sure Skibbitz noticed me on the way out. Steiffel, the fire marshal, the cops, they never even questioned me. What would I be doing over where the alarm got pulled, so far from the office and my class?"

"Who else knows about this? Besides Jeff, I mean?"

He shook his head and drained his glass. "Mori doesn't know. I told him I'd talk to Johnny and tell him to get somebody else to do his dirty work. Mori protested, and I told him to shut his yapper, it's taken care of."

"So Johnny thought Mori did it?"

Jake chuckled. "Nope. When Mori came to class without the alarm being pulled, I hear that Johnny was royally pissed off. He was ready to rip Mori's head off, and that's when the alarm went off."

"So Johnny Boe never found out?"

"Right."

It was disturbing, being the only one to know. Why would he choose to tell me? Why *me*, a guy he'd had almost no contact with in more than a decade? But then I thought about my father, who regarded the people he knew when he was 14 as the finest, most honorable folks he'd ever known, and man, weren't those the days.

I felt honored and perplexed, as well as saddened by the knowledge that Jake had kept all this to himself for sixteen years, while carrying around the guilt for that old man's death. Jake the Invisible Boy had become Jake the Invisible Man.

But here was the question that took hold of me and would

not let go: What makes him think I won't turn him in? Does he trust me so much? Or is he tired of toting his grief around? Does he not care if I bust him?

That line of thinking lead to other questions I would have to answer: Should I turn him in? Would I? Why would I do so? Or, why would I not?

While all of this passed through my mind, Jake watched me silently, dispassionately.

"Why are telling me this?" I asked. "Why now?"

"I thought maybe you'd understand, you know, why I did it. You and me – we were the only ones that ever looked out for Mori."

That comment led us into talking about Jeff's "acid trip". I told Jake about running into McClown and what a total disaster he was. I talked about how McClown's kid was pretty cool, well, except for that little ipecac incident. Jake laughed himself silly over that one.

Jake the Invisible Man and I still get together at Beats Workin' once or twice a year, but the subject of fire alarms never comes up.

Chapter 24 – August

As do many teachers, I suffered from RANS – Recurring August Nightmare Syndrome. It flared up in midsummer for two or three weeks, and then lay dormant for eleven months. My RAN typically plays like this:

It's the first day of school. I am late to 1st period because I cannot find my room. When I arrive thirty minutes late without lesson plans or shoes, I realize that no books were ordered for my forty students, most of whom are named Jerry, Jeff and Jebediah. Three administrators are observing me.

It probably goes without saying that my fly is down.

"Those of you who worked on setting academic standards four years ago will be pleased to hear that we are ready to take them to the next level." This was our first day back, and The Krabman was positively giddy at the prospect of implementing a new district program.

Winnie De Waart eyed our principal with unbridled hostility. "New standards? Again? Is the union aware of this?"

She had a point; this would be the third set of standards we had endured in five years. I looked around the library; would the troops rise up against this madness?

The Krabman, however, was not concerned in the least, having discovered that by softening up the staff with maple bars, blueberry muffins and the like, we'd swallow anything. Trays of pastries had been placed strategically throughout the library.

"New standards?" Betty Skibbitz screeched. "I remember back when Eisenhower was president; the Soviets had just launched Sputnik...." The Krabman picked up a tray of pastries and waved it seductively under her nose. "....and Ike was very concerned...." Stopping mid-sentence, Betty daintily picked out a cinnamon roll and nibbled off a bit of icing.

"Referring to your hand-out...." The Krabman rubbed his

hands together, like we were now in for a real treat. "…. you'll see the timeline for implementation of the new statewide assessment."

"Why can't they just call it a 'test'?" I grumbled to Uncle Fester, who finished off his cherry cheese danish and wiped a bit of red goop from his upper lip.

"Madness comes, madness goes," he replied.

It was good to see him and the rest of the staff after a two-month lay-off. Everyone had their stories to tell, and my safari photo album elicited oohs and aahs. But after sitting through three hours of meetings, summer was a fast-fading dream. Still, I looked forward to the day after Labor Day.

The Krabman said, "This assessment will be based on state standards, so they will be a vast improvement over standardized tests of the past. And then…." The Krabman lives for moments like these: "…. the OSPI will scrap our SLO's, whereupon the WSCSL will be developing GLE's and EALR's for K-12."

Heidi Blohmeyer asked him to translate.

The Krabman grinned and took a breath before speaking. "The Office of Superintendent of Public Instruction has directed districts to discard their Student Learning Objectives; the Washington State Commission on Student Learning will establish Grade Level Expectations and Essential Academic Learning Requirements for Kindergarten through 12th grade."

"Oh joy!" whispered Fester. "Have you noticed the shelf-life of educational acronyms is getting shorter? Once they lose that new-car smell, they're dumped like a year-old DeLorean."

"But this gives me hope," I whispered back. "Maybe if we adopt statewide standards, districts will quit floundering around, trying to come up with their own every few years."

"But the Commission on Student Learning is comprised of business leaders, like Warren Hamilton and his fat cat pals; he wants to make sure he's got enough computer geeks to fill up the labs in his "campus" up there on the plateau. There's not one teacher on the commission; no students either." On his hand-out Fester wrote: Wrong tern. He said, "Leo, can you snag me that donut with the…. no, to your left…. yeah, the one with the little orange sprinkles. Thanks."

"Still, if there is just *one test* for everyone, maybe we can stop re-inventing the wheel every few years. I'm hopeful."

"Well now," said Fester, "listen to Mr. Sunshine."

Back in my classroom, I counted textbooks and dug out lesson plans. If every minute of the first week was planned out, the rest of the year should be a breeze. I cranked up a tape of various artists, and said aloud, "Let's get 'er done."

"You know what they say about people who talk to themselves." I flinched and turned toward the door. Teri Zu had just entered, and she flung herself at me.

I set her back on the floor and said, "You know what they say about people who hear voices. How are you?"

"Good! We have a surprise for you!"

"We?"

"Anjuli and Calvin will be here in a minute."

"No Gizmo?"

She shook her head. "He and Calvin had a falling out. They both have it bad for Anj."

Anjuli and Calvin entered, singing "Happy Birthday". She laid a box on my desk and gave me a hug. "Mr. Haldini, you're 31 today, right? We made you a little something."

Calvin took the lid off the box and lifted out a square-shaped pie. On top they'd written in green icing "πr^2", referencing that lame old joke about the formula for the area of a circle: pie aren't square, pie are round. I cracked up, and it grew into one of those laughs where I had trouble breathing. The three of them were delighted with the prospect of me passing out.

"Look! This is for your Wall of Fame." Teri Zu handed me a photograph of the pie surrounded by all three of their faces. "So you don't forget us."

"Oh, I think there's very little chance of that. Thank you!"

"I hope you like blackberries," said Calvin.

"Love 'em!" I dug up paper plates and plastic knives. I served up the pie, mangling it in the process. We began eating it by balancing tiny bites on the knife blades, but soon gave up on that method. We resorted to holding the plates up to our mouths and shoveling the pie in. We listened to tunes as we ate.

Anjuli asked. "Is this your songwriter buddy?"

"That's him." Over a finger-picked electric guitar, Carl sang in falsetto:

Human heart, fragile in design
With agile mind, we chase away the gloom

"I like this," said Anjuli. "Does your songwriter buddy have a name?" My mouth being full of pie, I shook my head. "His rhymes are clever," she said. "I like this a lot."

I swallowed and said, "Me too. Hey, I'm going to miss you guys; I hope you know that."

Teri Zu responded right away. "No, you won't, because we'll come visit."

"Good. I'd like to see what you're all doing in ten years."

"Ten years?" said Calvin. "Will you still be alive?"

Teri Zu came to my defense. "C'mon, he's not that old. His hair isn't *all* gray."

Anjuli said, "You mean that shrubbery growing out of his ears?"

"All right, all right," I said. "What say we have a Be Nice To Your Teacher Day? What did you guys do this summer?"

"Worked at my dad's restaurant," said Teri Zu. "Mostly in the kitchen, but sometimes I got to do the bookkeeping."

Anjuli bumped her hip against Calvin's. "Your turn."

"I played guitar and babysat my three-year-old cousins."

"Nice kids or brats?"

"Haldini, it's weird! They're identical twins. Identical! If I brought them in here, you couldn't tell them apart, except that Mac is the nicest kid ever, and Jerome's a holy terror. When I make them sandwiches, Mac eats his. But Jerome takes his apart, eats one bite of bologna, then flings it against the wall to see if it'll stick. He rubs mustard all over his face, then rolls the bread up in a ball and chucks it at the dog. Haldini, how can they be that different?"

"Yep, that's weird, all right." I resisted the temptation to tell him my own experiences with J Boys. "How about another round.... um.... square, of pie?" I divvied up the last of it.

Anjuli asked, "Haldini, you went on a safari?"

Teri Zu was appalled. "You.... shot lions, and.... zebras?"

"No no, it was a photographic safari. It was the most beautiful thing I've ever seen."

Anjuli said, "I'm so jealous."

"Well, you got to go to California, didn't you?"

"We rented an RV and took an MFV – Mandatory Family Vacation – down the coast." Anjuli folded her arms and pouted. "Guess who had to take care of the mutants."

Though she loved her four younger siblings dearly, she felt overwhelmed by their presence and burdened by her responsibility for them.

"Your sis did her share of baby-sitting, didn't she?"

"No! Miss Kali, that skank, got a job, just in time to get out of going! And get this, the Torres family had such a glorious time, we're doing the same trip next year." She then brightened and said, "But I got my learner's permit last month. I got to do some of the driving."

"You learned to drive in an RV?"

"Don't tell my mom, but Grandma's been letting me drive for the last year."

"How are your parents getting along? Are they…?" How careless of me. I was tempted to slap myself silly.

"It's OK; these guys know what's going on. I still have hope, but keepin' the fam together seems like a long shot."

"Sorry to hear that."

"Yeah. Hey, you want me to send you a postcard next summer?"

"I would. Maybe from the Redwoods. You can let me know if one of the mutants accidentally gets eaten by a bear."

"Or if they accidentally eat poisonous berries." Rubbing her hands together, she let loose a wicked cackle and contorted her face into the essence of evil. "Gee, I hope none of them fall out of the RV at 70 miles an hour."

"You are a sick woman," I said.

"Guilty as charged," said Anjuli.

The pie was gone, and Teri Zu said, through berry-stained lips, "We have to take off now. This is sign-up day for cross country. Have a great year, Mr. Haldini."

"Thank you, thank you, thank you," I said to each of them. "I have the best job in the world, and you are the reason why.

Part III: 2003

Chapter 25 – September

When a company like Boeing develops a mission statement, I imagine a few middle-aged, middle management guys get together and hammer it out over lunch and whiskey sours:

> People working together as one global
> company for Aerospace leadership

It's not even a complete sentence, which is of no concern, because nobody, nobody, *nobody* at Boeing gives a hot patootie about mission statements; they've got jumbo jets to build.

Not so in education.

Today is the first Tuesday in September, and we held our third of seven sessions, spread out over 18 months, dedicated to concocting a concise, grammatically correct statement of the collective aspirations of our district's teachers, administrators, secretaries and custodial staff. Consensus, or at least the appearance of such, is valued above all else. Heading up the project is Dr. Krabke, our Chief Academic Director, and yes, he is widely referred to as our CAD. Tired of having his cutting-edge proposals undermined by "an uppity staff and myopic parents", he obtained his doctorate in something called "Systemic Reform of 21st Century Educational Paradigms", earning him a comfy position at The Head Shed, as the admin center is known across the district. Those of us who work here, except for The Big Wigs on the third floor, refer to it as Crazy Town.

"I would like to thank everyone for being on time." That was The Krabman's way of spotlighting the principal and two teachers who strolled in late. Accompanying that wicked twitch he acquired a quarter century ago, he now blinks furiously when speaking to a group. But whereas his cheek twitches in waltz time, he blinks with a two-count, resulting in a syncopated groove, an erratic mambo, known as The Krambo: *Twitch* twitchy twitch, *twitch*, twitchy twitch.

The Krabman began, "Research shows...."

Those two words sound harmless enough, right? But they often portend that all present will soon be forced to make an excruciating decision: Either challenge his assertion and then wade through the mountains of drivel that purportedly shore up his position; or concede the point and hope that no serious damage is done, like having the board decide that open-concept schools are the key to raising test scores.

"Research shows," he was saying, "that districts with clearly formulated mission statements outperform those districts lacking them. Every member of our district should be guided and inspirationalized by our mission statement."

Inspirationalized? Geez Louise. How did I get here?

This being the day after Labor Day, I should be feeling excited and anxious about meeting my five classes, my 150-or-so smart and curious and unmotivated and irreverent and kind students who were going to impress me and challenge me and learn with me and make my life complicated and crazy and fulfilling for the next ten months.

Instead, I am beginning my third year at Crazy Town. In June, I was offered the position of Chief Instructional Supervisor, along with a modest raise. Carl Martin, my songwriter buddy and now my boss, had scowled at my prospective title. "CIS? What kind of a worthless acronym is that?" But he then popped his head into my cubicle ten minutes later and said, "ChInSu – think of yourself as an educational martial artist, battling the Forces of Boneheadedness."

I will be assessing curricular materials, and then making recommendations to the Executive Council. I am currently working on a "Going Metric" proposal, with the intent of enacting a solely metric curriculum in the district next year. I will also be overseeing first-year teachers. Carl, as Director Of Curriculum, will oversee me; and yes, I sometimes referred to him as DOC.

Carl enticed me to come work at Crazy Town two years ago. "C'mon, it'll be fun," he'd said. "You and me, we'll be leading the charge. Teachers are buried to their butts in busy work; that's gotta change. And those asinine special ed policies? Gotta go."

Carl was effusive in his praise of my work. "Leo, I want to take what you do in a classroom and spread it around. Don't be selfish."

His offer was tempting. For years I had railed against inane district policies; at one point we actually changed from an A-B-C-D-F grading system to a 1-2-3-4 scale, the thinking being that numeric scores provided a less subjective measure of student learning. The problem came when students transferred to another district or applied to college, and we had to reconvert those number grades back into letters.

Crazy.

So if I decided to take a job at the Head Shed; it would be my opportunity to Take A Stand. Of course, I was blowing out of proportion the impact I would make in an entry level position. Still, my mindset was that I would Make A Difference, and in a small district like ours, maybe I could.

But.... but.... but I loved teaching. It had been frustrating, yes, but most afternoons I walked out of school with a joyous sense of accomplishment.

When I told my father that I planned on turning down Carl's offer, he had replied, "It would be foolhardy not to take it. Being a school teacher, now, that's all well and good, but writing the rules, developing policy, that's where the real power lies. Son, when I was growing up in Italy...."

Between my dad's prodding, Carl Martin's flattery, and the prospect of taking shelter from the ever-increasing avalanche of busywork and classroom distractions heaped upon teachers by the 3 P's – Politicians, Principals and Parents – I made the move to Crazy Town.

Though The Krabman is overseeing the Mission Statement

Project, the meetings are run by Penny Prismark, my fellow Fernwater alum, though she now goes by Penelope, a name that, in the words of Dr. Krabke, "tends to strike the ear as more empowermentalizing". While still teaching fulltime, she is also working toward obtaining her administrative credentials. A year ago, she expressed an interest in working in the "stimulating environment of Dr. Krabke's visionary directorship", and he agreed to mentor her.

Penelope began, "The purpose of our last meeting, like, was to, identify the responsibilities and goals of educators. I then combined responses that were similar, and I was all, like, Wow!" Smiling like Catherine Zeta-Jones auditioning for a toothpaste commercial, she passed around hand-outs. "Now, after you read through these, I am going to have you, like, get in groups of four and put stars by the responses your group thinks are, like, most relevant."

Penelope outlined our five-step process for generating a, like, rough draft of our mission statement. Halfway through the third step, Carl leaned over and whispered, "Step four better be, like, going out for beer."

I hoped for his sake that The Krabman hadn't heard him, but one look at that sourpuss left no doubt that he had. It was 8:07 a.m. and I wanted to, like, stab myself in the eye with a number two pencil.

As perky as ever, Penelope brings to mind Brutus III, my dad's cocker spaniel. In an effort to "re-professionalize" herself, she has traded in her floral print blouses for polyester pantsuits. When she showed up at the district office last year, I had not seen her since high school, and she immediately launched into a year-by-year, malady-by-malady, seemingly meal-by-meal account of the past twenty years:

".... and I taught 4th grade for, like, 15 years, but my doctor advised me to, like, change careers before – in her words – that peptic ulcer chews right through your stomach wall, and for goodness sakes, lay off those chimichangas, but my husband, he's, like, our night custodian here.... Well, you remember Johnny Boe! We met up at our 20-year reunion. He's, like, really a sweetheart, and, boy, does he love his Mexican food...."

At our first break, I was still reeling at the thought of Penelope Prismark marrying an ex-con – especially one named Johnny Boe – when Carl tapped me on the arm.

"What's up, DOC?"

He slid a piece of paper in front of me. "Whattaya think?"

Mission statement: Our school district is committed to developing an onsite decision-making model that will facilitate a paradigm shift toward the empowerment of various educational constituencies, implementation of world class standards and the actualization of a global, interdisciplinary framework, thereby bringing about a fundamental systemic reform and circumventing those coalitions whose sole aim is to preserve the pedagogic status quo.

"Don't let The Krabman see this," I giggled. "It'll give him a hard-on."

I felt hands on my shoulders and turned to find Penelope reading Carl's statement. I thought we were busted for sure, but she gushed, "That is like, totally awesome! I can't believe you wrote that in…. what, like, five minutes? Gold stars for you both!"

Carl was not, like, smiling.

By midmorning, Penelope put up a rough draft on the overhead:

Our schools provide a challenging, safe environment that guarantee the success of every student. Employees honor the cultural diversity of our supportive community, thereby fostering a healthy self-esteem in every student, each of whom we value as an individual. Motivation and retention are enhanced by relevance and pervasive caring.

And now began the madness. Get a bunch of educators together to edit a document, and our neuroses come gushing forth – we have a deep-seated, aberrant need to refine, revise, rehash and rephrase. Teachers love to edit. Teachers live to edit. Even those who profess that mission statements have no more redeemable value than a cold sore will jump headlong into the fray.

A brief sampling:

"Shouldn't that first sentence begin, 'Our schools *will* provide....'?"

"Or should it be '*Each* school will provide....'?"

"I think it should be '*Every* school will provide....' After all, this applies to *all* of us."

"The word 'will' implies that this is something that we *will do* in the future; leave it out."

"But the word 'will' also implies 'volition' and 'commitment', so we should keep it."

"There is a noun-verb mismatch in that first sentence. 'Schools' is plural, 'environment' is singular, and 'guarantee' is plural.

Let's see, $40/hour x 8 hours/day x 7 days x 25 people.... That's $56,000 to craft a document that nobody will ever look at. Most of my colleagues would be displeased with me for saying so, but this exercise reinforced my belief that public education is awash in money. We piss it away on mission statements, testing, special ed paperwork and administration.

What would my father do if he were here? I can't imagine he'd be sitting here as meekly as I, whining to myself. An image coalesced in my mind, of Dad playing Al Pacino's role of the blind retired soldier in Scent of a Woman, where he bellows from the witness stand, "I oughta take a flame-thrower to this place!" Then Dad, like the soldier, would revert to his glassy-eyed stare, focused on a faraway shadow with poorly defined boundaries.

It bugged me that I wasn't teaching somewhere exotic, Peru or Portugal. And it was odd that neither Penny nor any of my junior high buddies had moved away, as if there was an impenetrable energy field encircling Oxley; hadn't I seen all of this on an old episode of The Twilight Zone? Johnny Boe had gotten out of town by going to prison, but upon his release, an irresistible force snatched him right back here.

Carl leaned over and whispered, "You thinking what I'm thinking?"

"Depends. Are you thinking we should scare up a bottle of bourbon and a pair of scantily clad Filipino women?"

He faked a coughing fit to cover his laughter. I tuned back

in; the group was still debating that first sentence of our mission statement:

"Shouldn't it be 'safe, challenging, *healthy* environment'?"

"Oooooh, I like that!"

"But maybe the word 'healthy' should be placed ahead of 'challenging'."

"But if a school is healthy, it will also be safe, so let's *replace* 'safe' with 'healthy'."

The wordsmithing on that first sentence went on for 35 minutes before Carl raised a concern of substance: "Are we really going to *guarantee* the success of every student?"

Everyone read through the mission statement silently, and then a buzz of voices arose.

The Krabman shushed us and responded with a question of his own. "Are you suggesting that we don't want every student to succeed?"

"Of course not, but we can't guarantee every kid's success. We can encourage, we can inspire and sweet talk, but we can't force kids to think and do homework."

Penelope Prismark jumped in. "Students need to be held accountable. And teachers, like, should also be accountable."

"But legally speaking," said Carl, "if we guarantee success for every student, aren't we opening ourselves up to lawsuits?"

That buzz arose again, louder this time.

Prior to this moment, I had considered our mission statement project to be a colossal waste of time and money, but now I began to grasp its destructive potential. To avoid endless litigation, would we lower our standards? If so, by how much? In which courses and grade levels would we lower them? Or would some teachers lower standards when nobody's looking? Our mission statement might become a policy that could not be ignored, but there would be incentive to work around it.

"And how would we define success?" asked Carl. "Does 'success' equate to 'passing the WASL'? If so, how would we guarantee that every kid passes?"

Buzzzzzz.

Carl had a point. A student arriving in the US today from, oh say, Iran, speaking Farsi, will not be exempted from taking the WASL. Would we really guarantee her success? A decade ago, such a girl would have been welcomed at Fernwater and viewed as an asset, enriching and augmenting our ethnic mix.

But now? If we had to guarantee her success?

Bonnie Rhodes, a statuesque black principal from Alabama, cleared her throat loudly and deliberately. Every mouth in the room slammed shut. Her school, located in an affluent neighborhood, has the highest standardized test scores in the district, awarding her voice a considerable amount of credence.

"As educators," she said, "we must summon the courage and resolve to guarantee to our students, to the community, to each other, and most importantly, to ourselves, the success of each child in his or her quest for knowledge." She sermonized slowly and forcefully, as if we'd all be going off to fight The Battle of Armageddon after lunch. "If we are planning, ahead of time, for the failure of any of these children that have been placed in our care, then we are not discharging our duties in a responsible, professional manner."

The Krabman gave a little fist pump. "Well said, Mrs. Rhodes!" Recalling the day he cut 25 kids loose in 9th grade history, his enthusiasm struck me as ironic.

Penelope gazed at Bonnie with admiration. "I, like, totally agree." She turned back to us and said, "Now, your task is to, like, present this draft to the staff at your school, and then, like…."

But the teachers were not done editing that first sentence:

"We want our schools to be challenging, but not overly so. We don't want kids to feel…. oh, what word am I looking for?"

"Disenfranchised?"

"Overwhelmed? Threatened?"

"Horny?"

Bonnie Rhodes and I were the only ones that heard Carl say it. She gave him a yer-gonna-burn-fer-that-one look.

Chapter 26 – October

Every year or so, when Anjuli comes back to town, we get together for lunch or a beer or a hike in the Cascades. She called a few days ago and said, "I have a question for you."

Today I waited for her at an Italian restaurant in a recently constructed urban village down the road from her parents' house. The motley collection of trendy shops and tacky condos had been painted an eyeball-jarring amalgam of mauve, mustard and brick red. But it was a pleasant fall day, 65 degrees at noon, and I took a seat outdoors. I spotted her coming a block away. She had gained a few pounds and wore less make-up, and she projected, what, confidence? No, she's always had her fair share of that; she now seems almost cocky in the way she navigates the world. I greeted her with a quick hug and asked how she was.

"I finally got my degree – microbiology from U Mich – and I'm working in a lab. And I'm driving an ambulance on weekends.

"Congratulations."

"How about you?"

"Nothing that exciting. Guitars, gardening and going nuts at work."

"Two of three ain't bad. What's going on at work?"

"I'm losing faith in public education. Here's what I mean: A decade ago, business leaders were howling about the shortage of engineers and programmers. So we should have taken steps to increase enrollment in those fields by, say, 10%. Instead, we passed a law requiring all students to take more math and science."

"Doesn't that water down the curriculum?"

"Exactly."

How depressing; it had taken her all of ten seconds to see the problem. I asked about the mutants.

"Mini Mutant is a sevie at Fernwater – can you believe it?"

"The last Torres, the end of an era." The waitress took our order, and then I asked, "So, Anj, you have a question?"

"You are not going to believe this. For my birthday, my grandma, my mom's mom, is giving me a month-long trip, anywhere in the world. My question is: Where should I go?"

Anjuli had acquired a taste for travelling in her teens. She spent midwinter break of her sophomore year building homes in Haiti, and the next year she lived in Madrid for five months as an exchange student. While attending the U Dub, a category four hurricane laid waste to a good deal of Central America's population, infrastructure and farmland. She and her uncle flew down to his native Costa Rica and signed on as volunteers with a relief agency. Her mother had not been pleased, especially when Anjuli decided to stay for a year. Her letters detailed the damage from floods and winds. She also told of harrowing adventures, at one point riding on top of a train through the Andes. Upon returning, she spent two years living with her grandma in Detroit, working as a teacher's assistant in a poor neighborhood.

I whistled. "Now that's what I call a birthday present. Have you thought about where you want to go?"

"I've travelled around Central and South America. I want to go someplace different."

"If you're looking for 'different', go to India. Different food, different clothes, different beliefs; it even smells different."

"Is that a good thing?"

"Yeah, well, mostly."

"Tell me all of the places you've been."

Most guys probably wouldn't notice Anjuli walking down the street, but the second she opens her mouth, many of those same guys would think she's a knock-out. She exudes vitality, and when she listens, she is *present*. One of her professors, in a state of romantic agitation, advised Anjuli to "Get married, the sooner the better; enough hearts have been needlessly broken." I've met some of her boyfriends over the years; she tends to seesaw back and forth between accountants and bungee-jumping alligator wrestlers.

I said, "I stayed in a Tibetan monastery in Nepal where a guy from Idaho paid monks a quarter a day to quarry granite and build him a house." She leaned forward and focused those huge eyes on me. I could see how she'd made those college boys come unhinged. "I camped in the Amazon, laid on the beach in Rio, and

I've been to Europe. Then I spent a month in East Africa."

"Which trip would you say was life-changing?"

See, that's why I like this kid; she's a great question-asker. Although, being in her mid-20's now, she's not really a kid anymore.

"Well, I probably *saw* the most in Europe – you've got all that art and history staring you in the face. And Asia *taught* me the most, in terms of seeing how different, how fresh and heart-breaking life can be, and the people I met, for the most part, were kind and welcoming. But life-changing? Africa."

"Why is that?"

"I went on a safari, which is a pretty touristy thing to do, but the savannah is intense; it's beautiful, violent, heart-wrenching. I saw life as it's meant to be lived." I hesitated. Anjuli watched me with her wide-set, wide-open dark eyes, and I decided to give it a try: "I saw something idyllic and disturbing, wild and pure. It felt like being healed." Embarrassed, I paused. "This is really hard to talk about. I sound like a religious nut. But there you have it; I was.... ecstatic."

She nodded. "Any advice?"

"Keep your eyes open. Keep your mind open. Keep a journal. "

"Did you keep a journal?"

"Yeah, I have ever since 9th grade. Remember Uncle Fester? He told me it was good habit to get into."

The next evening, my phone rang during Letterman's monologue. "Hello?"

"I did it!" Anjuli never bothered to say who was calling. "I booked my trip to Kenya!

"Boy, you don't mess around."

"I'm leaving in three weeks."

"I'm so jealous! What did your folks have to say?"

"Dad's OK with it, but Mom's not too pleased. Grandma tried to calm her down, but she thinks I'll get blown up by.... oh, who knows? Al Queda. Oh, and I'll warn you, next time you see Mom, she's not too pleased with you."

"Whaaaat?"

I first met her mother a decade ago; she's polite, smart and considerably less adventurous than either her mother or daughter, both of whom make her nervous.

Anjuli laughed and said, "I heard Mom tell her neighbor, 'Damn Haldini! Sending my daughter off to Africa!'"

Part of my job is to mentor first-year teachers. Today I observed an 8th grade class at Oxley Junior High, taught by an exhausted young brunette. Smiley but stern, she collected a mound of homework from her 6th period class and placed it next to four other mounds. She arranged students into groups of four, with no more than one screwball per foursome, a variation on my divide-and-conquer approach.

The lesson involved finding the value of π. To each group, she handed out string, a calculator and a variety of cylinders and discs – soup cans, buckets, Frisbees, tennis ball cans, etc. She passed out meter sticks – rather than yard sticks, which pleased me greatly – along with the admonishment, "No sword fights."

Students were instructed to measure the circumference and diameter of each object, and divide the two numbers. Considering she's a rookie, it was a smoothly run operation. Most kids were focused, and she bustled from one group to the next, cajoling, clarifying, and riding herd on one kid who had apparently watched a lot of Elmer Fudd growing up.

"Be vewy, vewy quiet!" he kept yelling to buddies on the other side of the room. "We're hunting wabbits!"

"Jadolf," said the teacher patiently, "please use your inside voice."

Jadolf – are ya kidding me? *Jadolf?*

"I'll twy!" he called out. "Weally I will!"

The assignment out of the book focused more on writing than calculation or applications. After kids figured out the circumference formula, $C = 2\pi r$, they were asked to explain how they would go about calculating circumference, an unwieldy task that, to my way of thinking, the formula renders unnecessary. But such is life since implementation of the WASL and passage of NCLB.

Leafing through their textbook, I came across these instructions: If you have a question, ask your teacher; sometimes he or she might be able to assist you in ways that have not occurred to you.

The implication is that students, for the most part, need to figure all this stuff out on their own. The word "sometimes" and "might" did not sit well with me either. I pointed out those instructions to the teacher, and asked if they bothered her.

"Not at all," came her confident response. "My role is more of a coach than a 'sage on the stage'."

I asked how much work she took home.

Her shoulders slumped, and the confidence oozed out of her. "Last night was a good night," she said. "I got to bed before midnight."

I had taught out of a similar book my last year at Fernwater, as part of a district pilot project. It was a slog, wading through page after meandering page of poorly planned discovery lessons and writing assignments, and short on math. I stuck with it until the end of September, when I faced down a displeased group of parents at Open House, a night that I usually look forward to – go over the curriculum, crack a dumb joke, explain my grading system, play the intro to a Stan Wolowic tune, and thank parents for having great kids.

But that night the parents teed off, on our math books, on our school, and on me:

"How come there's no math in this math book?"

"I could not find one challenging problem in the first fifty pages. Mr. Haldini, do *you* think this is a good text?"

"What ninny picked this imbecilic book?"

My response was exceedingly feeble. "Your concerns are, uh.... valid. And I share them.... your concerns, I mean. I share your concerns. And, um, I will, uh, do my best to address them."

I knew many of these parents, having taught their older children. A decade's worth of trust had been built up between us. Looking into their worried but resolute faces, I could see that they wanted to trust my judgment, but it was clear that their sons and daughters, rightfully, took priority, and their trust in me could be washed away in an instant.

After the parents left that evening, I sat at my desk, dazed, replaying their concerns. I answered them with the responses I received from the publisher's agent, after having expressed similar concerns myself. The agent had given me tips about how to most effectively use this text:

"Some lessons may require scaffolding." In other words, students will likely be unable to make sense of these assignments until you teach them a bunch of other stuff not covered in the text.

"Feel free to enrich this material." Warning: In laboratory settings, this text has been known to induce narcolepsy.

"This book matches up very well with state standards." Whoop-de-doo.

Thumbing through the text, I attempted to get a debate going between parents and publisher. At each point of dispute, however, the parents kicked the publisher's ass. Examining the three authors' credentials at the front of the book, I was reminded that none of them had ever taught junior high.

I tracked down our swing shift custodian and asked if he could get me into the district warehouse.

"No," he said, "absolutely not, no way, no how." But then he gave me a curious look and asked, "How come?"

"I want to pick up a trunk load of old math books; books with math in them."

He had a 7th grade daughter at Fernwater. "Ohhhh! Well, shoot, why didn't you say so? Is midnight OK? I'll stop by there on my way home."

"Deal."

The next morning I took a math book off a kid's desk and kicked it across the room – that got their attention. I apologized for using substandard texts, and we exchanged their new books for the old, battered ones, filled with scribbles and graffiti. The tone of the class changed immediately; kids were asking questions, answering them, and debating amongst themselves. They were now being required to think.

When I bragged to my father about my "work around", I expected him to approve; his opinion of the new textbooks was even lower than mine. Instead he bawled me out for sneaking around in the middle of the night, rather than taking on the bureaucrats head on. He referred to my "midnight acquisitions" and "subversive activities" as "sabotage".

On Halloween I received an email, comprised of excerpts

from Anjuli's journal. The email had been sent to a dozen people.

Oct. 27rd
Dinner at the Ambassador Hotel. Authentic Kenyan recipe: boil up a slab of mystery meat and serve it on a bed of ugali, this ground-up, boiled corn mush that has the look, taste, and appeal of week-old oatmeal, and call it dinner. I shan't be eating here again.

Oct. 28th
Amazing!!!!!!! In the span of two hours, we saw lions sleeping in the grass, a cheetah toying with the remains of a gazelle, herds of elephants, a tribe of baboons knuckling their way down a path with babies hanging onto their backs and stomachs, and LOOK! A trio of giraffes posing in front of a gorgeous sunset, and THERE! Wildebeests charging across the savannah, and OVER HERE! Mongoose rustling through the grass. Vultures, topi.

Oct. 29th
I ate one bite of a thorny yellow fruit called durian, with the taste and consistency of rotten clams and partially digested onions. I spit it out, but could taste it hours later. Eeuuuww! I'm travelling in a van with Charlie the Driver, an Australian couple and their son Brian – he's smart, fun, and did I mention he's hot? Ahmde the Egyptian geologist is our class clown.

Masai village – huts made of sticks and cow dung, doorways 4 feet high. Fire pits inside with no ventilation. Animals everywhere – litter of kittens under the chicken coop, sorry looking dog lying under a sorry looking tree. Cows are brought inside the fence at night so they aren't eaten by lions. Flies. Flies! FLIES!

Chapter 27 – November

Like many businesses in Oxley, Beats Workin' has been given a facelift, courtesy of a booming economy. Ms. Pacman and the one-eyed, six-point buck have moved on, but the JFK-era pickled eggs are hangin' in there. Now dubbed a sports bar, Beats Workin' features six pool tables and three TV's, each the size of a chalkboard.

Carl slid into the booth across from me. With his soggy, curly locks hanging over his eyes, he looked like something the cat would not have dragged in. He wiped the rain off his cheeks and held out a glass.

"Beer me. Whoa! What kind of dreck is this, Haldini?" He held his glass up to the light. "Looks like camel whiz."

I took a swig. "Ahhhhh. I can't stand those beers that look and taste like transmission fluid. Besides, Bud makes the best commercials."

He eyed his glass sorrowfully. "Ah, what the heck…. just have to drink twice as much."

Consensus is that Carl had been an inspiring history teacher, an effective VP and a passable principal. But this is his fifth year at Crazy Town, and the stress is showing; when he sweeps the frizzy locks off his forehead, he exposes an increasingly furrowed brow.

"What's up, DOC?"

"Haldini, I got into education because I thought I could make a difference. And ya know what? I was right. So then I thought: A teacher affects 150 lives a year; administrators affect 800, or 2000. Being VP was a pain, but I taught kids how to make smart choices. Then, as a principal, I got paid more, and I bought a nice house." He stopped and swirled his beer. "And that's where things got weird. I no longer dealt with kids, mostly with teachers and parents, and I met with other principals who no longer dealt with kids. And then I went to work at Crazy Town. Jesus, Joe and

Jimmy Christ!"

"Yeah, we swapped teaching for debating policy with people who didn't like teaching."

"I'll drink to that. You know, I consider skepticism to be one of my finer qualities. But I tell you, I have moved way beyond skepticism."

"A toast to cynicism." We clinked our glasses and drank. "If I hear that phrase...."

".... 'research shows'...."

".... one more time...."

"Have you noticed how they *all* say it?"

".... I'm gonna duct tape somebody's mouth shut."

"Nah, that's a waste of good duct tape."

Yes, we were being churlish, but this was necessary therapy.

A barmaid came by to take our order. "Can I get you boys any....? Mr. Haldini! How are you?"

This happened all the time; I looked up into a cheerful, dusky-hued, vaguely familiar face, framed by frizzy black hair.

"I'm Jaime and Jeremiah's mom."

"Oh, right! What are those wild men up to?"

"Get this – Jaime's doing stand-up comedy in Hawaii."

"Oh, now that sounds like a hard life," I said. "And Bullfrog – what's he doing?"

"Are you ready for this? He's an 8th grade math teacher!" We talked about her boys, and she started to walk off, but then turned back. "Both of my boys swear they got their worst jokes from you." Her laugh was loud and raspy, but authentic. I pictured Jaime as a kid, trying out his new routines on her.

"But really," she said, "thank you; you were an inspiration to them." She laughed again and left.

"Maybe that's my problem, Carl; I miss having kids and parents thank me for doing my job." I took a long drink and asked, "Any tales from The Crap Shooters?" That was Carl's name for the group that met once a month to solve miscellaneous problems around the district.

"Haldini, I should invite you to sit in some time. Today we discussed what to do with a teacher who's been living at Oxley Junior High."

"What? What happens when…? Whaaat?"

"He's been living in the school's woodshop. It doesn't get used anymore."

"Why not?"

"Elective programs are getting the axe. Anyway, he had a microwave oven, an espresso machine and a cot set up back there. He moved in last April. Originally, he was planning to just stay for the weekend, until an apartment was vacated, but that fell through, and he got comfortable."

"Well, no commute – that would be nice."

"No rent…."

"…. and no utilities. Maybe he's on to something."

"But what do you say to dates? Hey, babe, wanna …."

"…. wanna come over and see my power tool?"

We must have been starving for levity. Our frivolity, however, was short-lived.

"OK, so get this," said Carl. "The next issue we dealt with – you know those cherry trees out front of Fernwater High?"

"My alma mater. That stand of trees is one of my better memories."

"Yeah, well, you can kiss your memories goodbye. The roots of a couple trees caused the cement to lift up and crack, and some klutzy kid tripped. Everybody's afraid of lawsuits, so we're cuttin' 'em down this week-end."

"They're cutting down two entire trees because of some klutz?"

"No, Haldini, they're cutting 'em all down. All twelve." He pushed the tangle of hair off his forehead and said, "It gets weirder. A teacher at Fernwater Junior High is being disciplined for an 'inappropriate interaction with a student'."

"Lemme guess. Some idiot claims to have found the love of his life in 1st period?"

This sort of thing happens every five years or so in our district. Trust between that school and the community takes years to rebuild.

"No, a basketball coach was giving a girl a ride home after practice."

"So the parents complained."

"No, they appreciate it. Both of them work late. The kid

had to quit the team; she had no other way home." In response to my confusion, Carl said, "Liability."

"Yeah, I can understand that, I guess. How is he being disciplined?"

"She. They gave away her coaching job to a teacher from another school." He took a drink. "Shoot, I used to give kids rides all the time. And didn't you host all-night Risk parties?"

"I did. Boy, that would never happen now."

He looked around the bar and asked if I missed teaching.

"Yeah, I do." My eyes lost focus. "Wasn't that fun?"

"It's scary, Haldini; I can't remember it clearly." Carl squeezed his eyes shut and rubbed his forehead. "Now we spend our days editing mission statements." He belched and said, "There. There's my e-mission statement."

"Carl, let's quit and start our own school."

"And what would we do to make our school exceptional?"

"We'd hire smart, good-hearted, curious teachers and let 'em teach."

"I'll drink to that." We toasted and then he gave me a hard look. "Haldini, I apologize."

"For what?"

"Asking you to leave the classroom." I started to object, but he waved me off. "It was lonesome down at Crazy Town; I needed somebody to keep me sane. And speaking of crazy, I got an offer from a publishing company to write and edit history textbooks."

"Yeahhh?"

"It would be a substantial raise, again, but with every raise, I get further removed from dealing with kids. I turned 'em down. Because I still believe in what administration could be. We could be, should be, making life easier for teachers, better for students." I nodded and he went on. "Hey, we're working on something really cool; I want you to be part of it. We're going to videotape teachers presenting lessons, and then we're going to transcribe it for teachers."

I looked at him incredulously. "You really *can't* remember the classroom, can you?"

"What?" Carl was annoyed, and I saw something akin to fear on his face. He was used to being one step ahead of the next guy, but in this case he had no idea what my response would be.

"Carl, the purpose of scripting lessons is to make sure we don't have atrocious teachers. But the flip side is that we won't have any stellar teachers. No, that path is a bid for mediocrity."

"We won't require teachers to follow the script; we're just making them available."

"C'mon, Carl. You know how these 'suggestions' tend to become 'requirements'."

"Jesus, you are cynical. And don't give me that look like I've gone over to the Dark Side." His voice had an edge to it.

I opted for a change of topic. "How are you and Tasha getting' on?"

He clenched his jaw and ran a hand harshly over his face. "I guess you and I haven't talked in a while. She's moving out this week-end."

"Sorry to hear that; you guys seem so good together."

"You know, we aren't. We're just too different. From her point of view, I'm restless, I take walks at midnight, I want to travel, I daydream. And her life is in an uproar; she's always got one crisis going, with two more on the back burner. And I hate that dumb techno-thump music. I won't miss her so much, but Riley...."

Tasha's six-year-old is a habitually cheerful kid who has trouble saying his r's and his l's. His own name comes out as "Whywe".

Carl choked up and his voice became a whisper. "We told him we were splittin' up yesterday. The look on his face just destroyed me. He wasn't angry at all, just confused. And so sad."

A quiet "damn" was the best I could manage, and we sat in silence for a minute. I offered to help move her out.

"Thanks; I'll take you up on that. I tell you, Leo, it's hard breaking up with a woman, but a six-year-old kid.... Riley hugged me as tight as he could and then looked at me with those little eyes, like he was memorizing my face, in case he never saw me again."

"Will you and Tasha stay friends?"

"I wish we could. But the other day, she really laid into me. It was like she'd rehearsed it. It was almost, um...."

"Scripted?" I said, tried not to smug about it.

"Yeah," he said with a weary sigh. "It was scripted."

A peal of thunder shook the building. We looked out through the propped-open double doors at the sudden downpour.

"Ahh, monsoon season," said Carl. "We got six months of rain and fungus to look forward to." His head sagged. "Well, Jesus, Joe and Jimmy Christ, I'm sure a joy to be around. Sorry."

"It's OK, my friend, I don't need an apology." I waggled my glass and nodded toward the pitcher. "But I do need a refill."

"I need a change," he said, and bonked his forehead with the palm of his hand three times.

An email from Anjuli was waiting for me when I got to work. She had again sent excerpts from her journal, except for the first entry, sent specifically to me.

Mr. Haldini, Oops! I mean Leo – it's still weird to call you that.

I'm miserable but happy. Bumpy roads are pulling my joints apart. The windows on our 3-year-old van don't close, we wear bandanas to keep from swallowing dust. I imagined you riding with us, writing a blues song that might go a little something like this:

Got dust in my nostrils, got dust in my shoes
Got dust in my undies, got dem ol' dusty blues
And I don't care if I don't see this van again
Got dem dusty blues, got dem blues, my friend

I woke up diz mornin', had dust in my mouth
I looked out da window, it be dusty north and south
I got me diz problem, and I got me no clue
How I'm gonna get rid of dese dusty, dusty blues!

Nov. 17th
Sat at an outdoor bar all day, 50 yards from the only watering hole around. Giraffes drank at one end, zebras the other. They all left, and a troop of baboons took their turn – they'd been waiting in the bush. Next came the break-dancing monkeys, a water buffalo and impalas (root word = impale?), like the whole thing was scheduled. "Bartender, another round of Cosmopolitans?"

My emotions run the gamut from elation to heartbreak, seeing how the Masai live, on increasingly small patches of land. 9% HIV infection rate, 38% unemployment. Charlie's world is threatened by Somali poachers displaced by civil war. Rhinos are killed, their horns ground up and sold in Asia as an aphrodisiac. Is that where "horny" comes from?

Nov somethingth
Zanzibar! Kids play soccer, cattle graze in a field on the Indian Ocean. In a few years it will be condos and restaurants. Gorgeous men! This island has been invaded by Arabs, Indians, Greeks, Europeans, Persians – stir all that together, you get these dark-skinned, white-teethed hotties. Or would that be hotten-totties?

Haven't slept in a week. My body forgot how. But I love it here! Extending my trip for a month to volunteer in a clinic in Kenya.

Chapter 28 – December

Carl Martin dropped by my cubicle just before eight a.m. He was really jazzed about something.

"Haldini, you know what I said about not being able to remember what it's like to teach? Well, here's my remedy: What if every administrator had to sub once a month?"

"Yeah, they might agree to that," I said. "And maybe we'll get a 40% raise this year."

Carl was more frustrated than angry. "Damn it, Leo. Are you just going to roll over and play dead?"

He was right, of course, and my dad would be appalled at my hesitancy to take on Crazy Town, because it's not like the Head Shed is some monolithic evil empire where nothing changes or gets done; buses run on time, teachers teach, and our district's on-time graduation rate, though stalled at a paltry 80%, is several percentage points above the statewide average.

Having said that, it strikes me as ludicrous that we'd spend over a year writing a mission statement, while also implementing new curriculum, new operating principles, a peer evaluation system, a new tracking system for failing students, the use of smart boards, and, again, new state standards! Off the top of my head, I could count 16 new programs in 16 months. And for the most part, this is an additive process, that is, the old tasks aren't retired – new ones get piled on top.

Most ludicrous of all is our goal of making all students college-ready, when 20% of them don't even graduate from high school.

Carl continued in a more conciliatory tone. "Look, there are things you hate about your job – same here – but admin needs good people, and if we give up, the whole thing is hopeless." He checked his watch. "Speaking of hopeless, we've got a meeting in two minutes."

Carl describes Susan Nysohr, our superintendent, as a "matron punk in a moo moo". A 60-year-old, six-foot behemoth, she sports a closely cropped metallic blue hairdo. Her forte is obtaining grants from high-tech companies headquartered around Seattle. She began our meeting with district principals by passing around two boxes of donuts. She licked her fingers and then dropped a bombshell:

"I am recommending to the Board that our district file a lawsuit against the US Government. No Child Left Behind, as an unfunded mandate, should either be rescinded or funds should be made available to implement the requisite changes."

Carl and I low-fived one another, prompting The Krabman to grumble, "Bush haters."

Ben Luzen was aghast. "Research shows that NCLB has increased student achievement in 13 out of 21 schools in our district."

Ben is our Director Of Remedial Curriculum, and yes, he is widely referred to as our DORC. As is the case with many upper level administrators, he is ten years removed from actually speaking with a teenager.

Penelope Prismark took exception to his claim. "26% of the student population at our school turned over this year. It isn't right that we are, like, judged on new arrivals."

Her school, located next to a government-subsidized housing project, serves a highly transient population with a large percentage of non-English speakers. They do not receive a lot of gold stars. NCLB dictates that if her school goes one more year without reaching specified goals, they would be required to provide transportation for students who elect to attend other schools. And if they miss their goals another year, her entire staff may be replaced. The year after that, her school could be shut down.

"Research shows," said Ben, "that US graduation rates have risen since passage of NCLB."

"True," said Carl. "But graduation rates have been rising steadily for the past century, and the rate of increase is slowing. The main problem with NCLB and the WASL is that they divert tens of millions of dollars, in Washington State alone, from programs that could work, or have worked in the past."

"In the past." Ben repeated that phrase with a dismissive shake of the head. "We are moving forward, Mr. Martin."

Before Carl could respond, Bonnie Rhodes flared her nostrils and barked, "Excuse me!" Silence. She welcomes the accolades bestowed upon her school, which has been one of the top five WASL performers in the state each year since the test's inception. Bonnie held up an 18 by 24 tagboard sign, precisely printed in block letters. It read:

YOUR CHILD LEFT BEHIND

"Ah found *this* hung above the door to the ladies' room. You dumbocraps would do well to remember that No Child Left Behind was a bi-partisan bill, championed by our president, Senator Kennedy and Congressman Boehner."

"It most definitely was," agreed Superintendent Nysohr. "But just because both parties erred does not absolve us from our responsibility to point out their error. Now, unless anyone has a new perspective on NCLB...." She waited all of three seconds and then said, "I will turn this meeting over to Ben."

Ben Luzen glided up to the front of the room. When he walks, he doesn't bob up and down, or sway from side to side, or swing his arms. His torso manages to stay perfectly stationary. Had he been walking behind a three-foot wall, visible only from the waist up, it would have appeared that a conveyor belt was whisking him across the room.

He began by trotting out the results from last year's Washington Assessment of Student Learning, the WASL, a standardized test administered each spring to all 4th, 7th, and 10th graders in Washington State. Beginning in 2008, passing the 10th grade WASL (rhymes with "fossil") would be a high school graduation requirement.

"Our goal today is to create an action plan, the purpose of which is to raise WASL scores. Now, as you are all undoubtedly aware, the 4th grade WASL covers mathematics, reading and writing. I have been researching how 4th grade teachers spend their class time."

Grinning like a chimp, he plopped his hands down on a six-inch-thick stack of paper. Ben's sole purpose in life, so far as I can tell, is analyzing WASL data.

"This is a bit of my recreational reading," he said. "Here is the daily breakdown for a typical 4th grader." He passed around hand-outs containing the following:

50 minutes	Writing, spelling
40 minutes	Reading
30 minutes	Math
40 minutes	Social Studies
25 minutes	Science
30 minutes	Art and/or music
35 minutes	Lunch
30 minutes	Recess, breaks
15 minutes	PE
20 minutes	misc: field trips, assemblies, etc

"As you can clearly see," said Ben, "these students spend approximately 2/3 of their school day involved in activities and curricula that are unrelated to the WASL." He paused to let that sink in, and then asked rhetorically, "Are we using the school day in the most efficient way? Simply put, we do not need to cover science, social studies, art, and music in 4th grade."

Most of the people sitting around the table nodded agreeably; the rest of us looked like we'd found an oyster in our jelly donuts.

"No science?" I asked. "How can you justify that?"

"Because we want to do what's best for kids."

That's one of Ben's standard responses, and it implies that anyone who questions him is planning to hijack a bus full of 9-year-olds and drive it into an alligator-infested swamp. In the middle of the table lay a staple gun. An image of Ben Luzen with his lips stapled shut took shape in my mind.

Ben continued: "Research shows...." Carl and I flinched. "…. that pruning extraneous subjects from the curricula raises WASL scores. 90% of kids catch up in their later years in science, as long as their fundamentals are strong."

"And there's the problem with the WASL, right *there*!" I jabbed my finger in the air for emphasis. "It not only determines what does get taught; it also determines what does not, which makes for a bland curriculum."

"For many years now," Ben replied, "teachers have had free rein in what they teach, and how they teach it. I hope they've enjoyed the ride, because the ride.... is.... over. We have state standards now, and the WASL measures how well those standards are being met."

I looked around for support. Most of the principals see themselves as team players who are doing their best to get on board with NCLB. And Carl had been fighting this battle for months; he'd shot his wad. On his notepad, he scrawled in large jagged letters:

> Minds conform!
> Define the norm!
> Hearts, renounce your passion!

Carl once pointed that No Child Left Behind is based on quite a lovely sentiment: Let's get every student to succeed. He then grumbled, "Gee, never thought of that."

The unintended consequences of NCLB are as pervasive as they are perverse. Besides being a sinkhole for time and money, the resulting pressure that comes from designating "Pass the Test" as our Prime Directive is a major reason cited by educators for leaving the profession. It should come as no surprise that *most* first-year teachers will flame out in less than six years on the job.

I said, "But science, if taught properly, teaches kids to be curious about the world, to test hypotheses, to question, to develop a sense of wonder. Is anything more important than that?"

Ben said, "We are, and will continue to be, a data-driven district. Nothing.... no *thing*.... is more important than getting the children under our care to pass the WASL."

There. He could not have said it more plainly. At best, the WASL had once been considered a measuring device, allowing each school, as well as each district, each teacher and each student, to identify academic weaknesses and then modify curriculum and study habits accordingly. But the WASL is no longer a tool; it has become an end in itself.

I gazed longingly at the staple gun. I pictured my father stapling his demands to this very table a quarter century ago.

Susan Nysohr said, "We are losing students to private schools that focus more on core curriculum. Increasingly, they consider electives to be frivolous." She shrugged apologetically. "I am no fan of the WASL, but we need to do everything we can to get kids to pass it."

Ben exhaled indignantly. "Speaking of which, a rather unfortunate situation has arisen." He held up a printout and shook it. "An email spoofing the WASL has been circulating amongst a rabble of junior high teachers. I want you to see for yourself the extent of the unprofessionalism we are dealing with here."

He took a moment to glare at each principal and then passed around copies of the email:

Sample 7ᵗʰ grade WASL math questions

1) Ali rode her bike to the store at 17 mph. The store is 6 miles from her house. She bought 4 Ho Hos at 57 cents each. How many calories are in 7 Ho Hos?

2) Visualize Idaho. The best estimate for its perimeter is:
   a) 760 miles   b) 761 miles   c) 761.7 miles   d) 760 spuds

3) Suppose your calculator is broken. If you multiply 9 by 4 and get an answer of 2, what would you get by adding 7 and 15?

4) Find the pattern and fill in the next blank: 2, 3, -17, 5.4, ___
   Explain your answer in words or pictures.

5) Find the pattern and fill in the blanks: 7, ___, ___, ___

The chuckles grew in volume as we read through the problems. Soon most of us were guffawing.

Ben Luzen laid into us: "I am appalled that you would be amused by such a disrespectful, bilious document as this, written by a mutinous clown who has the gall to call himself an educator."

Susan Nysohr half-heartedly hid a smirk. Several of us scooted our chairs back and fixed our eyes on the floor, lest we meet a colleague's eyes and again succumb to guffawing.

Prior to that meeting, the fake WASL had been seen by

maybe a dozen people. By eight o'clock the next morning, the problems would be seen by nearly every employee in the district. Sadly, the fake questions were not all that different from some of the real ones.

Over the past decade, dozens of Letters to the Editor have been published by The Seattle Times regarding the WASL, some praising it, some questioning its value, and some claiming that it is too difficult. Many take the position that it needs to be fine-tuned. The people writing these letters have one thing in common: None of them have seen the WASL. Outside of test writers, the only people who see it are students and educators. The main problem with the test is not its level of difficulty. Rather, many WASL questions, written under the guise of being "open-ended", are unclearly formulated. Carl claims the WASL was created by a fog machine.

In a sober tone, Ben said, "Updating our curriculum requires a Best Practices approach."

By invoking the phrase "Best Practices", Ben is granting himself license to brand anyone who challenges his proposals as a proponent of a Not-the-Best-Practices approach to education, or perhaps even the Worst Practices approach, wherein incorrect answers are rewarded with a severe caning. Even teachers using Pretty Darn Good Practices reveal themselves to be second-rate educators. Most teachers, thank goodness, dispensed with Crappy Practices years ago.

Ben went on. "As the fastest-growing district in the region, we need to make smarter choices about our course offerings."

Carl sketched a tombstone with an epitaph reading:

PUBLIC EDUCATION
(d. 2004)
smarter choices made
curriculum gutted, flayed

"Just to make sure I understand this," said Carl as he finished his sketch. "All students will be taught fewer subjects because some kids fail the WASL."

Ben replied, "We will maintain a more rigorous program for our gifted students."

"It doesn't seem right that the slower students drive our curriculum," I said.

Carl nodded. "High-end students get a first-rate education, because their parents are vocal; they get what they want. Low-end kids get an increasing share of our time, energy, and money each year, but I question whether it does them any good. Kids in the middle get the shaft; every year they get a smaller slice of the pie. If I were the parent of a so-called 'average kid', I'm not sure I would enroll him or her in our schools."

There it was. I considered Carl Martin to be the brightest, most insightful person in the room, and in all of 30 seconds, he had torpedoed his own career.

That afternoon, I got an email from Anjuli:

Leo,

Get THIS: I've been hanging with Warren Hamilton. Yes, HIM! The owner of Nanogration, Mr. Hi-tech Miniaturized Medical Equipment. Here I am, at a clinic in the middle of nowhere, he and his wife Marsha walk in. Weird place to run into a fellow Seattlite. I said, Warren, like we were buds. He laughed and said, Friends call me War. His foundation awards grants to organizations that address quality of life issues in Africa: health, literacy, poverty.

A man came running in, says his wife broke her leg. Our doc was going to run (run! we have no car) to help him. Warren offered to take him in his Hummer, so Marsha came with me on my rounds. Wambui is 20, pregnant, AIDS. Her asshole "boyfriend" stole her groceries, raped her. She was bleeding and had a nasty-smelling infection. Marsha is a champ. She cleaned her up and gave her an apple. The moment we left, Marsha was bawling. She had that helpless, hopeless look we all get when we first see this misery. But we kept going, giving shots, delivering meds.

At the clinic, Marsha helped with patients (sprain, spider bite). A woman and her pregnant teen-age daughter burst in, screaming, "Hurt like demon!" Aren't you supposed to boil water? I know of women being in labor for 23 hours, but a boy popped out in ten minutes! So gross, so beautiful. The new granny pointed at each of us, saying, "You, you, me, all mother!" We told them to wait for the doc, they smiled and left. Marsha was all hugs and tears.

I hope all is well. Love ya, Anjuli

PS I'm considering a trip to Pakistan next fall. Wanna come? Just a thought.

Pakistan, huh? With Anjuli. Now that sounds like a kick.

Today's meeting at Crazy Town left me seething. My stomach was still churning like a blender on its slowest setting, attempting in vain to digest our absurd district polices. I tried to convince myself that my colleagues and bosses were merely cartoon characters, incapable of inflicting serious damage, but having experienced firsthand the hilarity and imbecility of open concept schools, I am well aware of how much havoc can be wreaked by a dozen administrators sitting around a conference table.

Pakistan, huh? Yeah, maybe it's time for a change.

Chapter 29 – January

I got to work one snowy Monday morning and found three emails from Anjuli, sent specifically to me.

Jan. 13th
Marsha asked me to stay with her and War. They threw a party for a woman from the Ministry of Education and 3 philanthropists. I shot my mouth off about women's health and women's education in the third world. Good news – nobody deported me. Yet.

Next morning, Benji, their 8-year-old nephew, flopped on the couch, his head, knees, everything hurt. I took off his shirt and saw it right away, a black mark with a red circle, tic bite fever. It isn't dangerous, if treated with doxycycline, but it scared the bejesus out of Marsha – Benji's the closest thing they have to a son. He was better two days later. Marsha told me, We're not letting you leave; you know that, don't you?

p.s. What is a bejesus?

Jan. 14th
War, Marsha and I visited a school (cinderblock, dirt floor, no windows) to present the teacher with encyclopedias. She thanked us and set them up nice and square on the empty bookcase. She asked if we could get her some chalk. Her 47 kids applauded us! Marsha said the number is probably higher, girls skip school when menstruating, only one privy (bathroom) in the school, good luck finding tampons. New law: all kids must attend school through 8th grade. Adds a million kids to already over-burdened schools.

Kids mobbed me at recess, jabbering and reaching out hands to touch me. Is this Bono's life? I did a disappearing coin trick, they clapped and screamed! Should I take my show on the road? War gave me a how-do-you-<u>do</u>-this look. One little boy (adorable!) stood on tippy toes and reached up his skinny arms. I picked him up and carried him inside, when I put him down, he cried and took a fistful of my sweater with him. Does anyone ever hold him?

Jan. 15th
Get THIS, War and Marsha never give grants to individuals, but they're giving one to me! Question: If you had a pile o' money to spend on a worthy cause, what would that cause be?

Two weeks later, the phone rang at exactly nine o'clock on Saturday morning. "Hello?"

"So, whattaya think? If you had a pile o' money, what would you spend it on?"

"Hey, hey! Anj, good to hear your voice!"

"You too. Really, a pile of money – what would you do with it?"

"I've got an idea or two. How about you?"

"I've got an idea or two. I'm having lunch with Giz today. Wanna join us?"

It was gratifying to know she still used Gizmo's nickname.

"I can't do lunch. But let me toss out another idea – my buddy Carl is coming over to watch the Sonics tonight. How about if he and I nix the game, and the four of us get together for dinner? Spaghetti is a Haldini specialty, going back generations."

"Yes! I haven't talked to Giz yet, but trust me, he'll say yes."

I had not seen Gizmo in several years. His thick, curly black hair, always impressive, had grown out, literally, making it appear that his head was twice its actual size.

"Isn't it great?" Anjuli ran her hands through his hair and over his face. "And it's impossible to mess up."

After introducing them to Carl, I led them into the kitchen and uncorked a bottle of Merlot. "Your job is to entertain me while I cook."

I set to work chopping up mushrooms, tomatoes and bell peppers, as Anjuli recounted her story of running into Warren Hamilton in Kenya.

"Anjulita, how much money is he giving you?" Giz made an effort to come up with a new variation of her name every time he addressed her.

"That's the weird thing – he didn't say. Some people he gives $10,000; other grants are in the millions."

"Time line?" I asked. "What's he got in mind?"

"He would like a rough idea, an outline, by summer."

Carl made a "T" with his hands. "Hey, time out! I missed something. Why is he doing this?"

She flipped her hair coquettishly and offered up a dramatic sigh. "I guess he finds me charming."

Carl laughed, while Giz and I frowned at each other and shook our heads.

She said, "Actually, I think his wife Marsha was the driving force behind the grant. And they liked that I wasn't hitting them up for bucks like everybody else."

I said, "You guys like garlic?" Anjuli and Carl nodded.

Giz said he'd never eaten much spicy food. He then asked Carl what he did for a living.

"Mostly I commiserate with Leo over the state of education."

"Is it really that bad, Leo?" asked Anjuli.

"Whatever new program we try, it never works quite as well as it was supposed to, so every few years we're compelled to try something completely different, something shiny and new."

Carl added, "Two years ago there was a push to standardize curriculum throughout the district. This year, we're not just allowing non-conformity, we're mandating it. Each school has to spend 10% of its budget on new programs or a new paradigm. They were ordered to 'not follow the rules'. Our motto is: Innovate and Empower."

Anjuli asked, "Can schools spend the 10% however they want?"

Carl snorted. "That's what they were told. But Oxley High wanted to hire two additional English teachers, in order to limit their writing classes to 23, because it takes time to read essays. Their entire staff gave it the green light, but it was voted down by the district Executive Council. They told the staff, 'Wellll, no, that's not exactly what we had in mind.'"

"Why was it voted down?" asked Anjuli.

I said, "Because English teachers across the district would want to cap their classes at 23, and we don't want to fund it district-wide."

"Let's if I got this right," said Giz. "Schools have to come up with a good plan, but not so good that another school would want to try it."

"Exactly," said Carl. "Instead of 'Innovate and Empower', our motto should be 'Enervate the Empire'."

Anjuli chuckled. "Do you subversives have regrets about not teaching anymore?"

"Let me put it this way," I said. "Yes!"

"Sad, Mr. Haldini," said Giz. "You were a great teacher. Inspiring."

"Thank you, but knock off that 'Mr. Haldini' stuff. You're old now. If you want to get fed tonight, call me Leo." I crushed three cloves of garlic into the spaghetti sauce.

"OK, *Leo*, I'll try."

Anjuli said, "Yeah, I'm still getting used to calling you 'Leo' too. 'Cause you're not our teacher any more, and we're kind of like friends, but you're more like an uncle.... Uncle Leo!"

Oh, I liked the sound of that. I have always looked up to Fester as a paragon of educational excellence, and I've long been envious of his honorary "Uncle" title. He still signs off on emails using his "Uncle Fester" sobriquet. It's nice to entertain the notion that I would even be in his league as a teacher. It saddened me, however, that this title had not been conferred upon me until after I stopped teaching.

"I can live with that," I said, and then tasted the spaghetti sauce. "Could use some pepper."

Anjuli said, "Smells yummy."

I held out a spoonful of sauce. "Open up."

She took a taste, closed her eyes and purred, "Mmmm. Where'd you get the recipe?"

"Granny Haldini; she says the Holy Trinity of Cooking is garlic, oregano and basil. Her culinary prowess is spoken of in hushed and reverent tones up and down the shores of Lake Como."

"How about you, Giz?" asked Carl. "What did you do today?"

"Anjuliet and I were going to do lunch, but she called and proposed coming over here, so I went golfing at Oxley."

"I like that course. What did you shoot?"

"87, not great. But I got a range finder today; it's very cool." To Anjuli's questioning look, he said, "Binoculars – they tell how far you are from the flag."

I tasted the sauce one last time. "Delizioso! Go ahead and serve yourselves."

We sat for dinner, and after they had been satisfactorily effusive in their praise of my spaghetti, I said, "Anj, will your grant focus specifically on African concerns?"

"I've been assuming it should." She paused and closed her eyes. "But now that I think about it, Warren said over and over, 'Anything goes'.

"If that's the case," I said, "how about we address the traffic woes in this town? And the Mariners' bullpen could use some help." That opened the floodgate:

Giz: "How 'bout we fix my golf swing? I got a nasty slice."

Carl: "Let's rid the world of that dumb techno-thump."

Anjuli: "How 'bout we go down to Cabo and think this over for a coupla months?" She then amended her original statement. "War said over and over, 'As long as you do something for the good of the world, anything goes.' Let's brainstorm."

I hunted up a pad of paper and volunteered to take notes. "Gimme ideas, fast and furious, no editing."

Suggestions came at me rapid fire: Malaria. Recycling. Hunger. Cancer. Environmental concerns. Mental health issues. Overpopulation.

We took a break fifteen minutes later. I had two sheets of paper filled with ideas, punctuated with spaghetti stains. I was pleased to see that everyone headed back to the kitchen for seconds.

Anjuli said, "A lot of these ideas are beyond our scope, like cancer research. And recycling already has a cajillion people working on it. Let's focus on a unique issue. "

I said, "Maybe the question should be: Where do you get the best return?"

She nodded and looked over my list. "We can't discuss

every idea – we'd be here until Tuesday, and we'll run out of pasta and wine. So maybe we should just discuss the best ideas – mine!" Waving her hands over her head, she chanted, "Go, Anji! Go…. go…. go, Anji!"

Giz was the only one of us that didn't laugh. "Oh, girl, you are so confused."

Carl pushed his chair back from the table and patted his belly. "That was great, Haldini. I am stuffed."

I thanked him and asked if he'd been writing songs.

"Yeah, one or two."

"Wanna play one?"

"Oh, I don't know; they're not real cheery."

"That's OK by me," said Anjuli. "Most of my favorite songs are heartbreakers."

Carl brought my Martin guitar in from the family room, and played a blues riff. He then began finger-picking a progression of simple chords, but he placed surprising notes in the bass that kept it interesting and edgy. The second verse of his song stuck with me:

> The world is not a cruel place
> It does not plan your pain
> Has your angel, blue, lost faith in you?
> Heaven knows, but won't explain
> You play the odds, you pray to God
> And wait for soft reply

Giz and I focused intently on Carl's fingers. But during the last verse, we switched our focus to Anjuli, who turned away, but not before wiping her eyes. Carl finished the song, and everyone had the good sense to be silent for ten seconds. Anjuli asked him to play another one; he said he might later on.

I put my hands on his shoulders. "Great stuff, Carl. Let's head out to the back yard."

My three-bedroom rambler is nothing special. But my back yard, if I do say so myself, is a slice of heaven. Last summer I put in a brick patio and a koi pond with underwater lights and a cascading waterfall. Two raised flowerbeds are surrounded by Japanese knotweed, a type of bamboo that will take over if you let it, but its lushness simulates the feel of a jungle.

Disfiguring an otherwise idyllic setting are the grotesque piles of downed maples and firs on the lot bordering my property in back. Five acres had been clear-cut and hacked into quarter-acre parcels on which tract homes are being knocked together. Oxley is quickly developing itself into an anthill.

This being the last day of January, I loaded up my fire pit with newspapers, kindling and firewood. We had a healthy blaze going in two minutes. We sat on stone benches, Carl and I on one side of the fire, Anjuli and Giz on the other.

"Carl, I really liked that song," she said. "And your voice reminds me of someone, but I can't put my finger on who it is. Which is weird, because you have a totally unique voice."

She flashed him a radiant smile that caught Gizmo's attention. His eyes flitted back and forth between the two of them, and finally settled on Carl. I got the feeling Giz was appraising him, trying to discern his intent and trustworthiness.

Carl shrugged. "Always thought I sound like Neil Young with hay fever."

"Well, I like it. Do you write the music or lyrics first?"

Carl hadn't had a lot of female attention lately; he was lappin' it up. "Usually the lyrics, then the music, then I go back and rewrite most of the words. It's not a very efficient process."

Anjuli said, "That song had a lot of religious references. Are you religious?" When Carl balked, she said, "You're spiritual but not religious. That's what you were gonna say, right?"

"Yes, I was!" He shook his head in disbelief. "How did you do that?"

Giz mimicked her "Go Anji" chant. "Get used to it, man."

Carl persisted. "I mean it, Anjuli, how did you do that?"

"Here's what I've noticed: If someone is a believer or an atheist, they say so. If someone is 'spiritual', they hesitate, because.... well, I'm not sure." She waited expectantly.

"Spirituality is, at least for me, a mushy concept. It has to do with trusting your internal guidance system, rather than an external one. How about you? Are you religious?"

"My Costa Rican dad is Catholic, my Pakistani mom is Muslim. Me? I'm a mess. My parents argued about religion all through my teenage years, but they finally came to the realization that their marriage was more important than their individual concepts of God."

Carl said, "Boy, I wish the entire world could hear and understand that story."

"Yeah, it all worked out, but back then, I'd have done anything to get out of the house. I daydreamed about traveling all the time." She held out her open palms to the fire. "Mr. Hal.... Uncle Leo, I don't know if I ever thanked you for helping me through that period. You were my rock."

"Glad I could help." Fortunately, the firelight was too dim for them to see me blush.

"Confession time," she said. "Remember that night Kali and I came to visit you at home? We kinda lied to you. We had already gotten home from youth group, Mom and Dad were goin' at it, and Kali...." Anjuli swallowed hard. "I went into her room and found her with a bottle of pills. She said she was tired of their fights. She thought they were fighting over how to deal with her and her partying – isn't that wild? Anyway, that's how we ended up over at your house. You were the one person that I thought could talk her out of it."

"No," I whispered. Thinking back to that night, Kali had seemed cheery – maybe overly so? "I can't believe how clueless I can be."

Anjuli shook her head. "There's no way you could have known; she and I were really good at covering up. But you said exactly the right thing; you said something about Kurt Cobain leaving too soon. That woke her up."

"How's she doing?"

"Great. Two kids, married; he's not much to look at, but he's a good man." She placed a log on the fire. "Remember that song you played? I remember the lines 'Friends are gone as fast as you blink, as skipping stones in time must sink. Love them now, or forever think about it.' When Kali and I got home that night, I told her I loved her. I had never said that to her. Where'd that song come from, anyway?"

I smiled at Carl, who ducked his head.

"What?" said Anjuli.

Gizmo's head jerked up. "Carl, *you* wrote that? I've been hearing about that song since I was 14!"

"Leo!" said Anjuli. "You mean Carl is your songwriter buddy you were always telling us about?" She turned to face him. "That's why you sounded familiar! Uncle Leo was always playing your demo tapes before school. But he never referred to you by name. I need to thank you – my sister might not be.... Really, thank you."

Flummoxed, Carl gave an awkward nod.

We watched the fire for several minutes.

Anjuli finally broke the silence. "I've enjoyed tonight. Would you guys want to get together again and help me choose a grant project?"

"Absolutely," said Carl, and I echoed him.

Giz hesitated, and then said, "Count me in. Do we want to add anybody else?"

Anjuli answered immediately. "No, I like this group, just as we are."

Chapter 30 – February

Our new boardroom was apparently designed by a 14-year-old with ADHD named Joey. One wall is constructed of cedar shakes, another of brick, the third a disturbing shade of digestive green, and a pair of garage doors make up the fourth. The ceiling is a hodgepodge of acoustic foam tiling, ventilation shafts, 6x8 crossbeams and sheet metal. A picture of Bush had been taped high up on the brick with a caption reading:

YOUR CHILD LEFT BEREFT

Superintendent Susan Nysohr entered with four boxes of Krispy Kreme donuts. "Grab some breakfast 'n' let's get started." The box I opened was four shy of a dozen. Susan licked her fingers and addressed the assemblage of junior high administrators.

"Ben Luzen is here today to educate us about our Special Ed programs, to make sure we're in compliance with state and federal guidelines."

Ben glided up to the front of the room and took a seat. He clicked his mouse and brought up a PowerPoint presentation. "Good morning. As you requested, we are holding this meeting today to discuss last year's WASL scores. Now, referring to your hand-out...."

Every pair of eyes in the room checked out every other pair of eyes, asking silently: We requested this meeting? Really? Did you request it? Nope, not me, did you? Don't blame me, I didn't do it.

Three hands tentatively rose and a vice principal asked, "*Who* requested this meeting?"

Ben checked his notes. "11 out of 14 of you. I sent out an email last month – January 21st, to be precise – asking if you would prefer to meet today or tomorrow. The vast majority of you opted for today."

Oh. Eyes flitted around the room again, but nobody spoke up. We'd been had. 8:03 in the morning, and the blender in my stomach had already progressed through "blend" and "whip", and was now set on "puree".

"Now, let's discuss those WASL scores. If you refer to your hand-out...."

Carl and I had already heard this part of the presentation. He leaned over and wrote on my ChInSu notepad: Anj + Giz = item?

Giz had pursued her romantically off and on since 9th grade, but according to Anjuli, the timing was never quite right; she was always in the process of moving some place far away. At least that's what she'd told me, but I got the feeling that she was simply not all that interested. And that disappointed me, because at least on paper, they made a great couple. And their children – boy, they'd be something else.

As bright and inventive as he was, however, he seemed at home in the world, whereas she was restless and adventuresome, perhaps even reckless. Fortunately, they had managed to keep their friendship intact, except for a month-long span during their sophomore year of high school; he and Calvin had simultaneously vied for her affection, resulting in a lasting enmity between the boys.

On Anjuli's 21st birthday, I went out bar-crawling with her, Gizmo and two of her girlfriends in downtown Seattle. I drove, and we ended up in Pioneer Square at the Fenix, dancing to Ska Na Na, a reggae band with an outrageously soulful singer that looked like an ex-con and a female bass player that laid down a lazy, off-beat groove.

Around midnight, we took a break from dancing to Marley and UB40 tunes. Some jerk with a Mohawk and an iguana tattoo on his forearm started pawing Anjuli. After she told him twice to knock it off, I stood up and hissed, ala Mr. Hester, "Sssssstop it!"

Now, my teacher voice works on 99 kids out of 100, but locking horns with a stocky, bleary-eyed son of a bitch that has ingested fourteen pints of Hefeweizen is probably not what you'd call a Best Practices approach.

Swaying back and forth, Iguana Man leaned forward in a bellicose manner. "Now 'oo da fug are you, 'er gramma?"

He laid a beefy paw on my shoulder and gave me a shove.

Of course, I heard my dad intoning: Fight the good fight. If you don't stand up.... Oh damn! Am I gonna start a brawl in front of my ex-students? Really? I fingered the scar on my jaw, the 15-year-old reminder of the punch thrown by that pudgy trucker, intent on defend Mira's honor. By any measure, he had wholly succeeded. And now here I was, fists up, bobbin' and weavin', intent on defending Anjuli; at least that's how I sold myself on the gallantry of wading face-first into the impending free-for-all. Iguana Man was goin' down.

But Gizmo beat me to the punch, so to speak. Normally the gentlest of souls, he walloped the guy in the nose. Twice.

Oh, great.

With arms flailing, Iguana Man stumbled backwards and knocked a pitcher of beer off a table. He reached a hand up to his bleeding face and yowled, "Fug! By doze! He broke by doze!"

He took a run at Giz, but slipped in the spilled beer and twisted his knee on the way down. He grabbed his injured leg and whimpered, "Fug! By dee! By dee is brogen!"

His pals stuffed a couple cigarettes up his left nostril to staunch the flow of blood, and then hauled him to his feet. They draped his thrashing arms around their shoulders and dragged him out the door.

Iguana Man's voice faded into the night. "Fug! Dat fugger! He fuggin' broge by fuggin' doze! Lez go kig 'is fuggin' azz!"

We chugged our drinks, left more than enough bucks for the bill and hightailed it out of there before the bouncer figured out who had thrown the first, second and only punches. We were somber walking back to the car, until we heard Iguana Man hollering at us from a block away, threatening to kig ar azzes.

That revived us somewhat, and on the drive home, Anjuli and her girlfriends sat in the back, singing: "Get up, stand up. Don't give up the fight."

The song eventually fizzled out, and she asked, "Do math teachers always have this much fun? Do you always start rumbles in bars?"

"No, don't be ridiculous!" I frowned at her in the rearview mirror. "Sometimes we'll start a rumble in a grocery store, or a staff meeting, or at church, or ....”

"Wait a minute – I didn’t know you go to church.”

"Well, not anymore I don’t. They won’t let me in.”

"Cuz you start rumbles?”

I nodded sagely. "In my experience, religious rumbles are the worst.”

Sitting in the front, Giz said, "Haldini didn’t start that fight, Anjuloony. You were the one flirtin’ with that bozo.”

"I was not!” She thwacked him on his temple.

"Fug! By head! She broge by fuggin’ head!”

Giggling hysterically, she leaned over the front seat, grabbed his head roughly, and kissed him on the mouth. "I was not flirting, but thank you anyway, My Protector.”

I wrote on my ChInSu notepad and slid it over to Carl: Buddies. Why?

Of course I knew damn well why. And it was unnerving to have a colleague show romantic interest in one of my students.... well, *ex*-student, but still.... Should I be bothered? Anjuli has always been mature for her age. But having been her teacher, there is a generational gap between us. But Carl is a few years younger than me.... Doesn’t matter; I was definitely bugged. And here’s something else to consider: To some degree, she considers that song he wrote fifteen years ago to be the saving grace of her sister Kali, and if Anjuli was to hook up with him, would she be doing so out of gratitude?

Leave it alone, I told myself with a shrug; they’re adults.

But something was still pecking away at the edge of my consciousness, and it took me a while to identify it: If Anjuli is fair game for Carl, then how about me? Oh God, what a creepy thought. Or is it? She had floated the idea of a trip to Pakistan. As friends, of course. I would never pursue her romantically, but what if she jumped me? Nah, she wouldn’t. No. Or would she? And if so, would I be interested?

I volleyed that prospect around, and here is the line of reasoning that finally settled the issue for me: If I did get involved with 25-year-old Anjuli, people in my community – teachers, parents, ex-students – would wonder: Were they involved last year? How about two years ago? And then, whether they wanted to or not, their minds would creep back in time, inductively arriving at a vision of a 15-year-old girl and her teacher, and *now* we have reached true creepitude.

Still, who cares what those busybodies would think? Answer: I do. Though I am no longer teaching, I am a part of my community. Besides, it's a conceit to think that an attractive, happenin' young woman like Anjuli would consider the idea of jumping an old guy like me. And besides again, she calls me "Uncle Leo", which makes her something like a niece to me.

Carl wrote on my notepad: Curious.

"I've been doing research," Ben Luzen said ominously. "In our district, 7th graders in advanced math classes score 84.7% higher on the WASL than students in regular classes." He paused dramatically and scanned the room.

I foolishly took the bait. "And?"

"Wellll...." He paused again, hoping we dullards might catch up with him. "I propose that we place all of our 7th graders in the advanced class."

He leaned back in his chair, clasped his hands behind his head, cocked an eyebrow and smiled triumphantly, like he had just tossed a bar of gold bullion on the table. Several principals nodded enthusiastically.

Carl looked at me in bemusement, and being the more even-tempered of the two of us, he gave it a shot: "Ben, you have cause-and-effect mixed up. Students get placed in advanced math classes *because* they do well on the WASL and other tests. Students won't magically pass the WASL *because* they get placed in advanced math classes."

Bonnie Rhodes, always ready to preach a little hellfire and damnation, took over for Ben. "Are you then saying that you'd like to see some students *held back* in math?" She spoke as if she fancied herself a Southern Baptist Minister, addressing her flock of sinners and miscreants. "Ah am appalled that you would place limits on how much our students can learn!"

Carl responded more defensively than he would have liked. "I don't want to hold kids back. I just don't want to push them ahead before they're ready."

"I see the error in your thinking," said Ben. "It's our job to make sure they're all ready."

"Ready for what?" I asked. "Kids that take Algebra in 8th grade are on track to take Calculus as seniors. Will we now expect all students to take Calculus in high school?"

"If kids don't take Calculus, how can they expect to be accepted by the finer colleges?"

When a vice principal pointed out that not all students are going to college, Bonnie thundered, "How dare you! There are no jobs left that don't require a college education!"

I objected. "We're always going to need electricians, carpenters, plumbers...."

Bonnie cut me off with a ready response. "Let me make sure Ah understaaaaand." Drawing out that last word gave her time to make eye contact with each person in the room. "Are you proposing a two-tiered educational system? One for the 'haves', one for the 'have-nots'?" She shook her head sadly, as if I had suggested we banish a sizable chunk of our students to a leper colony.

"Shame, Mr. Haldini! Ah would not have pegged you for an elitist."

District administrators often lay out a nice spread for whatever group happens to be meeting that day. Today our buffet table was covered with Caesar salad, dill pickles, cold cuts, four types of bread, condiments, cantaloupe, éclairs, Perrier and an assortment of soft drinks. Like most days, someone had ordered twice as much food as we could possibly eat. When we finished gorging ourselves at 11:54, a newly hired principal gestured at the trays of leftovers.

"Who got the order wrong?" he asked.

Carl checked his watch. "No mistake with the order. Stand right there; I want you to see something."

Sure enough, one minute later the building sounded like it was caving in, and ten seconds after that, The Big Wigs from the third floor came charging down the stairs, Susan Nysohr in the fore, elbows a'flyin'. She rumbled across the foyer with her underlings in tow and stormed the buffet table. On her first pass, Susan snarfed up a sandwich, two pickles and a half dozen éclairs. After eating their fill, she and her colleagues loaded up their purses and pockets, retreating at precisely the stroke of noon.

The new principal said, "I've never seen a wheat field being Biblically assailed by a swarm of locusts, but I can now imagine it."

Carl intoned, "And the Philistines did layeth waste to the buffet table, lest one grain spoileth, and yea, it was good – 'specially those yummy little éclairs – and behold, it came to pass that the frock of the maiden Nysohr did seemeth to billow like unto a parachute, and verily, the Philistines did not rejoiceth."

The same group met in the afternoon, this time to discuss strategies that might better guarantee student success. "We have several proposals we'd like to share with you today," said Dr. Krabke, amidst a flurry of twitches and blinks. "I trust you will find them as exciting as we do." He paused, in hopes that we might soak up the excitement, the sizzle in the air. "For our low-achieving 9th grade math students, we will offer Acceleration Classes."

"Acceleration," I said. "That makes it sound like an honors class."

"It does have a positive connotation, doesn't it?" The Krabman swelled up like ex-power forward Shawn Kemp of the Seattle Sonics after Nate McMillan alley-ooped him the ball for a slam dunk. Taking a moment to bask in the glow of an imaginary spotlight, The Krabman crowed, "Some of you may not be aware that Mr. Haldini here is one of my former scholars."

Carl asked, "So the Acceleration Classes will take the place of regular classes?"

"No," said Penelope Prismark. "We have, like, a different approach in mind. Dr. Krabke?"

The Krabman grinned like a game show host about to give away a brand…. new…. car!

"Here is our plan: Students who fail the math section of the WASL will take a second math class, a WASL Prep class."

Several of those seated around the table looked like they'd been handed the keys to a Ford Pinto, and guess who was gonna have to tow it home, blown head gasket and all.

On the other hand, having taught my share of Pre-algebra classes, I could understand why we'd want to try something new. On four occasions at Fernwater, we had not offered a Pre-alg class.

One year we placed our 9ᵗʰ grade pre-alg kids back in 8ᵗʰ grade math and let them repeat it, which was a disaster – the leaders in a class tend to be the older students, who, in that case, happened to be the most troubled, least successful kids. Another year we gave the pre-alg kids a year off from math, which resulted in a different sort of disaster – when they went to take math in high school, they had by that time lost whatever skills they'd acquired, and then they were really behind. One year we stuck our pre-alg kids in Algebra and crossed our fingers. That was also a disaster; all but three of them failed and the rest raised hell on a daily basis. And finally, one year we tried a mix of these three approaches; all it did was spread the misery around.

Penelope Prismark said, "Research shows that, like, once kids get placed in a remedial class, they never catch up. That's exactly what happened to my husband Johnny. 93% of remedial students, like, stay in that track forever."

Carl scribbled on my ChInSu notepad: 86.13% of statistics are made up.

I asked The Krabman, "What about students who fail the writing section of the WASL?"

"They will take a WASL Prep Writing Class." His grin broadened, like he had just wrapped up the new car with ribbons and a bow, and attached balloons to the side mirrors.

"And what about kids that fail both sections of the WASL?" I asked peevishly.

The Krabman regarded me like I was a 14-year-old punk with a switchblade, sniffin' around his new car, ready to poke holes in the tires. Twitch twitchy twitch.

He said, "We need to do what's best for kids."

It required a gargantuan effort to resist asking what that meant. The Krabman nodded smugly, watching us choke back questions and emotionally strangle ourselves. My skull was ready to implode. This was my "Come to Jesus" moment; I found myself praying for a lightning bolt to appear out of the clear blue sky and smite him. Or perhaps the Creator could be persuaded to open up a meter-wide sinkhole and swallow The Krabman whole.

"Don't do anything foolhardy," whispered Carl, sliding the staple gun out of my reach. He took out his cell and put 911 on speed dial.

We resisted asking the inevitable question as long as we could, but it was like holding your breath – you can't do it forever.

Carl finally broke down. "Doing what's best for kids; exactly what would that entail?"

"They will take *two* Acceleration Classes." The Krabman was pleased as a papa of newborn twins.

I imagined some of my fidgety, lower ability students sitting in a desk all day. How will our present day Josh McClowns do without PE to burn off some excess energy or Art class to encourage creativity? Picturing Jeff Mori wrestle with algebra gave me heartburn. And what a joy it would be to teach Johnny Boe two math classes a day.

"So those kids won't take any electives?" asked Carl.

The Krabman's twitching and blinking accelerated. He looked like someone had pointed out a smudge on the car's candy apple red finish.

"No electives," I said. "Is that what's best for kids?"

Reuben Rapp, now Fernwater's principal, said, "With regards to the WASL, several teachers in my building express concern about how much time they spend teaching to the test. The consensus is…."

Bonnie had had it with this group of whiners and rabble-rousers. "*Excuse* me." We all clammed up. "If, by 'teach to the test', we mean 'focus on essential learning', Ah will need it explaaained to me what the problem is. If, by 'teach to the test', we mean 'encourage our students to excel', Ah will need it explaaained to me what the problem is." She glared at each principal in turn. "If, by 'teach to the test', we mean 'expect the best from classroom teachers', Ah will need it explaaained to me what the problem is."

The Krabman gave a tiny fist pump. "Well said, Mrs. Rhodes!" Revived by her preachin', he was set to launch into the next agenda item, but Carl was not finished.

"Just so I have this straight…." He looked morose, but he managed to keep his tone even. "Our least successful, least academically inclined students will be required to sit in desks for six hours straight?"

I tried unsuccessfully to keep the rancor out of my voice. "We are already short on math teachers. If we offer more math classes, who will teach them?"

Even Penelope piled on. "No PE, no shop, no music, no, like, art classes?" Two years of analyzing WASL data and writing mission statements had taken their toll on her perky attitude and team player mentality.

Reuben Rapp, wearing his One Good Tern sweatshirt, said, "One reason for offering a rich and varied curriculum is for kids to discover the value of academics. In photography and woodshop and music, it helps to know math."

The Krabman said, "For our gifted students...."

"*Excuse* me." Bonnie slapped the table with both hands. "Are not allll of our students gifted in their own way?"

Dr. Krabke had the look of a man who had made the mistake of parking his new car in one of the older, dilapidated neighborhoods of Oxley for thirty minutes. Upon returning, he found the car up on blocks, the stereo gone, in need of a paint job and a new set of tires.

Chapter 31 – March

I was cutting up mushrooms, onions and jalepenõs for the chili when Carl arrived. He noodled around on my 12-string until Anjuli showed up ten minutes later and Giz a couple minutes after that. Like our first dinner party, everybody hung around the kitchen.

Giz asked Carl to play an original. He thought a minute and said, "Haldini, you know this one; wanna help out?"

I picked up my Martin and tuned up. He began strumming and I joined in finger-picking. "North of Heaven" is my favorite of his songs, the last verse of which goes like this:

> We've all heard those travelling tales
> Somebody must have returned
> Whether myth or a memory
> We'll leave this island astern
> Thousands of blue miles ahead of us
> Somewhere, north of heaven

"Nice," said Anjuli. "What was your inspiration?"

"In general, it's about restlessness. Specifically, it's about the Polynesians that paddled 3000 miles to settle Hawaii a thousand years ago, give or take."

"Now that's what I call an adventure."

We were all emailing one another on an almost daily basis; Carl had offered to bring rum to make daiquiris. Giz brought strawberries and bananas, and Anjuli brought chocolate liqueur.

Carl and Anjuli filled my blender with strawberries and ice and then compared recipes.

She asked, "How many milliliters in a jigger?"

"How many ounces in a tablespoon?" asked Carl. "How many pecks in a bushel?" He dumped in a fourth of the bottle and set the blender on "liquefy".

"Giz," I said, "do you get the feeling these drinks are going to be strong?"

"Fo' shizzle.   Anybody know where the word 'daiquiri' comes from?"

With no hesitation, Carl said, "It's the name of a town in Cuba. Daiquiris were used by miners to fight off disease."

Anjuli was unsure whether to be skeptical or impressed. "It that true? Leo, how does he know stuff like that?"

"Got me.   But he'd kick some serious butt on Jeopardy."

Carl crossed his eyes. "Yep, my skull's full of all kinds of brilliant, worthless stuff."

Anjuli poured drinks and passed them around. "Fight off disease, huh? Then this will be good for what ails you." She held up her glass and toasted, "To friends, old and new."

"Geez Louise!" I said. "That's gooood medicine, but don't anybody light a match."

Carl nodded and then asked Giz about his golf game.

Giz shook his head woefully. "I've played three rounds in the last two weeks, and my shots are ten yards longer than they're supposed to be. *Consistently* ten yards longer – weird, huh?"

"It's a humbling sport," said Carl, then turned to Anjuli. "What's new? You said you were going to apply for a job at the hospital. I bet you interview well."

She flashed him a smile I'd never seen before. It was soft and wide-open, but not really a come on. Giz caught the look too, and knowing how protective of her he was, I wondered if he was bothered by it.

"They offered me the job, but I turned them down, because Giz here...." Anjuli grabbed his arm and squeezed. ".... got me a job at Pac En Con."

Responding to Carl's confused look, Giz explained, "Pacific Environmental Consultants, that's where I work. But I didn't *get* you job, Anjulius. You went in and ...."

Anjuli ran her hands through his jumble of hair. "Let's just say he put in a *very* good word for me. I start Monday, doing hydraulic analysis for the county, to protect streams and lakes." She looked back and forth between Carl and me. "How's life at Crazy Town, boys?" Though exuberant, she is not a conversation hog. Seeing Carl's pained look, she topped off his glass and asked,

"What ails you?"

Carl leaned over and bonked his head twice on the counter. "Susan Nysohr – that's our superintendent – is suing the federal government over No Child Left Behind. Leo, did you see the sign in the lobby today? NO SCHOOL LEFT BEFUNDED."

"Is that even a word?" asked Giz.

"Don't think so," I said. "There was another sign last week that said: NO CHILD LEFT BEFRIENDED."

"Who puts them up? Your superintendent?"

"Nobody knows. But they don't seem to bother her." I ground more pepper into the sauce and tasted it. "Needs oregano."

"And she's paranoid," said Carl. "She thinks Bush is going to – oh, I don't know – sic the IRS on her or something. It would be nice to have a leader."

Anjuli delivered her response with a straight face, "Sounds like you have a milli-leader."

"Ahhh, metric humor," I said.

"Uncle Leo, does Carl know the Russian Fags Story?"

"You tell it, Anj. You've heard it enough times."

Carl covered his ears and rocked back and forth. "I don't want to hearrrrrr this."

Giz waved his hand. "I know the story! Anjupiter, do you mind if I tell it?"

I said, "Anjupiter? Was that spontaneous, or did you plan et?" Carl scowled.

Giz didn't hesitate. "Good one, *Mars*ter Haldini."

Anjuli said, "Giz, he's gonna kick your asteroid and then write your *orbit*uary."

We kept this up until Carl covered his ears again and wailed, "Stop! Please stop!" He tentatively lowered his hands. "Is this what Haldini's classroom was like?"

"No," said Giz. "It was much, much worse."

Carl looked distressed. "Horrifying. What's the Russian.... story?"

Giz said, "See, Fernwater used to be an open-concept school, no walls, lotsa noise, paper airplanes and kumquats flying overhead, the average kid had the IQ of a sea anemone." He inhaled. "OK, here goes: Leo had a teacher in 9th grade that said, 'Every other industrialized country in the world had, unwisely in his opinion, switched to the metric system.' And this kid says, 'Nuh-uh, that only applies to foreign countries.' Another kid says, 'Nuh-uh, what about Canada?' *Another* kid says, 'No way! Canada's not a foreign country!' And another kid says, 'Oh, yes it is! Canada's part of Russia!'"

I prefer his version of this story to mine; it's more animated in the telling. Anjuli was clapping and squealing in anticipation of Gizmo's punch line:

"The last kid says, 'Yeah, and they're a bunch of fags!'"

Carl laughed along with us, but then he said, "No. That did not happen."

I held up my three Boy Scout fingers. "I swear it did. That's the problem with telling vintage Fernwater stories – they're hard to believe, unless you were there. But get this: that teacher was our very own Dr. James Krabke."

"No! What was that bit about 'unwisely in his opinion'?"

"Isn't that wild? The Krabman says the record for the hundred yard dash at the U Dub should belong to him. He still blames the switch from yards to meters."

Carl said, "He'll go ballistic when you make your Going Metric proposal."

"That's OK," I said. "I've talked to our superintendent about it, and she's on board. We're in good shape."

Speaking of ballistic," said Giz. "Did you hear about the space probe that crashed on Mars because some guys at NASA measured in yards, some measured in meters, and nobody did the conversion? A hundred million bucks and a cloud of dust."

An hour later, we sat for dinner and I bowed my head. Borrowing liberally from Carl's routine at the district luncheon, I intoned, "Thou hast gathered us here to breaketh this bread, verily, this corn bread, and to buttereth it abundantly; thou shalt dippeth thy bread in thine chili, which smoketh as a lake of fire and brimstone, though I knoweth not what brimstone is."

I lifted my head and everyone dug in. We discussed work, golf and, of course, my chili.

Acting the stern headmistress, Anjuli asked, "Did everyone do their homework?"

We mumbled in mock subservience, "Yes, ma'am."

"OK," she said, "whatcha got? Go around the table; tell me your first choice for this project. Giz, you go first."

"I don't know what the solution is, but I believe all major problems in the world can be traced back to fossil fuels. Many of the wars in the Middle East wouldn't have happened if not for oil."

"How about overpopulation?" said Carl.

"It wouldn't matter so much if oil weren't such a scarce commodity."

"How about climate change?" I asked. "Oh! Never mind."

Anjuli said, "Hunger?"

"If we weren't short of oil, it would be easy to produce more food. As for the solution, I'm not sure. Sea power? Wind? Ethanol's not great, because when you figure in the acreage needed to grow corn, and calculate the number of bushels produced, and then factor in the energy used to convert it into ethanol, you end up with this: To fuel one car with ethanol for a year requires seven times as much cropland as is needed to feed one American."

Anjuli said, "What exactly is a bushel?"

I saw that as my opening. "Who knows? Which brings me to my suggestion: A lot of problems in the world exist because people don't communicate well. The closest thing we have to a universal language is mathematics, and even that's not universal. It's a small idea, but I recommend changing to the metric system."

Carl asked, "Any idea how you'd approach that?"

"There are several ways – legislate it, change curriculum, change textbooks, lobby scientific and business communities."

"Would you change curriculum at the district level or state? Or national?"

"Good question; the higher up you go, the harder to change, but the more powerful that change would be."

Anjuli said, "Uncle Leo, remember how you taught us to do geometric proofs? You don't just start at the top and going roaring straight through. You work from the top a little and then work from the bottom, and you meet up in the middle. Effecting change is like that – it has to be both top-down and bottom-up."

I spread my hands and preened. "Did I do a good job or what?"

"Yes, you did," said Anjuli, taking a swat at me. "For a total nerd. OK, so far we have fossil fuels and the metric system.

I'll go next: Kenya's medical facilities don't even begin to address the needs of their malnourished children. This is happening *now*. Five million kids worldwide die every year from starvation."

I asked, "And what would you do about it?"

She ticked off the solutions on her fingers. "Prenatal care. HIV medicine. Education. Breakfast programs. I could go on and on."

Carl furrowed his brow. "I never know how to say this without sounding like a sociopath, but here goes: If we improve health care now, if we export food and drugs, we save lives, and that's a wonderful thing, but in twenty years...." He sounded sheepish. "Twenty years down the road, you have even more kids dying of hunger and AIDS."

Anjuli was incredulous. "So, you're saying we should cut these kids loose, so they can't...." She glowered at him. ".... so they can't *breed,* and breed more problems?"

Carl persisted in a quiet though impassioned tone. "No, I'm not saying that. Look, I've been to Nepal, I met people who live on a dime a day, I know what it's like to have 4-year-olds look up at you with outstretched hands, dark eyes pleading for help, flies feeding off sores on their lip. Believe me; my heart's been broken."

Anjuli sat smoldering with her arms folded.

Carl continued, "I see the value of feeding kids, I do, of bringing them medicine, but if you *only* do that, if you only think short-term, then you, *we*, are compounding the problem."

She asked warily, "Then what would you suggest?"

Carl took a deep breath. "There are too many people in the world. Billions of people live in conditions that wild animals would not tolerate. We've short-circuited natural selection; we keep everyone alive now, because we humans are so big-hearted. In the long run, though, we do ourselves a disservice. Every generation gets weaker and the bugs get stronger." He was ranting now. "If we don't rein ourselves in, nature will."

Anjuli glared at him. "So you're saying.... what? Maybe let a few billion die off so the world is less cluttered for *you*?"

I had never seen Carl angry before. "No, that's not what I'm saying! But we need to consider the future; we need to look more than five minutes ahead. We need to address birth control, we need to educate people and take on the Catholic Church, we need...."

Anjuli opened her mouth, but I cut in. "The world needs both of you." My inclination was to Take A Stand, one way or the other, but there was a more important issue at stake here. I said, "Without Carl's way of thinking, the world's problems increase exponentially. Without people like Anjuli, we would have driven ourselves off a cliff long ago. This is not an either/or situation."

Carl and Anjuli declared an unspoken truce, but it was obvious that both felt betrayed. We finished dinner and talked about various things, but our sense of camaraderie had dissipated. I had thought we might sit around the fire pit with a round of chocolate daiquiris, but it was not going to happen. Carl put on his jacket and went out to the backyard by himself.

I joined him five minutes later, and we watched the koi negotiate the underwater lights. Though this was the last day of March and fairly warm, he was shaking.

"Guess I blew that," he said.

I placed a hand on his shoulder. "No, I don't think you did. The two of you are looking at the same problem from different directions. And you both want to make the world better."

"Yeah." He nodded tentatively. "Yeah, I believe that. But...." He clasped his hands tightly behind his head. "Jesus! I came across as.... She thinks I'm a total ass."

I could not disagree. "I hope you two can find a way to reconcile your world views."

We went back inside, and Carl said, "Good to see you guys. I'm gonna take off."

Anjuli said she was leaving as well, and I saw them to the door. Giz offered to help me clean up, and I accepted. We started in on the kitchen, and I asked where he'd come up with his fossil fuels perspective.

He didn't hear me. "She can sure be stubborn," he said, while putting the leftover cornbread into a baggie.

"I guess, but was she more stubborn than Carl?"

"Yes. He was regretful; she wasn't. It will be hard for her to find a guy to settle down with. He'd have to be flexible enough to put up with her, but not so flexible that she'll walk all over him." He paused. "That was the problem between the two of us.

When she told me to be more assertive, I shrugged and said, 'OK'."

He chuckled and gave me an uncomprehending shake of his head.

Ten minutes later, the counters were clean and the dishes piled in the sink to soak. I made a couple of chocolate daiquiris and we carried them into the living room. Voices drifted in through the window, which I had inadvertently left ajar that afternoon. We tiptoed to the window and eavesdropped on Carl and Anjuli, who were sitting on my porch. Standing behind the drapes, we could only hear snippets of their conversation: "Kenya, the most....", "....star-gazing sometime...." and "metric humor".

We then heard a three-syllable chuckle from Anjuli, which at that moment was the most beautiful sound I could imagine. It was not clear to me, however, how that chuckle was received by Giz.

Chapter 32 – April

Forty emails were waiting for me when I got to work. Most were from teachers across the district, responding to a survey I had sent out regarding use of the metric system. It was gratifying to see that almost all of them, even those teaching outside of math and science fields, used the metric system on a regular basis, and most favored adopting an all-metric curriculum.

I also received an email from Anjuli. It had been sent at 4:27 a.m. to Carl, Giz and myself:

Boys, I had a great time last night. April Fools! lol   Uncle Leo, thanks for dinner. I still have dragon breath from the garlic, but K'boodle – that's my cat – doesn't seem to mind.

Leo, can we invite ourselves over again for dinner the first Saturday in May? ☺ My goal is to decide about the grant by June 1st. So I'm giving you boys another assignment (moo-hoo-ha-ha-ha ← that's my scary, wicked laugh). Actually, it's the same assignment as last time. Pick ONE IDEA (!!!) and research it. And so that Carl and I don't throttle each other (j/k, kind of ☺), the idea must address immediate concerns AND have a long-range vision attached. A tall order, but there it is.

I'm moving into an apartment in a few weeks. I love my fam, but I've had my fill. Could I get one of you to help me move some boxes Saturday evening the 25th?

Love you boys, Anj

p.s. Do you guys know about the Medici (pronounced: med' uh chee) family? What am I saying? Carl, I bet you do.

Giz and Carl had already emailed her back using the "reply to all" button. Giz couldn't help with the move, but Carl said he'd be happy to.

That day I was scheduled to meet with four aspiring teachers from the U Dub. I wanted them to see how a variety of teachers at Fernwater Junior High managed their classes.

I arrived early to walk the halls. This being my third year out of the classroom, it was the first year that none of my ex-students would be here. Each time I turned a corner, I looked for a familiar face, out of habit. It was disconcerting, navigating the narrow hallways, being jostled by adolescents, none of whom I recognized.

Most of the teachers were still here from three years ago, and it was good to see them, though disorienting; much of the banter that goes on between teachers involves concerns about administration or anecdotes about students. We no longer shared that common ground.

I poked my head into my old classroom. It was a shock to see my pictures, cartoons and paper maché creatures taken down.

"May I help you?" I had not noticed the tall, youthful woman standing in the far corner.

"Oh, uh, this used to be my room."

"Mr. Haldini?"

That was unexpected. "Yeah?"

"Last week I found a folder full of letters that had fallen behind a file cabinet. I was going to toss them, but…. Well, I read a couple of them." She blushed. "I couldn't bring myself to throw them away."

She rooted around in her desk and handed me a manila folder with a couple dozen letters in it.

I had searched for these letters on my last day at Fernwater. I opened one at random:

Haldini Meany,

I can't believe you're leaving – who's going to teach my little brother algebra? Who's going to tell him lies, like .9 repeating equals one? Who's going to make up taxi stories?

Seriously though, thank you for all you taught me, not just about math (which I liked this year), but about life and friendship. Thanks for asking about boys (by the way, me and Ben finally kissed!) and cheering me up when me and Mom got in a fight.

Enjoy your new job, but I predict you'll miss teaching. You're going to miss us!

Love, Cheetah

p.s. Get married!

I wished I could go home, brew a pot of tea and read them all. I thanked the woman, then wiped my eyes and left.

The four teachers-to-be were waiting in the office. After introductions were made, I explained that the big push in the district this year was "writing across the curriculum"; in an effort to improve literacy, all teachers in all subjects were expected to give writing assignments.

"But remember," I told them, "today we are focusing specifically on classroom management."

Our first stop was Heidi Blohmeyer's 8th grade PE class. It had taken her several years to realize that counselors don't have much time to actually counsel kids; mostly what they do is create master schedules, balance class loads, stare at computer screens, administer the WASL and then analyze the scores. So she had requested to teach PE, and though she is now well into her fifties, she has slimmed down and firmed up. In a word, she's a fox.

I introduced her to my charges, and Heidi told them the class would be performing an exercise in expository writing. Then, without saying anything or signaling in any overt way, she and I communicated back and forth:

Isn't this a crock? Her eyes said it all.

Certainly is.

Just doing what I'm told.

Know what you mean.

The bell rang, and I whispered to Heidi, "Enjoy your *suppository* writing. Hope you don't have any assholes in class."

She gave me a you-loser look and called out, "Find your places. Take out a piece of paper."

The kids sat on the floor in rows and columns, and opened their notebooks.

Heidi said, "I would like you to write an expository essay, explaining how to shoot a basketball."

Eyeballs rolled, heads drooped and kids gazed up wistfully

at the basketball hoops.

An Asian girl mumbled, "Holy crap! In PE?"

She must be new to our district.

Heidi picked up a basketball, dribbled a few times, bent at the knees and drained a three-pointer. "I want you to explain, or describe, how to shoot a basketball."

After a few grumbles, the students dutifully started in on the assignment. Some sat cross-legged on the floor; others leaned against bleachers. Heidi walked around, alternately checking their work and riding herd on two kids: a fidgety Hispanic boy – I'd have been willing to bet his name was Javier, Juan or Jorge – that kept singing the refrain from the Black-eyed Peas tune "Let's Get it Started"; and a girl that responded with "Let's get retarded."

Ten minutes into class, Heidi called out, "Finish this up tonight!"

The gym erupted with yelps of joy as students ran to get basketballs. The college students and I stood off to the side and watched for a while, then conferred.

"Observations?" I asked, and got no response. "Did you notice how Mrs. Blohmeyer handled the situation with the spiky-haired girl?"

Three of them looked at me blankly, but the oldest of the group, a middle-aged woman said, "Spike stole money from that boy in the striped shirt. Without stopping class, the teacher retrieved the money, made the girl apologize, and asked for her dad's phone number."

My guess was that this woman had raised kids of her own, and was now embarking on a new career.

Ten minutes later, I tried again. "We are focusing on classroom management. What have you seen?"

After a pause, the middle-aged woman said, "See that Asian girl, the one in blue? New kid; Mrs. Blohmeyer paired her up with that friendly boy with the long black hair."

It took me a moment to recognize Mini Mutant. Though he now stood about 5' 8", I could still see in him the exuberant three-year-old I met in Safeway a decade ago.

"Questions?" I asked my charges. "Comments?"

One of the teachers-in-training, an earnest looking young man in a blue shirt and white tie, asked, "Was she using the

Jamison Method to teach writing skills?"

"I…. Well, I'm not sure."

Our next stop was Felix Hester's 9th grade Language Arts class. Now in his late fifties, he sports a beard and a glossy white mane. I occasionally meet him for coffee on weekends, and I keep current with the series of editorials he writes for the Herald, entitled "Armageducation" and published under the pseudonym Ed U. Cajun. One of his columns, subtitled "Politicians, Principals and Parents", was based in part on one of my caffeinated rants about what's wrong with education.

Fester's latest column addressed the district's decision to allow 9th graders to take the 10th grade WASL, under the guise of "opening options". The Agin' Cajun, as Fester refers to himself, offered up another motive for making the change: It would tend to be the sharper, more successful 9th graders that opt to take the test, thereby goosing our WASL scores.

Boy, did the third floor Big Wigs work themselves up over that one:

"Who is this Mr. Cajun?"

"Can't we shut him down?"

"I wish he'd move back to Louisiana."

I sat in the back of Fester's class with the teachers-to-be and listened to a class discussion about *Huckleberry Finn*. The students had read about half the book so far.

A soft-spoken girl said, "Twain uses the word…." Her eyes scoured the class, landing on a Black classmate. "…. the N word." She said it apologetically, obviously disturbed by its very existence. "Why does he do that? How does he get away with it?"

A boy answered in a cocky tone. "That was what people called African Americans in the 1800's. It wasn't a rude term, at least not like it is now."

The girl said, "It's offensive, so how can we justify…. Why do we read this?"

A Hispanic boy said, "When we read that word now, we're not making fun of Blacks. I read it as – I don't know – anybody who uses that word is making a fool of himself."

Felix nodded approvingly.

A voice from the front of the room asked, "If this book was

written in 1885, and the Civil War was in 1860-something, how come they're still talking about owning slaves?"

Fester said, "It was written in 1885, but set in the 1840s."

The class discussed racial issues in the US after the Civil War and contrasted them with present day. Fester talked sparingly. Mostly he directed traffic, throwing out an occasional question or comment and making sure nobody hogged the floor.

"I want you to write for ten minutes," said Fester. He then turned on his overhead, where he had written two questions:

1) When Huck dressed like a girl and visited the woman in town, how did she know he was a boy?"
2) Do you consider Huck to be a moral person?

As kids wrote, Fester walked around the room and pulled aside three kids who had not answered the first question.

"Why didn't you read the book?"

Two of them mumbled, "Sorry."

"If this happens again, you fail the unit. Come to class ready to learn. Got it?" He sent them back to their seats.

The third kid was a sniffling six-footer that might have been Polynesian. The boy was on the verge of tears, so Fester led him out of class. Fester came back thirty seconds later, and the kid returned three minutes after that.

Opening his grade book, Fester said, "I'm going to pick a name at random to answer the second question. Was Huck a moral person?" He placed his finger on the grade book, looked down, and called out a name.

A boy in the back row flinched. "It's hard to say," he said. "Because, I mean, he was always trying to figure out what was the right thing to do, and then he'd do what he considered to be the wrong thing, but a lot of times it turned out to be the right thing, like helping Jim escape."

In rapid fire, several kids responded:

"From our point of view, he usually picked the right thing to do, but from the point of view of the times, it might have been the wrong thing."

"So Mark Twain was ahead of his time?"

"Hold on. How do we define what is moral?"

And so the conversation went; kids were thinking and talking and challenging one another. The U Dub students were seeing Fester at the top of his game.

At one point, the discussion turned to the Civil War, and a kid asked, "Mr. Hester, you fought in a war, didn't you?"

Before he could answer, a sassy girl said, "Yeah, World War I, wasn't it?"

In a gruff voice, he asked Sassy, "Do you understand sign language?" Without waiting for a response, Fester pointed at himself, then made a fist and pointed at it with his other hand. He then pointed, in succession, at her, his own nose, and back to her again. Finally, he rubbed his eyes.

She frowned and said, "You're gonna punch me in the nose, and I'll cry?"

"Good," said Fester. "We understand each other."

When the bell rang, kids filed out and the tall, dark-skinned boy came up to thank Fester.

"Lemme know if I can help." Fester put his hand on the back of the kid's head and gave him a gentle shove toward the door.

"What's goin' on with him?" I asked.

"His mom's in the hospital; might have found cancer." We then returned to business. Fester had set aside part of his plan period for us to think through the lesson, to figure out what worked and what could have gone better.

"Questions?" he asked.

A frail young woman asked, "What preparation do you do to get students ready for the WASL?"

Fester and I gave each other a bewildered look. If you had offered us a million dollars to guess what the first question would be, we never would have come up with *that*.

Fester said, "I can give you some websites with WASL prep material. What else?"

The earnest young man said, "The Grade Machine program; do you have it set up so parents can view their kids' grades throughout the quarter?"

"No, we don't have that capability. And I'm glad of it."

"Because I know of another district that does."

Fester shook his head. "Nope. Sorry. Other questions?"

One of my charges was a history major with something of a beatnik look about him – goatee, beret, shades. He said, "I noticed you put your hand on that boy's head. Is that OK?"

Seeing Fester's confusion, the middle-aged woman explained, "We addressed that in our Legalities in Education class, about taking a 'hands off' approach in dealing with kids. And in our Diversities class, we talked about how people from some cultures don't like to be touched on the head."

"Our purpose in coming here," I said, "was to have you watch a grizzled veteran – heh, heh, heh – work his magic. Do you have comments or questions about classroom management?"

The beatnik raised his hand – well, actually he raised a finger. "Students with Individual Education Programs – how do you accommodate them?"

What had they been watching for the past hour?

The teachers-in-training left a few minutes later to get back to their own classes.

Fester sighed. "What are they teaching in college these days?"

"Do you ever get disheartened? How much longer are you going to teach?"

"Oh, I could have retired comfortably two years ago. But I still get a kick out of coming to school. Yes, the WASL is the devil's spawn, and you and I have talked about a host of other problems, but…. you know what? As The Who once sang, 'The kids are all right.' And when you consider how things were when you attended Fernwater, life is heavenly."

Surprisingly, I had never made that comparison. And now, the issues that played a part in convincing me to leave the classroom three years ago seem downright trivial.

I said, "Considering how wild Fernwater used to be, how come you, and so many teachers, have stayed?"

"This place was hell when it first opened, but it was a great bonding experience. Believe it or not, it had calmed down by the time you came through. And it got better every year – walls, new administration, and then of course the earthquake. Some of us put down roots. And one of us.... well, one of us just got stuck here."

There was no need to mention Winnie De Waart by name.

Fester shrugged. "Madness comes, madness goes."

Chapter 33 - May

"Who is the Medici family?" asked Giz.

The gang was once again standing around my kitchen, yakking and drinking wine while I fixed the salad. On a base of mixed greens, I added gorgonzola cheese, apple slices and candied pecans. Lasagna was baking in the oven. After years of tinkering with my grandmother's recipe, I had finally come to realize that I was not going to improve upon perfection.

Anjuli looked at Carl. "Professor?"

Carl hesitated. "I don't know much about...."

"Oh, knock it off," I said. "You always say that, and then you give a three-hour dissertation on whatever it is you supposedly know nothing about."

"Not true. People get up and leave after two hours."

"Good point; take it away."

"The Medicis were a powerful family in Florence – they were popes and bankers, and more or less kicked off the Italian Renaissance. And Lorenzo Medici, Lorenzo the Magnificent, is arguably the most influential human being of the past thousand years. Hold it! Why am I doing this?"

"Boy, you do miss teaching, don't you? From zero to sixty in zero seconds." She gave him a playful punch on the shoulder and said, "Go on."

"Lorenzo would host these lavish dinner parties, and invite Michelangelo, DaVinci and Botticelli, and they'd talk about art, technology and the Greeks, and drink wine until the sun came up."

Giz said, "Let me guess, Anjuniper; are you suggesting that we are the reincarnation of the Medicis?"

Anjuli extended her hand with a flourish. "May I present Leo Haldini, our Italian host and chef. Giz and Carl are brilliant and well-read. And I.... love wine!"

"Hmmm, the Medicis." I wrote down the word "meta-cheese" on a paper towel.

Carl and Giz applauded.

Anjuli asked, "What does 'meta' mean?"

"One meaning is 'transcending'," said Carl, raising his glass. "A toast; to transcending cheese."

We clinked glasses and solemnly repeated, "To transcending cheese." Anjuli burst into laughter in mid-swallow, squirting a geyser of wine out her nose.

"Nice, Anjuvenile." Giz grabbed her by the wrist and led her over to the sink. "C'mon, let's hose ya down."

While drying herself off, she said, "I brought up the Medicis for a reason – see, when Lorenzo hosted dinner parties, his home became a classroom." She looked intently at each of us. "Uncle Leo, that's how I think of your kitchen – it feels like a classroom, just the opposite of ten years ago – your classroom seemed like home to me, back when my parents were talking divorce." I was set to say something sappy, but she gave me a sly smile and said, "I like it better now cuz you feed us."

"I do my best. Speaking of which, you guys ready for appetizers?"

"Yeah," said Carl. "But could we appetize outside?"

We brought our wine out to the backyard and nibbled on Muenster cheese, crackers and sliced pears.

Carl turned his face up to the sun. "After hibernating for six months, I am starving for vitamin D."

Giz noticed that Carl and Anjuli were sitting elbow to elbow. He said, "Maybe you need to move to a sunnier climate."

Yikes! I thought the two men had bonded. Was Giz now trying to edge him out? Could be, but he didn't seem miffed.

"OK, people, focus," said Anjuli. "We've put forth four ideas: Fossil fuels, health clinics, overpopulation and the metric system."

Giz choked on a cracker and blurted out: "Carl, I didn't tell you! You know how all my golf shots were ten yards too long? It turns out my range finder was set for meters instead of yards."

"I rest my case," I said smugly. "Changing to the metric system would relieve human suffering. Inches and ounces are the root of all evil. Golf will be more fun, and daiquiris will be easier to make – no more converting ounces to jiggers to bushels."

Carl added, "And Russian fags will be happier."

Anjuli scanned her list. "OK, next up, fossil fuels." She looked at Giz expectantly.

He answered, "We don't have the expertise, contacts or funds necessary to address alternate energy concerns. As far as conservation of fuel goes, the biggest wastage comes from flying."

Anj, Giz and I responded with some variation of: "What do you mean?"

"I hate to say this, because I know how much you all love to travel, but when you look at the economics of flying, it gets disturbing in a hurry. If you take a 737 flying from Seattle to New York – that's 3000 miles, 150 passengers, 2 *gallons* per *mile* – it works out to 40 gallons per person, one way. That's how much gas an American uses in a month, assuming 12,000 miles per year in a car that gets 25 miles per gallon."

Carl was skeptical, so Giz asked for a pen and paper and laid it out for him. Carl massaged his forehead and moaned.

To clarify his point, Giz said, "So if a family of three takes two trips per year to the east coast and back, they use enough fuel to drive another car. Wanna talk about European vacations? Or carbon dioxide emissions?"

"Thank you for that uplifting presentation," said Anjuli. "Got any other cheery news?"

"I have an idea to run by you, but it can wait."

Anjuli started to respond, but then let it go. She looked at her list. "Next: population concerns or health clinics?"

Carl said immediately, "I vote for health clinics. What do you have in mind?"

"First off, remember that we want to think short term *and* long. So, I've considered using the grant money to open up a clinic in Kenya; it wouldn't just be about healing people, it should also be about education, teaching people how to take care of themselves, about HIV and birth control."

She looked at Carl, her expression a mixture of hopefulness and resolve.

"I like that," he said. "I like it a lot. Would you work as an EMT or a nurse? Or would you manage the clinic?"

She threw her hands up. "See? That's what so frustrating. I know nothing about running a business, and a nursing degree is years away. Med school is even further. And how do you go about finding doctors willing to work in the middle of nowhere?"

I asked, "Is Kenya short on nurses and doctors?"

"Ahem," said Giz.

Anjuli said, "I've heard that doctors...."

"*Ahem!*" We turned to Giz, who said, "I assumed that this project would end up back in Kenya, so I took the liberty of running off what are known as 'background notes'." He got up and retrieved a manila folder he'd left in the kitchen.

Carl called, "What are background notes?"

Upon his return, Giz smiled broadly, taunting him. "The professor doesn't *know*? Oooh, I am soooo pleased. If a senator, or anybody, is going to travel abroad, they go on the State Department's website and pull up background notes on that country – five pages or so of economic stats, a capsule history, population, education, type of government, current events. And they keep it up to date, within a couple weeks."

Carl said, "So if Dick Cheney told Bush to take a trip to, say, Austria...."

I jumped in. "Dubya would say, 'Oh, goody, kangaroos!'"

"Cheap shot," said Giz. "Poor Dick 'n' Bush, our humble *pubic* servants."

Anjuli said to Carl, "Wasn't Bush an idiot on 'Meet the Press' last week?"

He looked startled, and she immediately began reading the background notes aloud: "82% literacy rate, first eight years of schooling free and compulsory, per capita income $432...."

They'd become skittish all of a sudden. Why? Why be embarrassed about "Meet the Press"? I had seen that interview Sunday morning, and there was nothing that would have ....

Hold it. Meet the Press, Sunday morning.... *early* Sunday morning, after Carl helped her move in the night before. Carl, you sly devil! I had seen him every day this past week, and he'd made no mention of Anjuli. Oh well, at least he has good taste. And so does she. Pleased with my detective work, I kept my eyes open for more clues.

".... the Kikuyu are the dominant ethnic group, one fifth of the populace are farmers.... This is good stuff. Thanks, Giz, but it doesn't give stats about health or the causes...."

"Ahem!" Giz held up a sheaf of papers. "I found other

websites that offer up stats on health, education, industry."

Anjuli patted his cheek. "Giz, you da bomb."

Carl gave her a bemused look, and I said, "You've been out of the classroom too long. 'Da bomb' – it's more or less an update of 'phat' or 'rad' or 'groovy'."

Carl struck his best hip-hop pose, elbows out to the side and fingers splayed, which on him looked just plain goofy-assed, and said, "Fo' shizzle."

Anjuli's looked at him with a peculiar mixture of affection and revulsion. She said, "You know, if guys were vegetables, you'd be a rutabaga."

Carl acted flattered. "Thank you, my dear."

"Hopeless." Shaking her head, she said to Giz, "Pass those around, would you?"

We spent the next ten minutes reading and tossing out random statistics:

"Infant mortality rate, 6.6%, more than ten times the US."

"Doctor/patient ratio, 140 per million, compared with the US, 2500 per million."

"$1 US = 80 Kenya shillings."

I went inside to put the finishing touches on dinner, and opened the kitchen window to listen in on their conversation.

Giz said, "Anjubilant, how did your cat get the name K'boodle?"

"I got him when he was three weeks old, and named him Kitten K'boodle. He's an Angora, a big white fluff ball."

While drizzling lemon vinaigrette over the salad, I called out, "I *love* those!"

Giz called back, "Leo, how come you don't have a cat?"

"I'm thinking about getting one; I'll be home this summer."

"K'boodle's a sweetheart," said Anjuli. "But he's freaked out by the dog next door. He's run away twice."

Straight-faced, Carl said, "So you had to do a CAT scan?"

With a roll of her eyes, she said, "If comedians were currency, you'd be a shilling."

Carl responded immediately. "And if analogy-makers were animals, you'd be an amoeba."

"Oh, yeah? Well…. if people were pizzas…. you'd stink!"

Giz and Anjuli cracked up and pointed at Carl, who was

alternately smiling and wincing from having landed on his keister. He'd laughed himself right off the bench.

I placed the lasagna in the middle of the table and called them inside; Anjuli snagged the seat next to Carl. My guests were lavish in their praise of my culinary skills. We resumed our discussion of medical facilities.

"I'm stuck," said Anjuli. "Even if you build a medical clinic, how would you staff it?"

Carl nodded. "And even if you found people to staff it, you'd just be taking people away from other facilities. You wouldn't be addressing the problem."

I said, "Somehow there have to be more people *trained* in the medical profession."

"But in order to go to college," said Anjuli, "people have to go to secondary school first, and…. where was that stat about tuition?" She rifled through Gizmo's manila folder. "It costs 15,000 Kenyan shillings to attend high school, which is…. what? $200, and if…."

Carl broke in. "Hold on, $200 for high school?" He picked up a paper he'd seen earlier. "And the per capita income is 450? No way! Most kids can't afford high school. Not even close."

I said, "And even if they could, they'd be attending classes with 40 or 50 kids in them."

Giz had been so quiet that we hadn't noticed the goofy smile plastered all over his face.

The three of us said, "Whaaat?"

"Isn't it obvious? It's not a clinic you need to open up, it's a school."

I said, a bit more sharply than intended, "But you heard Anj – there aren't enough teachers to fill the schools."

Giz was patient with us. "Right, you need to open a school that will *train teachers*." He was right – it *was* obvious! To drive home his point, he referred us back to a question I had asked last winter: "Where do you get the best return? Education. Or rather, educating educators."

Anjuli eyed him suspiciously. "Was this the idea you said you wanted to run by us? You creep; you let us wander all over…. Well, it won't work anyway. I know nothing about running a school."

Giz rubbed his shoulder and winked at me. It suddenly became clear that he had set this plan in motion hours ago, or maybe days or even weeks ago.

"That's OK," he said. "Carl is coming with you. Leo, dish me up some more lasagna, would ya?"

I backed him up immediately. "Kenya is beautiful. Carl, you will love it."

Anjuli and Carl were dumbfounded. Giz hooked a thumb at him and said, "He's been a teacher, a VP, a principal, and he's worked at the district office."

"And he's not all that fond of his job," I pointed out. "Anj, you'd be doing him a huge favor."

Giz said, "You'd be liberating him, Anjulita. And he's been to Africa. What more could you want, girl? Could I have some wine over here?"

Anjuli and Carl had not yet looked at one another, and both had apparently lost the power of speech.

I said, "Oh, and Carl, no more Seattle winters. Giz, how 'bout those Mariners?"

"Go M's! Leo, the lasagna is exquisite."

"Thank you, my good man; Granny Haldini's greatest hit."

"Oh, Carl, research shows...." Giz was enjoying himself immensely. ".... that improving women's education usually acts to *decrease* population, so you need to open up a girl's school. Aaaand, in case you haven't noticed, Anjina, Carl is smitten; his heart only beats for you. Yo, Leo, more wine, her glass is getting low."

We rubbed it in until Carl and Anjuli finally worked up the nerve to look at one another.

"We been busted," she said, then skooched her chair over and rested her head on his shoulder. I thought he was going to die, from a mix of embarrassment, bewilderment and joy.

"But what about K'boodle?" asked Carl. "We can't take her with us."

"No problem," said Giz. "Leo's gonna take her."

Anjuli looked at him through narrowed eyes. "When you said that Carl should move to a sunnier climate.... Giz, if guys were diseases, you'd be dweebitis."

Chapter 34 – June

Assorted cousins, second cousins, aunts and uncles were playing a raucous game of croquet in my parents' backyard on a warm, breezy afternoon. Mom smiled grandly, pleased with the festive atmosphere of the Second Annual Haldini Reunion. Now 72, she's slowing down, but she's as congenial as ever; maybe more so, in an effort to counterbalance Dad's grumpiness.

Uncle Marco was in fine form. Sitting at a picnic table, he poured a round of sangria and said, "Abbiamo trombato come ricci!" We screwed like hedgehogs.

My uncle's wife, his third, understands less Italian than do I, but she still knows enough to be good-naturedly insulted. "You beast!" she shrieked.

I had just asked Marco about their first date. Dad was annoyed, as usual, that I not only understood his brother's bawdy language, but found it entertaining.

Terry and Jerry, Ella's nine-year-old identical twins, tugged on my arms, asking, "What did Marco say? What'd he say, Uncle Leo?"

The twins are affectionate and boisterous, that is to say, Terry is affectionate and Jerry puts the "boi" in boisterous.

My niece Lucia, now an astute 17-year-old, looked appraisingly back and forth between us adults; though she understood not a single word of Italian, she knew sex talk when she heard it. With her unusual combination of blonde hair and brown eyes, she was developing into a striking young woman. According to Ella, boys were calling night and day.

"You beast!" Marco's wife screeched again, raising her cane to smack him.

He let loose his ragged old man's laugh and fended off her blows with bony elbows and a compliment: "Lei e una ragazza a posta." She is a respectable girl. But the moment she lowered her cane, he cupped a hand around his mouth and whispered to me,

"Lei e una macchina da sesso." She is a sex machine.

"What's the old goat saying about me now?"

"Like I've said before, Auntie, I don't speak Italian."

"And like *I've* said before, you understand it." She threatened me now, and I made a crack about raising cane.

Marco puckered his lips at his wife and said, "Mi dai un bacio, piccola cucciola." Give me a kiss, my little puppy." Geez Louise, what a crusty old horndog.

Terry jumped onto my lap feet first, missing my groin by mere centimeters. "What did he say, Uncle Leo? What'd he say?"

Jerry grabbed my hand and applied his patented bend-his-little-finger-back-'til-it-snaps-off brand of torture, saying, "You better tell us."

I am fond of Ella's kids. The twins are entertaining, and Lucia is personable and forthright. Their presence serves to remind me how much I miss being around young people. Now that I'm no longer teaching, it occurred to me that maybe it's time to have a child or two of my own. Of course, there are problems with that scenario: First, women are not exactly busting down my door to bear my children; and second, even if I did get married and have, say, a daughter in the next few years, I'd be sixty before she was out of her teens. Sixty! I'd be paying for her prom dress with my social security check.

The breeze died down at dusk, and we got dive-bombed by mosquitoes. Most of the clan thanked my parents and took off, but when Ella's husband volunteered to take the twins home, allowing Ella and Lucia to stay, Uncle Marco and I decided to stick around as well. We moved the food and drinks inside, and sat around my parent's dining room table.

Ella told me, "I'm considering going back to school, to get a teaching degree. What do you think? I could do my student teaching next spring."

Lucia was alarmed. "Please tell me you won't be teaching at Fernwater."

"I could be."

"Mo-ommm!" She and Ella got along reasonably well, but the thought of having her mother at school for her senior year was too much.

Ella asked me, "Any thoughts?"

My head flopped back and I focused on a crack in the ceiling. "Ah sis, I'm not sure I could recommend education as a profession."

"Why not?"

"Oh, maybe I'm just getting crotchety, but on a typical day, teachers spend an hour emailing parents, half an hour messin' with the WASL, and half an hour filling out special ed paperwork. And in a couple years, they'll be expected to post grades online every Friday. Need I go on? There's no time to *teach* anymore. Oh, and get this...." I slapped my own face. "I'll shut up. Sis, you'll make a great teacher."

My bitching brought Dad to life. "You've got to stand up to the people who make these despotic rules. It's not like a Haldini to give up the fight so easily."

Because of his arthritis and the liver spots on his face and hands, Dad now looks like the older of the two brothers.

Shedding his happy-go-lucky veneer, Marco said, "God knows you were willing to fight sixty years ago, little brother."

Dad and my uncle have a tendency to slip back into the roles they developed as kids; those ancient dynamics and rivalries are ever vigilant, ready to pounce.

"That was a different time," Dad grumped. "And it was a different place, *brother*."

"Yes, and our neighbors were different people."

Marco gazed at the ornately framed picture of the partially burned Italian villa. Mom and Ella both got up to straighten it.

Lucia cut straight through the tension. "Was that Grampadini's home in Italy?"

Though I was an inquisitive sort as a boy, I'd heard bits of the growing-up-during-The-War talk enough times to make me want to pound nails into my ears. But I actually knew very little about Dad's life, and nothing at all about that picture, which I had always assumed to be my grandparents' home. Whenever we'd move into a new house, that photo got hung up first thing.

And now here was Lucia asking about The Old Days; I sat up and tuned in. No one had answered her, so she asked Uncle Marco, "Was that where you and Grampadini lived?"

"No, and yes."

Being as confused as I, Lucia tried a different tack. "How did it get burned? And why do you keep the picture?"

"I didn't live there." Marco sighed. "Your grandfather did, when he was 14, with some of his.... compatriots. 1944 was a bad year. We were hungry, and Mama cut up her wedding dress to make us clothes. It was cold that winter; all we had to cover our feet were zoccoli, just wooden soles with leather straps."

He was rambling now, and Mom, clearly uncomfortable with where this talk might lead, gave him a quick shake of the head. But my carefree, horny, lovable, cantankerous uncle generally preferred to say what was on his mind and then pick up the pieces later.

"Gianni kept the picture...."

Dad interrupted, "....as a reminder what happens when you don't stand up to bullies."

Lucia pressed on fearlessly. "And who were the bullies?"

"Damn communists! Wanted to run the world!" Dad spit the words out. "Mussolini had the backbone to take them on. He had le palle!" Testicles.

Lucia was incredulous, as was I. "Wait; you fought *with* Mussolini?" she said. "But, didn't he join up with Hitler?"

Ella placed a hand on her daughter's arm and asked if she had homework. Everyone ignored her.

Dad was fuming. "Yes, just as Roosevelt joined up with Stalin! America made a deal with the devil, even as the devil was killing 15 million of his own!"

"Don't tell me," I said through clenched teeth, "you and Mussolini stood up to them."

Dad sat silently with clenched teeth of his own.

"And the picture," said Lucia. "What's the story?"

"Arson," said my uncle.

Finally, catching a headshake from my mom, he zipped his own lips shut. We looked to Dad for an explanation.

My father, whose emotional state has always gravitated toward sadness, now eyed the picture with a melancholy that seemed to ooze from his pores. "We didn't intend to damage the house. We only meant to scare them away." Dad hunched over and stared silently at the table. Then he rallied and defended himself. "They were traitors to my country!"

A lifetime of dad-isms washed over me: You allow evil and ignorance to breed if you don't Take A Stand. Silence gives consent. The *Resistenza* knew how to fight. People who make the rules – *that's* where the power is. I took things from good people that were worse off than I. If you don't stand up to bullies....

His eyes boring in on Marco, Dad amended his statement: "Traitors to *our* country. Like Papa."

"Papa had sense enough to admit that he'd backed the wrong horse."

"Nonsense. Papa lived by noble principles, and then bailed out when it was convenient."

"If we're going to discuss convenience," said Marco, "we should start with Il Duce's marriage of convenience to the Pope."

"Il Duce was a pragmatist."

"And was a pragmatist worthy of your worship?"

"To fight communism, we did what was necessary."

I could not believe what I was hearing. Growing up, I had always considered Dad to be good-hearted – though inexplicably broken-hearted – and I assumed he'd been part of the *Resistenza*. Yet here I was, coming up on my 40th birthday, just now learning about my father the fascist, the arsonist, an accomplice of the Black Shirts, and, in his own eyes, a champion of the downtrodden.

Marco said, "When you get right down to it, brother, there was not much difference between fascism and communism. Both rained down ruination on the world; both knew how to 'disappear' people."

Ella, always the one to try to lighten things up when things got tense, sat there shell-shocked, zoned out. Her ability to focus melted away. I had long thought of her as a younger version of our mother, and it was distressing to see my father's melancholy descend upon her.

Unaware of his daughter's despondence, Dad soldiered on. "There was a world of difference, brother! Under communism, there is no incentive to work – they'd have torn the guts out of our country! We stood up...."

Instantly, I hit my flashpoint and stood up. "And WHO.... stands up to YOUUU.... DAAAD?" I was ready to charge at the slightest provocation.

"Leo, don't you dare speak to your father like that!" Mom was incensed, like I had never seen her. "It's easy to make judgments of those who lived in another time."

I was infuriated, bewildered and, just for a moment, proud that I had stood up to The Old Man. But even in my state of fury, I realized that I was standing up to the old bully, *as* a bully, and my triumph rang hollow. Winning did not feel like winning.

"How come you never *told* me?" It was discomfiting to hear to such venom in my own voice.

"I *did*." His sneer carried venom of its own. "I've been telling you since you were five. You didn't want to hear it."

That stopped me cold; it's true that I had been tuning him out for decades. *Had* he told me? Had I chosen at some point not to hear it? Was it my preference to believe that he'd fought with the good guys? But then I caught a sly look in Dad's eye, and I shook my head.

"No no no, I'm not falling for that. Dad, you never said you fought with the Fascists."

"You don't listen! I was not fighting *with* anybody! I was fighting *against* communism!"

Put like that, it almost made his cause sound noble and his efforts praiseworthy. Almost.

"I have always been fighting!" he said. "I still am! *We* still are; the Cold War never ended. We'd do well to sleep with one eye open!"

Put like that, he sounded like a scared, harmless, embittered old man. I was embarrassed for him.

"You stole a.... a house?" Lucia stared incredulously at her grandfather. "When you were 14?"

"We were caretakers."

"Call it what you will, brother." Marco turned to Lucia. "It wasn't all your grandpa's doing. He had help from his friend Herr Luther, or, as I've come to think of him, Heir Looter."

"It was never my intent...." Dad's voice trailed away. He struggled to his feet, and Mom, ever the loyal companion, guided him down the hall toward their bedroom.

My uncle and I were content to let him go, whereas Lucia leapt up and hugged him fiercely. "Good night, Grampadini. I love you."

Being two generations removed from the madness that had been his childhood, she had the capacity and willingness to forgive him any and all transgressions. Dad had never been the huggy type, but he put his arms around her and squeezed. He wiped his eyes and allowed Mom to lead him away.

Uncle Marco stood and said, "I guess I've caused enough trouble for one night." He was gathering up his things as Mom returned. "Sister," he began contritely, "if I have...."

She interrupted and said firmly, "No, sit. Please. And finire la storia." Finish the story.

Whaaat? Mom knows Italian?

Over the course of the next hour, Marco filled us in on the gruesome details of our family history. His tale took us up through the spring of '45; the Germans withdrew from northern Italy, and Mussolini was caught and hanged by Communist partisans. The townsfolk turned against my father. And my uncle, always the charmer, devised a way to immigrate to the USA with his underage brother. The New World offered sanctuary for my father and adventure for my uncle.

Mom said, "Marco, you told the truth, and nothing but the truth, but not the whole truth."

"Oh?"

"You remember when Gianni and I moved to Italy.... oh, a dozen years ago? We did so because he wanted to set things right with his father. And the owners of that villa – we tried for two years to track them down, but...." She shook her head. "Gianni made amends with people in town, and he made a generous contribution to the library, but it was clear that he, *we*, would never belong." She then turned to me. "Leo, there are times when it is commendable, even necessary, to take a stand and do battle. But usually, when men go off to war, they do it simply because they enjoy the fight." The tears in her eyes conveyed love and sorrow. "Leo, it's rare, so very rare, that battle is necessary."

In that moment it became clear to me that, for all of my father's bluster, Mom had become the strong one, the wise one, in our family. Or maybe she always had been.

Uncle Marco stood and kissed my mother on the forehead. He walked into the kitchen to retrieve the carafe of sangria, and upon returning, he patted me roughly on the cheek and said, "Old

Italian saying, Leo: You'll never complete your journey if you stop to throw a stone at every dog that barks along the way."

I hate it when people try to psychoanalyze me, like when a girlfriend points out my shortcomings as she's dumping me, or, for that matter, when I'm dumping her.

But there I was on the drive home, doing my best to sort out my father's life, his drive, his intentions, his pathologies. For decades, I had interpreted the message in his growing-up-during-the-war diatribe as: Son, stand up to people like I do. But now I see those rantings in what I believe to be a clearer light: Son, stand up to people like me.

After a lifetime of regret, was he wondering why no one had stood up to him? Did he keep that photograph prominently displayed in his own home as a self-imposed penance? Or, did he still believe that villa to be rightfully his? Or was I was reading too much into this? Even taking into account the fire damage, it's still a gorgeous estate, and a beautiful photograph.

I fingered the scar on my jaw, and it occurred to me that by Taking A Stand with as much zeal and as little discretion as I often did, I had spent much of my life fighting my father's war, throwing stones at every dog that barks along the way.

Chapter 35 – July

Carl, Anjuli, Giz and I had left my car at Anacortes, 90 miles north of Seattle, and rolled our suitcases onto the ferry that was now weaving its way through the sparsely populated San Juan Islands, considered by many to be the most beautiful part of Washington State. The outside deck was cool and breezy, but none of us had the slightest inclination to head inside.

The sun was low in the sky when we pulled into Friday Harbor on San Juan Island. Hiking up to Front Street, Anjuli let out a yelp when she spotted Marsha Hamilton, and the women flung themselves at one another. Marsha has gray hair, gray eyes and even a gray sweater, but there is nothing gray about her personality. They finally let go of one another, still yelping, for God's sake.

"These are my friends!" said Anjuli.

Marsha gave Carl and me quick hugs. "I've heard about you guys!" Giz looked pleasantly bewildered when she ran her hands through his tangle of hair. "Anjuli told me I should do that."

Marsha led us to her car, saying, "I'm glad you accepted our invitation to stay the weekend. And you better be hungry."

A half hour later, we pulled up in front of the Hamiltons' two-story "cabin", which is three times the size of my house. It lay nestled among a stand of pine trees on a bluff overlooking Haro Strait. In the distance lay Vancouver Island, the southernmost point of Canada on the West Coast.

We entered the cabin, and Warren Hamilton descended a pinewood staircase. In his mid-60s and standing 6'5'' or so, he projects an aura of vitality. "War" gave Anjuli a bear hug and said, "Let's go out on the deck. Watch the sun set."

During press conferences, he delivers his observations and proclamations about medicine, technology and education in a formal, precise manner, the result being that he comes across on camera as being stiff, if not downright frosty. I contrasted that image with this convivial man before me who tends to speak in sentence fragments.

Marsha grabbed Anjuli by both wrists and tugged. "C'mon, let's get dinner before it gets dark. Giz.... *Giz*? Can I call you that? You come too."

The three of them disappeared down a precipitous flight of stairs off the back of the deck.

Carl looked baffled. "Is there a Safeway at the bottom?"

Warren let out a raspy chuckle. "Not exactly. Get you fellas a beer?"

With Hefeweizens in hand, we settled into plush oversized lawn chairs and watched as the sunset infused patchy clouds with shades of red, orange and peach.

I said, "Boy, if I lived here, I'd never get out of this chair."

Warren nodded. "Got that right. Wish I could spend more time up here. Go crazy workin' in Seattle as much as I do."

After we swapped travel stories, Warren said, "I hear you two are educators. Got three passions in life, four, countin' my wife: my medical business; health issues in the third world; and a desire to improve education. I talk to superintendents and senators, but rarely get a chance to speak with real life teachers. Tell me, what's it like in the classroom?"

"It's a beautiful evening," I said. "You sure you wanna ask that?"

He chuckled again. "Yes, I do. Give it to me straight."

"First the good news," I said. "For the kids who can handle the flood of information, we are turning out the finest young men and women the world has ever seen. They're smart and curious, and they're informed about the world." I nodded to Carl.

"I concur," he said. "Given the choice between teaching this generation and my own, I'd pick this generation, hands down. Any other good news, Leo?"

"Nope, that about covers it. We've both been out of the classroom a few years, but here's the bad news, in no particular order: Our math books still present problems in feet, miles, quarts and pounds." I was pleased to see that Warren grimaced.

Carl said, "Schools need to offer a vocational ed program. We teach all kids as if they're college-bound. They're not. Nor should they be."

"The WASL is ill-conceived and poorly written. Have you actually seen it?"

Warren's scowl reminded me that he had played a vital role in creating the WASL.

"Special ed teachers used to teach," said Carl. "Now they spend hours a day filling out paperwork, because of state and federal regulations."

"Fourth grade teachers don't teach basic multiplication, like 7 x 8 = 56. They're too busy getting kids to pass the WASL. So parents are told that teaching times tables is *their* job."

"And district meetings...."

".... oh man, consensus must be reached...."

".... or at least an appearance of consensus...."

".... by forty people, and that's not the worst of it...."

".... the most vile phrase in the English language is....."

We finished in unison. ".... research shows."

Warren had been listening impassively, but he suddenly burst into a full-on belly laugh. "Good grief! You remind me of *me*, dealing with mid-level management!" He sobered up instantly and looked each of us in the eye. "You boys have a lot of work to do."

Marsha, Anjuli and Giz appeared at the top of the stairs, talking excitedly. Anjuli plopped down a bucket, filled with a writhing mass of claws, shells, antennae and tiny eyeballs.

"We got 13 of 'em!" she said. "Check 'em out!"

Marsha explained, "We put out crab pots with bait this morning. Crabs can get in, but they can't get out. We just rowed the boat out, pulled up the pots, and voila! Dinner! Let's get you settled in and then we can eat."

We followed her upstairs with our luggage. Anjuli and Carl had assumed they would be sharing a room, but when Marsha pointed out four guest rooms, my friends did not challenge her.

Two hours later, we were taking our first bites of Dungeness crab, served with baked potatoes stuffed with chives, butter and sour cream.

"I guess I've never had fresh crab," said Carl. "This is amazing!" He cracked a leg and the meat almost jumped out of the shell; no digging was necessary.

Marsha asked me, "So what kind of student was Anjuli?"

I told her about the man-with-the-rock-in-the-boat-in-the-lake problem, and how she solved it with lip gloss. I also told about the time Anjuli slugged me.

She pointed her crab cracker at me. "You had it comin'."

Marsha looked like she wanted to adopt her.

After dinner we adjourned to the living room; Warren served coffee, tea and lemon cake.

Marsha lit a fire in their floor-to-ceiling fireplace, saying, "War and I look forward to the day we can live up here full time."

"Would you ever get lonely?" asked Carl.

"He's got friends he plays chess with. I go sailing with some girls in Roche Harbor."

Warren waited a moment, and then said, "Time's come to talk about why we're here. Anjuli informed me that she has decided on a direction for her grant. 'Parently you all had a part in this decision? Anjuli Torres, what is your vision? And how did you come by it?"

She peppered her account with vignettes from our dinner parties, but she reads people well and knows when to get down to business.

"Kenya has a shortage of teachers, and secondary tuition is prohibitively expensive for most kids. So we'd like to open a school that focuses on preparing students to obtain teaching degrees. We would identify highly capable students that are at risk of dropping out, and offer a two-stage scholarship: free tuition, room and board at our school; and a scholarship, in the form of a loan, for tuition at an accredited teacher college. If a graduate teaches for five years, we would pay off the loan. Because of the plight of women in Kenya, we would specifically provide this opportunity for girls."

Warren massaged the back of his neck. "First question: Who is 'we'?"

"Carl and I would like to pursue this venture. He's been a teacher, principal and district administrator. He would teach social studies and English, I'd take math and science. We would both teach PE and music. He plays guitar and I play flute."

Warren sized up Carl and asked, "Spent time in Africa?"

"Two years in the Peace Corps, early 90's, Ghana and

Sierra Leone." Was Carl aware that he had adopted Warren's abbreviated form of speech?

Warren's warm, fuzzy demeanor toughened up. "You deal with the bureaucracy?"

"Some. My passport was stolen in Lagos. Got a new one at the American Consulate, and then began the nightmarish process of obtaining a new visa. Here's what I learned: If someone won't help, you ask, 'Who's your boss?' They hated me for that, but they'd eventually take me to their boss, and I kept climbing until I found someone who would help."

"And if they were uncooperative?"

"I did my best to go around them. One time I couldn't, and, well, I bribed him."

"I remember the first time I bribed somebody. Went home and took a shower afterwards. If you don't stand up to corruption, you give people license to misbehave."

Geez Louise! My dad would love this guy.

Warren looked back and forth between Anjuli and Carl. "How long you known each other?"

Carl blushed. "About five months."

"Aw, Christ!" He slapped his massive thighs. "There's a continent at risk over there! We're tryin' to help a generation survive! I'm there to heal and educate, not provide a damn photo safari for young lovers!"

Carl glowered and opened his mouth to speak, but Marsha beat him to it. "War, may I have a word with you in the kitchen?"

They left, and Giz said, "That didn't go exactly like we hoped."

We couldn't quite make out what the Hamiltons were saying. Their tone was intense, but they were clearly making an effort to remain civil. Warren came barging through the swinging door three minutes later, asking, "Any chance you all could stay a few days?"

We all nodded, except for Giz, who said he would try to get Monday off.

"If need be, we'll get a float plane to take you back." Warren pointed two fingers at Carl and Anjuli. "I'll need to speak with the two of you tomorrow morning for several hours." He then spoke to Anjuli gruffly. "Marsha thinks you're somethin' special."

She met his gaze undaunted, and he added, "What it's worth, so do I." He eyed Carl. "Not sure what you're all about, but we're gonna find out."

Giz and I were playing chess on the deck Saturday morning when Warren poked his head out of the French doors long enough to say: "Lunch in twenty."

Carl emerged, wearing a worn-out grin. "I see why they call him 'War'."

"C'mon," said Anjuli, "he's a teddy bear."

"I'll tell you, Leo, I'd take this over district meetings any day. He's tough, but he's smart and fair. We'll get a thumbs-up or a thumbs-down by Monday.

Anjuli grabbed my arm. "I have a question for you. Let's take a walk."

The skies had darkened and a cool wind kicked up. Anjuli put her arm around my waist and we wandered off into the pines. She inhaled deeply and leaned her head on my shoulder.

"Uncle Leo, am I doing the right thing? Running off with a man I hardly know?"

"Now that is ironic, asking me for romantic advice." I paused, wanting to get this right. "Anj, I know nothing about making romance last. But I do know about making friendship last, and it all comes down to trust. Do you trust Carl?"

She frowned. "How do you mean? Are you asking if he'll lie to me?"

"Yes, but I mean more than that. Do you trust him to care about you? Could you rely on him is a dangerous situation? Will he listen to you?"

She stopped walking and faced me. "Well, *you* know him better than I do."

"Doesn't matter what I think. Do you trust him?"

She looked up through the towering pines at the threatening sky. "Yes, but I've been wrong about guys before."

"What does Giz think?"

She gave me a wry smile. "He says I have rotten taste in guys. Except for Carl; Giz tells me I'm strong and soft around him. I'm not sure what that means, but he trusts Carl."

I put my arm around her shoulder and steered her back

toward the cabin. "Me too."

After lunch, all six of us met to discuss a time frame, number of students served, support staff, permits, etc. Mostly Giz and I listened, but a few times Warren had IT questions for Giz, and Carl asked me about schools I had visited in Kenya.

Warren said, "Carl, I know you've been to Africa, but travel is one thing, doing business with the government is another. Just so's you realize the extent of the corruption we're talking here, let's begin with the Goldenberg scandal in the 90's; the Minister of Education was involved in a gold-exporting scam that siphoned off as much as ten percent of GDP."

"You'll be faced with conspiracy theories," said Marsha. "Kenyans see do-gooders, and they're afraid their children will be kidnapped, taken to Europe and have their organs harvested."

We talked until 4:00, at which point Warren announced, "Let's wrap it up for today." He checked his notes. "Got a few people I need to contact here. You're on your own 'til six."

Feasting on crab again that evening, Warren reverted to being a relaxed and gracious host. "Where did you get the name 'Giz'?"

Giz pointed at me. "Ask this guy."

I told the Hamiltons about his coat full of gizmos and his flute that could play two notes, and about how he had asked for more challenging homework in 9th grade. Anjuli pointed out that the school-for-teachers idea was really his.

Warren asked, "Giz, would you come work for me?"

Giz blushed like crazy. "Doing what?"

"What kind of schooling do you have?"

"Bachelor's in Computer Sciences."

"I'd find something for you to do. I get too many kids out of college with their heads buzzin' with formulas and clutter, but no ability to think."

"Uh, thank you. I would need time to...."

Warren broke off a crab leg and said, "I'd make it worth your while."

When Giz and I returned from hiking the next morning,

Anjuli and Carl were waiting on the front porch.

"It's a go!" she said.

Giz said, "I thought Warren wasn't going to decide until Monday."

"Carl knocked the Old Man's socks off." She regarded him with something approaching awe. "How do you know so much about British colonialism?"

He shrugged. "I crammed for the test."

I said, "He reads like a cheetah runs, and he remembers it."

"We still have issues," said Carl. "Not all Kenyans speak English. Anjuli speaks a little Swahili, and War said he'd hook us up with tutors. She'll need to get teaching credentials, and we have to figure out where the school gets built, but we're leaving at the end of August."

Marsha exited the front door and said, "Time to go, Giz. I already loaded up your suitcase." He had not been able to find anyone to fill in for him at work, so she had offered to drive him down to the air harbor.

"Be there in one minute," he said and then turned to Anjuli. "If women were food, you'd be a Dungeness crab." She was ready with a comeback, but he put a finger to her lips and said in a tender voice, "I am.... so.... *proud* of you."

He then turned to Carl, and I expected him to say: Listen, bub, you better look after her. Instead, his eyes turned watery, and he said, "Anjuli, take care of this guy; be good to him."

Without waiting for a response, Giz hopped into Marsha's car and they took off.

That parting remark to Carl threw Anjuli off-balance. A look of sadness crossed her face, but it was sadness devoid of regret and tinged with relief. Carl slid his arm around her waist and told me they were going for a hike, to talk about their upcoming move to Kenya. She rested her head on his shoulder in a weary but contented way, and they disappeared into the forest.

And just like *that*, I was alone, looking out at the ships passing on Haro Strait, feeling utterly lost. Though pleased with my friends' good fortunes, I was painfully aware that they were passing me by, getting on with their lives. And I was left behind, treading water.

Contemplating the upcoming school year filled me with

dread and despair. I had but one consolation: Susan Nysohr is on board with Going Metric. Whoop-de-doo.

Warren poked his head out and invited me inside. We sat ourselves in front of the fireplace on a plush white couch.

He poured two cups of Market Spice Tea and asked, "Like your job?"

"Boy, I sure used to. I got to hang out with people like Giz and Anjuli all day."

"Sounds terrific. Anj was talking about you behind your back this morning; said you were the best teacher she ever had." He gave me a hard look that did not match up with those warm, fuzzy words. "Mind if I ask why you left the classroom?"

"I wanted to teach teachers, to choose better textbooks, to adopt the metric system. And I got a raise. But mostly I changed because Carl asked me to; he can be very persuasive."

He raised an eyebrow. "Let me ask your advice. This school-for-teachers project – he the right man for the job?"

"If anyone can do it, Carl can. He's a True Believer, in people and education."

Warren got up to stir the fire. He said, "The other day you expressed dissatisfaction with the WASL. 'Ill-conceived and poorly written', is how you put it. Mind explaining that?"

I had long fantasized about this moment; my response was ready: "An academic discipline not specifically covered on such a high-stakes test won't get taught, or at least it will be seriously de-emphasized. As for being poorly written, some problems intended to be open-ended are simply worded unclearly. Some of them border on being nonsensical."

"Can you give me an example?"

"I could, but business leaders need to look at the test."

"Just so you know, I was one of the prime movers in creating the WASL."

"I know that. And I believe you had nothing but the best of intentions. But the WASL has become a beast with a ferocious appetite; it devours obscene amounts of resources, money and time. I implore you: Please find a way to see the test."

He grunted and got up to place another log on the fire. "If I did take a look it, would you be willing to sit down with me and discuss it? Maybe bring a few colleagues?"

"Warren.... War.... Yes, I would."

We stared at the flames. After a few minutes, he asked, "You a Boy Scout?"

"Yeah, I was. Made Eagle. You?"

"Made Eagle. Remember the Boy Scout motto?"

"Ummm.... Be prepared. Why do you ask?"

"Just thinking about you and that job that's drivin' you crazy. Sounds like you get blind-sided in meetings." While I chewed on that, he said, "Be prepared."

Chapter 36 - August

Susan Nysohr had resigned as superintendent in late July, citing a desire to be closer to her family back east. But word around Crazy Town is that she was about to be canned because of her open opposition to the Bush administration's educational policies. She believed the feds were snooping around, covertly accessing hard drives and reading emails. The week before she left, signs had been hung up around Crazy Town reading:

NO PHONE LEFT UNTAPPED

In July, many of my colleagues had come to the conclusion that it was Susan putting up the signs, but there was a new one hanging above the main entrance this morning:

NO CHILD LEFT WITH DIGNITY

As usual, the neatly printed capital letters were precisely squared up on tagboard. I was the last one out of the building last night, and according to Johnny Boe, our surly, sleep-deprived night custodian, I was the first to arrive today.

Speaking of Johnny, his head still swivels as if welded to a gun turret, but now, rather than looking to cause a ruckus, he's constantly looking over his shoulders to see who's coming up behind him. I guess prison does that to you.

As for those tagboard signs, I must have heard ten people say this morning: Gotta be somebody who gets here early or stays super late.

The last time the school board chose a superintendent, they conducted a nationwide search to find the most highly qualified candidate. This time, when the board expressed a desire to hire in-house, Ben Luzen and Bonnie Rhodes jockeyed for position to replace Susan, but their abrasive personalities and smarmy politicking alienated all but a few at Crazy Town. The board let it be known they were searching for "a veteran educator with 20-20 vision of 21st century educational practices, a team player with local values, willing to make the tough decisions".

Translated: They were looking for an old guy with an advanced degree, a toady who had never left Washington State and had no qualms about pissing off teachers.

Betty Skibbitz was retiring, and this morning she was being recognized by the board for her decades of dedication. A state senator was in attendance, as were four prominent business leaders who had been her students. A reporter and photographer from the Seattle Times were on hand. The remainder of the audience was made up of colleagues, past and present, as well as Betty's older sister.

On the dais in the conference room stands the oak table assaulted by my father 25 years ago. Our new superintendent's high-backed leather chair, conspicuously empty today, occupies the center position behind the desk. Board members seated to either side of the vacant chair were visibly annoyed.

Ben Luzen, filling in for our superintendent, called Betty forward. Her hair is now a wispy white and she is perceptibly shorter than when I taught with her, but she strode to the dais with grace and purpose.

"You are an inspiration to us all," Ben gushed as he stepped off the dais to shake her hand. "And we know the Fernwater Math Department will sorely miss you."

He then presented her with a plaque reading "68 Years of Meritorious Service". Cameras flashed and all present applauded. Ben readied himself to address the next agenda item, assuming that Betty would return to her seat.

Think again.

In her raspy voice, she began, "I have to tell you a little story about when Jimmy K was in 4th grade; see, I knew him from my kindiegarten class...."

Jimmy K! Oh man! Why had I not taken a front row seat?

".... one day he got pinched for shop-lifting; he made off with a snazzy yoyo from the five and dime on Elm, and the men in blue caught him before he flew the coop...."

The board members looked for a spot to jump in, but she stared them down, one by one, her 90-year-old steely blue eyes ready to strike down anyone audacious enough to interrupt.

"…. he razzed a kid about having big feet, and this twerp, he was fulla piss 'n' vinegar, he gave Jimmy K a knuckle sandwich…."

Shadow-boxing now, she delivered a surprisingly quick right cross. Board members were in a panic, but, really, what were they so upset about? Yeah, she was taking up board time, but so what? This would likely be her last chance to shine.

The boardroom door squeaked, and Betty took a break from her monologue. The Krabman walked to the dais, took the middle seat, and straightened his shiny new nameplate:

> Dr. James Krabke
> Superintendent

All assembled waited expectantly as he straightened his tie and cleared his throat. Cameras flashed as he began speaking.

"My BMW has a gauge that indicates how far you can drive with the amount of gas on board. It was set for kilometers instead of miles." Twitch twitchy twitch. Looking out at the sea of confused faces, he added, "I… well, I ran out of gas on I-5."

Betty took issue with that. "Oh, horse feathers, Jimmy K! Even in kindiegarten, you were never on time, but you were always ready with some cockamamy excuse."

What? Jimmy K and The Krabman, one and the same! He twitched and blinked like he was facing a roomful of Joshes, Jeffs, Jakes and Johnny Boes. His indignation rose above the laughter.

"Damn Europeans and their damn kill-o-meters!"

The hubbub died once we realized Betty had resumed her narrative: "Jimmy K would rather shoe a mule than read a book, but get a load of this: Back when Truman was president…. "

Two hours later, waiting for Anjuli at a Thai restaurant two blocks from Crazy Town, I thought about those two new signs. I wanted to thank whoever was hanging them up, for adding some much needed levity to my life. And with The Krabman running the show, what sort of train wreck awaits us?

"You look sad, Uncle Leo." I hadn't noticed that Anjuli was standing beside me, her face filled with concern.

"Oh, hey. Sorry. I am very happy and excited for you and Carl. But I feel adrift."

She grabbed me by my wrists, pulled me to my feet and gave me a quick hug. As we sat down, she asked, "Why not go back to teaching?"

"Oh, I don't know, Anj. I'm not sure I made much of a difference."

"Yeah," she said. "I can see how you'd think that."

"What?" I'm sure my face registered surprise and more than a touch of indignation.

"Well, you didn't enjoy teaching, you weren't real good at it, and – let's face it – your sense of humor needs some work."

I tried my hardest not to smile, and ended up frowning and laughing simultaneously.

Anjuli thwacked me on the shoulder. "You goof! Leo, if not for you, I probably would have lost my sister, I wouldn't have gone to Africa, and I never would have met Carl. And that's just me; how many students have you had? Hundreds? Thousands? Millions? Remember the question I asked you six months ago: If you had a pile o' money to spend on a worthy cause, what would that cause be? And then, after considering all options, Carl and I decided to teach. We're going to teach teachers. We could not come up with anything more important."

She smiled radiantly. "I cannot wait to be a teacher."

"Oh, Anj, you already are."

Returning from lunch, I mulled over my conversation with Anjuli, and I came away with one thought: We are all teachers, and hopefully we never quit being students.

Back to teaching, huh? Maybe I should try elementary or high school this time around.

Nah. As much as I love Ella's kids, the 9-year-old twins are not yet capable of the level of abstraction I crave, and 17-year-old Lucia, though she likes me well enough, has no real need of me, or any adult, for that matter. At least that's what she believes, or what she says she believes. In any case, she does not seek my counsel.

Walking across Crazy Town's parking lot, I braced myself for the upcoming Executive Council meeting.

"Be prepared," I said aloud, while admiring the gray BMW seven series parked in the space reserved for the superintendent. I was not surprised to see Dr. Jimmy Krabman sacked out in "his new baby", where he often sought noontime sanctuary. As usual, his spine appeared to have jackknifed at the neck. His mouth hung open and his nose pointed skyward, a position Carl dubbed NAP, Not Administrating Posture. As uncomfortable as that had to be, he looked curiously peaceful. In sleep, he is given respite from his perpetual facial spasms.

At two minutes before one o'clock, I entered the conference room and took a seat at the oak table next to Penelope.

Reuben Rapp, Fernwater's principal, sat down across from me. He smiled and said, "One Good Tern."

"Deserves Another," I replied.

Penelope frowned in befuddlement at my new attaché case, from which I removed several documents. She said, "Since when do you carry a briefcase?"

I leaned toward her and whispered, "No Child Left With Dignity, that's my favorite sign yet. Gold star for you."

She feigned ignorance, in hopes that I was fishing, which I was. But her blush confirmed my suspicions, and the last time I saw her express such abject terror involved Josh McClown and a bottle of Jack Daniel's.

It had occurred to me while waiting for Anjuli that Johnny Boe, as night custodian, would have been able to hang his wife's signs at his leisure. It was then that I recalled Penny had always printed with precise block capitals, even back in 9th grade.

"Your secret is safe with me," I said. "I love your signs."

I counted the number of principals present: 13 out of 17 schools were represented. Good.

"We have several curricular issues on our agenda," began Ben Luzen, checking his watch. "Superintendent Krabke will be along shortly. Mr. Haldini is proposing that our district adopt a mathematics curriculum that would be strictly metric. Is that correct?"

"Yes, the metric system is a superior, simpler system of measurement that our country has been intending to adopt for decades. The scientific community...."

Ben interrupted. "Research shows that the cost to the American economy...."

I interrupted right back. "Research *shows* that in 1999, NASA lost $125 million when the Mars orbiter crashed because everyone forgot to convert from English to metric."

I floated a print-out from CNN.com across the table to him.

Ben said, "The business community in Washington State will resist converting to metric."

"May I read a brief email I received from Warren Hamilton yesterday morning?" When Ben hesitated, I read aloud:

Leo,
Glad you could make it up to our cabin. Good luck on Going Metric. Let me know if I can help. Time is past due for a change. Be prepared. Talk soon, War

p.s. Marsha says she's going to kick our butts at Pinochle next time you visit.

"In case you're not aware of it," I said, "War is Chairman of the Washington State Business Council."

Ben looked pleadingly at Bonnie Rhodes. She cleared her throat and straightened her already ramrod-straight posture.

"Be that as it maaaay, this body...." She extended her arms to include everyone at the table, ".... lacks the power to make decisions of this nature in the absence of Superintendent Krabke, and knowing how he feels about the metric system...."

I plopped a bound document on the table; it made a nice "thunk" when it landed. "Here is a copy of our District Operating Principles. We have 13 of our 17 schools represented here – more than the 75% required for us to act. This document...." I laid my hand on it, as if taking an oath. ".... clearly states that if we have a quorum of administrators present, we *do* have the power to make decisions of this nature."

Penelope leaned toward me and whispered, "You go, girl!"

This was the first time I'd seen her Catherine Zeta-Jones smile in months. Her perkiness had always bugged the bejesus out of me, but it was good to see her coming back to life.

Ben faltered. "Where *is* Dr. Krabke?"

I deadpanned my response. "I saw him ten minutes ago; he's in NAP."

Bonnie pursed her lips. "What, may Ah ask, is the NAP?"

I shrugged. "All I know is that it's very time-consuming."

Having heard Carl's jest about Not Administrating Posture, Penelope snickered and snorted into her palm.

Bonnie regarded Ben accusingly. "Why, *whyyy* would the NAP take precedence over the Executive Council?"

Ben's hair, clothing and demeanor are generally impervious to, respectively, wind, wrinkles, and wise guys. But he was now sweating like a leeetle peeeg een a beeeeeeeg blanket.

"I don't know," he said. "I propose that we research Leo's proposal, and at our next meeting...."

I interrupted yet again. "As Chief Instructional Supervisor, I've *done* the research." I slid another paper across the table to him. "Item Three of my job description reads: Collect staff input regarding curricular issues and make recommendations to the Executive Council...." I extended my arms, ala Bonnie Rhodes. ".... that best fit our academic objectives." I held up several sheets of paper emblazoned with my official ChInSu letterhead. "I collected input, and the response from teachers and administrators overwhelmingly supports exclusive use of the metric system. I move that we adopt an all-metric curriculum in our district."

Penelope jumped all over it. "Like, second!"

"A motion has been made and seconded," said Ben. "All in favor?"

All except Bonnie raised their hands. She glared at Ben's tentatively raised arm.

"All opposed?" Arms fell. "Motion carries; we are Going Metric. OK, next item: We were set to vote on acceptance of our district's proposed mission statement, but Dr. Krabke is not satisfied will the statement's exact wording, so he would like to take us, in his words, 'back to the proverbial drawing board'."

Jaws dropped, shoulders sagged, and eyes bulged like Marty Feldman's in <u>Young Frankenstein</u>. Several of us had been involved in the 18-month process, which I would not have been alone in describing as "excruciating".

Three of us said, "I move that we adopt...."

Ben Luzen wagged his index finger at us. "Ah, ah, ah. We don't want to be hasty about this, and I for one would like to get Dr. Krabke's perspective on this matter."

Hasty? After 18 months? Heat spread across my face, and I was tempted to challenge him, but having already scored a major win today, I decided not to push my luck.

Bonnie stood up. "Ah move we take a 15-minute recess. Perhaps our superintendent will be finished with his NAP by then. If he's still a no-show, Ah say we vote on this abominable mission statement and be done with it."

With that, she turned and walked out. Most of us followed.

Carl called as I stepped into the foyer. He had taken the day off to obtain an international driver's license, get vaccinations, and meet with the people who would be renting his house.

"Haldini," he said, "how's Crazy Town?"

"Crazier than usual; I have stories. Wanna get a beer?"

"Sure. Beats Workin' at five?"

"Make it 5:30; I have to stop by home to feed K'boodle. Are you guys ready to leave?"

"Almost. One week and we're out of here. Hey, I'm looking forward to this move and all, but I'm sorry about bailin'."

"It's OK. I'm not going to be workin' here this year either. I gave what I had to give; I learned what I had to learn."

For the past three years, I have told myself that once I figured out how to play the game at Crazy Town, I would enjoy my job. As I discovered today, however, even when you win here, it feels rotten.

"Jesus, Joe, and Jimmy Christ, Haldini! You're *quitting*?"

"No, but it's time to move forward, which for me means taking a step back. Fernwater has an opening for a math teacher."

For three years, Reuben has told me that he could always make room for One More Good Tern at Fernwater.

My favorite dad-ism played in my head: Decisions you make when you're 14 stay with you always.

Yes, 14 is a pivotal age, which makes junior high the place to be. During that wondrous three-year window of adolescent accessibility, friendships form and heads get fed, or spirits warp and wither.

This is a terning point, I told myself. Nyuk nyuk nyuk.

Let's pull a U-tern.

"Carl, I'm not sure if you've noticed, but my sense of humor never progressed beyond that of a 14-year-old. Junior high is where I belong."

"Goes for both of us. But, hey, maybe you ought to think this over for a day or two."

"No. This is only the second moment of absolute clarity I've had in my life."

Out in the parking lot, Betty Skibbitz and her older sister were peering through the windshield of Dr. Jimmy Krabman's Beemer. Shielding their eyes from the sun, they bent at the waist, inching back and forth to get a better look.

"Hold on a sec, Carl. I got a little situation here." Exiting the building, I crept up behind the women and listened in:

"Why, that's Jimmy K," said Betty. "Is he all right? Go tap on the window."

"Not me; I don't think he's breathing. You best call 911."

"Maybe he's asleep. I'll go check." Betty began hobbling around to the driver's side.

"What's the problem, ladies?"

Both women began chattering at once. Miming The Krabman's NAP, Betty almost toppled onto her backside. I helped her steady herself.

"He's fine, ladies. He had a...." I looked around, leaned in and lowered my voice. "He had a bit of a hard night. It's best to let him be. I'll keep an eye on him."

Betty's sister grabbed my hand with both of hers. "Why, thank you, young man!"

"I do what I can."

Betty thanked me as well and then led her sister away, saying, "Jimmy K was a student of mine, back when Roosevelt was president – Franklin, of course, not Teddy...."

"Carl, you still there? As ChInSu, I propose that we change the meaning of NAP to 'No Appreciable Pulse'. And research shows – heh, heh, heh – that Superintendent Krabke is 72.185% more effective while unconscious."

The last words I heard from Betty Skibbitz as she and her sister rounded the building were: "Jimmy K, same ol' cockamamy excuses."